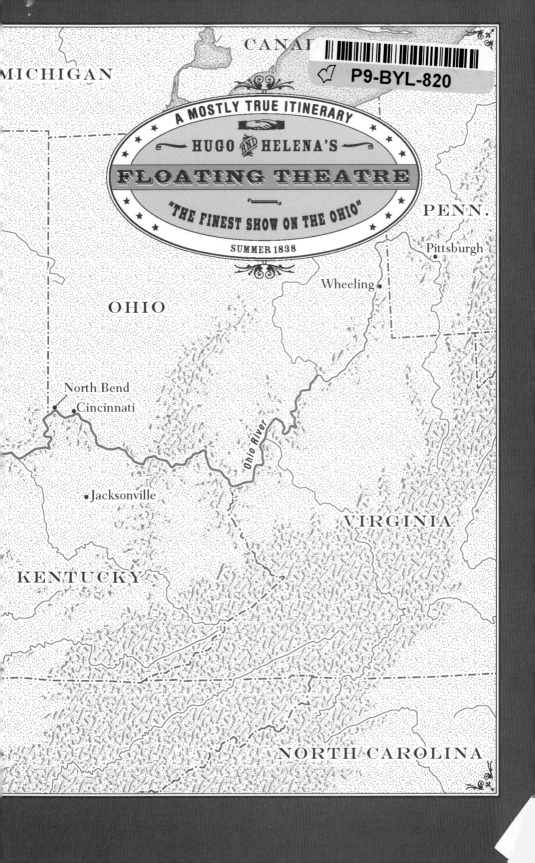

MICHIGAN

CANADA

P9-BYL-820

A MOSTLY TRUE ITINERARY

HUGO *AND* HELENA'S

FLOATING THEATRE

"THE FINEST SHOW ON THE OHIO"

SUMMER 1838

PENN.

Pittsburgh

Wheeling

OHIO

Ohio River

North Bend
Cincinnati

Jacksonville

VIRGINIA

KENTUCKY

NORTH CAROLINA

ALSO BY MARTHA CONWAY

Sugarland

Thieving Forest

12 Bliss Street

THE UNDERGROUND RIVER

Martha Conway

TOUCHSTONE
New York   London   Toronto   Sydney   New Delhi

Touchstone
An Imprint of Simon & Schuster, Inc.
1230 Avenue of the Americas
New York, NY 10020

First Touchstone hardcover edition June 2017

TOUCHSTONE and colophon are registered trademarks of Simon & Schuster, Inc.

For information about special discounts for bulk purchases, please contact Simon & Schuster Special Sales at 1-866-506-1949 or business@simonandschuster.com.

The Simon & Schuster Speakers Bureau can bring authors to your live event. For more information or to book an event, contact the Simon & Schuster Speakers Bureau at 1-866-248-3049 or visit our website at www.simonspeakers.com.

Interior design by Jill Putorti

Manufactured in the United States of America

10 9 8 7 6 5 4 3 2 1

Library of Congress Cataloging-in-Publication Data
Names: Conway, Martha, author.
Title: The Underground River : a novel / Martha Conway.
Description: First Touchstone hardcover edition. | New York : Simon & Schuster, 2017. | A Touchstone Book.
Identifiers: LCCN 2016050548 (print) | LCCN 2016057448 (ebook) | ISBN 9781501160202 (hardback) | ISBN 9781501160257 (trade paperback) | ISBN 9781501160264 (ebook)
Subjects: | BISAC: FICTION / Historical. | FICTION / Family Life. | FICTION / General.
Classification: LCC PS3603.O565 R36 2017 (print) | LCC PS3603.O565 (ebook) | DDC 813/.6--dc23
LC record available at https://lccn.loc.gov/2016050548

ISBN 978-1-5011-6020-2
ISBN 978-1-5011-6026-4 (ebook)

For my father, Richard Conway,
who toured the Ohio River with me.

1

When the steamboat *Moselle* blew apart just off its Cincinnati landing, I was sitting below deck in the ladies' cabin, sewing tea leaves into little muslin bags and plotting revenge on my cousin Comfort for laughing at me during dinner.

I had many ways of getting back at her. Sometimes I put a few darts in her cuffs so that when her wrists swelled, which they always did when she was performing, she would have to cut the cloth later to get her arms out. Or I snipped her lace ties just a little, which kept her from pulling her corset as tightly as she liked; or I sewed a small pigeon feather into the back of one of her costumes so that when she walked across the stage the shaft scratched at her skin.

I was Comfort's seamstress, dresser, and trunk packer. And a hundred other things as well. She was the Famous Comfort Vertue. That was her stage name.

But she was not famous, and she was not related to Lord and Lady Vertue of Suffolk, England, as she claimed at dinner. Comfort was nearly thirty but gave her age as my own, twenty-two. In the last six months, offers for ingénue roles had begun to dry up, but she was not yet willing to move on to stately matriarchs or widows, since those parts received second or third billing at best. Instead she booked us both tickets to St. Louis on the steamboat *Moselle* in search, as she put it, of new opportunities.

We had quarreled about it in Pittsburgh. I wanted to take an over-land coach to New York, where there were more opportunities. But Comfort had had enough of New York.

"We haven't enough money for that, Frog. Anyway, I've got an offer from the New Theatre in St. Louis. The director is putting together a company."

She smiled at me. She was a very beautiful woman, my cousin, with bright, reddish-gold hair that I curled in rags for her every night, and clear blue eyes, and good teeth. Although her nose was ever so slightly crooked, it called attention to the cleft on her chin.

"A *firm* offer?" I asked.

She liked to say that she rescued me after my mother died, but that was not true. She recognized an opportunity is all. Like the opportunity she now saw in St. Louis. No one knew us there. She could be twenty-two and just starting out, instead of almost thirty and stumbling along. I would be who I always was: her dark-haired cousin who sewed for her and stayed well off the stage. I could be twenty-two also. Which I was.

On the afternoon the *Moselle* went down, we'd already been on board for six days and expected to be on it for six more. At dinner, Comfort and I sat at a large table near the center of the dining room with seven or eight other guests, all of us pulled up close to the white cloth with its small dots of gravy stains spattered over it, while men in white jackets brought out platters from the kitchen: broiled and fried chicken, breaded cod, cold ham, hot bread, pickled peaches, pre-served cucumbers, and big ironstone bowls of steaming vegetables. The dining room smelled of roasted meat and turpentine, and there was a low but constant roar from the boilers, which we had to speak over. This was no problem for Comfort, a trained actress. One of the ladies at our table, Mrs. Flora Howard, a red-faced abolitionist—I called her Florid Howard to myself—was someone we'd begun to eat all our meals with. She was telling us a funny story about a mule, and I suppose I must have been smiling, because another one of our party, Mr. Thaddeus Mason, an actor like Comfort, suddenly said, "Why, May! What a beautiful smile!"

I immediately felt self-conscious and pulled my lips together.

"Now see what you've done," Mrs. Howard said. "I do believe I've never seen May's teeth before."

"The smile that is all the more entrancing because it's so rare," Thaddeus said in his poetry-reciting voice. Thaddeus was a shade shorter than average and wore his curly blond hair rather long, like a younger man. We knew him from the Third Street Theatre, where Comfort played opposite him for a month. Mrs. Flora Howard had been visiting her brother in Shippingport and now was going to visit another brother in Vevay. She was a heavyset woman who wore long ropes of pearls and silver chains every day over the drapery of her silk dresses. A great many yards of fabric went into each dress she wore, and I wondered if the cost alone wouldn't induce her to slim down a bit; but Comfort told me that Mrs. Howard was a wealthy widow with a large, beautifully furnished house in Cincinnati—Comfort always seems to find out about such things—so perhaps she felt she could afford her weight.

Comfort tilted her head at Mrs. Howard and smiled her dimpled, childlike smile; she was used to being the one who received the attention and she didn't like sharing it with me. Nor did I like taking any share, for that matter.

"You have a great deal of talent," she said to Mrs. Howard, "if you can make my cousin smile. And if you can make her laugh, why, I'll give you a dollar. I believe I've heard May laugh only twice in all of my life."

An exaggeration. I dislike exaggerations.

"I laugh sometimes," I said.

"I'm sure you have a beautiful laugh," Thaddeus put in. "Like your smile."

Comfort frowned. Attention, to her, was what sewing a perfectly straight hemline was to me, and we were both willing to work hard to get what we wanted.

"Why, look at that: Is that girl going to sing for us?" she asked loudly, changing the subject. "I do believe I'm right! I do believe that girl is actually going to sing for her supper!"

I turned. A tall woman wearing a rose-colored dress was standing on a small dais, preparing to perform. Next to her a man with a violin under his chin played a few tuning notes to get our attention, and when the room quieted he pointed to her with his violin bow and said: "Ladies and gentlemen! Miss Helena Cushing, from Hugo and Helena's Floating Theatre."

The closed glass doors of the dining room cast a diffused afternoon light onto her pink dress and her lovely soft face. Above us, the chandeliers swung as the boat made a slight course adjustment, and then Miss Cushing spread her arms and began to sing:

"Drink to me only with thine eyes, and I will pledge with mine
Or leave a kiss within the cup and I'll not ask for wine . . ."

She sang in a composed and relaxed manner, not at all as if she was standing in front of a hundred strangers with napkins tucked into their collars and their forks halfway to their mouths, but rather like someone alone in a room, letting her tea grow cold while she followed her own thoughts to their rightful end. When she finished, there was some polite applause, and then people began ringing their bells for more bread.

Miss Cushing turned to the violinist and began speaking to him energetically. All in a moment her lovely stillness was gone.

"Well, that's just terrible," Mrs. Howard announced.

I followed her gaze to a nearby table, where an elderly woman in a dark green dress was being waited on by a young Negro boy.

"She's brought her slave boy with her," Mrs. Howard said.

The boy was standing behind his mistress's chair, wearing white gloves buttoned tightly at the wrist and a little brown necktie over a freshly ironed white shirt. I'd grown up in the North and had only seen slaves a few times before. Although his shirt had clearly been made over for him—the line of the shoulders was not quite right—he or someone else took great care to keep it clean.

One of our dinner table companions, a man with mutton-chop whiskers and a ring with an emerald stone on his smallest finger, leaned forward.

"In St. Louis I hear the slaves all speak French," he said.

"He's like a piece of luggage to her," Mrs. Howard went on in a loud, indignant voice. "She just picks him up and carries him with her wherever she goes. Someone should snatch him away right now and take him to Canada."

The man with the pinkie ring scowled. "That's theft; they could hang you for that. Take that man Lovejoy: all he did was run a few antislavery articles in his paper and they burned down the press and him in it. Or shot him—I can't remember which."

But this just made Mrs. Howard more adamant. "Slavery must be eradicated, not tomorrow but today. I'm sure everyone at this table agrees."

For some reason her eyes rested on me. Getting no reaction—I was not sure what she wanted—her gaze traveled to Comfort. "What do you think, my dear?" she asked.

But Comfort was still looking at the singer. "Oh, she has a pleasant enough voice to be sure," she said. "But nowadays you need to know a bit of everything. A pleasant voice is not enough. Why, I was at a theater in Boston where they wanted me to dance a jig. A jig! And they all want someone singing 'Jump Jim Crow.' I could kill Tom Rice for writing that down. I know him, of course. We performed together in Tarrytown. He heard the song from a stable hand in back of the theater. I was on the stage at the time."

Not true. More than an exaggeration—a lie. I wiped my hands on a dark brown napkin that seemed already greasy.

"May was there, too," Comfort went on, giving me a sly look, and I saw that she was not done teasing me. "She heard the stable boy singing it herself. If she had been quicker, she might have written down the song first and made us our fortune."

"Is that so?" Thaddeus asked, helping himself to another piece of cod. The food on the boat came with the price of the ticket.

"No," I said. "It is not. Tom Rice heard the song in Baltimore, not Tarrytown. And I was nowhere near."

Comfort burst out laughing. "There—did I not tell you, Mrs. Howard? May cannot tell a lie! She simply cannot do it!"

I looked at her sharply. Had she been talking about me before I sat down? But Mrs. Howard was still staring daggers at the woman with the slave boy.

"She never in her *life* has been able to tell a lie," Comfort said, this time addressing everyone at the table. "Not even to say she likes your hat when she does not. Once I heard her tell a bride on the morning of her wedding that the weather would certainly not get any better that day. And it was raining only very slightly at the time."

The man with the emerald pinkie ring looked me over while still chewing his food, as though I were a curiosity. A dark anger rose in me.

"And then of course May was right: a storm hit while they were in the church," Comfort went on gaily, "and they missed their wedding breakfast, afraid to leave for the lightning. We ate it ourselves. Isn't that right, May?"

I felt my face flush hotter and crossed my fork and knife carefully over my plate. I did not want to speak—I do not like speaking in groups—but I had to say, "No. We did not."

Comfort laughed again. She had everyone's attention now. "See! She can't tell a lie, not even to let me save face, and I believe she is most fond of me in all of the world."

Mrs. Howard, Thaddeus, and the man with the emerald pinkie ring all turned to look at me. I pinched my wrist, willing the conversation to be over. I did not like speaking in a group, I did not like being teased, and I did not, above all, like everyone watching me. This was my punishment for smiling.

"You *are* fond of me, Frog, aren't you?" Comfort teased in her flirtatious voice.

I looked away. I am fond of my cousin, it's true, but at that moment I hated her.

After dinner Comfort and Mrs. Howard went for a walk around the deck, and Thaddeus Mason accompanied the man with the emerald pinkie ring to smoke cigars. I went by myself to the ladies' cabin to sew and plot revenge on my cousin.

The ladies' cabin was a large square room, fitted up rather shabbily compared to the men's, which Comfort and I had peeked into when we first came on board. Ours had a couple of thin rugs on the floor and only two framed pictures, but at least there were no spittoons. Fifteen or twenty women were already in the room when I entered, sitting in upholstered straight-backed chairs in little groups of three or four, all of them reading or talking or sewing.

I found an empty chair near a window where I could look out on our westward progress. Since the Ohio flows downstream from Pittsburgh to where it meets the Mississippi River in Cairo, Illinois— passing four more states in between—we were going fairly fast with the current, and, sitting down, I could hear the rhythmic thrashing of the paddlewheels as they churned up the water.

I arranged my light shawl over my knees, which get cold, and pro-

ceeded to take out a needle and thread and a squat jar of tea. I was
sewing little tea sachets that I sold for extra money, an invention I
thought of myself: shredded tea leaves, measured out for one cup,
folded inside a square of absorbent muslin and then sewn closed. I
used to take around a box of them during intermission at whatever
theater Comfort was performing, explaining to the theatergoers how
they could dip the sachets in a cup of boiling water for a convenient
single serving of tea. I always gave the theater managers ten percent
of my profit, and I was careful to calculate their amount to the penny,
although I could have easily cheated them, they paid so little attention to what I did. But I would never cheat them, because cheating
is the same thing as lying.

Comfort was right when she said I could not lie. It's not on principle. For reasons I can't explain, I feel a great need to give a pointedly
accurate account of the facts. And since I don't always understand
what people mean outside of their words, I might be more honest
than is necessary or even desired. My mother used to blame this on
the loss of hearing in my left ear. I could not hear the undertones,
she explained, and that was why I didn't pick up what other people
might from a conversation. For instance, if a woman said to me, to
use Comfort's example, *I am not sure about this new hat I bought,* I
probably would not guess that she wanted me to tell her I liked it.
Instead I would try to list what I saw as the hat's good points and bad
in order to help her reach a conclusion. I don't know why Comfort
laughs at me when I do this. It's just who I am, and she knows this.
Why should someone lie about a hat?

However, pushing a needle in and out of a small space always
soothes me, and as the boat veered to stop at one of Cincinnati's
outlying landings, rocking gently forward and back over the thrum
of its boilers, I began to forget my irritation with Comfort. I'd been
on steamboats before and didn't mind the smell of wet wood, cigar
smoke, and roasted meat from meals long past that pervaded every

cabin and deck, and I enjoyed the sight of the Ohio River with its long line of willows bending to bathe their leaves in the water. The river was the natural division between the North and the South, with Ohio on one side and Kentucky on the other. Along the shore I could see crooked shacks where the woodcutters lived, and a little boy with a bluish-white complexion waded along in the mud leading a half-starved cow. He looked up as the *Moselle* steamed past as if it alone were his instrument of redemption and here we were, passing him by. I snipped off the end of thread with my scissors: another tea sachet finished.

"After Chautauqua I may take the water cure at Malvern," one of the ladies opposite me said in a dry, feathery voice. It was the elderly lady from dinner who had brought her slave boy with her, although the boy was not with her now. She sat with her old, gnarled hands folded on the dark green silk of her dress, and a couple of shiny gray ringlets hung from beneath her matching green cap. As I cut more muslin into squares I could hear the steam on the boat rise to an unusual pitch while we waited for the newcomers to board. Later I heard that the captain of the *Moselle* was overly proud of his vessel, which had recently set a record for the quickest journey from Pittsburgh, and that on this particular day he wanted to beat the steamboat *Tribune* to the next landing. The new passengers pushed their way onto our crowded vessel, the captain raised his arm, and we were off, hoping to make up the time. But the wheel of the *Moselle* did not even make one full rotation when all four boilers burst at the same time with a sound like a full stockade of gunpowder all exploding at once.

It was a noise I felt like a hit. For a moment it seemed as though the air itself had cracked open and the boat lurched sharply, causing all of us to fall from our chairs. The unlit oil lamps crashed to the floor, and above us the chandeliers swung crazily as everyone in the room tumbled toward the bulkhead. My face swept over someone's gown and I was momentarily pinned by the elderly woman who wanted to go to Malvern.

"What's happened?" she asked in her old, feathery voice.

"She's blown!" someone cried.

The boat lurched and stopped. For the first few minutes all any of us could do was try to stand up and help others get up, too. Everyone was saying the same thing: "Are you hurt?" "No, are you?" The old woman who wanted to go to Malvern was hugging her elbow. "Are we sinking?" she asked me. Without waiting for an answer, she said, "We must get to the deck before we go under."

Her cap had been partially knocked back and I saw that her shiny gray ringlets were fake, sewn onto the inside of the cap, and that her real hair was wispy and scarce. Although there were easily fifteen of us in the room, after the explosion my world shrank to the two or three people around me. Somehow the Malvern lady and I and another woman with her child made it our business to help each other. The air in the room was dangerously smoky and my ears hurt from the sound of the blast, but the walls, I noticed, were still level.

"Is the boat on fire?" the woman with the child asked.

"Let's get up on deck," I told her. "Surely some boats will come to come help us."

My voice seemed to come from my ears and everything looked like it was outlined in black: the doorframe, the edge of the steps. We were all trying to get out of the cabin now, and for the moment everyone was still orderly, although later I found bruises on my arm that I couldn't account for, sharply yellow and round as buttons. In all this time I did not think of Comfort—that's how dazed I was. I thought only of myself, the Malvern lady, and the lady with her child. But once we got up to the deck we were separated, and I don't know if in the end they were saved or not, if the elderly lady ever got to Malvern, or if the mother drowned with her child.

On the deck I was pushed all the way to the rail by people com-

ing up behind me, and when I finally could stop and look around, I
saw that our situation was even bleaker than I had imagined. There
were still several hours of daylight left; that was one good thing. But
the upper deck of the vessel in front of the side wheels had been
blown to splinters. Anyone unlucky enough to be standing there
when the boilers exploded had almost certainly been killed, and I
could see a dozen charred bodies floating in the river. So far there
were no boats coming out to save us, although where I stood, on the
lower deck behind the wheels, was crowded with people scanning
the banks.

I searched for my cousin in the throng but could not immediately
spot her. One man, someone in uniform, was trying to give directions: ladies here, gentlemen there. He had a moustache like wet
straw and a blue coat, and his stiff collar was spattered with blood.
I'm not sure anyone was paying him attention. It was hard to know
what to pay attention to. Without steerage, we were drifting with the
current, moving farther and farther away from the Ohio embank-
ment. Kentucky, on the other side of the river, was even farther away.
A dry, gunpowdery smoke hung above us, and I could see several fires
burning in the bow of the ship.

How long could we remain afloat? That's what people were asking
each other in high, frightened voices, and there was a good deal of
jostling as people tried to move as far back from the front of the boat
as possible. Some of the wounded in the river were trying to climb
back on board, and, looking down, I saw a man's burned hand, unat-
tached to a body, in our wake.

My stomach turned over. "Comfort!" I shouted.

The hand had an emerald ring on its pinkie finger.

"*Comfort!*"

The man in the blue uniform said sharply, "Keep calm." He had
a thunderous voice, and even just speaking it carried farther than
my shout. A moment later the boat, which had been drifting toward

Kentucky all this while, stopped abruptly as if it had caught on some-thing. Everyone turned and looked out to see what it was.

For a moment, nothing. Then the boat tipped. Only a slight tip, but we all felt it. Leaning back instinctively as though my body could right this imbalance, I felt a powerful urge, like a trapped animal, to get away, to be elsewhere. On the Kentucky side of the boat people began to shout, and on the Ohio side there was a lot of shoving and movement. I gripped the railing hard every time a person pushed against me in their effort to cross to the other side, where, anyone could see, the situation was no better. I turned my deaf ear toward Kentucky and watched the crowd on the Ohio side swell and pulse like a heart. Sweat ran in a thin line down my spine. It had been a warm day, but the fires on the bow made the air positively hot.

People began to panic and jump into the river. A few feet away from me a man stripped off his clothes and dove into the water hold-ing his wallet in his teeth. Seconds later a young woman jumped in after him fully clothed. She never resurfaced.

"Dov'é il mio papa?"

I looked down. A girl in a clean brown-checked dress was looking up at me. She was Italian and must have mistaken me for Italian. It's happened before—my black hair and black eyes. I could see faint lines where her hem had been let down, and there was a small cross-stitched patch near her shoulder. Comfort was twice in an Italian operetta, so I was able to reply, *"Non so."* I don't know. The girl was eight or nine years old and she held her hands in front of her like a supplicant or someone in prayer.

To my right I heard another loud splash as someone else dove into the water. Besides the burned bodies from the initial explosion, the river was now littered with a second front of corpses: foolish women like the one I'd seen jumping into the water a few moments before without regard for their boots and their heavy dresses, their mutton-shaped sleeves floating out at their sides, their fleshy arms and legs hidden beneath yards of sodden cloth—striped, burgundy, checkered, a few tartans, some of the colors more visible than others. There were drowned men, too, a few of them faceup. The water near the boat had become very crowded with bodies both dead and alive, although the deck didn't seem any less populated. Where were the barges to pick us up? All I could see were a row of warehouses on the waterfront and tall factory chimneys behind them. Although the Ohio River is almost a thousand miles long, it's only a mile across at its widest, and we were more or less in the middle of it. A few men on the shore had waded into the water and were trying to reach the first set of people swimming for land, but still I could see no boats.

Every one of us would live or die on our own; I understood that now. A woman a few feet away from me began to scream, and the noise was like glass breaking inside my ear. The front half of the boat, still aflame in parts, was tipping in small, jerky stages into the water. In a quarter of an hour we would be completely submerged, but it was the scream that finally spurred me to action. The little Italian girl was searching my face as if to say, *What now?*

I looked again for Comfort—I shouted her name again—but it was useless: there were too many people, and I could not think clearly. When I glanced down I saw that I was still holding the pair of fabric scissors I'd been using when the boilers exploded. Had I been holding them this whole time? I couldn't feel them in my fingers.

I knew one more piece of Italian: "*Io mi chiamo May,*" I said. Then in English: "What is your name?"

"*Mi chiamo Giulia.*"

"Good," I said. "All right, Giulia. Look. I have a pair of scissors here, do you see? I'm going to cut your dress off. We don't have time for all these buttons. We need to cut off our clothes so they don't drown us." I looked at the riverbank again. I had swum across the Tiffin River near my girlhood home many times, and it was about as wide as where we were now from the shore. My mother taught me to swim, and it was something I did better than anyone else, even Comfort. When I was swimming, all the noise of the world receded and I was alone with the feel of water like silk against my skin. I liked that feeling. I thought I could do it.

Giulia's eyes were wet with fear but she didn't cry, and although she opened her mouth to put her tongue between her lips, she made no sound when I began to cut her dress off, starting from her small pointed collar and proceeding down. The noise around us was getting louder, both wailing and shouting, and a group of women had knelt down with their foreheads on the railing and were praying aloud. Occasionally hot cinders from the bow fires floated back onto the deck, burning our hands and faces. I couldn't take a deep breath for fear of them. After I was finished cutting the girl's dress off, I began cutting off my own.

When we were both in our muslin shifts, I tucked my father's pocket watch, which hung from a silver chain around my neck, under the fabric. Then I looked for a place to ease our way into the river. If we jumped, we would go down a long way before coming up again, and Giulia might panic. Other people were climbing down the port side of the boat—their feet on the window ledges, then the latticework, then the edge of its muddy hull—and after looking for a better way and finding none, I did the same with the girl holding on to my neck.

2

My mother's only brother had drowned when she was a girl, and for that reason she made sure that I knew how to swim at an early age. We lived near a small town on the Tiffin River about fifty miles southwest of Toledo. Our property was on raised land above the riverbank, but, even so, the Tiffin flooded us and everyone else every five or six years until at last funds were raised to build a levee. When I was six, one of our barns got swept away. I still remember the sight of its buckled and splintered wood leaning against a couple of mud-encrusted trees where it landed, a good half mile from where it had been built.

I loved to swim. I liked feeling the slight pressure of the water like an eggshell around me, and I liked being at a distance from everyone else. My mother tied a red ribbon around my head so she could watch my progress. She always wore a faded blue wraparound dress with two cloth ties instead of buttons—the dress she cleaned in—and she sat on an old oak stump on the lowest part of the bank to watch me.

The river ran behind our house and heavy white oak trees grew down nearly to the waterline, so she probably felt it was private enough for that dress. My mother cared quite a lot about privacy, as well as prompt housekeeping and regularly paid accounts. She liked everything to be neatly arranged and organized efficiently—"my German side," she used to say. She was an excellent dressmaker, and her seams and hems were straighter than anyone else's, although unlike me she never used a measure. I remember how she would touch a hem I was working on to show me where it had veered off a little. She had me touch it, too, as if the misalignment was something I could understand better by feel. Then she would tell me to pull it out and start again.

I wanted to pull it out. I wanted my hems to be as straight as hers. I don't know if I inherited my feelings from her or if I learned them, but I always took great pleasure in neat, straight lines and even seams. When I was older, my sewing became a matter of pride to my mother, something she showed people when they visited.

"May did this when she was only six years old," she said, passing around a gingham dress I'd made for my doll. "She learned how to sew buttonholes without asking one person."

What she didn't tell people—what perhaps she did not even know—was how she lifted her eyebrows slightly whenever I asked her a question, as though she found it strange that I did not already know the answer myself. This was less about her confidence in my abilities than a general ignorance of what children learn by themselves and what you must teach them. My mother was forty years old when I was born, and I think that she never quite got over the surprise of having me. My father was one month shy of fifty-five. They had been married almost twenty years, and whatever thoughts they might have once had about children must have been long past when they found out I was coming. My father raised cows; he died when I was eleven. His hair was fully white by the time I was four, and by the time I was nine he walked with a cane. He had but one tease and that was to say when I did something careless, that he would send me back to work at the glass factory if I did it again. Then he would smile and pinch my arm gently to show he was joking.

My mother's father was from Germany, and from him she got the habit of drinking a glass of hard cider every night after dinner. Then she came up to my bedroom and sat on my bed. "Good night, May. God be with you," she would say. Sometimes she said it in German, and I wondered if this was what her parents had said to her when she was a girl. I understood that the cider she drank each night from her father's heavy yellow glass, cloudy with age, was her way of honoring her past, and that sitting on my bed and her words to me—the only time she mentioned God to my memory—was her way of telling me she loved me.

Other than this, she did not show much emotion. She always dressed in dark blue or brown and moved quickly, erectly, and with concentrated purpose from the moment she got up until her glass of cider at night. One of her interests was the price of pig iron, and she kept a little book in her apron pocket where she recorded each day its fluctuating prices. It was my belief that she owned some shares of pig iron, and that belief I found out to be true when she died.

My father took care of the animals and the outbuildings, and he constructed and repaired the light wooden wheels for the cheese. My mother oversaw the two dairymaids who milked our cows, and she also made it her job to teach *them* how to swim. And when Comfort and her mother moved to the little town near our farm the summer I was nine, Comfort was told that she must learn to swim also.

It was the first time we met. I was just coming up to the house after visiting the cows—something I did every morning—and I saw her standing by the back door with my mother and a woman who looked like an older, thinner, unhappier version of my mother.

"May, come meet your cousin and your aunt," my mother called to me.

Comfort was already grown up, at least to me, for she was sixteen years old and stunningly beautiful, while I was nine and still awkwardly growing. She and her mother had been living in Europe with

Comfort's stepfather, who was Dutch and a gambler, which meant they moved constantly from town to town. He died after falling from a horse late at night, drunk, and after that Aunt Ann took to the stage for a few years, playing the matronly roles that Comfort would come to despise. But Aunt Ann had quit that life now and was moving to America to be closer to her sister.

"Comfort, do you know how to swim?" my mother had asked that first day. They would stay with us the entire summer and then rent a few rooms in the nearby town of Oxbow in the fall. My aunt Ann thought this would give Comfort "more opportunity" than living on a dairy farm. Opportunity always carried great weight with both of them, perhaps an effect of the gambling nature of their early days.

"A little," Comfort answered, looking at me and winking.

For some reason her wink thrilled me.

"I'll teach you," my mother said.

As I made my slow way across the Ohio River holding on to Giulia, however, I couldn't think about Comfort. I could only think about the bank: how far away was it, could I reach it, and could I keep my grip on the girl? Only later did I remind myself that my mother had taught Comfort how to swim, hoping this meant that she was alive.

With one arm crossed over Giulia's little chest and under her arm, I paddled very slowly north toward Ohio. I can remember only a few things about that twilight swim: the feel of Giulia's wet hair pasted against my neck, the sight of two men in the water clinging to the corpse of a mule, and the cries of those drowning around us. Also—but I might have dreamed this later in one of my nightmares—I remember seeing fragments of some silky material floating by me in the water. At first I thought they were the muslin tea sachets I'd been sewing on the boat, but then I realized they were bits of burned skin.

I had to stop a number of times to rest and tread water. After the first time Giulia understood what I was doing and, holding on to my shoulder, scissored her legs alongside mine, both of us facing the bank. The water was cold and the slight current pushed us away from where we wanted to go. Treading water let me rest my arms and lungs but made me colder, and as soon as I could I pushed off again, which I signaled to Giulia by squeezing her arm.

Her thin, barely clad body was a long, heavy sack that grew heavier the longer I swam. The slithery water fingered my skin and heaved itself against me, and I tried not to think about what was swimming beneath us: the whiskered catfish I'd seen fishermen haul up from among the rocks as the steamship trudged past them. My left arm grew numb and seemed to harden around Giulia's little body while my right arm propelled us gradually forward.

Our progress seemed impossibly slow, but when at last my foot found the river's bottom, my relief was like a sob in my belly, and then I remember nothing more until Giulia and I were sitting side by side on newspapers that someone had spread out for us on a dry log on the bank.

But even here, out of habit or in need of her warmth, I held her close, and she pressed her little body against mine. A woman gave us blankets and another woman took down our names. My relief melted into a kind of stunned exhaustion, and I looked out at the river we had just swum across as if I needed, even from here, to make sense of it. Of course, there was no sense to be made. With my good ear I could still hear people in the water crying for help.

Giulia moved her wet head from side to side, looking at every man who walked by us as the sun fell over the horizon. Small boats and rafts had finally begun picking up the swimmers, but more shouted for help than there were boats to help them. I looked for Comfort in the water but I was too far away to make out anyone's features, and exhaustion held me in place. I had no sensation in my arms and legs, and my breath felt like a quietly wheezing animal inside my chest.

Suddenly, Giulia shouted, "Papa!" with a voice strangely loud and deep for a girl so young, and she seemed to spring with one motion off the log and right into a man's arms.

The man was barefoot and hatless and wore only wet long johns under his blanket. He was not very tall and his shoulders were stooped, but he had Giulia's nose and something of her bearing. There was no mistaking him for anything other than kin, and I felt then, as I feel now, that it was a kind of miracle that they both had made it off the *Moselle* alive, considering how many had not. Giulia's father wrapped his wet arms around Giulia, and I felt the cold air come into the space under my arm where a moment ago I'd been holding her. I watched them embrace and cry. He was sobbing openly, something I had never seen a man do before.

When Giulia led him back to me, he said something in Italian in a voice that cracked. He stopped and cried some more and then started again. I listened to him, not understanding a word, and I tried to look him in the eye as my mother always reminded me to do. I was glad they were alive and I was glad that they had found each other, but I was embarrassed by his attention. When he finished speaking, Giulia hugged me and I let myself be hugged, trying not to stiffen. After she let go I relaxed, and then I looked at her face carefully so I would remember it. I must have gotten a good image of it in my mind, for it often came back to me later in my dreams, but in my dreams she was not smiling; she was scared.

"*Grazie, grazie, che il buon Dio con voi,*" Giulia's father called back.

I watched them until Giulia's little head became just a dot in the distance. Then it was gone. The lamplighter began lighting the lamps alongside the river, and when I looked out at the water again I saw that it was streaked with the deep purples and blues of sunset. The cool evening air seemed to blow down from the town and up from the river both at once, and I pulled my blanket closer around my shoulders and stood.

I needed to find Comfort. She was wearing her chartreuse dress. She had her favorite hair ornament in her hair, a silver bird with a turquoise eye. I tried to remember other details. But although I stumbled barefoot along the debris on the beach, looking at each face I passed and at all the faces of the waterlogged dead pulled up from the river, I could not find her.

Early the next morning, the Cincinnati City Council appointed twenty-one men to retrieve the remaining bodies from the river. Some men cut back the saplings and brush that grew down into the water in order to make the bank wider, while others pulled the bodies onto flat sheets and arranged them faceup with scraps of clothes or personal articles alongside them to help with identification. By the time I got back to the riverbank, a large tent had been erected over the bodies to protect them from the sun: for April, the weather was unusually mild.

The corpses were laid out with their feet pointing toward the river like an accusation, and their clothes were stained with mud and blood. The woman in front of me, Mrs. Alma Stoke, her face swollen with crying, pinched her nose with her fingers as she looked at the bloated faces. The night before Mrs. Stoke and I had both been given lodging in the home of a city gauger named Nedel. Mrs. Stoke was looking for her husband and three children.

When we came to the last row in the tent, a man with a city emblem on his coat said, "There's more at the morgue, taken last night."

This was a one-story yellow brick building a few blocks away. A line had formed at the door, and we were led inside in groups of five. Here the bodies seemed more dignified, lifted off the ground and laid out on low tables with sheets up to their necks and their hair brushed. The floor and the lower halves of the walls were tiled with teal-blue tiles, and in the middle of the floor stood a drain.

Comfort was not among those on the tables, but Mrs. Stoke found her husband and two of her children. Before that moment the five of us looking were silent, and then all at once her wails filled the room, echoing off the tiled floor. I turned my good ear away from the noise and found myself staring at a metal counter with unmarked toe tags, needles and sewing materials, a bone saw, and other tools of the trade. Bile rose in my throat. I was beginning to feel desperate.

Back out on the sidewalk, a boy with a brown jug gave me half a cup of water even though I didn't have a penny to pay him. People were gathering with signs: "Looking for: one child, gray dress, yellow stockings, called Anna Weaver" and "John and Edward Sunbury lodging at 2 West Circle and looking for their mother" and "Frank Jewett! I am alive and staying on Cross Street at Mrs. Vernon's, on the corner." Horses pulling wagons with company names painted on the sides passed me in a steady stream, and I stood there staring at them for a long time, not knowing what to do next. She knows how to swim, I reminded myself, but I was by now sick with anxiety.

"Well, well, if it isn't the girl with the ephemeral smile."

I turned to see a man walking toward me with shoulder-length curly blond hair: Mr. Thaddeus Mason. His left arm was in a sling made of soft black cotton dotted with irregular specks like the night sky on a very clear night if stars were light green and not white. He held a jar of jam in his injured hand and a spoon in the other.

A warm flood of relief washed over me. "Mr. Mason!" I said.

"Thaddeus," he corrected as he led me to a bench in the shade. "My dear, I was worried about you!" I could tell he hadn't given a thought to me until he saw me this moment, but I didn't mind: I was just glad to be speaking to someone I knew.

Thaddeus licked his spoon and put it in his jacket pocket. Despite being an actor and not rich, Thaddeus always dressed well. Today he was wearing a dark green jacket with a wide striped tie and light-colored trousers—certainly borrowed, and yet the clothes seemed tailored to fit him. When I asked him what had happened to his arm, he said, "A little sprain from my fall; nothing serious. Now, what news do you have of your beautiful cousin? Please tell me you are waiting here for her, that she's just gone to post a letter or to collect a check."

I don't know why actors are always going to the post office looking for money in the mail; in my experience they either get paid promptly in person or not at all. Two young women came strolling toward us arm in arm, taking care to keep away from the pigs, which in Cincinnati roam freely in the streets. One of the women had hair the same reddish-gold color as Comfort's, and all at once I felt tears stand in my eyes.

"I fear that she's dead," I said.

Thaddeus said in a kind voice, "Oh, my dear," and I looked down at my lap. But when he took my fingers in his, I blinked back my tears and concentrated on easing my hand away. To my surprise, Thaddeus laughed and his manner shifted.

"You don't take much in the way of sympathy, do you?" he asked, and for once his voice sounded genuine. "Listen, they're printing up a new broadsheet now. I'm guessing that with all the confusion Comfort didn't think to give her name last night. I'll just pop over to the newspaper office and see what I can find out. Here," he said, fishing out the jam jar from his sling. "Sour cherry preserves."

He didn't leave the spoon, but in any case I wasn't hungry. I watched him stride down the street in his usual confident manner. When I first met him, Thaddeus seemed to me like an opportunistic man with most of his opportunities behind him. For all his long yellow hair he was aging: there were small wrinkles around his eyes and laugh lines at the corners of his mouth. But he was not unattractive, and if he worried about his own prospects, he never let on. He had a way of looking straight at a woman as though he could see her hidden self and he liked it. I'd seen him look this way at Comfort whenever he wanted something from her. A loan of money, usually.

It felt a long time until he came back, but when he did he was carrying a folded newspaper in his good hand and he was grinning.

"There," he said, opening it up for me to see.

On the page, three columns of names were printed in dark type: "Dead," "Missing," and "Saved." Comfort's name was just below Mrs. Flora Howard's in the category of "Saved." The print was very small but there was no mistake.

Comfort Vertue. Of course she would save herself; why did I doubt that? As I held the long paper I noticed my fingers were shaking, and the page folded backward in the wind.

"But where could she be?" I asked. I cast around in my mind for an explanation. "With Mrs. Howard?"

"The woman boasted of having a large house." Thaddeus grinned at me. In direct sunlight he looked even older. "Now's our chance to see."

Mrs. Flora Howard had not exaggerated about her home, which was an immense sand-colored stone house, three stories high, with a round turret on the left. The cabdriver—Thaddeus persuaded him to give us a free ride, since we were "victims of the *Moselle*, don't you know"—let us out at the corner, and we walked up to the house between tightly clipped shrubbery, which flanked the drive like armrests. As we came to the front door I felt my heart give two hard beats against my ribs and then settle itself into a faster rhythm.

Thaddeus rapped the large brass knocker. A moment later the blackest man I'd ever seen opened the door. He was immaculately dressed in a brown suit with a white shirt, and his eyes went straight to the hem of my skirt, which I knew was too short.

"We've come to see Mrs. Howard," Thaddeus said. He gave our names and explained that we were all on the *Moselle* together. "And Miss Comfort Vertue, if she is here."

"Is she here?" I asked.

The man kept his hand on the door. His suit coat was so crisp that it looked as though it had been cut from mahogany wood instead of cloth, and I wanted to tell him that my shawl, visibly mended, and my short dress were both borrowed.

"May we come in?" Thaddeus asked.

Still the man did not answer. He shut the door.

The color rose slightly on Thaddeus's face. "Well!" he said, drawing back his chin. The man's silence had surprised me, too, but he hadn't looked completely blank when we asked about Comfort, so that gave me hope.

After a few moments the man opened the door again and stepped aside to let us into the hallway, which was very wide, almost a room by itself. A long wooden settee painted black stood against the wall to our left, and three framed pictures hung in a precise line above it. Mrs. Howard was coming down the hallway, wiping the back of her neck with a handkerchief.

"I don't know why you felt compelled to come in person when a note would have done just as well," she said. She took my hand for a brief moment before letting it drop. She was wearing a dove-gray gown with long silver chains over it, one of them supporting a small bottle of perfume.

"Mrs. Howard," Thaddeus said. "I'm so happy to see you alive and well!"

"Yes, yes, it's been quite a remarkable few days, and I must return the compliments, of course, so happy to see you both, and so on. But I expect you've come to inquire about Comfort. I thought at least we'd have a day or two to recuperate first, but here you are already. Well, never mind that; I suppose it's natural." She frowned at me.

"So Comfort is here? She's well?" I asked.

"Of course she's here; isn't that plain by what I am saying? She received a nasty blow to the head, but Dr. Penrod has seen her twice

and declares she is in no danger. Well, these doctors are overly san-
guine sometimes, but I daresay he's right as long as she is adequately
nursed, which I am more than capable of, considering how I nursed
Mr. Howard in his last illness for over a year—and that was a bad
case, let me assure you." She paused to frown at me again.

"A very bad case," I said, for I thought she was waiting for my response, "considering how it ended in death." Last illness, she'd said.

Her face became very red, and I thought of my private nickname
for her: Florid.

"Well, Comfort is not so bad as that; no, indeed! And it was not
my fault that Mr. Howard . . . No one could say I didn't do everything
possible. And I am quite just as careful with Comfort . . ."

She went on talking without a break and without leading us out
of the hallway. She put me in mind of a stout operatic singer I once
knew, capable of talking over anyone and with terrible breath besides, but Mrs. Howard smelled of mint and violets. Her bottom two
teeth grew in toward each other, and I found myself watching them
while she spoke.

". . . and the oarsman swung around at the shout and hit Comfort
with his oar. She nearly fell in the river again but for me. And then
when I chastised the man, he had the effrontery to remind us he had
just saved our lives!" She was telling us about her adventures, which
I wanted to hear from Comfort.

"I'd like to see her," I said.

But Mrs. Howard paid no attention; perhaps she did not even
hear me. "Fortunately, Donaldson was waiting at the river with the
carriage—he came as soon as he heard what had happened, which
was quite soon, he's remarkable that way—and we rushed home to
where Dr. Penrod was waiting, thinking I might need some care. I pay
for his boy's schooling, you know; they've sent him back to England
for that, better mathematics and science over there."

"You must let me see Comfort," I said, and when Mrs. Howard

continued talking, I said loudly, "Mrs. Howard, excuse me, I'll just make my way upstairs." That stopped her.

"Oh, no! No, no!" She actually took a step sideways, blocking my passage. "You mustn't disturb her, not now: I've only just gotten her to sleep!"

"You talk as if my cousin were an infant." I looked over at Thaddeus, who was wearing an amused smile. This annoyed me further.

"She just needs rest and good nursing; she'll be perfectly fine. Why won't you take my word on that? I know what I am about. Anyway, she is asleep. Donaldson!"

The black man appeared with a lacquered tea tray. He placed it neatly on the table next to the wooden settee and then turned one of the cup handles to match the direction of the other.

Thaddeus bent to take a look. "Mm. Is that ginger cake?"

"Don't bother to ask him anything; he can't speak," Mrs. Howard said of Donaldson without so much as a glance at the man. "Now I must go. Dr. Penrod is waiting in the kitchen and I want to consult with him. After that, I'm gone to the apothecary. You may leave a note for Comfort if you wish. I hope tomorrow she'll be able to sit upright . . . I'll tell her you were here." She turned to the kitchen and I realized she meant for us to take our tea in the hall.

"She intends to keep Comfort to herself," Thaddeus said in a low voice.

"What do you mean?" But Thaddeus only smiled his annoying smile. "I'm her cousin," I said, and he shrugged.

Donaldson stood by the door with his hands at his sides. If he was surprised that we took up the offer of tea in the hallway, he didn't show it; but I was hungry and thirsty, and Thaddeus never refused food. He cut himself two thick slices of ginger cake and sat down beside me, resting his plate on his knee.

This was not the first time I had been shut out of some room Comfort was in. All too often she met with admirers after the last bow or the curtain call, then the flowers, a final adieu followed by the sweep of her dress as she made her way through the narrow passageways of some theater or another going back to her dressing room (not always the largest—she was not always the star). Perhaps I would be sent to find more wood for the dressing room stove, and when I returned the door would be shut and I would hear her laughing. "Don't come in yet, May!" she would call, and I knew that someone else was in there, untying her laces. It was always chilly in theater hallways. It was not unusual for me to be locked out without a shawl and she would laugh, later, to find me with an old curtain over my shoulders. If the hall porter saw me, he might fetch off a boy to get me a half-pint of beer and some bread. One porter once gave me half of his dinner and let me have his stool while he stood. The clergy like to say that the theater is not a respectable profession, but I have found hall porters to be, to a man, honest, good folk.

In Mrs. Howard's hallway I drank my tea slowly and listened for any noise from upstairs. As I sliced a second piece of cake, Mrs. Howard called out to Donaldson from the kitchen.

Donaldson glanced at us but did not move.

"Donaldson!" she boomed again.

For a moment I thought he was going to open the front door to usher us out, cake in hand, rather than leave us alone, but instead he walked back to the kitchen. How old was he? Forty? Fifty? Seventy? None of those ages would have surprised me. He had wide shoulders and a good build, and he was careful with his clothes, which I approved of. When the door closed behind him, I put my plate down on the settee and stood.

Thaddeus looked up and winked, his mouth full. As I walked silently up the carpeted steps, I could hear Mrs. Howard's loud voice at the back of the house. Upstairs I opened one door and then another until I found Comfort—not asleep in bed, as Mrs. Howard had claimed, but sitting on a white and blue upholstered chair looking out the front window. Her head was bandaged and she was wearing a loose white gown with a white pelisse over it, not tied and not properly ironed.

She turned to look at me as I stepped into the room. "Why . . . May!"

"Don't stand up." I went to her and took her two hands. After so many fittings and costume changes, I was as used to the feel of her skin as I was of my own.

"May! Oh, May!" was all she could say at first, squeezing my fingers, and then, in spite of my words, she stood up and pulled me into a hug. I felt her warmth for a moment before I drew back.

"Did you think I had drowned?" I asked.

"Of course not! No! Well, I don't know! I was trying not to think," she said, and that sounded right to me. "Flora was planning to get the afternoon paper—she'd been checking the names—but I'm not supposed to read any fine print for a day or two. Oh, May, I'm so glad to see you! My little May," she said, although I am now taller than she is—something she always disputes.

"You should rest. I'll be back tomorrow. I just wanted to see if you were really all right."

"Of course I am."

Of course she was. Her hair smelled freshly washed, and the bandage on her forehead was as clean as if it were part of a costume.

"I feel fine," she said, "just the tiniest headache. Of course, I suppose I play it up some; you know how I am."

I looked her over carefully. Her face was paler than usual.

"You should lie down," I told her.

"Oh, all right, but only if you'll come with me, Frog. The bed is heavenly."

I helped her to the bed, and after she was settled I took off my shawl and carefully folded it up into a square, laid it on the end of the mattress, and stretched out next to her with my shoes on the shawl. I looked up at the ceiling. Comfort was right: the bed was very comfortable.

"It's pleasant here, don't you think?" she asked. "A beautiful house. You must move your things in; there's plenty of room. What an ordeal! Did you have a hard time?"

"Mrs. Howard tried to keep me downstairs."

"I meant getting off the boat."

"Oh." As usual I tried to be precise. "Not hard, exactly. Swimming to the bank took a long time. At least, it felt long."

"I can't remember much, and I don't want to," Comfort said.

I turned my head to breathe in the faint rose scent of the pillow. Relief, I sometimes think, is a feeling that doesn't have any feeling: when it happens you hardly notice—you've already turned your mind to other things. Lying on the bed next to my cousin, I began thinking about money and how we could get ourselves to St. Louis. I could always sew or do alterations. Two tickets probably wouldn't cost more than twelve dollars, and in New York or Pittsburgh, when Comfort wasn't in a play, I could make that in a couple of weeks. Or we could tap Mrs. Howard, who was rich and clearly fond of Comfort. She might give us a loan. Thaddeus, of course, was a dead loss.

3

The next morning I was awakened early by the hoarse lowing of cattle. Like most women in the neighborhood, Mrs. Nedel owned her own cow, but the city was too built-up for private stables. Instead the cows, like the pigs, roamed freely in the streets, going into the hills at night and coming back by themselves in the morning. Mrs. Nedel had given me a room on the third floor next to the attic; its only window looked out over the narrow back alley, where I could hear more than one cow lowing angrily for breakfast. I picked up my father's pocket watch to look at the time, forgetting it was waterlogged and broken from my swim across the river. A couple of hams were hanging in one corner of the room to dry, wrapped in cloth bags to keep the insects out, and in the other corner stood a covered rack with Mrs. Nedel's winter dresses. The room smelled like a smokehouse strewn with camphor. I dressed as quickly as I could and went downstairs.

There was coffee already made and set out in the dining room, and as I poured myself a cup I set myself the task for the day: coming up with a plan to make money. I had never intended to be Comfort's dresser, but it was work that suited me. I had gone to visit her in New York after my mother died, not planning to stay. My mother and I had been living in town ever since we sold the dairy farm, and when she died she left me, as I suspected she would, all her shares of pig iron.

It was a handsome amount, although not quite enough to live on. A few weeks later I received a letter from Comfort on heavy, cream-colored paper.

March the 2ⁿᵈ, 1832

My dear May,

I just received your letter. I am so very sorry to hear about the passing of my aunt Constance. It is very bad for you, I'm sure. Why don't you come visit me for a while? Jasper is still recovering from his pneumonia, which gave me quite a fright, and although he is much better now, he tires in the afternoon. That is very dull, and the idea came to me even before I read your letter that the person I would most like to cheer me up is you.

New York is glorious. The fashions here would amaze and delight you, I am sure. The best dresses come from Belgium, but there is no one in Belgium or anywhere else who can turn a dress like you. Please come for a month or two so you can have a change and keep me company, and I will try my best to persuade you to make one or two dresses for me while you're at it.

I've enclosed money for your tickets. Now, don't say no, Frog. Life is too exciting for no.

Your loving cousin,
Comfort

Comfort and her husband, Mr. Jasper Sinclair, lived in the country in Flatbush, Long Island, but according to Comfort's letters they drove into the city three or four evenings a week to have dinner or to go see a play. Mr. Sinclair's father had made his fortune from oyster crackers, and Comfort met the younger Mr. Sinclair when he stopped in our little town to look at some land, thinking to build a new factory. Whether she was in love with him I don't know, but he was rich, and he was a way out of small-town life. She married him, and by her accounts—her infrequent letters—she was happy. However, he was not an attractive man, Mr. Sinclair, with his long nose, his close-set eyes, and the deep pits on his cheeks from childhood smallpox. He suffered from poor health all his life, and by the time I reached Flatbush, twenty-two days after I received Comfort's letter, he was gone.

"Dead," Comfort told me at the front door, which she answered herself. "And it seems that he lied to me about his great fortune."

She was wearing a black dress with uneven side seams. The funeral had been a week before, she said, and she met with Mr. Sinclair's solicitor the day after that.

"One thousand dollars." She was not one to keep anything back. "That's all he left me. I've had to dismiss all the servants. Even the house isn't mine: he's been leasing it all these years. Oh, Frog! I'm so glad you're here. I've eaten nothing but bread and cheese for three days. Let's go into New York for dinner—I didn't want to go by myself."

I had hardly put down my bag. We were still standing in the house's round foyer, and the cabbie bringing up my trunk knocked at the door. "I haven't even washed off my travel," I said.

"Then wash!" she told me. She threw herself down in a chair with an embroidered seat cover, letting me answer the door.

Although I was sorry that Mr. Sinclair had died, I was glad to be useful and to think of something other than my own grief. As soon as I could, I hired a part-time domestic to help me with the cooking and cleaning—Comfort was useless in the kitchen—and I sold whatever furniture could be sold. Comfort was right: Mr. Sinclair had lied about many things. He owned no property anywhere, and his paintings were all copies. His father may have made a fortune from oyster crackers, but now both father and son were dead and the fortune spent.

One thousand dollars. No one in New York could live long on that.

But Comfort was not without ideas. Might she take up miniature painting? She had a good hand, and they were very popular at the moment. Or she could invest in a coffee farm or a tea plantation and live off the interest. I could always go back to Oxbow, though there was nothing and no one waiting for me there. But one morning Comfort told me that she had fixed on a plan:

"I'll go on the stage."

It wasn't the most practical decision, and it was one based, I suspected, on vanity: Comfort was proud of her looks and her voice, and she knew something about the life, since her mother had been an actress for a few years in Europe. Still, acting—or, rather, learning to act—cost money. We moved into a cheap women's boardinghouse near Gramercy Park, and Comfort began taking fencing lessons to learn how to "loosen her limbs," as her trainer—an old actor who began drinking at noon and could no longer reliably perform at night—put it. He also taught her how to walk across the stage, how to stop and turn, and how to present herself in a three-quarter view to the audience. After lunch she exercised her voice with a former operatic singer—the one with very bad breath whom Mrs. Howard reminded me of—to increase its power.

We agreed to use my money from the pig iron shares to offset the cost of all this training, and to use Comfort's inheritance to live on before her debut. But the costs of both the training and the living kept mounting, and even after Comfort began getting paid work, we often had to dip into our own savings to pay the rent at a rooming house or for transportation to a theater at another city or a hundred other things. By the time we reached Pittsburgh, six years later, all the pig iron money was gone. So, too, was Mr. Sinclair's one thousand dollars. The amount of cash we still had was small enough to be carried with us, and subsequently lost, on the *Moselle*.

The good news was that Comfort had an offer to join a company in St. Louis. The question was: How to get there? As I drank my coffee in Mrs. Nedel's dining room, I thought of the banknotes I'd had in my purse on the *Moselle*. All gone. However, even that lost sum would not have kept us in salt long, as my mother used to say.

"It's funny, you being a seamstress," Mrs. Nedel said to me when she sat down to breakfast. "*Nedel* being German, you know, for needle."

She was a heavyset woman, not young, but still wearing her brown hair in tight ringlets like her daughter, Elizabeth. She surveyed the array of dishes with a pleased expression—turkey, ham, hotcakes and waffle cake, custard, hung beef, warm bread and biscuits—as she asked her daughter to pass her the coffeepot. Breakfast was a serious meal in this house, although Mr. Nedel, I was told, took his breakfast every morning at a coffeehouse near his warehouse. I had yet to meet him.

"Now, my dear, what plans have you made for your departure?" Mrs. Nedel asked me mildly. Her eyes were tiny and blue, and her nose was like a little sausage roll in the middle of her face. "If it is not too impolite to ask. Of course, you may stay however long you need. I know you're waiting for your sister to get well. And then you two are off to . . . Chicago, was it?"

"My cousin," I told her. "And we're going to St. Louis. Mrs. Stoke was the one going to Chicago." Mrs. Stoke had left the house the day before; I never learned if she'd found her third child.

"Poor Mrs. Stoke," Mrs. Nedel said. Like many ladies that year, she wore a good layer of pulverized starch on her face and arms and neck. When she dabbed her mouth with her napkin, I saw tiny white flakes float down toward her coffee cup. I pulled my own cup slightly closer to me.

"Do you have family in St. Louis?" Elizabeth asked. She was only fifteen, but the starch on her face was nearly as thick as her mother's.

"My cousin has been offered a role at the New Theatre. She's an actress," I explained.

In spite of her powder, Mrs. Nedel's cheeks turned red and she glanced at her daughter. "An actress! Goodness!"

There were still plenty of people, and not only clergymen, who believed that actresses took work as paid companions at night. In case Mrs. Nedel was one of those people, I sought to put her right.

"Of course, you know that actresses aren't prostitutes," I said.

Mrs. Nedel made a strange sound like the rubber top to a bottle coming off. "Oh, my dear! We don't speak like that in Cincinnati." She lowered her voice. "We call them *public women*."

Public women. I could remember that.

"I made all of my cousin's costumes," I said after a pause. I was proud of my work, although everything was now at the bottom of the Ohio River.

"I have absolutely no talent for sewing," Elizabeth said, buttering a biscuit. "Mama can vouch for that."

"I certainly cannot! You just need more patience."

"It doesn't signify anyway. We have someone in every Easter to make our spring clothes, and then again in October. Miss Justine."

I was curious about this, since doing alterations seemed the most obvious way for me to earn money. "How much do you pay Miss Justine?" I asked.

Elizabeth blushed, looking for a moment like her mother.

"We don't speak so plain about money here," Mrs. Nedel said a little hesitantly. "Maybe it's different in New York."

I reflected to myself that it wasn't so different; I had only forgotten. "I was thinking about ways I could earn my passage to St. Louis, that's all."

Mrs. Nedel reached for the jam jar, looking thoughtful. After a moment she said, "We give her twenty cents for the day."

The room darkened, and through the three long windows I could see heavy clouds gathering in the sky. Twenty cents! I didn't see how anyone could live on that.

"It's on account of Cincinnati being so close to Kentucky," Eliza-

beth explained. "The white seamstresses don't get paid so well because there's slaves to do the work instead."

"Slaves? There are slaves in Ohio?"

"Oh, no. But, you see, if someone has family on the other side of
the river, why, they might just borrow one of their slaves for the day.
We get my aunt's girl Minnie about once a month when we turn the
mattresses, and she sometimes makes over a dress if I want."

Lending slaves across the river. I had never heard of that.

"Do you pay Minnie?" I asked.

"She's not used to getting money," Elizabeth told me.

"We feed her dinner, of course," Mrs. Nedel said, dabbing at
something on her dress.

I thought of the slave boy I had seen on the *Moselle*. Twenty cents
a day was more than dinner but not by very much; I would be a pau-
per in no time at that rate. Mrs. Nedel was still dabbing at the mark
on her dress, and now she began to cluck at it.

"If that's jam," I told her, "I can get it out if you have a bit of pearl ash."

"Pearl ash?"

"And a clean cloth."

"I've never heard . . . But of course you would know about such
things, helping your sister and so on. Pearl ash. I believe I might have
some in the cellar; I'll just have a look after breakfast."

Outside, the rain started suddenly, a quick torrent that hit the
windows sharply like a cat's claws. "You know," Mrs. Nedel said, raising her mild voice over the noise, "I think I have an old dress that
might suit you. And as we're talking about, I have a blouse with a
stain on the front; maybe you could look at that, too? I've nearly given
up on it, and it was once quite my favorite."

I'd been invited back to Mrs. Howard's house that afternoon, and
Mrs. Nedel—pleased with my work on her clothes—gave me a ride

there in her carriage. Standing once again at the front door, I was aware that the rain had brought out the smell of ham in my clothes and my hair, but there was nothing I could do about that. Donaldson took the umbrella Elizabeth had lent me, and Mrs. Howard herself led me into the parlor, saying that Comfort was feeling much better and would be downstairs presently.

"We'll drink our tea in here," she said, sliding the pocket doors open. Apparently today I was allowed to go farther than the hallway.

The parlor walls were lined with baby-blue wallpaper with scenes of milkmaids at their work. Mrs. Howard called my attention to the intricate carvings on the long mantel all done by a penknife, she said. Can you imagine? The house was over a hundred years old, and when Mr. Howard bought it they discovered pig hairs in the ceilings upstairs.

"That was what they used back then to strengthen the plaster," she told me. "But it made them furry." She smiled. Was she joking?

"The ceilings were furry?"

"With the pig hair in it," she explained.

She looked at me as if waiting for something.

"Never mind," she said. "Now, May, I want to have a serious discussion about your cousin. She and I had an interesting idea last night. Why don't you sit—no, take that chair; it's more comfortable. I want to put something to you."

I preferred straight-backed chairs, but I sat on the low upholstered one by the window that she directed me to. The parlor was in the turreted part of the house, and I could see the dark mass of pachysandra planted all around it shifting back and forth in the wind.

Mrs. Howard picked up a small brown book from a side table and pulled out a letter in use as a bookmark. She unfolded the letter and, after a quick scan, found what she was looking for: a sentence or two about the moral weakness of slave owners and the unsound logic of those in the North who support them.

"That was written to me by a man in my own organization," she told me, removing her eyeglasses. "The Ohio Association for the Abolishment of Slavery and the Betterment of Mankind. I truly believe that, if not for the sin of greed, slavery would have been abolished before the time of Noah. That is the sin we face here in Cincinnati: greed. Greed and ignorance. Few in the North know the true facts about slave conditions, the terrible lives these pitiable men and women lead, and the poor little babies taken away from their mothers before their thumbs can even find a way to their mouths, deprived of a comforting bosom." Her own bosom swelled as she spoke, and from time to time she looked at me with a severe expression as if at any moment I might say something she would not like. I did not think I was someone who had fallen prey to backwards morality or weak logic, but up until now I had spent most of my time in the North. After a while I stopped listening and watched her two crooked bottom teeth. Her lips stretched up and down, hiding and revealing them in turn.

"And that would be Comfort," Mrs. Howard finished.

"What would be Comfort?"

"A woman ideally suited to promote our cause: someone used to public speaking, possessing a strong voice that can reach to the back of a hall, and, of course, lovely to look at; that's important, too, I've come to realize."

"You want Comfort to give speeches?"

"For our association, yes. Go from town to town. Set the facts straight but in a pretty way. She could do that very well, don't you think? We would pay her a salary, of course. That is, I would."

My first thought was that this would save us from going to St. Louis, and my second was that now Comfort wouldn't be forced to take the matronly roles that she hated. Mrs. Howard was watching me closely.

"What does Comfort think?" I asked.

"Why, naturally she likes the idea! It would pay better than the theater. And she can do it as long as she likes, or until slavery is finally abolished in this country. If she's good at the job, she might be out of it soon." Another flash of crooked teeth.

"What would she wear?"

"Nice dresses. Sedate. The best quality, of course."

"Where will I get the material?"

Mrs. Howard looked at me. She clasped her hands behind her back like a man and faced me in her rocklike way. "May, I'll speak plainly, as you're someone who likes the truth. There isn't a place for you in this proposal. You don't want to speak in front of a paying public, do you? And Comfort won't need what she used to need—costumes and so forth, help with dressing—and whatever help she does need, I am more than adequate to supply myself. But you needn't worry: I know you're in a bit of a fix right now, so I can pay your fare back home. Of course I would do that. You come from New York, is that right?"

"No, near Toledo."

"As close as that! Well, I can certainly pay for your fare there. And you can finally leave off sewing for Comfort. My, you must be tired of that; how many years has it been? You'll have a chance now to really be independent—I can see it clearly." Her voice began to take on the force of a steam train pushing itself uphill. "I know a change would suit you; my Uncle Jacob always said that change was good for the soul, and, like absolutely nothing else, he was right about that. He was a slave owner himself, you know, which is why I understand slaves' lives so intimately. I used to watch them in his fields when I visited: always hunched over, always working. In Uncle Jacob, ignorance and greed were combined in equal measure. But I believe Comfort has the charm and skill to turn even a man such as he was, God rest his little soul. And you, May, you will no longer need to pin and hem and wait for the curtain to drop as I know you have had to do so often . . ."

I tried to sit up straighter in the upholstered chair, but the back was designed for leisure. I looked behind her at the scenes of milk-maids on the wallpaper, which were not accurate depictions: their dresses were too formal and their hair ribbons ridiculous. Her arguments were like the wallpaper, idealized and untrue, and if she broke off for two seconds altogether I would be able to reply to each of her statements; but like the steam train she would not so much as pause, and I felt myself losing the argument without even beginning my case.

"I don't want any change," I said.

Mrs. Howard didn't appear to hear me. ". . . a life spent until now in the wings, if I might borrow a metaphor from your world. But now you'll be able to step out and develop your own interests. Why, I almost envy you this turn at a new life . . ."

What new life was she envisioning? I grew up on a farm near a town so small it did not even have a regular coach stop. Everyone made their own clothes. A sound made me turn my head: Comfort was opening the pocket doors. She wore the same white gown as yesterday and a mint-colored shawl. The bandage over her forehead was gone. Mrs. Howard was still talking about this new life of mine, and for a moment I thought Comfort would interrupt—*Oh, no, no, May will stay with me of course!*—but she was looking at Mrs. Howard, not me, and her face was soft and compliant, like clay waiting to be made into something. She stepped into the room and, with a trick she learned from an actor in New York, pulled herself up to find another half inch of height.

Mrs. Howard didn't take a breath, didn't break off her monologue, even as she turned to address Comfort. She still would give me no room to argue.

"I've been telling May all about our little scheme, dear," she said. "And you have no cause to worry. I can tell that she sees it all clearly, how good it will be for you and for our cause, and how she will have a chance now to be on her own. You have always struck me," she said, turning back to look at me, "as quite independent in spirit."

*　　　*　　　*

I fared no better with Comfort when I could get her alone. Mrs. Howard asked her to show me the "lovely garden" now that it had stopped raining. "Meanwhile I'll tell Mr. Salter to get the horses ready," she said with the air of conferring a great favor, "and he can drive May back." I saw that I would not be offered a room in her house, nor even an invitation to supper.

The back garden was not lovely, it being only April and muddy from all the rain, and it smelled like rotting leaves. As we walked among the clipped hedges and the lemon trees standing in pots, I began protesting strongly against Mrs. Howard's proposal.

"There is nothing in it for me. Mrs. Howard said so herself. You expect me to go home?"

Comfort said no, of course not, I didn't have to go home if I didn't want to. "But don't you see how this is better than traipsing about from city to city," she asked, "holding a six-week engagement here, a month engagement there? I can't be an actress in my old age."

"You're only thirty!"

"Twenty-nine. But, Frog, think of all those short old ladies. Who wants to play those parts?"

"You've never been interested in slavery," I said. What I should have said was: *You've never been interested in anything except yourself.*

"Flora can be very persuasive," she told me.

She was staring at the back of Mrs. Howard's house, which from here looked magnificent: the stones fit so precisely, they seemed like lines carved into one giant rock that rose wholly formed from the earth. However, it was not Mrs. Howard and her house I was thinking of as I stood there but rather Comfort's late husband, Jasper Sinclair. When he came to our little town, he stood out dramatically by his finely cut clothes and his brushed hat and the gold watch fob that he checked constantly, as if even in the middle of rural Ohio he had firm appointments he couldn't be late for. I didn't think Comfort was in love with him, but while he lived I believed she was happy. Maybe love was not something she looked for in a companion. Or maybe she was just being practical. Being practical was in both of our natures. Our mothers were sisters, after all. As we stood there, Mrs. Howard's face appeared in an upstairs window like a full white moon with a puff of hair. Did she know we could see her? She stood there for a long time.

"Flora has beautiful taste. She tries to preserve the original look of the house," Comfort said. "She restored the old farmer's harpsichord, although no one can play it. And she has real marmalade imported from England."

"Why keep a musical instrument that no one can play?" The idea was absurd to me.

"Oh, Frog, wouldn't it be nice to settle down at last? *Zoals het klokje thuis tikt, tikt het nergens,*" she said in Dutch. The clock ticks at home as it ticks nowhere else. She had always been good with languages, and she resorted to Dutch—which she used to speak with her stepfather—when she was feeling sentimental.

"Come dine with us tomorrow," she said, starting back toward the house, "when Flora has time to order something nice."

That sounded like a promise concocted for later only to get rid of me now, and I felt my blood swell beneath my skin. I was like a child being sent away and not knowing why. When Comfort opened the door, I told her there was no reason for me to go back inside, that I would meet Mrs. Howard out in front.

"I'll see you tomorrow, then." She kissed me hurriedly, as though relieved our tête-à-tête was over. This plan was better for her, and that was the beginning and end to it.

After she left, I waited for a minute or two by the back door. Then I pushed it open again slowly. Like everything else in Mrs. Howard's house, the hinges were well maintained, useful, and silent.

I walked quietly on the thick carpeting toward the front of the house, and if the two maids I passed—one carrying an armful of folded linen—thought it was odd of me to wander the house alone, they were too well trained to show it. They nodded and averted their eyes. They had work to do. So did I. I wanted to know more. I followed the sound of Mrs. Howard's incessant buzz back to the parlor, where the pocket doors were partially open. Standing in the hall with my good ear trained toward the room, I heard her say, "She is quite comfortable with the idea. I'm sure of it."

Someone closed a door somewhere and I missed what Comfort said in reply, but Mrs. Howard answered in her booming voice, "Believe me, my dear, I'm a good judge of character."

"But what will she do? She can't make a living by herself."

"That's why I'm sending her back to your people."

What people, I wondered? There was only Comfort's mother, my aunt Ann, a sour recluse who ate a boiled egg for breakfast and a coddled egg for supper, skipping dinner in order to save money.

"She's stood behind you all these years," Mrs. Howard went on, "in your shadow. It's not healthy for her or for you to let her live off you this way! I've provided a nice, clean break for both of you."

For the second time that day I thought of the slave boy I'd seen on the *Moselle* standing behind his mistress's chair, and my face grew warm. I'm not a servant, I thought angrily. I haven't been staying in her shadow all this time. I could make a living on my own.

"She's younger than her years," Comfort said.

"Well, more's the shame and pity," Mrs. Howard replied. "That's her mother's fault for spoiling her, and yours, too. But now is her chance to grow up. Ah, the horses are here. Do you see her on the drive?"

I was in no mood for more creeping, so I went out by the front door and closed it loudly behind me, not caring if they knew I'd heard them talking. But Mrs. Howard, perhaps used to her servants opening and closing the doors all day, came out moments later saying she hoped I hadn't been waiting there long.

"I'm not Comfort's servant," I told her.

But even then Mrs. Howard didn't blush. She had her agenda and was following it doggedly. She handed me Elizabeth Nedel's umbrella.

"Of course not, no. Not a servant. A helper! You have been so helpful to her all these years. And now good-bye, my dear," she said, opening the carriage door for me. The wind picked up and blew against her but she didn't alter her stance. She was a block of wood like her manservant, Donaldson. "We'll see you tomorrow. We dine early, six o'clock."

After supper that night I brought the plaid dress Mrs. Nedel had given me into the parlor, hoping that ripping the cloth seams apart to remake it would help me recover some sense of myself. In the course of one afternoon I'd been flattened and reshaped into something else altogether, a construct of Mrs. Howard's: Comfort's hapless cousin, her servant, a seamstress with no life of her own. Elizabeth sat in the armchair beside me, toying with a bit of fancy embroidery.

As I unraveled the stitches I replayed Mrs. Howard's speech in my mind. I didn't want to go back home. I didn't want to live with Aunt Ann. When I came to a stronger line of stitching, I borrowed a thick needle from Elizabeth in order to pick out the thread. Underneath each sleeve was a gusset I would have to recut, and then I would need to smooth out the pleats. After a while my work made the memory of Mrs. Howard's mosquito-like voice recede a little. There were theaters in Cincinnati; perhaps I could find work in one of them.

When the hall clock chimed eight o'clock, Elizabeth went over to the piano, turned the wick up on the lamp, and began to look through some sheet music. A minute or two later Mrs. Nedel came into the room, and Elizabeth sat down on the piano bench to play a mazurka, although she played it very badly, missing notes and running up the beat in a way I found almost unbearable.

"Bother!" she said in disgust, breaking off suddenly. "I've forgotten this one entirely."

"Dearest, your language," Mrs. Nedel reproved her mildly. "Anyway it sounds very nice." She was sitting on the upright chair that Elizabeth had abandoned, examining Elizabeth's embroidery. After a moment she pulled the needle out from where it was docked and began adding a few stitches. I wondered how much of the cover had actually been stitched by her. Maybe all of it.

"Do you play the piano?" Mrs. Nedel asked me. When I said I did, she prevailed on me to play a tune. I'd learned to play as a child, and as an adult I sometimes filled in at the theaters where Comfort worked if the regular player was ill; consequently I became very good at sight-reading. In the middle of playing the mazurka, the parlor door swung open and Mr. Nedel poked his face in.

"Knew that couldn't be our Lambie," Mr. Nedel said, stepping in. That was their nickname for Elizabeth. "Not enough mistakes." He carried in a newspaper and sat down on one end of the sofa. "Continue," he said, so I did.

When I finished, Mr. Nedel thanked me "for the pleasure of the piece." He was a slight man, slimmer than Mrs. Nedel, and his eyes and nose and mouth were very neatly arranged in perfect symmetry on his wide face, although rather bunched into the middle of it. He wore a well-cut dark jacket that made me think again of his name, Nedel: with his long fingers, he would have been well suited to tailoring. However, whiskey inspection no doubt paid better.

As I took up the plaid dress again, Mr. Nedel asked if I had been able to form any plans for my future—although I could stay here as long as I wanted to, he told me with a smile, if I would play the piano for them every night. But when I said I might try to find work in a theater downtown, his eyes seemed to move closer together and he frowned.

"I thought you had a friend—or a sister? Someone you were traveling with?"

"My cousin. She's staying with Mrs. Flora Howard."

"Ah, yes, the abolitionist," Mr. Nedel said. "I met the husband once years ago; he made a small fortune in paper. Wonder what he'd think of where that money was going to now. Well, you know," he said in a louder voice, as though I had just stated some opinion, "these abolitionists just cannot be discouraged. Some of them actually try to steal slaves away—a man's own property! Around here they're hung for that. We don't take to thieves kindly. In my opinion, hanging's too easy. Well, I'm old-fashioned that way."

I began pulling out the stitches around the gusset, close work that took some attention.

"And while I do not condone slavery," Mr. Nedel went on, "I do say let those creatures stay as they are and let our commerce continue with the evils and the advantages fixed as such. Everyone knows that if we were to abolish slavery the whole of the southern economy would collapse, and then where would we be?"

I said, working the edge of my scissors under the thread to loosen it, "Of course, you use slaves yourself."

Mr. Nedel puffed out a breath of air. "We have never owned slaves! Ohio is a free state."

"Well, I meant Minnie."

The gusset was proving hard to unstitch with scissors. I reached for Elizabeth's thick needle again, and as I did so I saw that Mr. Nedel was looking at me with a fixed expression that might be called outrage. His face was very red. Mrs. Nedel and Elizabeth, with much paler complexions, were both looking anxiously from his face to mine.

I said, "I'm sorry, am I mistaken?"

Mr. Nedel rose from the couch. "That is a family matter . . . What a family does . . . our own private exchanges . . . Are you an abolition-ist, too, then?" He glared at me.

"My dear, she's from New York . . ." Mrs. Nedel's voice was very weak. I saw that I had trespassed and I tried to apologize.

"I didn't mean she was your slave. You don't pay her, but you feed her dinner, which I'm sure is very nice."

"Now you insult me with sarcasm?" Mr. Nedel snapped.

"I am never sarcastic."

"Enough," said Mr. Nedel. He pulled open the parlor door and left the room abruptly, leaving his newspaper still open on the couch.

All the lamp flames wavered with the sudden opening and closing of the door, and when they settled I saw that Elizabeth was studying a page of sheet music with unusual attention. I could still feel Mr. Nedel's angry presence, which seemed to pull air from each corner of the room. For a long while no one spoke, and I wished—not for the first time—that I could say what was expected instead of what I thought. At last the half hour struck and Mrs. Nedel quickly said good night and left, with Elizabeth following her. Molly, the domestic, came in to extinguish all the lamps except the one nearest me, and I wanted to speak to her, but her face looked like a tightly closed door. After she left, the darkened room felt larger and my place in it very small.

Mr. Nedel's newspaper still lay on the couch. In it I found notices for a few theaters, one on Columbia Street and one on Third Avenue and Vine. No doubt I could find a room to rent nearby, but I would be sorry to leave here. I had already grown used to Mrs. Nedel and Elizabeth, and even to the smell of ham in my hair.

4

Cincinnati's Columbia Theatre stood pat in the middle of Columbia Street, a large white building designed in a classical Greek style with a tobacconist shop renting out the first floor. Although yesterday's rain had moved off, a mineral smell remained in the air. As I made my way across the street I tried to stay away from the snuffling pigs running loose and making every effort to bump up against me. I thought to myself how surprised Comfort would be when I told her that I'd found my own job. Younger than my years! That's what she called me. My chest still burned when I thought of it.

Yesterday I missed my sewing box most, but today I missed all the costumes I'd sewn over the years, all those gowns and bodices and capes I'd so carefully rolled and folded into Comfort's green costume trunk—now sunk. Most actors' costumes are terrible, some of them even pinned instead of hemmed, and with no sense of what is historically accurate. However, I'd had a book to guide me: Walter Daugherty's *Dress Through the Ages*, given to me by a retired mistress of the wardrobe, an Englishwoman, whom I met in New York. It had drawings of everything from a Swiss soldier's uniform to Italian dresses in the fifteenth century. Even if the play reviews were bad, the reviewers always mentioned Comfort's strong voice and her beautiful wardrobe. I believe that an accurate costume greatly adds to the effect of a role. But how could I demonstrate my abilities?

There was quite a bit of loose garbage outside the theater, since no one came to collect house scraps: they were just thrown by the bucketful into the streets for the pigs. But the theater's stone steps were newly washed and smelled of lye, and in the lobby a workman was cleaning the wallpaper with pipe clay and water. When I asked him where I might find the manager, he pushed his chin in the direction of the stage without stopping his work.

I pulled open the heavy door that led to the seats. The house was dark and smelled like damp wool, and up on the stage two actors faced each other, rehearsing a scene. After a few moments I spied the manager sitting in the third row, so small that at first I mistook him for a child. He had a plank of wood balanced on his lap with an inkwell and paper on top.

"Mr. Kreuger?"

He turned his head, sneezed, and then sneezed again. He had a fearsomely unruly red beard, perhaps to convince others that he had in fact reached adulthood. After sneezing a third time he called to the actors to take a break and blew his nose loudly. "Hay fever," he explained.

I was standing in the aisle. "I'm looking for work," I told him. "I'm a seamstress. I worked in the Park Theatre for many years in New York, and in other theatres, too. My last job was at the Third Street Theatre in Pittsburgh."

Mr. Kreuger looked me over. "Actors see to their own costumes here," he said. This was common practice, even in New York. We were slow to catch up to the advances in England, where wardrobe mistresses oversaw the whole show and everyone in it. That was something I would very much like to do, but of course I couldn't afford the passage to England.

"I can be useful in other ways, too. The ballet girls often need help

with their shoes, and in between acts, when the ladies need changing, I can help them as well. Also I play the piano. I can sight-read
and transpose."

"What would I pay you?"

I had thought about this. "Two dollars a week," I said. Comfort
often got as much as five.

But he just laughed, which made him sneeze again. "I haven't got
two dollars to spare," he said. "Nor even a nickel. They say they're
closing me down this week." His creditors, I supposed.

"They always say that." I handed him my clean handkerchief, and
his expression softened as he took it, thanking me. I was encouraged.
"I noticed some lobelia growing in the park there on the corner. It's
very good for hay fever. You should try it."

"That so?"

"You just grind up the root and put it in tea. But it's a considerable
diuretic, so I would be careful about the amount."

Now he looked at me strangely. I thought he didn't understand.

"Too much can strongly affect the bowels," I explained.

His face turned beet red and he folded up my handkerchief
quickly.

I said, "But it has no power of curing syphilis; that's a mistaken
idea." I thought I should tell him everything I knew about the flower,
in case something proved useful to him.

"Syphilis! Now, listen here, I haven't got that!"

"Well," I said, surprised at his vehemence, "some men do."

His face turned an even deeper shade and he held out my handkerchief. "I haven't got work for a seamstress and I'm in the middle of
rehearsal. Be off with you now. Go to the saloon if you want drama."

I had no more success with the next two theater managers, although I
tried to impress the last one with my knowledge of theater life: Never

put a hat on a bed or shoes on a makeup table; no peacock feathers; and no yellow costumes.

"Actors believe all sorts of nonsense," I said. "I've learned that it is no use treating them like people guided by logic."

"Is that so? Well, I'm an actor myself," he told me, waving me out. "And at the moment my logic tells me that I don't need a seamstress."

Back on the sidewalk with the pigs.

By this time the bells were chiming two o'clock, and I was hungry. I decided to walk down to the river, where pushcart vendors were selling food to the merchants and boatmen along the pier. It was very noisy there, with all the men calling out prices and haggling with each other or shouting directions to the Negro rousters loading or unloading cargo. I spotted a man smoking a pipe with a stem as long as his forearm who was selling rye rolls from a basket. As I leaned against an upright barrel eating my roll, I watched the wind ripple the river water into waves no bigger than mice. An old-fashioned keelboat rang its bell for departure, and when it pulled back I noticed a small, two-story flatbed boat tied up to the dock behind it. It was painted white with green trim and had a green flag on its staff with the words "Floating Theatre" in fancy script.

A theater boat? Curious, I swallowed the last of my roll and walked along the raised pier to get a closer look. I could smell salt in the air, but the Ohio River is not a salt river; the smell was coming from a popcorn vendor in front of a stationary pushcart. He was young and darkly handsome, wearing a uniform that looked like striped red pajamas.

"Popcorn! Fresh popcorn here!" he called out in a thick Irish accent.

A group of maids with wicker baby carriages stood around his cart eating popcorn from red-and-white-striped paper bags while sneaking looks at him. Once I got around the crowd I could see the *Floating Theatre* more clearly: a narrow white barge, maybe a hundred feet

long, with a kind of house built upon it, like a box on a box. The green
flag unfolded itself in the wind:

"Hugo and Helena's Floating Theatre."

Two figures were standing on the lower deck at the stern of the
boat. One of them might have been Hugo, but as I got closer I saw
that the other one was certainly not Helena: it was Thaddeus Mason,
eating popcorn from a red-and-white-striped bag.

"What ho, May!" Thaddeus called out when he saw me, as if he
were practicing for a nautical part. I noticed he no longer wore his
arm in a sling. The other man turned as I came up the gangplank;
like Thaddeus, he wore his hair long, but his coloring was darker and
he was half a head taller. There was a band of black crepe around his
straw hat, and his shirtsleeves were rolled up past his elbows. Thaddeus introduced me.

"Captain Hugo Cushing," the man said in a British accent, touching his hat.

"May and I were on the *Moselle* together," Thaddeus told him; was
that to be his introduction for me from now on? But he went on to
say that Hugo's sister Helena had been on the *Moselle*, too. "Do you
remember the singer at dinner? Helena Cushing, of Hugo and Helena's Floating Theatre?" Thaddeus took off his hat. "Sadly, she was
not as fortunate as we were."

I looked at Hugo and tried to think of something kind to say. I remembered the singer in her pink dress with the light shining behind her.

"The captain let her on to perform," Hugo said. "We often made
a few extra dollars this way. She was going to get off at the stop after
Fulton. I was just pushing off to meet up with her there when the sky
broke up with the explosion."

"Oh," I said. "That is—that's very bad . . ." I trailed off awkwardly,
but Thaddeus came in with a string of platitudes, which he spoke
with great conviction and aplomb—"a terrible disaster," "an immense
misfortune," the captain was a "dastardly fellow."

"Where do you go?" I asked Hugo when Thaddeus finished. "Or do you stay here?"

He looked at me blankly.

"On this boat. Your theatre. Where do you perform?"

"Oh, well, then, down along the Ohio, of course. We dock at a different town every day, put on a show, and then the next morning pull up and head for the next town. We go all the way to the Mississippi, playing towns until the weather turns. Then we get pushed back up the river; I hire a steamer." I could see that his boat, a flatboat, had no steam power of its own. "Fourth year at it," he told me. "My sister and I put it all together. But now . . ." He made a gesture that I took to mean that, for him, like me, his old partnership was over.

"And if that weren't enough, his boat was damaged by the explosion," Thaddeus added. "The captain was just telling me. Part of the *Moselle*'s paddle box shot in like a cannonball."

"Even worse, my leather boat pump got punctured," Hugo said. "Don't know how I'm going to fix it, and a new one costs twenty dollars more than I have."

"How much does a new one cost?" I asked.

He looked at me as if I were a fool. "Twenty dollars."

"Where is your company?" Thaddeus asked him. "Maybe you could take up a collection."

"They skittered off into town. Probably drinking their way into even more uselessness. Damn actors. Excuse me," he said, but I wasn't sure he meant the apology for me, since he was looking out at the river. I wasn't offended in any case. I had seen actors humiliate themselves in a variety of ways over the years.

"I can help you with that hole if you like," Thaddeus told him, taking off his coat. "My father was a boatbuilder."

I had heard Thaddeus say, in the course of the two months that I knew him, that his father was an actor, a playwright, a wheelwright, and a steam engine designer, but I'd never heard boatbuilder before.

Hugo Cushing glanced at me again with a stern expression, perhaps expecting me to leave so they could get on to their work, but I re-crossed my shawl and made it my turn to look out onto the river. A passing steamer pushed heavy clouds of black smoke into the air, and after a moment I felt Hugo's small boat catch its wake.

Here was a theater, I was thinking. Here was the possibility of employment.

But I was a terrible advocate for my own cause; this morning had shown me that clearly. Thaddeus, on the other hand, like Comfort, was at his most eloquent when arguing for his personal gain. I waited while Hugo and Thaddeus conferred with each other on how best to mend the hole, and when Hugo went off to get more oak nails, I turned to Thaddeus and told him as quickly as I could about Comfort's new employment and how I was out looking for work.

"Little Comfort off to give stump speeches?" he asked. "Well! Good for her! Wouldn't I like to be on the payroll of some wealthy benefactress."

I didn't want to discuss it with him; I only wanted to lay out the facts. "Listen, would you help me ask for a job? I don't know what Mr. Cushing's sister did, but I could probably do it—all except sing. Wardrobe, props, playing the piano, keeping the books—I could do all of that."

"I was looking for a job with him myself but I'm not sure that he's hiring. Plus there's the matter of the boat pump. Anyway, why stick around here? Or don't you have the money to hightail it back home?"

"It's not that. Florid told me she would pay for my ticket. Flora, I mean. Mrs. Howard."

"'Florid'?" Thaddeus laughed. "I like that. 'Florid Horrid.' But why not take her up on her offer? It's always easier finding work among people who know you."

Florid Horrid. Yes, that was what she was. And although I was used to Comfort telling me what to do, I did not want Mrs. Howard to feel that she had the same right. But to Thaddeus I just said that there was no employment for me back home, which also was true.

"How much for the coach ticket?" he asked after a moment.

"If I had to guess, I'd say near ten dollars. But I told you, I don't want to go back."

"I was thinking of the boat pump," he said.

Before I could ask what he meant, Hugo Cushing came back with oak nails and a canvas folding chair for me, as if by now he guessed I had nowhere else to go. While they worked, Thaddeus told Hugo about his last run in Pittsburgh, taking particular care to describe the three costumes I'd made for Comfort, one for each act. But it wasn't until a few of the boat's actors came up the gangplank that Thaddeus broached the matter of employment. The actors were carrying one of their company, a drunk heavyset man who had tripped over a sugar barrel in town, badly twisting his ankle. But they needn't have bothered carrying him back: as soon as Hugo saw the condition of his foot, he gave the actor the sack. How could he have a performer who couldn't walk across the stage? he asked angrily. This left an opening for Thaddeus. And once his place was secured, Thaddeus began arguing for mine.

"Don't need a seamstress," Hugo, who was picking up his hammer again, told him.

"She's more than just a seamstress—she's a *costume designer*," Thaddeus said. "I wish you could see how beautiful her work is, but, sadly, it's all being eaten now by the fish."

"My people see to their own costumes."

I pinched the inside of my wrist nervously. I could hear Hugo's actors—whom Hugo had ordered up to the galley to get themselves strong cups of coffee—laughing and banging pots.

"I understand," Thaddeus said. "But if you don't mind me asking, what did your sister do"—he took a moment to remove his hat in respect—"besides sing?"

Hugo looked down at the plank he was nailing. He had taken off his straw hat and his dark hair fell over his forehead.

"Played the piano," he said, striking the nail. "All the cue music and mood music and the actors' specialties; also the community sing at the end. She painted scenery. Repaired props and wardrobe. Made up the show bills and the tickets. Handled sales." With every task he named, his hammer seemed to get louder. "Advertised the show, talked it up at every landing, found out who she should give free tickets to and gave them free tickets."

"You can do all that, can't you, May?"

"I can play the piano, but—"

"May is a wonderful seller!" Thaddeus talked over me. "She'll get you more tickets bought than ever before. And her musicality is just what it should be. She's played piano for shows in New York and Philadelphia and Pittsburgh. Isn't that right?"

"Yes, but I've never—"

"And she can transpose just about anything! I know because I've had her do that for me, and it takes her no time. Sight-reading is no problem, either. And she can play by ear if need be."

Hugo gave a few last taps to the nail, looked at his thumb, and then looked over at me with a frown that I was already getting used to. "Can she, now," he said. "Well, our Mrs. Niffen can play the piano. She's one of the company. But she can't sight-read and she can't transpose."

Here I felt more comfortable. "I can do both," I told him.

"There's still the matter of the pump," Hugo said, rubbing his hand down his pant leg. "Can't leave the dock without it." He looked around for another nail.

"You're in luck there, too," Thaddeus told him, handing him one. "If you hire her, May can help with that as well. Just a loan, of course."

Hugo turned to me.

"You have twenty dollars to loan?"

"May can bring it to you tomorrow," Thaddeus told him. "The whole twenty dollars. You'll have your boat pump and be off before the week is out."

"Well . . ." Hugo hesitated. He looked at me in a thoughtful manner.

"Right, then," Thaddeus said. "Now I'll just go fetch my things. You never know: that chap's ankle might suddenly improve once his head clears up." He put on his hat and picked up his coat from the railing.

"Mistimed his entrances anyway," Hugo said. "Not even an actor; he was a scene shifter when I met him."

The waves lapped lightly against the boat with the sound of a kitten at its milk bowl as I followed Thaddeus down the gangplank. I wasn't sure I was hired, but Thaddeus seemed to think that I was. I could tell he was very pleased with himself by the way he swung his jacket over his shoulder, and he made long strides up the sand, leaving me to struggle behind him. It was getting late, and the Irish popcorn vendor, the maids, and the babies in their carriages all were gone. Up on the sidewalk Thaddeus turned and waited for me, his curly hair blowing back in the wind.

"Now for that money," he said.

5

Comfort exclaimed over Mrs. Howard's china, which was white with swirls of blue floral sprays and red cranberries along the rim. In the tradition of allowing me into one room per day, this evening Donaldson led me straight to the dining room, where Mrs. Howard and Comfort were already waiting. Tonight he was wearing another stiff dark suit and starched white gloves, and he served and cleared and took instructions all without moving a muscle in his face. When his eyes met mine, I felt I was back at school and awaiting directions, but of course none were forthcoming.

"So lovely!" Comfort said, looking at her plate. "Is the pattern from England? It must be English." I noticed she was using her ingénue's voice.

"I bought the set just after Mr. Howard's last illness. I needed something pretty to cheer me up. We all need that, don't we?"

Mrs. Howard looked at Comfort in the same manner as she looked at her food. She was a very hearty eater and made no apologies for it, and she urged us to eat heartily, too. Donaldson served a light-colored fish boiled in a light-colored sauce, followed by venison in peach syrup. After that, he came around with dishes of custard, cucumbers, string beans, and baked beans, and then he set a platter of warm rolls in the center of the table.

Although eating took some attention—Mrs. Howard's dinner knives, though graceful and perfectly shined, were more decorative than effective when cutting the hard squares of meat—I found myself looking up whenever Mrs. Howard turned to address Comfort. Tonight Comfort was wearing a simple mouse-colored dress with high sleeves and a low neckline. I wondered if Mrs. Howard had hired a seamstress for her: the dress was simple enough to have been stitched up in a day. To my surprise I felt some jealousy, although why should I care who made Comfort's dresses? I was just used to doing it myself. The candelabra cast shadows on Mrs. Howard's pretty wallpapered walls—in this room, red scenes of birds feathering their nests—as I struggled with the blunt point of Mrs. Howard's pretty knife. In spite of the fire in the fireplace, I was cold, and I wished I had another shawl to put over my lap.

Lying is easy, Thaddeus had told me on the wharf. All you have to do is create the space for it. I didn't see why I should lie to Mrs. Howard to get money for the boat pump, and I told him so. "If she's willing to give me money for my ticket home, I said, surely she'll give the same to help me secure employment here." But Thaddeus disagreed.

"She wants you out of the way. She wants Comfort all to herself. These abolitionist ladies, they like other women, don't you know. All abolitionists are like that. Teetotalers, too."

I had never heard such nonsense.

"Listen, May. Look at it this way. If Florid says no, then that's our chance gone. Better just to say that you've decided to take her up on her offer. It would only be a little lie. It would in no way blemish your natural honesty."

"It's not that. I just can't do it. It's not in me."

"Sure it is! Lying is part of the human condition. It's what separates us from the beasts in the wild. Listen, May. We need that money. You want a job, don't you? I'll teach you how to do it; you can use an old acting trick. Do you know the Greek alphabet?"

I did not.

"Good," he told me. "Because it's hard to remember."

Unlike Thaddeus, I did not think being an abolitionist meant that you liked other ladies, but, watching Mrs. Howard at the head of the table at supper, I noticed her flushed cheeks and how often she patted Comfort's hand. Comfort sat on her right and I sat on her left, and the polished mahogany table between us grew darker as the candles burned down. I was never good at guessing someone's thoughts by looking at their faces, even Comfort's, but tonight, chatting about the china and the food, she seemed happy. I thought of two women who had lived in the boardinghouse where Comfort and I passed our first winter in New York: Miss Linsome and Miss Bates. "Sapphos," Comfort told me. When I didn't understand, she said, "They love each other, like a married couple." While Donaldson cleared our plates I tried to remember what I thought about Miss Linsome and Miss Bates. I remember noticing Miss Linsome's hat, which was made of black sealskin—unusual, for a woman's hat—and it struck me as quite stylish.

"I have gone once or twice," Mrs. Howard was saying, "but it's mainly a man's affair." She was talking about the theaters in Cincinnati. "I have neighbors who boast they have never once seen a play in all of their lives! Well, this is hardly surprising in a city where billiards and cards are forbidden by law. Do you know that to sell a pack of cards you might incur a fine of fifty dollars?"

She paused to take a sip of water. The meal was almost over. Soon it would be time for me to leave, and I needed to get this business over with before then. My regret—one of my regrets—was that if I followed Thaddeus's plan, I couldn't tell them that I had found myself a job, and I wanted to tell them that.

Instead I said, "I've decided to take you up on your offer, Mrs. Howard."

Mrs. Howard put down her glass. I'll say this for her, she never pretends not to understand anything that she understands perfectly well.

"I'm glad," she said. "I'm so glad. And when do you plan to go home?"

Alpha. Beta. Gamma. Delta, I recited to myself slowly, looking at the red wallpaper. "Think of it as a script," Thaddeus had told me. "Memorize your lines, and then recite the Greek letters in your head before you can say anything else. That's the way to lie."

"As soon as I can buy my ticket," I said instead of what I really wanted to say: *I won't be going home. I need the money to repair a boat so the owner will hire me to do what his sister used to do because she died on the* Moselle, *unlike Comfort and me, who survived but lost the little we still had . . .* I swallowed. "Tomorrow, if I'm able."

"That's just grand. And how much is the ticket?"

Alpha, beta, gamma . . . "Twenty dollars," I told her.

I waited for her to say that that was absurd—a single coach ticket could not possibly cost so much, and what was I really planning to do with the money?—but when the silence continued I looked up to see that Mrs. Howard was smiling broadly at Comfort. Comfort was looking at me.

"Are you certain you want to?" Comfort asked. Her ingénue voice was gone.

"What else would I do?"

"She's right, she's right, my dear," Mrs. Howard said quickly. "This is by far the best plan."

"But surely you needn't go right away." Comfort looked at Mrs. Howard. "She can wait a few days, Flora, maybe cut out a dress or two? Do some alterations for you? To give May a bit of pocket money for traveling."

"Oh, I'm prepared to give her something extra—say, another five or six dollars. Let's call it twenty-five dollars. She's your cousin! I would not hire her, my dear, that's absurd." The irony that she was hiring Comfort to go on a lecture circuit did not seem to occur to her.

Comfort slid her chair back and came over to my place to put her arms around me. "May, May," she said, leaning over me. For some reason this made me cross.

"Well, it's too late for that," I said.

"I know. I'm sorry." She drew back and looked at my face, and I found myself staring at the cleft in her chin. It was small and perfect, like a tiny almond, and because of a trick of the candlelight it seemed raised rather than receding, an almond I could pluck and take with me. "Do you hate me?" she asked.

I thought about this. "No," I told her.

"Girls," Mrs. Howard said, rising from the table. "No sentiment, please. Donaldson!" He came in before she even finished saying his name, as if he had been standing all this while with his white glove on the doorknob, waiting to be called. Mrs. Howard told him we would take our dessert in the parlor, and although I am not given to fancies, when his eyes slid over mine I had the strongest sensation that from the other side of the door he had heard my lie and understood it as such. My stomach felt both tight and queasy, and in the parlor I did not look twice at the dessert he brought in on a shiny silver platter, a white cake with two thick layers of cream frosting.

Later, with a fold of Mrs. Howard's bills in my pocket, I said good-bye to Comfort. The bills were so crisp I wondered if one of the maids had ironed them along with the linen, and I felt them crunch when Comfort hugged me. Even with the money I did not feel victorious, however. Instead, strangely, I felt even lower than I had when I'd arrived. Perhaps part of me thought that even at this late hour Comfort might change her mind and fight for me. But as we stood at the door waiting for the horses, she said nothing except that I must write her with news. When I looked back at her standing in the foyer, I had to admit that she went very well with the pretty house and the pretty furniture, and Mrs. Howard must have thought so, too, because her eyes kept straying to her even as she said good-bye to me.

The night air had a slight chill to it, and after Donaldson helped me into the carriage he arranged a wool blanket over my knees. Then, to my surprise, he cleared his throat. I had a moment's feeling that he was about to say something to me, either a reprimand for my lie or perhaps something sympathetic. But he only shut the door, checked the latch, and then put his hand up to signal to the driver that I was ready to go.

I did not look out to see if Comfort was watching me leave from the window. I did not think that she was.

6

The morning that the *Floating Theatre* was fully repaired and ready to depart Cincinnati, I was up and dressed a few hours before sunrise. Since it was too early even for her cow to arrive at the back door, Mrs. Nedel gave me a knuckle of ham and a piece of pound cake wrapped in a clean sheet of paper in lieu of breakfast. The night before she'd taken down from the attic a cracked leather carryall with rope straps, into which I packed my clothes and a half dozen handkerchiefs that Elizabeth gave me, her initials loosely stitched in the corner; I thought I could easily pull those out. Elizabeth also found an empty cigar box I could use for my new sewing supplies, which I'd purchased using a dollar of the "extra money" that Mrs. Howard had given me: needles and thread, nested embroidery hoops, two sizes of scissors, a thimble, a piece of chalk for marking up, and pins. I'd earned a dollar and a quarter from Mrs. Nedel plus another one of her discarded dresses for doing some alterations, although I used fifty cents of it to have my father's watch repaired.

Four dollars and seventy-five cents, three dresses, and my sewing supplies. That was everything I had.

Outside, it was still more night than day. The sky rippled out above me in yards of gray linen, and small points of stars shone out where the clouds had thinned. However, the street already had a fair amount of traffic: milk carts, bread trucks, and a few tradesmen walking briskly along the sidewalk, their shoes already coated with Cincinnati's pervasive white dust. As I waited on a corner for some carts to pass, I read a broadside nailed to a tree trunk. Looking back, the notice had the feel almost of an omen, although I didn't take it as such at the time:

RANAWAY from the subscriber on the night of 22nd March, a handsome negro boy named Philip, assisted by a tall white man with a scar down the right side of his face. The WHITE THIEF is thought to live in Cincinnati; he is a LAW BREAKER and will decoy more slaves away if not stopped. If the organized courts are not up to the task, then Old Judge Lynch will soon sit upon the bench.

"Well, now," said a man in a gray felt cap who had stopped at the corner, too. "That oughta frighten a soul. Judge Lynch, that's who takes them down, no one but."

"Is he a judge in Cincinnati?" I asked.

"Haw haw haw," the man laughed.

A space between carts opened up, and I crossed the street thinking no more about it. I could now make out the wharf in the distance, and the Ohio River, vast and heavy, the largest tributary of the Mississippi—in fact, when the two rivers met, I was later told, the Ohio was the greater body of water—looked like a dark shadow beside it.

You might think that after living through the destruction of one boat I would not want to embark on another, but I am not sensitive in that way. Besides, there were obvious differences: One, the *Floating Theatre* was a flatbed, not a steamship, so it had no boilers to overstoke. It was poled downstream with the current, and at the end of the run it would be pushed back up the river by a hired steamer. Two, Hugo Cushing was not interested in breaking any kind of record traveling from one town to the next, or in outracing another boat, or in any other way putting his life (and ours) in danger. He was a man, I would soon learn, for whom theater was everything. All he wanted to do was to get to the next town so he could put on his show. His company consisted of five actors and three actresses. In addition to acting himself, Hugo was the director, manager, accountant, and owner, and he also held captain's papers good from the head of the Allegheny to the lower Mississippi. Most of the company called him Captain, or Captain Cushing, but in my mind I always thought of him as Hugo, perhaps because of the green flag waving on the jack staff, "Hugo and Helena's Floating Theatre," which was the first thing I'd noticed.

I hadn't seen Hugo since I'd given him the loan of twenty dollars three days before, but as I came up the gangplank I spotted him at the end of the boat winding a line around an oversized spool, getting the boat ready to embark. Thaddeus and two other men were on deck helping, all with their backs to me. Although the wind had not yet risen, the boat leaned slightly like a tree against a steady gust. I put my carryall down next to the ticket office window and hugged my shawl more tightly around me.

Small steamboats were already chugging past us, coughing up smoke. In comparison, the *Floating Theatre* seemed more like a barge: a box with another box nailed on top of it. Still, its fresh paint and green trim made it stand out from the other barges lining the pier, which were rusty and workmanlike, with dark barrels full of cargo roped onto their decks. Hugo's boat was something in between commerce and pleasure. It was painted white like a two-tiered frosted cake, and like a cake some places needed more frosting than others to cover the dents. It had two decks with narrow walkways around them called guards, and evenly spaced square windows, and a striped green-and-white awning over the upper porch at the stern. The theater and the small ticket office took up the lower deck, whereas the upper deck was divided into living quarters: the galley, the dining room, and the staterooms—which were our bedrooms—all of which I would find as compact as the inside of a toolbox, useful without being pretty.

I stood on the lower deck uncertainly, not wanting to interrupt the men's work but looking for the chance to say, *Here I am; where should I go?* Usually Comfort was the one who said this whenever we arrived somewhere new, smiling and using a great many more words. I recrossed my shawl and waited for an opening. No one noticed me. Meanwhile, Hugo was speaking loudly to the men while he pulled up the lines.

"Now, Leo, remember to keep her to the middle of the river; the water will begin to rise as we leave the city. But listen here, half a mile out there's a sandbar, so keep closer to the right there. Now take care to knot that line up tight. You have it? Good man. Hold up! Bells starting!"

Today was the one-week anniversary of the sinking of the *Moselle*, and, according to the newspapers, at sunrise the bells of St. George would ring out twelve times to honor the one hundred and eighty dead. The man Hugo called Leo wrapped his arm around a long pole that he'd stuck down into the muddy bottom of the river, anchoring us, and then he took off his hat. Although the rest of us turned to the east when the bells started, Hugo turned to the west. I wondered about that. I watched his face soften as he looked out over the water.

The sound of the last bell was still echoing when he turned and noticed me. His face returned to a stern expression. "You're here, then, are you? All right, well off the deck now. We have work to do."

"Where should I go?" I asked.

The slightest pause. Then gruffly: "To Helena's stateroom, I suppose."

"Where is that?"

But he had already turned around, and if he said something more I didn't catch his words. Leo left his long pole and walked over to a little bell strung up near the boat's stern, ringing it to signal our departure. Although Hugo was a tall man, Leo was taller by nearly a head, and his copper skin—he was part Seminole Indian, I learned later, and part Negro—was already shiny with sweat. He went back to the pole, which the boat had drifted slightly away from, pulled it out, and began poling us expertly into the middle of the river.

Thaddeus came up to me with a can of lamp oil hooked over his forefinger. "I'll show you where to go. Just let me take this to the theater first." He'd been living on the boat for less than a week but carried the air of an old-timer.

"Don't track mud onto my stage," Hugo called after us. "And don't fiddle with anything!"

We entered at the back of the auditorium, which was narrow but long. Two rows of benches had been nailed to the ground in front of a small stage, which was divided from the audience by a painted proscenium. The stage floor and walls were white—Hugo repainted the stage floor himself once a month—and five or six of the smallest kerosene lamps I'd ever seen were lined up on the floor at the proscenium line.

"Seats almost a hundred," Thaddeus told me as we walked up the aisle between the two rows of benches. "Risers in the back for free blacks. Back behind the stage is the green room."

We went up the three or four steps on the side of the stage and then around to the small room at the back of it, which had more furniture and crates crammed into it than seemed possible. At one end there was a couch and two straight-backed chairs all rather tightly pushed together, and at the other end was a makeshift kitchen: a squat portable stove sitting in a box of sand, a shelf of cups and saucers above it, and a kettle on the floor. Someone had hung up an unframed picture of the English actress Mrs. Siddons, but other than that the walls were peeling planks of bare wood. One small window looked out onto a slice of river without giving much of a view, and wooden crates of various sizes had been stacked on either side of it.

Two women were sitting on the couch: a young, pale, pretty

woman and an older woman with a thick mantle of white hair piled on top of her head. They stopped running lines to look at us when we walked in, and I saw that the woman with the white hair was younger than the color of her hair implied, maybe only forty. Mrs. Niffen was her name.

"Pleased, I'm sure," she said when Thaddeus introduced me, "although I must say that I certainly could have done Miss Helena's job as well as my own. I told Captain Cushing that. I told him how I helped her all last year doing everything—the tickets, the props— and I'm quite a fine seamstress."

"Mrs. Niffen is principally an actress," Thaddeus said to me with a smile that seemed to convey something other than pleasure. "And Mr. Niffen plays all the mayors and shopkeepers."

"Doubles on the fiddle," Mrs. Niffen told me. She had a sharp nose and small eyes and her face made me think of an illustration I'd once seen in a storybook of a very clever rat. Her skin was softly pink and nearly unwrinkled, a curious complement to her white hair.

"I'm Lydia Fiske," the younger woman said. "Please call me Liddy." She had a full, round face with pretty downturned eyes that seemed sad, and a pleasant upturned mouth that seemed happy. The contrast was fetching. Here was a younger Comfort: pretty, used to playing the lead roles, and charming—she smiled at me as though she had already decided she liked me, in marked contrast to Mrs. Niffen, whose frown seemed to deepen whenever she looked at me. I stepped forward to take Liddy's outstretched hand and tripped on a box.

"Careful," Liddy said. "I don't know why we keep these crates. There's something moldering somewhere in one of them but we can't discover what."

Mrs. Niffen assured us all that she knew what was moldering and she was dealing with it in a timely way, and also that there was always something moldering on theater boats and one could never be sure entirely what it was; she seemed to be arguing both points at once.

While she was speaking, the floorboards shifted beneath my feet and I felt my body dip and move as the boat pitched forward. A strong odor of mud blew in from the partially open window.

"Whew! That's a smell for you," Thaddeus said, and all at once my stomach seemed to tighten and take notice. All this while the water had been pushing up at the boat from below, trying to move it, and yet I had been standing as though the ground were as stable as plowed earth. But it was not stable, I realized now, not at all. As we lurched again into the current I put my hand on the wall. I swallowed and then swallowed again. Liddy looked out the window.

"A little rough today," she said.

Mrs. Niffen decided that she should be the one to show me Helena's room, for reasons I could not follow. As the boat rocked over the choppy water my attention became riveted on my stomach, which seemed to be rising inside my chest. While we were climbing the outside stairs, the boat pitched forward and my stomach fell with a funny twist. The top deck consisted of a line of narrow rooms ending with the dining room and kitchen galley, each room accessible only from the outdoor guard, although the galley also had an interior door to the dining room.

Helena's room was on the other end at the stern of the boat, just above the ticket office. Captain Cushing's room, Mrs. Niffen told me as she opened the door, was the next one over. All the staterooms were small, less than ten feet across; but, being on the end, Helena's room was a little bit longer than most. Inside, there was a narrow cot with two trunks at its foot forming a long T, along with the usual chipped washstand, chipped basin, and short oak cabinet. I was used to boardinghouse furniture, but here everything was about three or four inches smaller in width. On the far end was a door leading to a small outdoor porch overlooking the river, and near the solitary window stood a drop bucket attached to a rope so that I could pull up my own water, Mrs. Niffen explained.

"I thought about asking Captain Cushing to move Mr. Niffen and me here; it's the biggest room next to his—next to the captain's, I mean. But I have been so busy attending to everything that Helena would normally do . . . well, someone had to step in, and I am by far the most useful person on board; you will soon see how much I'm called on to do, and with so much on my hands, I just haven't had the chance. But the room is much too large for you—for one person, I mean. Of course, you haven't unpacked yet."

"No," I said putting down my carryall. My stomach rose with my words and I sat down on the thin mattress. A wave of heat seemed to enshroud my body, followed by a run of cold shivers. I had always felt perfectly fine on the *Moselle*, but that had been a much larger ship. The *Floating Theatre*, which was light enough to be jolted about with every wave, lurched in the current, and my stomach swayed in the opposite direction. I waited for Mrs. Niffen to leave so I could lie down, but she just stood in the doorway looking around.

"It would take Mr. Niffen and me no time at all to change."

"To change what?"

"To change rooms."

"Where would you go?"

She looked at me with her little pink rodent eyes and made a deliberate frown. Then she noticed my hand over my stomach. "Are you sick? Now, don't tell me . . ." She shook her head but at the same time seemed a little bit pleased. "*That* would put the Captain off. Shall I fetch him?"

Alpha. Beta. Gamma. Delta. "I'm fine," I said. I stood up to demonstrate. A mistake, but I tried to pay no attention to my stomach.

She folded her arms and noticed something on the floor. "Goodness, here's Mr. Niffen's lure box—what he loaned to Miss Helena. I'd forgotten about that!" She picked up a small scratched box with a metal handle. "I'll just take it back with me. Oh, and this little jug. Helena once told me I could have it." She picked up a few more objects—a candlesnuffer, a pair of gloves, a book—claiming either that I wouldn't need them or that they were hers, and sometimes claiming both. Her face, looking around the room, wore an expression very like the one I'd seen on traders down at the wharf as they assessed the contents of open barrels. Meanwhile my stomach rose and flattened as the boat bounced along. I saw Mrs. Niffen eyeing the bedsheets but I could say nothing. For a moment I thought I would be sick. I leaned against the wall and swallowed the strong acidic taste that rose in my mouth.

"I bought these in Wheeling," Mrs. Niffen said, gathering the sheets up. Then she took the pillowcase off the pillow. When I saw her looking at the folded cot blanket, however, I sat down on it to prevent her from taking that, too.

"Well!" she said. "I suppose I could let you borrow that until you can buy your own. But now what to do about Helena's trunks with all of her costumes and such? If I had a free hand I would go through them." She had no free hands. "I think there are a few items in there for Oliver. That's Leo's dog. Goes on stage, you know. Really, I ought to keep the trunks in my own room. Let me just fetch Mr. Niffen to carry them."

I swallowed. "No," I said carefully. "Don't."

"Oh, but you wouldn't know what to do with them."

"Don't," I said again.

She cleared her throat in a growly way. "Well . . ."

"Good-bye, Mrs. Niffen," I told her.

Her eyes rested on my hand, which was again over my stomach, and I pulled it away.

"Bell for breakfast should be soon, now that we're off. If you want any," she added with another half-satisfied frown. What I wanted was to lie down, but I wouldn't give her the satisfaction of seeing me unwell, or risking the chance that she might call Hugo and inform him that I could not possibly take a job on a boat. My independence would be over before it had properly begun. But at last she left the room without bothering to close the door behind her, and I listened to the clip of her boots going down the guard.

In spite of my stomach, however, I was now curious about Helena's costumes, so instead of lying down I carefully lowered myself to the floor and opened the smaller of the two trunks. In it I found a top shelf of handkerchiefs and shirtwaists and necklaces that made me believe this was Helena's private trunk. I found the costumes along with some outdoor gear—fishing rods and tackle—in the second, larger trunk: unremarkable dresses, a couple of old-fashioned dress coats with half-sewn trimming, a few waistcoats and breeches that had been altered and were partially sewn up, and a white apron trimmed with insufficient ribbon.

"Helena carried a few of the costume dresses with her on the *Moselle*, since she wasn't sure what she'd sing. That's what she usually did."

Hugo was standing at the open door with his straw hat in his hand. He came in and picked up a garment I'd set aside, an afternoon jacket with one sleeve coming loose.

"My sister was not much of a seamstress," he said, looking at the sleeve. "Too impatient, I expect. Well!" He put the jacket back down. "I've come to see how you're doing." His voice sounded formal and loud, more commanding than welcoming, but his words were kind enough. "We're a small troupe, but we think of ourselves as family. For three months, at least. Anything you need, you let me know."

"I'll need some more thread if I'm to repair these costumes. Most of them will have to be completely resewn."

"Surely it's not as bad as that."

"Oh, yes it is, it's very bad. They're very poorly sewn. What's more, they have no sense of time or place, they might all be from the same period. There's nothing here to distinguish them. I'm surprised that you used them on a stage."

His voice got gruffer. "Costumes aren't all that important. Helena used to say all we need to do is give the audience the idea of the thing. It's up to the actors to do the rest."

"Not important? Of course costumes are important! You want to give an accurate rendition." The boat leaned suddenly portside and my stomach tightened. "If you give me a list of what you'll be performing, I can get a better sense of what is needed."

"I don't have time to write out a list! I have a boat to run and a new actor to train!"

"I'll sit in on one of your rehearsals then and see for myself."

"No good. Closed rehearsals," Hugo snapped. I looked up at him. His face was red and his English accent had become very pronounced. "Bother the costumes. My sister did an altogether fine job with them. She worked very hard."

"But—" I started to get up from the floor and had more trouble than I had anticipated. I leaned forward to put my hand on the bed before I sat down on it. For a moment or two I looked at my knees, willing myself not to be sick.

"What we need more immediately are tickets and show posters. You know how to make those up?" Before I could start up my Greek, he said, "Good. I'll leave you to it, then."

He was angry. I wasn't sure why. The bell rang out for breakfast just as he turned to leave.

"And find some ginger to put under your tongue," he said. "If you're no good on a boat, you'll soon be off mine."

When he was gone, I lay down on the sheetless cot without bothering to take off my shoes, and I brought my knees up to my chest. Although my arms were cold, my face was hot. I could hear loud talk as people walked along the guard to the dining room, and, closer at hand, herring gulls called out like the squeaks of a fast-rocking

rocking chair, *hya-hya-hya-hya,* marking their territory or looking for mates. I tipped myself up off the cot and got myself over to the drop bucket and was sick in it. Then I went back to the cot and closed my eyes. Helena's room smelled like kerosene and damp wood and ashes. My room, I reminded myself.

When I woke up later, the sun was streaming through the open porch door and onto my bed, making an angled design like a carpenter's square. Looking out the window, I saw that we were tied up at a small cove studded with branchy maple trees and tall weeds. I didn't know if I felt better because I had slept or because the boat was no longer moving, but I went along to the kitchen galley anyway to see if I could get that ginger Hugo had suggested.

Cook was a red-faced man with stringy salt-and-pepper hair. I never learned his true name, since everyone just called him Cook. When he wasn't at his stove, he was sleeping; he had no stateroom of his own but kept a hammock strung up in the galley, and that's where I found him.

Swinging himself out of it, he told me, "Up too early for a full night's sleep, getting breakfast for Captain and the others what are moving the boat. I nap when I can."

He found a withered hunk of ginger, sliced off a piece with a knife as big as a cat, and handed it to me.

"Where is everyone?" I asked.

"Rehearsal. Can't you hear?"

We both looked at the door as if that would improve our hearing, and then I turned my good ear toward it. After a moment I could make out muffled voices from below.

"Hugo asked me to make the tickets for the show. How do I do that?" I asked, holding the slightly slimy ginger slice with my thumb and forefinger. Now that I had it I found I didn't want it.

Cook nodded at it. "Go on, pop it in," he said.

He couldn't help me with the tickets. I went back outside, but before I got to my room I pitched the ginger over the side of the boat. As I did so, I noticed the poleman, Leo, who was sitting on a canvas chair on the bank, holding a fishing line. A small dog sat next to him, and that gave me an idea. I went into my room and looked through Helena's costume trunk for a piece of leftover silk, and then I drew out a pattern on some muslin and pinned the silk on top. Measure twice, cut once. Audiences love animals on the stage with little clothes on them, and I thought I could make a neck ruffle for the dog. Oliver, Mrs. Niffen had called him. Once I had the pattern, I could sew a small ruffle in less time than it takes to milk a cow.

It felt good to have a needle in my hand. When it was finished I made a shirttail hem—a thin hem folded twice over—and then I spread the ruffle on my lap, pinching the pleats up with my fingertips. I was pleased with it.

As I came off the boat, Leo did not look at me, but I had the feeling he knew I was coming, and the little dog turned his head. The smell of fish and mud rose in the air as the river licked at the bank.

"Is this Oliver?" I asked, although obviously it was. I held out my hand to him. He was black with little white and gray spots along his back, and short upright ears. He turned his nose from me. There was nothing on my hand of interest.

"I'm May Bedloe," I said to Leo, standing up again. "I've made Oliver a ruffle."

"A ruffle? Is that so?"

"For the stage. I heard he performs?"

Leo stood from the chair and pulled out something that looked like a glistening green string from his fish bucket.

"Sit," Leo said. Oliver sat. "Up." Oliver jumped. "Up, up, up." Oliver jumped and rotated in a circle at the same time. His tail curled over his back like a fingernail cutting.

Leo gave him the piece of fish gut. "Catahoula leopard dog on one side. Other side pure mutt."

"Do you think I could try this on him?" I asked, holding up the ruffle. "I want to get a measurement so I can put the ties right."

I wrapped the ruffle around Oliver's thick neck, folded the ends back, and pinned where the ties should go. Then I said without looking at Leo, "Captain Cushing wants me to see to the tickets. But I don't know how to do that."

"Hunh," Leo said.

"Do you know where I might find an old one? Something I can copy?"

"An old ticket? No, I don't. Miss Helena did those in the office."

"How did she do them?"

"Well, now, I don't know."

Oliver barked once to get our attention. The ruffle sagged a little to the right as he sat back on his haunches. Leo laughed. "He do look cute."

"Was it something like this?" I drew out of my pocket a piece of paper I had worked on before coming down the stairs. It was about the size and shape of a one-dollar bill but a little bit shorter, and I'd drawn a curlicue border around its edge. In the middle I'd printed "Admit One."

Leo took it from me and held it up to his eyes. "I don't think there was this little pattern round the sides. Also, she wrote more."

"What did she write?"

Leo turned the paper over to its blank side, and with my pencil drew a squiggle on the upper left corner and a squiggle in the middle. Along the bottom edge he drew a long squiggle in an unbroken line from end to end.

"Something like that," he said.

The squiggles represented words. I realized he didn't know how to write, nor read either probably.

"You're sure there was no decoration?" All the tickets I'd seen sported some pattern or maybe a little emblem of the theater, like a long black hat. But they were printed up in cities, not written out by hand.

"Miss Helena didn't have time for all that."

"Do you know where she got her paper?"

"Office, probably." He tilted his head in that direction.

The ticket office was not locked, and once my eyes adjusted to the light I saw that the space was not unlike a mop closet. A desk was built out from the ticket window, and underneath it were some shelves where I found a book of blank paper and several jars of ink but no quills. These proved to be in a box on the floor, next to the cash box.

Arranging the paper and ink on the desk in front of me, I sat down on the high stool and took my shawl from my shoulders and covered my lap with it. Then I set to work. With Leo's example in hand, I wrote the tickets like this:

Tonight, after sunset   20 cents
ADMIT ONE
Come to see some river entertainment—music and comedy and song

The theater was directly behind the ticket office, and as I dipped my pen in the ink I could hear Hugo shouting at the actors. I did not take this to mean that they were an untalented group, however. Directors shout for emphasis, Comfort told me when she first started acting, and I learned to turn my bad ear toward any director approaching me.

"Every moment you are on stage, you *want* something," Hugo was shouting at some poor player. "The moment you stop wanting, the audience loses interest."

It occurred to me that if Hugo was facing the stage, which he would be if the actors were rehearsing, I could sit on the risers in the back and he wouldn't see me. Closed rehearsal, he had said, but I needed to get some idea of the costumes. I'd made only ten or twelve tickets so far, but I thought I could both write out tickets and watch rehearsal if I was careful with the ink.

"What is it you want in this scene?" Hugo was shouting as I un-latched the door between the office and the auditorium. Then: "No, don't tell *me*, I'm asking for *your* sake, it's for *you!*"

A few figures were up on the stage and Hugo, as I'd expected, had his back to the seats. I quickly went up to the top riser, where I set down the ink and paper and placed the quill box on my lap to write on. Hugo walked backwards a few steps to the front-row bench and put one foot upon it, leaning forward.

"Right, then. Go on," he said.

When the players started up, I could tell at once what they were rehearsing: the buck basket scene from *The Merry Wives of Windsor*, a favorite at that time. Thaddeus stood with his leg thrust forward, and he stuck his chin out as he spoke.

". . . but I love thee," he said, "none but thee; and thou deservest it."

Liddy: "Do not betray me, sir. I fear you love Mistress Page."

Thaddeus: "Thou mightst as well say I love to walk by the Coun-ter-gate . . . which . . . which is . . . *line?*"

"Which is as hateful to me . . ." Hugo prompted.

Thaddeus: "Which is as hateful to me as the reek of lime."

Hugo: "The reek of a lime-kiln!"

Thaddeus swept his hand forward. "Which is as hateful to me as the reek of a lime-kiln."

"Stop!" Hugo shouted. He jumped up on the front bench and

stood on it. "Stop! All of you, listen to this—this is important. Come out here, come out!" Mrs. Niffen came out from the wings, followed by a young girl with a spindly brown braid down her back and four male actors whom I hadn't met, though I recognized a couple of them as ones who had helped move the boat. The shortest actor had a cap on his head marking him as a boy, but, other than that, no one wore a scrap of what might be taken as costume.

"Your voices, all of them, are terrible," Hugo told them. "Have none of you ever learned the importance of breathing? Have I not spoken about this before?"

A short silence.

"Pinky?" Hugo asked the short actor.

"I can't—I don't recall that you have," Pinky answered.

"You must breathe from your back! That's the secret!"

"Your back?" Liddy asked.

"Yes, yes, your back; there's room in the back. Think of the back of your ribs and reach for the air there!"

All eight players looked at him, waiting for some further explanation.

"What do you mean, Captain?" Pinky finally asked.

"Inhale! Deep breath! All the way from your back!" Hugo shouted. "Like this." He jumped off the bench and onto the stage with so much energy it seemed to escape from every part of his body at once. Then he spread his legs like a warrior and turned so that I had a view of his profile.

"Percy Hotspur from Henry the Fourth. He's just been given a mortal wound and he's dying. Imagine a man breathing his last."

He took a long breath that seemed to pull him in several directions. "O Harry," he began, "thou hast robb'd me of my youth!" He said the next few lines in the same breath, and then he inhaled and opened his arms. "O, I could prophesy, but that the earthy and cold hand of death lies on my tongue"—another breath—"no, Percy, thou art dust . . ."

For a moment he seemed broken, although he stood as upright as before. Then, as if a string had been pulled, Hugo lifted himself up out of the role and turned to face the company.

"Well?"

A long moment. Then, alone, Mrs. Niffen began to nod. "Yes, yes, quite right," she said. "I saw it very well. Breathing from the back. Nicely done."

"That's wonderful," Hugo said. "I'm glad you could see it. And now, Mrs. Niffen, please explain to the others *why* you breathe from the back?"

"Because . . ." Mrs. Niffen looked around at the other players for help, but they looked back at her blankly. "Because. . ." She frowned and looked out past him. "Why, who is that? Is that Miss May up there? I didn't know you were sitting there. Did you know she was sitting there, Captain? Isn't this a closed rehearsal?"

Hugo turned. I said quickly, "I had a question about the tickets," and in a moment he was striding down the aisle between the benches with the manner of a man who might take a fancy to knock one of them over as he passed, though they were nailed down. At every second I was expecting him to raise his voice against me, and I turned my head so that only my bad ear would catch it; but when he got to the risers, he merely took the inky sheet of paper from my hands and held it up to the light.

"Good God, is this what you've been doing? How much paper have you wasted? This is terrible! Utter rubbish! Where's the date? Doesn't matter if everyone knows the showboat's in town today so the show will be tonight—they want to see the date. And what's this? 'Come to see some river entertainment'?" This he read in a character voice, scoffing. "What kind of send-up is that? Where's the spark? Where's the spur to the imagination? You need something to drive folks here, you understand?"

"I could make up the tickets, Captain; it would take me no time at all," Mrs. Niffen called from the stage. "I know how to draw in a crowd. No one is better than me at drawing in a crowd."

Hugo ignored her. "Try this: 'Riverboat theatre at its finest.' Or: 'The entertainment of the year.' Or even: 'The finest show on the Ohio.'"

"Is that true?" I asked.

"Is what true?"

"Is it the finest show on the Ohio?"

"You don't think I'm capable of producing the finest show on the *Ohio River*?" he shouted at me.

The boat rocked sharply for a moment as if lung power alone could unmoor it. Hugo reminded me, and then he turned to remind everyone, that he had been trained in London, he had acted in Oxford, he had directed comedies in the very town where Shakespeare was born. He had been on the stage with the best, and so on and so forth. I found myself staring at the knot of his tie; I was surprised that, given all his vocal assertions of the last hour, it still showed no signs of loosening. The material would probably do well as a sash if a military figure was needed. After a while Hugo finished spooling off his accomplishments and looked at me expectantly.

I said, "The boat's name, the *Floating Theatre*—that should be written on the ticket."

"Oh, really? The name of the boat but not the date?"

"Next to the date, perhaps."

"And why is that?" He was testing me as he had tested Mrs. Niffen about the breathing. I knew what I meant, but I wasn't sure how to explain it. Earlier, while I was listening to him give Hotspur's dying speech, a slight upheaval in the river made the riser seat shift beneath me, and a picture came into my mind: a flat stage surrounded by lit candles floating downstream. Hugo was standing, giving his speech within the frame of candles, and an audience floated alongside on another barge to watch. In my mind the sound of Hugo's voice carried out over the water toward the riverbanks, the flatlands of the north on one side and the sloped hills of the south on the other. A floating theater. Of course, this wasn't an accurate representation of what the audience would see once they paid for their tickets. I knew that, of course.

"It . . . well . . . it brings up a picture," I told him.

A short silence. Hugo narrowed his eyes, looking at me.

Then: "I agree with May," Liddy said from the stage. "I always liked that name. It sounds like a fairy tale. If you're talking about drawing in an audience." From that moment on, I considered Liddy my friend.

Now Hugo turned to look at her instead of me. She blushed and took a deep, dramatic breath and reached back to feel, with her fingers, the end of her spine, trying, I suppose, to breathe from her back—a ridiculous notion if ever I heard one.

7

Two by two, like the animals on Noah's boat, I met the actors and actresses on board. Mrs. Niffen and Liddy, of course, were the first, and after rehearsal Liddy came to me with a young girl in tow, the one with the brown braid I'd seen on the stage.

"This is Celia Oxberry," Liddy said, stepping into the office, where I was busy rewriting the tickets after Hugo sent me away. "Mrs. Niffen's niece. We share a room. Rehearsal's over and we've come to take you up to the dining room. Cook usually has tea."

Celia was a thin, pale girl who seemed to sink under the weight of her thin cotton dress. She was fourteen years old, she told me, and was here because her mother had gotten remarried last year and was now expecting another child and the pregnancy was a difficult one and so her new father's mother was attending her only there were but two bedrooms in their house although it was a new house right inside town—her words came out in a rush while she looked steadily at the corner of the ceiling. After a while Liddy said kindly, "Enough now, Cee, we've come to take Miss May and see that she eats something," at which point I said, "Please call me May," and Celia looked at my face for a quick moment before resting her eyes on my shoulder.

Jemmy Grieve and Sam Trotter were next. We found them in the dining room eating sandwiches they'd slapped together themselves with cold meat and Cook's fresh bread. Jemmy (James on the play-bill) played mostly villains—bankers and governors, he told me. He sported a long moustache and was about my age. Sam Trotter was younger and partial to light comedy, he said, but he could also play villains, as he did once with a pasted-on moustache made from mule hair when Jemmy fell ill last season. All of the company except Celia and Thaddeus had been on the boat last year, and many had been on the year before that as well.

"A good job," Jemmy told me. "No coaches to catch while we struggle with our costumes and such, going from town to town with our acts. Guaranteed a full season, no traveling or living expenses—why, last year I came away with near two hundred dollars!"

Celia had started to put together a sandwich like the men until she saw that Liddy had buttered her bread and was cutting up her meat neatly in pieces, so she took her sandwich apart and tried to butter the bread, now greasy with meat juice. Considering my stomach, I thought it wise to stick to salt crackers.

The next two actors walked in carrying a line of fish between them; as if in a play, one was tall and one was short. I recognized the short one as the one Hugo had called Pinky, who'd worn a boy's cap at rehearsal.

"Francis Winter," he said, introducing himself. He held up the little finger to his left hand, which was only a stub. "Everyone calls me Pinky."

"Did you have an accident?" I asked, about the missing finger.

"Sure did," he said. "I was born."

The tall actor was Mrs. Niffen's husband; I was told later that he was very charming when he talked but that this was not often. He did not say anything now but only made a slight bow to me and then got right down to his food. Everyone called him Mr. Niffen with some formality, even Mrs. Niffen, although they'd been married for twenty years. Mr. Niffen spoke to his wife as rarely as he did anyone else—not that it mattered, since Mrs. Niffen had voice enough for both of them.

"Captain's saving up to buy himself a steamboat," Pinky told me. "Small ones getting cheaper all the time. If it works out, next year we might forget the Mississippi and steam up some of these side rivers and back down again, like the Monongahela and the Green."

"And the Kentucky River," Jemmy added. "Good fishing there. The Mississippi, in my opinion, has got itself too crowded."

"What about you, May?" Liddy asked me. "Do you act?"

"Act on the stage? Never." I must have said this with some vehemence, because everyone looked up from their plates. Here is where, if I were with Comfort, she would say something like "Don't mind May, she just says what she thinks," or "May isn't interested in plays, she's only interested in sewing." I'd gotten used to her explaining me to new people, but now I would have to do it myself.

"I sew. I play the piano . . ." They waited for more, looking at my face. Mr. Niffen, sitting at the next table, didn't join the conversation but ate steadily while reading the side of a newspaper. For a moment I wished I were at his table, where I wouldn't have to speak.

"I was hired to do what the captain's sister used to do," I said. "Before she was blown up on the *Moselle*."

Liddy cast me a surprised look, and I saw that everyone else wore near the same expression. "Apt to be literal" was another way Comfort described me.

"Yes, we know," Liddy said gently after a moment. "She was our friend."

They were all looking at me, not unkindly, but waiting for something. An explanation?

"I have . . . I can be very literal," I told them, "when I talk. That's what my cousin used to say. I say what I think."

Another short silence. Then Pinky said, "I guess I can tell you're not an actor, then, ha-ha!"

Sam and Liddy laughed, too.

"What do you mean?"

"Well, we theater people aren't exactly known for saying what we think," Liddy told me.

"Rather we say whatever we would like to be true," Pinky said. They all laughed again.

"Or what we *believe* is true, which is never the same as what we *think* is true," Jemmy put in. More laughter.

After this bump in the conversation, everyone except Celia—who never spoke much—resumed telling stories. Liddy kept a small cloth purse on her lap, even while she ate, and her face colored attractively when she laughed. Celia's eyes kept straying to her. So did Pinky's.

"I found him on the guard with a fish on his line," Pinky said to me, but he was looking at Liddy, "and I said, Where's your wig? They've just said your cue."

Jemmy laughed. "I knew you were having me on."

"Got your hair on double quick, though, didn't you?" Pinky countered.

They could laugh at each other, and they didn't take what I had said very much to heart. That was good. Liddy asked where I was from and seemed genuinely interested in our dairy farm. "I'm also from Ohio, but closer to Akron," she told me. She asked me if I liked to swim, and when I said yes, she invited me go to the river with her in the afternoons. "I'm teaching Celia how to dive," she said. "I could teach you, too."

Later, walking back to my stateroom, I decided I liked this new crop of actors. They were cheerful enough and didn't seem to be overly shocked by what my mother called my straightforward nature. Maybe I didn't need Comfort to explain me to them. That thought, or my lunch of salt crackers, made me feel much better until I opened the door to find Mrs. Niffen kneeling on the floor of my room, going through Helena's large gray trunk.

"Just doing an inventory," she said, taking her time standing up.

There was a keyhole in my door but no key to fit into it. I had to do something about that.

We were tied up near the little town of North Bend, Ohio, not at the town's proper landing but at a smaller bend farther downstream, where it was cheaper to dock. The plan was to stay here for three days rehearsing the show with Thaddeus before putting it on for the people of North Bend. That meant I had three days to get the costumes in order.

I wasn't sure it could be done, given what I'd found in Helena's trunk. I was also supposed to put up posters and advertise the show in town, but I kept circling back to the problem of the costumes: I needed to shorten Jemmy's knee breeches and make a vest for Thaddeus and fix Mrs. Niffen's red wig, which was matted at the nape. For that, I usually use cooking oil, and afterwards I rub a little perfume into the wig to diffuse the smell.

The boat itself took some getting used to also, and I don't mean my initial seasickness, which was no longer a problem now that we were docked. The smell of my stateroom, like wood soaked in fish oil, and the way the morning light came across my bed, starting from the left instead of the right as it had in my last room, and the texture of the light, which bounced off the river water, giving it a silvery quality, not to mention the rough walls, which were not wallpapered or painted, even badly, as they would have been in a boardinghouse—all this pulled at my attention in a vague but unsettling way. And that was only my own room. Every time I took a step out, I was barraged with new details—the slant of the guard, the white paint that pimpled along the upper deck's port side—and when I went down to the lower deck, I took care to accommodate for the uneven spacing of the stairs. If I could have, I would have just stayed in my room and sewed.

But the light left my room after mid-morning, and so I sewed down in the auditorium, which got the most sun if the heavy curtains were tied back. Fortunately by this time Hugo had eased his rule about closed rehearsals.

"But don't say a word, and for God's sake don't clap. Chances are you'll clap when they've done something wrong, and then I'll have a deuce of a time getting them to change it."

I didn't want to clap; I only wanted to sew. When I sewed, I forgot the unfamiliar and the strange; my world narrowed to the ends of my fingers, which was a sight I was used to and liked. It reminded me that I was still the same person. And it made up for the empty space I felt beside me, which was Comfort. Of all the strange things I needed to get used to, her absence was the strangest.

Every time I thought to myself, *In an hour I will walk into town and paste up some show posters,* I found that, before that hour had passed, something new had sprung up that needed my attention: a button off a cape, or a loose hem, or Pinky telling me that it was very important that he have a red necktie and what could we use for that? And so the three days became two days, and the two days became one, and still I hadn't set foot in town. The thought that my job in town was to talk to more people I didn't know, complete strangers, did not help matters.

On the morning of the show I woke early and put the show posters into Helena's satchel along with a stack of complimentary tickets I was to give away. Then I ate breakfast. Then I sewed a button on Pinky's breeches, and Liddy asked me to look at her bonnet, and Sam or Jemmy wanted something, too. When at last I walked down the gangplank—here called a stage plank, something else that was new—it was almost noon. And I'd only finally gotten myself off the boat because Hugo had said, "Come along, now, May, let's do one last round in town." I didn't tell him that this last round was also my first.

We walked up the path Leo had cut through the willow trees, Hugo wearing his captain's hat and me with my satchel of homemade posters and tickets. Leo couldn't read or write but he could draw, and on each handbill he had sketched a woman in a long, flowing dress with her mouth open in a circle as if singing. Underneath the drawings I had printed:

The Floating Theatre.
Sunset, May the Fifth, ½ mile upstream from town landing.
Best Show on the Ohio River.

"Right, very nice," Hugo said when I showed him. "And it is indeed the best show," he added proudly. I was determined that the costumes would be the best costumes, too, and I worried about the work I still had to do: I needed to sew a gathering stitch on the bottom of Jemmy's shirtsleeves to make channels for the ribbons, and I wanted to add more lace to Liddy's bonnet.

"Some of these towns," Hugo was telling me, "have a feed store as well as a grocer's. In that case you'll want to put up a handbill there, too." He had tied a bit of blue silk around his walking stick, and it waved back and forth with each step. His voice carried over the wide road, and his English accent, though not refined, combined a clipped sense of business with pleasure.

"Here there's just the one store, Brown's. You've gone there already, I expect. Now, make sure you go up to that bluff there . . ." He waved his hand toward a purplish rise in the north that looked more like a cloud than a piece of land. "Paste some bills on the higher trees so the farmers notice. They'll see something's up and go have a look. Have you met the justice of the peace? In these little towns, that's what goes for a mayor."

I was wondering how I was going to disguise the fact that I hadn't gone to town earlier, had given away no tickets, and had put up no posters, but Leo saved me from that. We heard a shout and turned to see him running up the road.

"Broadhorn snapped, Captain," he said when he got to us.

"What? What was it doing in the water?"

"It's fixable, but I thought you'd want to come see it."

Hugo pulled at his collar with two fingers and looked at me with a frowning expression, as though I had snapped the broadhorn myself. "Take Miss May into town, would you, Leo? See that the rest of those show posters get up."

I watched him turn back, pulling his walking stick under his arm like a riding crop. He wasn't running but was so energetic, he seemed to draw movement from the very air around him.

"How're you liking the boat, Miss May?" Leo asked me as we walked. We passed the town pier with several barges tied up to it and bales of cotton piled neatly on the dock like a row of corks. I told him that at the moment the boat felt more like a boardinghouse.

Leo looked at me sideways and laughed. He had a wide, intelligent face and heavy eyelids. "With it docked, I guess it do. Now, tell me the truth: You haven't been up in town yet, have you?"

I was surprised, but then I guessed that he saw everyone go on and off the boat. "I kept meaning to, but something always got in my way."

"Well, you have a speck of work, then. Here, let me take some of those posters. I can help put 'em up."

The main street in the upper town was neither cobbled nor paved, and a raised sidewalk ran along a line of attached wooden houses that served as stores. I was used to cities farther north with brick buildings and cobblestone streets; here it was like stepping back in time: the post office was still a log cabin. However, compared to the little towns I would see as we traveled farther down the Ohio River, North Bend was absolutely modern and new.

The grocery store stood by itself up from the main road. It had a small porch with a red awning over it and a handwritten sign in the window: "Brown's Goods." Leo told me that Helena always gave two free tickets to the grocer, Mr. Brown, in exchange for a bucket of water and some flour to paste up the show posters around town. While he waited on the porch, I went inside, determined to get through this business as quickly as possible. It was past noon now and the show would start at about eight, when the sun went down. That gave me only a few more hours to finish the costumes. As I waited for the grocer to finish tying up a cardboard box of nails for another customer, I looked around for spools of dyed lace to trim Liddy's bonnet.

"Well, now." Mr. Brown finally turned to face me. He was a tall man with a hefty gray moustache like a bit of mop stuck to his face. "You're not from around here."

"No, sir. I'm from the showboat. I'm here to give you a couple of free tickets."

"The showboat. Is it that time of year already? Where are you all tied up? I haven't heard you were here. And"—examining me with no change of expression—"you're not Miss Helena."

"Miss Helena had an unfortunate accident. I'm May Bedloe." I held out my hand. "I was hoping—"

"What happened to Miss Helena?"

"She was on the *Moselle*."

"The *Moselle*? That the steamer that went down? What was she doing on that?"

There was no one else in the store and Mr. Brown was in no hurry. After we finished with Helena's accident, he wanted to know whether I acted or sang.

"Mostly I see to the costumes. And put up show posters. I was hoping to get some flour? And a bucket of water? To put them up."

But hearing about costumes made him want to tell me about the show last year, and it was another ten minutes before I managed to obtain a paper cone of flour and some water.

"Man sure can talk," Leo said when I finally came out, taking the water bucket from me. "That's why I don't bring Oliver when I come here, he get too hot."

We pasted the show posters on the trees and fence poles near

Brown's, slapping the paste on with a paintbrush, and then I went into the log cabin post office and asked if could I put up a notice on the outside wall. After that I wanted to get back to the boat.

"Miss Helena always went to put a few up on some barns, too," Leo said. "And don't forget up that bluff."

"I don't have time anymore to go wandering about."

When we got back, everyone was in the theater rehearsing—even Hugo, who was playing Sir Hugh Evans in the Falstaff scene wearing a green cravat and a tall black hat, the whole of his costume. I thought the boat shirt and trousers he was wearing took away all semblance of character, but he told me that morning, when I asked him if he needed anything, that he considered a hat costume enough, so I counted it as a small victory that he decided to add the cravat.

At supper there was the usual bustle, the actors and actresses too excited to eat (except for Mr. Niffen, who always ate slowly and methodically) but never too excited to talk. The sun slanted into the dining room on its way down and a rising wind blew loose willow leaves against the glass. "I hope it won't rain," everyone kept saying to each other. "Will they come if it rains, do you think?" Some said yes, some said no. It was the first night they would perform with Thaddeus, and two new acts had been added including the buck basket scene. I told young Celia that after supper I would help with her makeup. This, Liddy told me, was Celia's favorite part of the show.

"She's a crowd filler. She doesn't have any lines but she likes to be made up just as well."

In the green room Celia found a tin of Pears's White Imperial Powder and applied it liberally, giving her face the shade and texture of rice flour. Afterward I held her chin and drew on eyeliner with a toothpick.

"Here, May," Liddy said, holding a box of pink lip rouge. "Let me do your mouth."

"I'm just playing the piano," I protested. "No one will look at me."

"How do you know they won't look at you? Anyway, you're on stage. You have to have a little something." She outlined my mouth, and as she leaned in I felt her warm breath on my cheek. "I wish I had your lovely long lashes," she said.

Comfort almost never gave me compliments, and certainly not about my appearance. She was the pretty one. When Liddy finished my mouth, I took up a hand mirror to study my face.

Liddy began ironing her Falstaff dress and she thanked me for all the changes I'd made to it. "I never felt like I was in a proper costume before tonight," she told me. "Of course, I wouldn't complain, but I do think it makes a difference."

"My cousin always said a good costume helped her feel the part."

Liddy smiled. "She's right."

"Sun's behind the tree line," Celia said from the window.

Liddy looked at me. "You'd better get out there, May."

I decided that the first song I would play would be "O Swiftly Glides the Bonny Boat," and after I helped collect tickets I went up on the stage to play it while people found their seats. The piano was the shortest upright I'd ever seen, fitted with small wheels so it could be rolled out of the way. The show opened with a poetic address given by Hugo, followed by the Tambour jig danced by Mrs. Niffen with Mr. Niffen on his fiddle. Next, a scene from the farce "'Twas I!" and then Liddy and Thaddeus sang two songs together. After the intermission, Mrs. Niffen sang a solo, and then Jemmy and Sam did an act whereby they drew a story with changing characters on a large square of white paper. The show ended with the Falstaff scene, always a crowd-pleaser, especially when Oliver the dog danced around the large basket of soiled laundry where Falstaff was hiding. Hugo instructed me to play "something jaunty" after the show, when the audience took up their lanterns to walk home.

I was pleased because I had done everything I wanted to do— even added the lace to Liddy's bonnet. The mistake I made was believing that the costumes would mask my other deficiencies. That night only ten people came to the show. And it wasn't because of rain: the clouds had moved off and the evening was cool but clear. They just didn't come. One man, seeing that he had a whole bench to himself, stretched out along it and fell asleep with his hat over his face. Another man laughed loudly and stamped his feet at the end of every act but left at the intermission. I kept playing the piano as I was supposed to, adapting to Mrs. Niffen when she realized she could not hit a high note and abruptly changed keys, but at intermission Hugo informed me with a very red face that there would be no community sing after the show. The sleeping man woke up when Oliver came onto the stage and danced around the laundry basket, and he talked to him like he was his own dog and there was no one else in the room. "What's that, then, a rat in there? What have you got? Show old Joe what you've got."

At twenty cents a ticket, we made two dollars. That almost covered our landing fees.

When the show ended, the remaining nine men unhooked their lanterns from where they hung on the walls and made their way down the stage plank and back up the riverbank into town. From the auditorium window I could see the dots of their lights moving away as the actors and actresses came out onto the stage so Hugo could give them their notes.

"Sam, you were late on your cue. Come onto the stage while Jemmy's still talking."

His voice was firm and loud, not quite raised to a shout.

"Celia, my darling, don't touch your hair when you're on stage: we all can see you and it takes our attention away from the action. And, Mrs. Niffen, fix the key you want to sing in and keep to it. All right, that's it, everyone. Good show."

We were all in low moods. Although Hugo waved us off, Pinky said, "What about the house, Captain?"

"What about it?"

"We can't make a living off of that."

"You do your job," Hugo said gruffly. "Don't worry about the house. I'll take care of that." Then he turned to look at me. "You. Wait."

"If you're going to close up shop," Pinky continued, "give us some warning. And do it near a real town, will ya? Not out where we can't get back from."

"I'm not closing up shop," Hugo told him, but he was looking at me like I was the one he would close up if he could.

Liddy glanced at me and then at Hugo. She said, "Captain, I asked May to do so many alterations to my costume. I probably asked too much, but she did every one." She looked like she was going to say more, but Hugo cut her off: "I know that; be off with you now."

I watched them all file out, some into the green room behind the stage and some down the aisle and out the side door. Mrs. Niffen took a particularly long time to leave and then stood out on the guard with Celia without closing the door until Hugo called out, "Thank you very much, ladies. Good night!"

When we were alone he asked me what had happened in town that afternoon.

"I did what you said. I gave free tickets to the grocer and hung up the posters."

"Who else did you give free tickets to?"

"Who else? No one."

"What about the bluff? Did you go up there?"

"I didn't have time."

We both looked back as the door from the ticket office opened and Leo walked in with Oliver. "I've come to bed down," Leo said. At night he slept on the stage on a straw tick, which could be rolled up out of sight in the morning. Oliver was still wearing his costume ruff. I thought, *I need to rescue that before he sleeps in it.*

"Give me a minute here, Leo, if you please," Hugo said.

Leo backed up and whistled to Oliver. When the door shut behind him, Hugo thrust his hands in all of his pockets looking for something. We were standing in front of the stage, and I could see some of his face in the partial light; two small lanterns were still glowing at the foot of the proscenium. My hair was coming down my neck, and as I reached up to re-fix a pin, he stopped searching his pockets to look at what I was doing with a fierce expression. I put my hand back down without changing the pin. But I found I could not do both—keep my hands still and also wait silently for him to give me a scolding.

I said, "The costumes looked good from where I sat."

The very worst thing to say, and I knew it at once. I was spending too much time on costumes and not enough time on the other parts of Helena's job—wasn't that what he was about to tell me? But still I went on; I couldn't help myself.

"If I had a bit of chain, I could make a clasp for Thaddeus's cape. I noticed the ties came loose while he sang with Liddy, and after that he had to hold the two ends together to keep it from falling. And I'd like to make a loose strap for Pinky's cap. And the women in the Falstaff scene should all be wearing bonnets, even Celia."

I kept talking and talking. I could not seem to stop. Every point I brought up was true, but that wasn't why I continued on, hardly taking a breath, like Mrs. Howard. Maybe I thought that if I spoke long enough, Hugo would forget to fire me. Or maybe I would say something that might make him think in the future I could be more useful. I liked working on so many costumes at once instead of just one, Comfort's. It felt like progress. A promotion. I did not want to leave.

"May," Hugo said.

I didn't look at him. "If you tied your cravat a bit looser, you could take it off for the final bow and wave it in your hand. The audience loves that," I said. "And—"

"May." This time he touched my arm, and at that I finally stopped. He took a long breath, as if getting ready to raise his voice, and I turned my bad ear toward him. But to my surprise he spoke in a lower tone than before. "You need to find the important people in every town and give them tickets. The justice of the peace, the sheriff, the man who owns the biggest house—anyone who has half a pull. If they come, the others will follow. And always give them two so they can bring their wives. Wives talk to other wives. And don't skimp on the show posters. Get them up far and wide, understand?"

He felt his vest pocket and this time drew out a packet of tobacco. "All right?" he asked.

I waited for more. "All right," I said when no more came.

"Leo!" Hugo called out. "We're done here."

I left the auditorium as quickly as I could, my face burning with embarrassment and an urge to cover myself. As I made my way up the stairs to my stateroom, I caught a glimpse of Mrs. Niffen's skirt sweeping around the corner on the lower deck. It would be like her to stand outside the auditorium door so she could hear every word. My face burned again, this time with a shot of anger mixed in with the shame.

I still had no sheets—another errand I'd meant to do in town—so I wrapped myself in my blanket like a swaddled baby. After a while I heard Hugo come into his room, the room next to mine. I listened to the scratch of his pen as he wrote in his log and then I heard his footsteps crossing over the floorboards and the creak of a window opening. My window was closed but I could still smell the river. I would grow used to that smell in time, like everything else, and even later come to miss it, but that night I turned my face into my pillow and breathed in its scent of feathers and old smoke, only marginally better than river mud. I thought about the boxes and trunks in the green room, which Liddy thought might contain torn costumes and props. Hugo's window creaked again, and then I heard the creak of his cot. Mrs. Niffen would probably know what was stored in the trunks, but I would rather break open the locks with a crowbar than ask her.

8

The next morning I woke to the sensation of movement. I went outside to the guard to find that the boat was already unmoored and we were traveling down the current in the middle of the river. Below me, Leo was working his thirty-foot oar hard to keep us there, and I could see Hugo steering the boat with a long, rudder-like sweep. He had his captain's hat on and a thick linsey-woolsey coat with a broad yellow stripe, the kind of coat I'd seen on many a boatman but never yet on a stage director.

"Heave her head to port!" he shouted.

The river was at its widest at Cincinnati and now it narrowed, moving faster, the water as dense and brown as unplowed earth. A long keelboat was shoving itself as fast as possible downstream and three men on the starboard side—the side I could see—were poling hard. They crossed our wake and left us behind. It was exhilarating to be out in the moving boat with the wind in my face. I'd been on deck on the *Moselle* many times, but here the movement felt much closer to my body, almost as if I were advancing the boat with my own limbs. I felt no seasickness; perhaps it had only been nerves after all.

I'd probably been standing there for three-quarters of an hour, watching Leo and the river, when Hugo tethered the sweep and began walking up the stairs. Halfway up he stopped and shaded his eyes with his right hand.

"Is that you, May? Lend me a hand, would you, and knock on Jemmy's door: we're about ready to land."

Jemmy came out in his nightshirt and breeches. They were landing the boat on the Kentucky side of the river today, and Sam and Pinky came over from the other side of the boat, where they'd been working the starboard sweep. As we neared the bank, Hugo rang the bell three times. "All right, now, Pinky, get the spring line! Leo, on the stern! Ready with that head line! Sam, move us in! All right now, Jemmy, jump! Jump, Jemmy, jump!"

Jemmy jumped into the muddy water with a two-inch hawser tied to his waist, found his footing, and then waded heavily through the muck until he was near enough to grab an overhanging willow branch that he used to pull himself up onto solid ground.

"Splendid! Right, then, Jemmy, tie her up to that cottonwood!" Hugo shouted. "I've got the spar pole out. Wrap her up tight!"

Jemmy began wrapping the hawser around the thickest tree trunk, his pants and the bottom of his shirt dripping wet. The boat jerked like a horse suddenly reined in, and I tightened my grip on the railing, which I was now holding with both hands, as the boat rocked itself in increasingly quieter waves. My breath caught like a breeze inside me and I found myself excited, even thrilled, by the men's skill. Hugo ran to the upper deck taking two steps at a time and threw a second line to Jemmy, who found another cottonwood tree to tie it to before he stretched out on the ground to catch his breath.

When the boat was secure, Hugo came over to where I was standing. He said, "Welcome to Kentucky. Ever been here before?"

I shook my head. "Jemmy looks done in," I said, for he was still lying prone on the bank with the crook of his arm over his eyes.

"Landing is hard work. Leo's better at it but he won't tie up here."

"Why not?" I asked.

"Won't set foot anywhere in the South. His mother was a slave in Carolina, don't you know. Ran away to Florida with her brother when she was a girl. That's where she met Leo's father, the Seminole."

"But why does that mean Leo can't step foot in the South?"

"Didn't say can't; said won't."

The town was called Jacksonville, and as before we tied up a little ways down from the town's main pier to save a few dollars. When the bell rang for breakfast, I went to my stateroom to fetch Helena's satchel with the show posters and tickets. My plan was to go into town immediately after breakfast. I was determined to do better today.

But as I walked back down the guard I could hear Mrs. Niffen's loud voice coming from the dining room.

"I know it well. I used to have an aunt who lived here, though she died some years back of the diphtheria, poor thing. I could easily sell more tickets than there are seats. And you wouldn't have to pay me anything, what with the repairs, the new pump, and everything so topsy-turvy . . . In short, I would be delighted to take on this job, and I know you'll be pleased with how—"

I opened the dining room door to see, as I expected, that she was talking to Hugo. They were sitting at the nearest table, and Mrs. Niffen didn't bother to stop when she saw me.

"Oh, May, there you are, and isn't that lucky you have the posters with you. That's Helena's satchel, isn't it? Let me take it. I was just telling the captain that I can go into town to sell the tickets—that is, if you've made them up? If not, I can easily write them myself; I know just where the paper is and I have my own ink, so no expense to you there, Captain. I always stock up in Cincinnati; I know a little shop . . ."

She wore a large white apron over her dress like a farmer's wife and produced from its oversized pocket a stoppered inkwell.

"Always keep some with me," she said.

I wondered what else she always kept with her.

"I'm sure Miss May will have no trouble," Hugo told her.

"No expense to you," Mrs. Niffen repeated. "None at all." She held out her hand for the satchel and I looked cautiously at Hugo. Certainly I would have to do whatever he decided, but my heart sank slightly, feeling the reproof.

However, "Thank you, Mrs. Niffen," he said, "but I'm sure Miss May will have no trouble at all today."

He put a roll and a hard-boiled egg in his pocket and stood up from the table. "I have to see to the landing fees. If you want"—this to me—"you can come with me into town."

I put a hard-boiled egg in my own pocket and followed him.

"Why does Mrs. Niffen want to do Helena's jobs?" I asked when we got outside, having first stopped in the galley for a bucket of water and some flour so we could put up show posters before we got to the town.

"No doubt she wants the extra pay," Hugo told me.

"But she said she would do it for free."

"Oh, that. That means nothing. I've seen that trick before. Someone offers to start without pay and then later they come to you with a pressing need for money."

We walked down the stage plank and started up to the bank through a dense jungle of hickory trees toward the road. Hugo gave me his arm as we climbed the muddy rise, our boots squelching with every step; and when I started to slip, I felt his fingers slide more firmly under my elbow and pinch the bone. I was walking the opposite way than I usually did, with my bad ear instead of my good one toward my companion, because I thought there was a chance that he would start up again about last night's show. He hadn't shouted last night but that didn't mean he wouldn't shout today thinking back on it. I cast about for something to say to distract him; however, all I could think of were the locked trunks with the old costumes inside and how I would get into them, but I didn't want to bring up any mention of costumes. For once, I was trying to be strategic. It felt very uncomfortable, like the horsehair blanket against my wet skin that I was given after I swam across the river with Giulia.

"I was wondering if there was a key to my stateroom," I said, landing at last on a topic. "The door has a keyhole but no key."

"What do you need a key for?"

I looked at him. What did he mean? "To lock the door," I said.

He moved the water bucket to his other hand and took hold of a tree branch to heave himself up the last bit of bank. Then he turned and held out his hand to pull me up, too. His touch felt as impersonal as if I were just something else—like his boat—that needed to be moved. That suited me. Comfort used to take any opportunity to raise her companion's emotions; here she would have said something provocative or suggested that Hugo had led her here just so he could touch her hand. It always embarrassed me when she did that. As soon as I found my footing at the top of the bank, Hugo let go of me and began scraping the bottom of his muddy boot against the grass. I did the same.

At a sound he looked up. "Aha, and here they are," he said, as if we'd been talking about someone. I followed his line of sight: four young boys were coming toward us, riding across the meadow on ponies, their legs dangling out of the stirrups.

"Mornin', sir. Y'all from the showboat?" the largest boy asked Hugo after he reined in his horse. He had a squat-nosed, sunburned face and long yellow hair, and his Kentucky accent was so marked that it took me a moment to unravel his words.

"That I am! I'm the captain." Hugo held out his hand. The boy took it a moment, looking down at him as if from a great height, but the pony was small enough so that he was nearly on eye level with Hugo.

"Where's yer captain's hat?" he asked suspiciously.

"Back on the boat. You're a tall lad. How old are you, twelve?"

"Nearly," the boy said.

"More like nearly ten!" another one shouted, this one almost an exact copy of the first with his long yellow hair and snub nose, only smaller.

"Well, that's splendid. And don't you have some fine ponies, here. If you go down to my boat, Cook'll give you some carrots for them. You tell my man Leo there to show you up to the top deck. But first, stop a moment, let me see." Hugo fished in his pocket and came up with a handful of boiled candy wrapped in twists of paper. "These might do better for you boys than carrots."

The ponies came nosing up to his hand, but he reached around their bridles to give the candy to the boys one by one. A round of thanks came up from the group, but not until after the candy had been quickly unwrapped and lay safely inside their wet mouths. A snowfall of white wrappers landed on the grass, which the ponies bent forward to sniff.

"Coming to the show tonight?" Hugo asked the boys.

"I sure hope so!" "Yessir!" "Pa says we could might!" The fourth boy only nodded, moving the candy around in his mouth.

"It's a fine show we're putting on. This is Miss Bedloe, who makes our costumes, the best you've seen! Capes and fancy dress, you name it. We're lucky to have her."

I looked at Hugo in surprise, wondering if he meant it or if this was just part of his promotion.

"You tell your folks. Twenty cents for them, only a dime for you. And if you get there early, I'll let you try on my captain's hat. I think it'll just about fit some of you."

"Not you, Jackie!" the yellow-haired one said to his little brother, which made Jackie reach over to try to shove him off his mount, and then all at once the ponies took off together across the scruffy grass. The boys reined them in with the nonchalance of English lords and turned them toward the river. At the edge of the meadow they jumped off and, throwing the reins over the ponies' necks but not bothering to tie them up, they scrambled down the bank in a shouting mass on their way to the boat.

"Do you always carry candy in your pocket?" I asked Hugo.

"Lesson one: Never underestimate the power of children. Those boys'll be after their fathers and mothers all day, God willing, to go to the show."

Boys, grocers, postmasters, and the justice of the peace, if there was one. I was amazed that Helena ever had time to do anything but give out tickets. No wonder the costumes all had a half-finished look—but I didn't mention this to Hugo, who was whistling happily, his eyes squinting into almonds in the sunshine.

This was my first time in Kentucky, and indeed my first time anywhere in the South except for Baltimore. As Hugo and I walked into town I noticed a few dark-skinned figures on the road and in the yards we passed: slaves going about their masters' business. I looked at their faces curiously. In Cincinnati there were all kinds of rumors about the slaves in the South: how they were all in chains, or how in truth they were well treated, or how the abolitionist movement was all just a plot formed by England to try to destroy America. Having lived all my life in the North, I hadn't seen many slaves before. Closer to town we passed a notice hanging crookedly on a tree:

Any SLAVE thinking of crossing the river —
BEWARE! The yankee is not your friend and will send you
to Cuba when you arrive, if you have not drowned first.

Whoever put it up used no paste but merely punctured the paper on the end of a dead tree branch, like a meat hook.

"You'll learn to stay away from the emancipation fight," Hugo said when he saw me reading it. "I've seen men come to blows more times than not over the issue. Tempers run hot, let me tell you. You'll need more paste for that one," he told me as I began to put up one of our posters on the opposite tree.

We walked by two slaves using a mangle in a yard, their faces hidden from me, and on the road we passed a tall woman, another slave by the looks of her, leading a small goat by a string. When the goat stopped to try to eat something along the road, she scolded it, and something about her firm but gentle voice and her very straight carriage reminded me of someone. A few steps later it came to me: my mother. In truth I don't know what I had expected. I suppose, like Hugo, I felt it wasn't my fight, but rather the fight of someone like Mrs. Howard and her well-organized Association for Slavery Abolishment for the Bettering . . . the Betterment . . . I couldn't remember its long name.

Hugo and I came to the town square and pasted our show posters all around it so that people could see one, Hugo explained, from whatever direction they came from. Most of the main street consisted of narrow wooden stores, but, as in North Bend, there were a couple of log cabins still wedged in here and there. Farther up the hill I could see planted fields and orchards. Jacksonville was a typical little river town that kept itself going mainly by farming—"plantation" being too grand a word—and, more recently, river commerce. We stopped in at the grocer's to give him free tickets. Back outside, an old white woman with a straw basket over her arm took the handbill we gave her and looked it over carefully through a pair of spectacles with yellowing glass, as if she were certain there must be a misspelling somewhere and she would be the one to catch it.

"Let's hang the last one here," Hugo said in front of the post office, "then we'll go back."

"What about the justice of the peace? Shouldn't we give him a couple of free tickets?"

"Good for you," Hugo said with a laugh. "You remembered. Now I won't have to send you back to the glass factory."

I looked at him, astonished.

"That was a joke," he told me.

"I know. It's what my father used to say to me sometimes."

"Is that so? All right, then, I'm off to find the justice. Why don't you take the post office yourself. After you give the postmaster his free tickets, ask him if you can put up the notice. And remember to smile."

I must have looked uncertain, for he said, "Just spread your lips and show your teeth."

The post office was a narrow two-story building with a dry goods store on the top floor. Inside it smelled like the lit oil lamps in the back, where a couple of men and one boy were busy sorting letters and magazines, and I could also smell paper and another odor like the inside of hats. The counter was unmanned. A stained white card had been propped up against a cloth-bound book with the message *Postmaster Mundy back in 10 minutes.* There was no time or date on the card.

While I waited for the postmaster, I stood looking at the notices already plastered along the wall near the counter. Jacksonville, although small, had a few lectures this week: "'The Secret Nature of the Sun,' by Astronomer John Findlay lately of Edinburgh, Scotland, which will prove by means of singeing tobacco that the Sun is a lens made out of ice"; and "'Coronation Rituals Explained,' for those interested in the upcoming ceremony for the new English Queen, Victoria." But nothing about slavery or its abolition.

"You won't find Comfort speaking here," a voice said behind me.

I turned to find Thaddeus standing just inside the door with a rolled-up newspaper in one hand and a half-eaten apple in the other. Thaddeus was always eating; he was like a young boy in his second growth. A small belly was beginning to protrude from his shirt, which he took pains to hide, but I had seen it fitting him out for his costumes. I wondered how he knew I had been looking for her.

"She wouldn't dare lecture in the South," he told me. "The people here would string her up in a tree. Why, just last week a man was shot in the back not too far from here, and all he did was give food to a runaway slave girl. Look at this." He pointed to a notice I had passed over, an advertisement for capturing a runaway slave named Hamp. Unlike Leo's show posters, this was printed up professionally, with a black-ink drawing of a hand pointing to the bold $200 reward.

"'Dark, about six feet high, wearing a swansdown vest. Plays well on the violin,'" Thaddeus read. "'Payment made for information or return. Anyone assisting the runaway will be hanged.'"

He tucked his rolled newspaper under his arm and put the apple core in his pocket. "Hand me one of our posters," he said, and he pasted it right over the one about the runaway slave.

"Are you allowed to do that?"

"You have to start thinking like a man of business, May. There's no better spot for it. Now let's be off."

"I can't go until I give tickets to the postmaster," I told him.

"Is that right? Let's see 'em."

I gave him the tickets and he went up to the long counter and looked around. Then he rapped twice on the wood. "You there! Boy!"

The young boy working in the back came trotting over, his hands and face covered with newsprint ink. Thaddeus asked him if he knew the postmaster.

"What, you mean my pa?"

"Your pa! Terrific! Yes, Postmaster Mundy, your pa. Why don't you come around here to me. Do you have a pocket on you?"

The boy came around the counter and stood before us, feeling his various pockets as if to show us how many he had.

"Hold one open for me, will you? I have a present."

The boy looked at Thaddeus for a long moment as though not sure if he was friend or foe. He was wearing dark trousers buttoned at the knee with loosely knit gray socks tucked up underneath, and ankle-high boots that were so big, they must have been his father's, though I could see why he wore them: they were made of good, supple leather. He cleared out one trouser pocket of its pebbles, penknife, and rawhide string and then held the empty pocket open with his finger and thumb while Thaddeus slipped two tickets inside, whistling their descent.

"Two complimentary tickets for your pa and your ma," Thaddeus told him. "Now, what about you. You like dancing? There's some very fine dancing on the program tonight. And I sing two songs with the most beautiful lady you ever saw; she has dimples and golden ringlets."

The boy looked at me as though trying to transform what he saw before him into the picture Thaddeus was painting.

"Not me," I told him. "I play the piano." Then, remembering Hugo's instructions, I opened my mouth slightly to show my teeth.

"We've got jokes, too, and a good scene at the very end that will make you laugh. You like dogs? Our show's got the best actor on all of the Ohio River, and he's canine."

"He's what?"

"He's our dog! Now, you give those tickets to your pa quick as you can. You got any brothers or sisters?"

"No, sir, there's just me. My mother had a deal of trouble and didn't think she could have a baby, but I'm the angel sent to her by God."

He said this most seriously, his hands clasped behind his back.

"And for this they have you working the store?" Thaddeus teased.

Still the boy was solemn. "My pa says he couldn't do without me."

That stopped Thaddeus a moment. Then he said more seriously, "Your pa told you that? Well, that's fine, that's just fine. What's your name, son?"

"Charles Mundy."

"Charles Mundy, what about I give you a complimentary ticket, too, eh? If I do that, will you tell all your friends and their parents to come? Only ten cents for boys, tell 'em. You can show 'em your ticket.

But yours is a special one, specially marked." Thaddeus looked at me and I fished in my satchel for another ticket. But when I held it out to him, the boy didn't take it.

"What about magic?" he asked.

"What about magic?"

"Any magic tricks in your show?"

"Suuure!" Thaddeus said. He smiled showing his very white teeth. "Best magic on the Ohio. You do magic?"

Charles Mundy took the ticket from me and tucked it carefully into his pocket without bending the stiff paper. "I know a trick, but I need horsehair and a comb."

"Now, don't you go climbing trees with those valuables in your pocket," Thaddeus warned him. He picked up his newspaper from the counter and slapped it playfully against his thigh.

"I won't, sir," Charles Mundy said seriously.

When we were outside on the street I said, "Why did you tell him we have magic? We don't have magic."

"May, May, what did I say before?" Again the gleam of white teeth. "Think like a businessman! You don't want a repeat of last night's performance—that weak crowd! Anyway, I liked that boy, that Charles Mundy. So solemn! I was never in my life as solemn as that; I even laughed when I was hiding from my mother when she needed wood cut. And isn't that a wonderful thing for a father to tell his son? 'Can't do without him.' That's just shining. If I had a son, why, that is just what I would tell him. May! Do you have a pencil? I have to write that down."

I wondered if, like so many other actors I knew, he was writing his memoirs. It was a common statement among them: "I'll put that in my book" or "You'll read *that* story in print one day." I suppose that now I am the one writing a memoir, but I must rely on my memory, for on that afternoon, like most afternoons, I did not have a pencil with me. It didn't occur to me then or for a long time afterwards that I had anything to memoir about, and I never used a pencil to do anything but mark cloth for a seam. So Thaddeus just took off his hat and scratched above his ear as if he could commit the thought to memory in that way.

The setting sun cast a crimson glow on the river, and from my little stool in front of the ticket window I saw the townspeople start to arrive.

Leo had swept the stage plank, and one by one men and women walked up it wearing their good clothes and carrying lanterns for the walk back. I took their money and in return gave them a stiff gray stub, a souvenir. One man offered a sack of cornmeal in payment for himself and his wife, and when I hesitated, Hugo, who was greeting people at the top of the plank, said in his rolling English accent, "Splendid! Of course! And I thank you for it!"

More people lined up. It was going to be a good show, I thought, my heart beating high with excitement, and I was right. That night we had almost sixty people in the audience, with only a few back rows left untaken. Mrs. Niffen sang her song without changing keys, and the new chain on Thaddeus's cape kept it in place perfectly. Of course, tonight I noticed other things: Pinky's cap, even with the strap, was too big for his face and sometimes hid his expressions—Pinky was wonderfully expressive, something to capitalize on, not to hide—and Mr. Niffen wore the wrong sort of tie for a shopkeeper. But the show as a whole went off beautifully. People left the auditorium laughing and repeating phrases to each other while I played them out on the piano. After they were all gone and I'd rolled the piano off to the side, I went into the office to retrieve the long silk bag of change; another part of my job was making sure Hugo took this with him to his room every night.

Outside I found the townspeople still lingering on the flat spit of land. Their lanterns swung in the night, and I could hear children laughing with tired hysteria up in the trees while the wind combed the long grass underneath. My fingers were tired from piano playing, but I felt good, and the bag of change was satisfyingly heavy. I looped its string over my wrist, and then I stretched out my hands and made two fists and stretched them out again, loosening exercises I'd learned from a piano player in New York.

"What's that?" I heard Hugo say. "Who told you that?"

I made out his figure just ahead standing with a small boy and a tall man in a dark suit. The boy turned and in the light of his small, child-sized lantern I saw it was Charles Mundy. I smiled and started to walk up to him but stopped when I saw his face was wet with tears.

"She did!" he said, pointing to me.

I started to say "No I didn't," for by now I guessed what this was about, but Hugo said quickly, "May, right, the change bag. Open it up for me, will you?"

He stuck his hand in and pulled out three nickels. He gave one to the boy and one to the tall man—Postmaster Mundy, I assumed—and made the third appear under his own hat, in his inside vest pocket, and in Charles Mundy's oversized boot. He took the coin back from the postmaster but then the postmaster found it in his palm again. Soon the boy was smiling, and when Hugo coughed a nickel up and took it from his mouth, he even laughed.

"You keep this one," Hugo said, rubbing the coin on his elbow and giving it to the boy. "I can't stand the sight of my food after I've eaten it."

I watched the boy slip his free hand into his father's as they walked away, and then he let go to run to his mother, who was standing in a knot of women underneath a tree. She bent to look at the coin he held out to her. Then, his miniature lantern swinging, Charles Mundy left his parents alone to skip ahead, his overly big boots bothering him not at all in this endeavor. All children, I've noticed, can work with any manner of footwear when it comes to skipping for joy.

Hugo turned to me. I started to say I wasn't the one who said any-thing about magic, but he spoke first.

"Never promise something you won't deliver, May. The audience has to believe they can trust us. It's part of our job, don't you see, to let people know what their dimes will get them. That's what keeps them coming back every year. You're new to this, May, I understand that, but you have to do better. I didn't realize how much you didn't know. You have to do better than this."

He shook his head, disappointed in me. A film seemed to harden around my heart. I wanted to say I wasn't the one who promised the boy magic, but a crushing feeling came over me along with the sense that it didn't matter; I'd already gotten another bad mark. What's more, Hugo might say what I was now thinking: that in any case I should have spoken up when Thaddeus lied.

The townspeople began to climb the bluff with their lanterns held out in front of them. From the corner of my eye I could see a light up in the galley of the boat, and then some more lights blinked on in the dining room: someone was turning up the oil lamps. The actors were hungry, I guessed, and, armed with bread and cold meat, they'd be sitting around the tables, dismantling the night's show, discussing what worked and what didn't, everyone with an opinion, their voices getting louder as they joked about someone in the audience with a stuttering laugh or an ill-timed cough, and then they would move on to joke about each other. Down in the auditorium, Leo would be sweeping the stage before bedding down himself.

"Do you want me to leave?" I asked Hugo. My bones seemed to stiffen as though in spite of my question I might tether myself to the spot by their very rigidity. In the moonlight I couldn't make out Hugo's expression. I would have to take a steamer back to Cincinnati, I was thinking. Or find room in a barge. Surely he'd let me stay until morning.

"Leave the boat?" he asked. "Why? Do you want to go?"

"No, I don't."

He paused, and for a moment I felt a terrible weight. But then he just said, "That's all right, then. You've made mistakes, that's all. We all do. I'll tell you something I've noticed, though, which is that you care about the show. I could tell that last night, when you paid such close attention to what worked and what didn't—well, I'm talking about the costumes, of course, capes falling off and so forth. I hadn't thought about any of that very much, to be perfectly frank, and it surprised me. I think you understand more than you let on about putting on a fine performance. That's worth more to me than a few mistakes."

I could hear the gentleness in his voice. "I do care," I said, and although I was still too shaken to smile, I remembered to open my lips to show my teeth.

Something passed over his features, a brush of an expression I couldn't read.

"Don't worry, May, We'll get you all sorted before long." He took my arm and began to walk with me back up to the boat. "Anyway, you'll want your twenty dollars back, and I don't have it. But if you give me that change bag I'll cut you a share of tonight's house, and you can put that down toward what I owe you."

9

It did not take me long to learn the habits of the *Floating Theatre*. Hugo and Leo woke up well before dawn to move the boat before the wind rose, and Cook was up even earlier, brewing dark, bitter coffee and frying up muffin-shaped doughnuts that he rolled in brown sugar. Once the boat was unmoored, Hugo stood at the bow drinking his coffee from a little white enamel bucket with a lid, about the size of a small water dipper, wearing his chalk-colored blanket coat with the yellow stripe and shouting out directions.

I liked to get up early to watch the men move the boat, first fetching my own doughnut to eat while I stood on the upper deck out of their way. Leo worked one of the side sweeps, which is what I learned to call the long oars, while Pinky and either Sam or Jemmy worked the sweeps on the opposite side. Hugo steered the boat with a short front sweep called a gouger. Occasionally he called out names of the sandbars coming up—"Petticoat Ripple! Owl Hollow Run!"—in his thunderous English accent. I wasn't sure if he was warning the crew or if he just liked saying the names. This was Hugo's fourth season on the Ohio, and he could fathom its depth just by the color of the water. He counted aloud the number of snags—dead trees partially submerged in the river—and recorded the number in his oversized brown leather logbook at the end of every jump.

Watching Hugo pilot the boat, I sometimes wondered if this was like another stage role to him—the captain with his blanket coat and his river jargon—but other times I had the feeling that moving the boat downstream every morning was his favorite part of the day. He kept a long, narrow copy of *The Navigator* in his outside pocket with its detailed information about sandbars, harbors, channels, and creeks, as well as all the towns and settlements along the Ohio and their businesses: the saddleries and weaving houses, the brass foundries and breweries. I enjoyed the feeling of movement as we made our way downriver, and I also liked watching the steady stream of river commerce in the blue morning light, the barges on their way to New Orleans with barrels of pork fat and buttons and tea and molasses and nails, the steamers with their roped cargo or sleeping passengers, and our small flat riverboat theater moving among them, always last.

Since the *Floating Theatre* was unmoored around three in the morning, by the time the actors awoke we were usually already tied up at the new landing. Breakfast was available until nine. At noon we ate dinner, and the supper gong rang at five. Normally we played one night in each town and then traveled four or five hours the following morning to get to the next one. We didn't stop at every town, only ones large enough to draw a crowd. We played in Ohio and crossed the river to play in Kentucky, but, north or south, all the towns and villages were laid out very much the same: a long, wet pier before a line of two-story wooden buildings facing the water—taverns with a room or two to let, boat shops, warehouses, sometimes a tobacco-cutting shop—and the ever-present men sitting on horse carts on the wide dirt track next to the pier, waiting to unload or load their goods onto the packet boats. The track led to higher ground where the town proper was laid out, although often that was only one block long. From my balcony on the upper deck I could usually make out farms and orchards in the distance, wattle fences separating properties, and a creek or two snaking down to the river.

Every morning after breakfast I went into town with Leo or Hugo, though after a couple of weeks Hugo felt I was sufficiently trained to go by myself. In the afternoon, if it was fine, I swam in the river with Liddy. Good as her word, she was teaching Celia and me how to dive.

"Give a little jump with your toes, Cee," Liddy instructed. "Look at how May does it. May, you're a natural!"

In the afternoons Leo sat fishing, and after swimming I often took my sewing outside to sit beside him and Oliver on the riverbank. Leo was very much like me in some ways with his own private interest, fishing, which he pursued as doggedly as I pursued my sewing. Most of the time we sat without talking, which suited us both, but sometimes he told me about Florida, where he grew up. "The swamp started at the back of the house," he said. "I guess that's why water feels more natural to me than dry land." When I asked him, he showed me how to reel in a fish and then how to clean and gut it.

He wound his long, tapered fingers along a filet knife and sliced in through the gills. "You sure you don't mind this? Some ladies don't like the looks of all that."

I didn't mind. I always cleaned hares with my mother when she wanted a stew; my father, even using a cane, was a very good shot. Leo had a slow way of speaking and he always looked right at me, which ordinarily made me uncomfortable, but it didn't with him.

"Now you take the knife and try it with this one. That's a smelt," he said. He worked the knife into position for me under the gill. "You take it from here."

He knew every kind of fish and every kind of barge. But I noticed Hugo was right: Leo never left the boat if we were in the South. He didn't even sit on the riverbank but instead he fished from the boat deck. In some ways the towns to the south of the river looked just like the towns to the north, but there were differences, of course. I never saw a slave auction, but at one town I did see rough stone blocks in front of a small hotel, on which the men and women would stand to be inspected and bid upon; the stones were so narrow, I didn't see how an adult could balance on one. And once I saw a slave being led into a slave jail, where his owner paid a man fifty cents to whip him for some misdeed while young white boys scrambled for positions at the window to watch.

I saw all this, but I don't think I fully understood what I was seeing. Sometimes now I wonder whether, like swimming, when you first submerge yourself in a new environment, you lose some of the power of your senses—your ears clog, you shut your eyes—as you try to get used to it. I was learning a new trade and learning to live with people in a way I'd never done before. Most of my thoughts were focused on succeeding in these two endeavors. When I was with Comfort, we always rented rooms in a boardinghouse but we never much mingled with any other boarders. And although we spent a great deal of time at the theater, we usually ate alone in our room to save money. Or, if Comfort went out to a public house for a meal with an admirer or some fellow actors, I would go back to our room and eat by myself, sometimes only chocolate, and then go to bed when I liked.

On the *Floating Theatre* everyone ate at the same time, family-style, and on Sundays we pushed the tables into one long row so we could all sit together. By law we could not perform any show on a Sunday, so there was no hustle to be finished, and everyone relaxed, content to sit for hours in the dining room and talk.

"Here's all you need to know about flatboats," Hugo said one Sunday evening over coffee and a piece of Cook's lumpy pecan pie. "Keep the boat as much as possible in the swiftest part of the current, avoid river cut-offs, and never tie up alongside a fallen bank. There! Now any one of you can be captain. What do you think, May? You've seen us move the boat enough now. You'll be wanting your own captain's papers before long."

Mrs. Niffen frowned. "Oh, Captain Cushing, no one knows all that you know," she said. "If I studied the river twenty years, I could not come up with half the facts you tell."

"Leo here's been on this river only two years and he knows more than I do already," Hugo told her. "But I can make my way upstage to down if I keep my wits. So far we've stayed upright, I guess." He smiled at Mrs. Niffen and she smiled back uncertainly, clearly at a loss as to how serious he was. Unlike me, she hadn't seen him every morning with his little bucket of coffee in one hand and the gouger in the other, steering the heavy boat with one arm and landing it every time in the exact part of the current he aimed for, his blanket coat flapping behind him.

"But you have your captain's papers," she said in a tighter voice.

"That I have! Course, any fool who can read can get those."

"Ha-ha-ha," Mrs. Niffen laughed weakly, looking over at her husband, who winked at her. I'd noticed that although Mr. Niffen did not speak overly much, he made good use of gesture.

By my third week on the boat I was feeling more capable. It was mid-May, and the *Moselle* had sunk at the end of April. I'd had no news of Comfort, but of course she didn't know where I was, and I didn't write to tell her. I still felt her absence sometimes, usually in the morning when I used to watch her do her exercises while I made our morning tea. But soon enough the tasks on the boat and in town distracted me even from that. Every night Hugo gave me a share of the house, usually a dime, toward the twenty dollars he owed me. We had good crowds most nights, or at least good enough to have made the stop worthwhile.

I had only one nagging worry: Mrs. Niffen. Twice I had come upon her in my room, looking at my things. The second time she was holding my father's pocket watch, which, going down early in the morning one day to bathe in the river with Celia and Liddy ("Prepare to be cold, May!"), I'd left by my bed.

"This watch looks just like Mr. Niffen's; I thought he might have loaned it to Helena," Mrs. Niffen said, not handing it back right away. I was fairly sure that if I had returned a mere two minutes later it would have already been in her pocket.

"Have you been able to find that key?" I asked Hugo after supper that night.

"What key?"

"The key to my stateroom. Mrs. Niffen keeps going in while I'm not there."

"Oh, don't worry about Mrs. Niffen; she's harmless. Well, fairly harmless," he amended. "She only wants whatever anyone else might have." He laughed, but I did not see the joke.

"That doesn't sound harmless to me," I said.

The next day we crossed out of the state of Ohio and into Indiana; on the other side of the river, Kentucky went on and on. June was still a week or so away, but the summer heat seemed to have settled in early. After my swim with Liddy, I thought I might try to rearrange things in the green room so I could put Helena's trunks in there, too: they were still pushed against the cot in my stateroom. Whenever I asked Hugo about Helena's belongings, his face seemed to grow a hard layer and he turned away from me, saying, "Yes, yes, I'll work something out." I don't think he was lying, exactly, but after the third time he said it, I realized that if anything would be worked out, it would not be by him.

Liddy told me that Hugo and Helena had been very close. "They built this business together. He probably can't bring himself to look at her things yet."

So, with my hair still wet, I went along the outside guard to the back door of the green room to see if I could find space for the trunks in there. But as soon as I stepped inside, I realized that the room could barely contain what was already in it. Instead I decided to pry open the crates to see what was inside them, hoping for some useful costume material and props, and maybe I could consolidate a few of them to make more room.

I found I could open every crate but two without a key. Inside, it was true, there was a lot of moldering cloth, which I set into two piles: the fabric I could recut into bodices (Liddy) or matronly capes (Mrs. Niffen) or gaudy vests for a villain (Thaddeus); and the fabric so far gone that it had to be thrown away. I was disappointed because there were no hats and nothing like a cane, which I particularly wanted. In spite of the small window cut into the back wall, the space felt dark and closet-like, and it reminded me of the small room off the dairy where my father kept his cleaning equipment.

I opened one of the side doors to let in more light, when I heard a voice coming from the auditorium. Although it was directly behind the stage, the green room had two doors on either side that led to stage left and stage right, where the actors waited for their cues—technically the wings, I suppose, although the space was as cramped as an upright coffin—and I went out there to see who it was.

Hugo was standing on the stage facing an imaginary audience. "In the old country," he was saying in his broadest English accent, "magic was street entertainment."

I must have made some noise, for he stopped and turned his head.

"Who's back there? Mrs. Niffen? Come out here a minute if you don't mind."

When I walked onto the stage, I saw with some surprise that the velvet curtains in the auditorium had been rolled down to block the afternoon light, and six small lighted lanterns formed a circle around a wooden chair that faced the audience. Hugo stood within the lanterns' dim light with his hand on the back of the chair. Next to him, also within the circle of light, was a small table with a folded handkerchief and a glass of water.

"May! I thought you were Mrs. Niffen. No, no, even better," he said as I started to leave. "Sit here in this chair, will you? I want to practice my patter. All that nonsense with the postmaster's boy made me want to try out my act again. But I do better with a live volunteer."

I noticed that he had stuck a few cotton handkerchiefs into the cuffs of his shirt, and as he waved his hands they shifted a little with the movement, but not much. Silk would work better, I thought.

"I'm not a volunteer," I said, removing the tea towel I had draped over my shoulders on account of my dripping hair. "Rather conscripted."

He made the smallest of smiles, just a movement of the chin. As I sat down on the chair I could smell the mixture of washing soda and powdered ammonia that Leo used to clean smoke from the lantern glass. I'd never before been on the stage, facing the audience, imaginary or otherwise, and I was glad there was not really a line of coughing and spitting men who stomped their feet if they liked something and booed if they didn't. In New York theaters there was more distance between the actors and those who watched them, but on the *Floating Theatre* it seemed as if good manners alone (and those not always prevailing) drew the line. I was wearing my plainest brown dress, something I would never allow onstage on anyone else because it bled right into the woodwork.

"In the old country," Hugo began again, "magic was street entertainment."

He produced a coin from behind my ear just as he had done a few weeks before with Charles Mundy. He said, "Gasp as though you're surprised."

I gasped as though I were surprised.

He showed the coin and two more like it to the imaginary audience, fanning them in the mouth of his fist. I guessed what was coming: an old trick called the Jumping Coin, which I had seen many times. I knew what couldn't be seen from the audience: a fourth coin palmed in his hand. With a limp flourish—the cotton handkerchiefs still refusing to flutter—Hugo dropped one coin into his pocket and wrapped the other two in the handkerchief.

"Magicians often performed in private homes in London during the season. My own father was once in the home of Lady Margaret of Kent and made a Spanish doubloon appear from her bodice."

He unwrapped the handkerchief to reveal all three coins inside. He put one coin in his pocket and then tapped his leg and found it in his boot. He put it back in the handkerchief with the other two coins and then shook the handkerchief out, but now nothing was in it.

"I daresay you think moving a coin into the bodice of a lady the height of impertinence."

He took my hand and shook it. A coin dropped from my sleeve onto the stage floor.

"So did Lady Margaret. She sent him off on the next boat to America."

He shook my hand again and another coin fell.

"And so you see me here, happily plying my trade in America, all because my father found his coins in the rudest of places."

He gave me the handkerchief and I opened it. Inside were all three coins. I lifted them out to show the empty benches and Hugo clapped for himself.

"Your father was sent here by Lady Margaret of Kent?" I asked as Hugo folded up the handkerchief and put it in his pocket. He pushed the table an inch upstage and looked at it. In two steps he was off the stage and in the front row, evaluating the table from there.

"No, of course not," he said as he jumped back up on the stage to move the table again. His movements were like the forest pucks my mother used to tell me about as a child: one minute here, one minute there, his gait something between a leap and a skip.

"My father never set foot in America. That's just my stage patter. There is no Lady Margaret of Kent."

My face heated suddenly. "No Lady Margaret? All that's a lie?"

"Not a lie. I told you. It's stage patter."

"Stage patter," I repeated. A hot, dark circle seemed to start under my rib cage and radiate out. I'd been so ashamed when I saw little Charles Mundy crying, and I hadn't even been the one who lied; I was remorseful because I didn't *correct* the lie. But here Hugo was actually practicing a falsehood without the slightest compunction at all.

"I don't see any difference between saying your father was sent here by a lady in England who doesn't exist, and telling a boy that there will be magic in the show when there is not," I said with some vehemence. But Hugo only glanced at me and then went over to the windows.

"The difference, May, is that my act is a kind of fiction and the audience knows it. When a man gives me money and I give him a ticket, we've made ourselves a deal: I will try to make him believe something that is not true, and he will to try to believe it."

He rolled up the velvet curtains and wound the rope ties carefully around the wall hooks as if he were securing the boat to a tree. Sunlight poured in, hitting the stage at a slant.

"That's just buffalo talk," I said.

"Oh, no, May. Not a bit of it. Think back on when you're sitting in an audience. At first you're aware that you're on a plush seat, or a hard bench, or maybe you're standing in the pit, but in any case there are people around you who, just like you, paid to be in this place, and you spend some time looking at them, what they're wearing, who they're talking to, and so forth, maybe even listening to what they're saying." He went to the next curtain and began rolling it up. "You might know some of them, but even if you don't, you know that you are all from the same place and speak the same language and so on. Then the bell rings and the actors come out on the stage and the scene begins—let's say it's a country scene and maybe it's in Italy or somewhere else far off—and for a moment, even as the players start their speeches, you are still you and the town you live in is still just outside the closed theater doors. But then, rather quickly if the actors are any good, something happens and somehow you drop into the fiction of the Italian countryside, and there you are. You forget all about the people around you because the only people that exist are the actors onstage, and the only world is the world they are playing out for you. You've lost yourself in the fiction. Afterwards, do you feel cheated? No. You might have liked the performance, you might have hated it, but it doesn't strike you as a *lie* . . . it's more like a window. And you're complicit. You wanted to look in that window and you did."

The puck was gone; the director-teacher had returned. There were eleven curtains on each side and they were so heavy and thick with dust that so far he had raised only five. At night no one would notice the dust—especially if, as Hugo was trying to convince me, they so fully believed in the story on the stage that for them there were no curtains, there were no windows, there was no boat. But could that really happen? It had never happened to me.

"I never sit in the audience," I told him. "I'm always offstage helping."

"Yes, yes, I know. But on the other days, when you aren't working . . ." He went to the next window.

"I never go to the theater when I'm not working. I've never sat in an audience in my life."

Hugo stopped and turned to look at me. "You mean to tell me you've never seen a play from the seats?"

"No."

"Why?"

Why? A fair question. I didn't like to sit for any length of time without doing something with my hands—that was one answer. Another answer was that I simply had no desire to do so. Hugo watched me as though my face might answer his question as well as any words. Above us the bell sounded for supper.

"Well, why should I?" I said at last, defensively, when I saw that he was not going to stop waiting for an answer.

Hugo frowned, and then laughed, and then shook his head. "You are a strange duck," he said, "living with actors all year round and not interested in seeing a play."

"Are you interested in costumes? In sewing?"

"Not the same thing."

"Why not?"

The bell rang again. I was annoyed because I hadn't finished going through the crates in the green room and because Hugo was a hypocrite, notwithstanding all of his fine words about what was a lie and what wasn't. But mostly I was annoyed because he now knew that I didn't like plays. I don't know why that last bothered me so much except that I wanted to keep my job and I knew how much theater meant to him.

"Look here," he said instead of answering me. He came up to me and showed me the same three coins again, and then palmed them.

"I'm hungry," I said impatiently. "All the pie will be gone."

Hugo said, "There are a few things you ought to learn if you're working in my theater. One is the willful suspension of disbelief." He rolled the phrase along in his strongest English accent. "Ever read Coleridge, May?"

"No."

Once again he made the coins appear from behind my ear, then in one of his pockets, and then in the other one.

"We want to believe a story is true. We use our imagination to convince ourselves. We can't help it. Now, you know that I didn't find this coin in your palm"—he was shaking my hand—"but here it is, and so your imagination says it must be so. And what a delightful feeling it is, believing something that we know isn't true!"

"My cousin has always maintained that I have no imagination."

"If we can believe something that isn't true," Hugo went on, "the possibilities become endless. And then surprise, when it comes, is no longer frightening but rather a pleasure. And you know, May, that there is always a surprise at the end."

Now he drew close enough to put his hand in my pocket, and for a moment I could smell the dark, rich balm he put in his hair, a spicy smell that seemed to bring with it the very taste of a faraway place, but one that I could never get to either by boat or by land. His fingers found my dress pocket and slid in, and for a moment his warm arm pressed against mine. Then he drew something out of my pocket and stood back.

He held out his hand. "Look what I found."

It was a long brass key. The key to my stateroom, I guessed. And at that, I confess, I did make a short gasp in surprise and pleasure.

"Right there in your pocket all along," he told me.

In my travels with Comfort I'd had many keys given to me: heavy iron keys and small thin keys that might just as well have been hatpins, keys to dressing rooms or boardinghouse rooms, keys to prop cabinets. My mother kept all her keys on a ring, which she carried in a basket. She used the same keys nearly all her life, but my keys changed with the theater season. Some landladies gave Comfort and me only one key for our shared rooms, and one wouldn't give us a key at all. "My people are all respectable," she'd told us, "and I trust you are, too."

I was unusually pleased to have this new key, and later, at supper, I found myself reliving the moment when Hugo leaned in to put it in my pocket. I was surprised at the rush of sensation and the pleasurable tingle that stayed with me, which I prodded like a sore tooth, though it wasn't painful—rather the opposite. He remembered I wanted the key, he had looked for it and found it, and he had given it to me in a surprising way, to amuse me, as entertainment. I knew it wasn't magic, but I still felt happy. At the table I sat where I usually sat, between Liddy and Celia, but every once in a while I touched the brass key through the fabric of my dress pocket.

"Aren't you hungry, May?" Hugo asked me from across the table. I looked at his eyes, trying to determine if he had felt the same pleasure giving the key as I had felt getting it. Liddy was telling a story about how once, when she was playing Juliet, she became so far gone into the part that she actually drank the poison (black ink) instead of miming it, and while she spoke Pinky stared at her intently. I noticed how Pinky's eyes shone whenever he looked at Liddy, and I fancied he liked the excuse—listening to her tell a long story—to watch her face, which was, indeed, very lovely with her downturned eyes and happy smile. She carried a small yellow pocketbook around with letters inside it, and sometimes she opened one and read it under the table. Were they love letters? I wondered. Pinky, if he noticed her reading one, went a bit red in the face. His ears drooped forward but other than this he was a handsome man with a fine straight nose and cornflower-blue eyes that crinkled like an Irishman's when he smiled.

"Way I see it, an actor can't be too familiar with himself and his own reactions," he said when Liddy finished, "since every night you have to say your lines as though for the first time. You have to feel it each night."

"This new style, what they call the American style—lots of feeling there," Jemmy put in.

Sam, sitting next to Jemmy, nodded. "Quite loud," he said.

I thought of Sam as one degree beyond Mr. Niffen: Sam spoke, but not much, and usually only words of one syllable.

Thaddeus warmed to the subject. "That's just the ticket! Make your words sound important and put the audience all in a maze and a muddle. Edwin Forrest and his lot, they never just walk through their parts. They have strength, you know, and power. I met Forrest once."

"To my mind those blokes go too far. It's a lot of empty ranting," Hugo said. He held a piece of pie in his hand and as he spoke he waved it around, scattering small flakes of crust.

"They get the audience's attention, though," Thaddeus said.

"Only by tearing up the language." Hugo waved his pie again. "Too much mouth, in my opinion, and not enough art."

Cook put another pot of coffee down on the table. "Let me get you a fork, Cap'n," he said.

"No, no," Hugo said. "Don't bother. I come from farm people in the north. Sheffield. We all eat our pie this way."

I decided this was probably a joke, since I knew from all our talks as we walked into town together that his parents had both been stock actors in London. But Mrs. Niffen leaned toward him and said, "Quite right, Captain, quite right. Pies were originally like sandwiches, you know. A fine old tradition. The plowman taking his break. We should all eat our pie in just that way." She declared that from now on she herself would always eat her pie with her hand and would encourage everyone else to do the same.

"Isn't that right, Celia?" she asked her niece. "You and I will eat our pies with our hands like the fine farm folk in, er, Neffield."

Celia, who unlike her aunt had not yet finished her pie, put her fork down, her face reddening. Hugo winked at her from across the table.

Satisfied that the issue was settled, Mrs. Niffen wiped her mouth with the corner of her napkin and said she must now "see to her housekeeping," a phrase I never understood (it was her usual way of quitting a room), since it was Leo who did most of the chores: emptying our stove ashes every morning, for instance, and sweeping the floors, and scrubbing the barrels that held our drinking water.

After she left, I waited for a minute and then I left, too. Down the guard, as I suspected, Mrs. Niffen stood with her hand on the doorknob to my stateroom. She looked over as I approached with no indication of wrongdoing either in her expression or her manner. Her hand remained on the doorknob.

"I've been looking for a book I've misplaced," she said evenly. "I thought it might be here in Helena's room, in one of those trunks."

I pulled the long key from my pocket, fitted it into my door lock, and turned it. For a boat lock subject to wind and moisture, heat and cold—and possibly all that in one day—it was surprisingly smooth. The mechanism turned over with a satisfying click.

Mrs. Niffen looked down at the key and then up into my face with surprise. The nights were getting warmer now, and her silver-gray hair was curling near her forehead with the humidity. Her face looked even pinker than usual.

"It's my room now," I told her. "And the book isn't here. There is nothing of yours in here, Mrs. Niffen."

I turned the doorknob while pushing the door with the flat of my hand to make sure it was locked, and then I returned the key to my pocket and walked back to the dining room, leaving Mrs. Niffen standing there with nothing to do.

A few days after this Hugo made an announcement at breakfast: he wanted to change up the show midsummer, right about the time the Ohio met up with the Mississippi River, and put on a three-act play.

"It's never been done on a riverboat that I've heard of," he said. He had risen from the table to address us all, first beating a spoon against his water cup to get our attention. The hair on the right side of his head stood straight up, probably from him running his fingers through it, and as he spoke he began walking backwards, still talking, toward the windows. I was reminded, again, of a puck.

"We'll be the first! A real three-act play right on the river. Introducing the interior of America to the finer dramatic arts." He was framed by the window light now, which seemed to emanate from his limbs rather than shine through the glass. A three-act play! I thought of all the new costumes that would require.

"We only have about a month, so we'll have to rehearse every morning until then. It's not Shakespeare, mind," he said, looking at Thaddeus, "no important speeches. We have to remember the audience we have—farmers and merchants wanting a bit of an escape. But you'll be able to sink yourself into a role for all that."

"That's the idea!" Thaddeus said. He seemed to puff up with satisfaction.

"And we'll need a whole line of new costumes," Hugo went on, looking at me. Although I'd been thinking just that, when his eyes met mine, all my blood seemed to rush out toward the tips of my fingers. I wanted to begin right away.

"Have you chosen a play?" I asked. Hugo was holding a script in his hand on oversized paper bound in oilcloth. As an answer, he waved it up and down like a flag.

"*The Midnight Hour*," he said. "*Ruse Contre Ruse* in the French."

Two of the windows behind him were open and I heard a steamboat puff hard like an old woman pressing her lips together and then blowing out air to show her disapproval. Hugo was smiling broadly. His enthusiasm seemed to go around the room like someone tapping us each on the shoulder. The actors and actresses seemed just as excited as he was, except Mr. Niffen, who looked different only in that he had put down his newspaper to listen.

Pinky glanced at Liddy, something hungry in his face.

"I've seen that," he said to Hugo. "It's good fun. Who will play the marquis?"

"That would be Thaddeus. And Mr. Niffen will play Sebastian. Liddy will be Julia, of course, and I'll stand up for the General."

Pinky's ears drooped forward in disappointment, but Liddy's face positively shone.

"Wonderful idea. But won't the audience grow bored?" Mrs. Niffen asked, as usual mixing her compliment with a complaint so that you didn't know which she truly meant.

"It's a comedy," Hugo told her. "And it's short." He bounced up and down on his toes and looked at our faces, resting at last on mine. His smile broadened. "What do you say, May? Think you can pin together a wardrobe in three or four weeks?"

I felt myself smile in spite of his suggestion of pinning. "I can try."

*   *   *

We were tied up in Listerville, Indiana, and as soon as we could, Liddy and I went up into town to look at fabric. Celia trailed a few steps behind us reading a book while she walked. There was a high wind coming off the river and the tree leaves waved this way and that as if, Liddy said playfully, they were avoiding a conversation.

She was in good spirits. We all were. The prospect of a new play and all the costumes that it would need made me happy and restless. I would be overseeing an entire production from scratch, and I wanted to start everything at once. Hugo had given me a list of the characters—the Marquis, the General, the young ingénue, and so on. The ingénue—Liddy—would be the easiest.

"Something pastel, of course," Liddy was saying. "Youthful. Maybe a large hat? Does it take place in the summer?"

"We don't want to hide your face. Celia, watch yourself!" Celia had just tripped over a root in the dirt road. I held out my hand for the book. It was a slim leather volume with a title etched in gold. "*Songs Along the River*," I read aloud. Liddy turned her face away but not before I'd gotten the impression she was blushing. Then she said quickly,

"What's that boy got?"

Underneath a large sycamore tree at one corner of the town square sat a little black boy about six or seven years old.

"Happy in a box!" the boy called out when he saw us. Nested in his lap was a muddy cardboard box. "Come see happy in a box, only a penny a look!"

When we came up to him he smiled, showing a space where his two front teeth had once been; now two stony white nubs were beginning to show themselves. He was barefoot and wore a too-long shirt with the cuffs rolled up. His eyes were bright and friendly.

"I'd like to see what happy looks like," Liddy said, opening her purse and giving the boy a penny.

He was careful to keep one hand on the box lid. "Have to crunch down over it, ma'am," he instructed.

The three of us knelt on the grass. Then the boy lifted the lid a couple of inches and I saw a very small sand-colored toad inside, with a couple of stalks of curved green grass in the center next to a small gray stone.

"This is happiness?" Liddy asked. Celia poked her finger in, trying to make the toad turn.

"Happy," the boy corrected. "You notice how his color's that unusual? And look here at these little red spots downside his back: that's what make him lucky."

An older man suddenly walked up to us as we knelt there. He was short and wore good clothes and had a moustache with long waxed ends. A rolled newspaper was wedged under one arm and he carried an air of knowing better than anyone else what was what.

"Happy in a box, sir," the boy said to him uncertainly. "A penny a look."

The man leaned over and pulled up the box lid without paying. He peered inside. "What's this? A frog? You've asked these ladies to pay to look at a frog? Why, they could see twenty or more if they just stepped over toward the creek! Give them their coin back at once!"

He had a southern accent although we were in the north, in Indiana. The boy opened his palm and the man took the penny. But he did not give it back to Liddy at once.

"I'm sorry, ladies. This boy ought to be whipped. I would do it myself if I had a whip on me." He took his rolled paper out from under his arm as if that might do in a pinch. "Imagine! Asking folk money to see a frog!"

I looked at Liddy, unsure what to do. A kind of stubbornness crossed her face. She stood up and took the penny from the man and gave it back to the boy.

"It's a frog in a box," she said. "I could see twenty in a creek, but I've never seen one in a box before."

The man pulled his chin back, astonished, and his face became red with anger. Celia and I stood up now, too, bolstering Liddy on either side.

"You'll ruin him for good, honest work," the man told her in a booming voice.

Liddy ignored him and turned to the boy. "Why do you call him Happy?" she asked.

The boy looked at her carefully, as if uncertain whether he should talk. He stood up and pulled the box closer to his chest. "Because he haps about," he said.

"Get along now, you," the man said roughly, prodding him with the end of his rolled newspaper. "Don't come back along here with your tricks, d'you hear?"

The boy scampered off down the street, holding the box in his hands in front of him like a tray. Once he was far enough away from us to feel safe, he slowed down and began skipping.

But the red-faced man wasn't finished with us. "If you think you've done that boy a good turn, you're mistaken. Hard enough to get them to understand honest work. This is what comes from freeing them. Damn liberals. Damn abolitionists. It's you women," he said.

"Oh, did women write up the legislature for the free states?" Liddy asked. Her face had become as red as the old man's.

"Now, don't be smart. You make men soft is what you do. Soften them up like the sun."

Like the ends of his moustache, I thought, which were beginning to look oily in the heat.

Liddy turned her back to him in an exaggerated, theatrical manner. When we were out of earshot she said, "Imagine bullying a young boy like that. A young, harmless boy."

For a moment the wind blew hard against us, and Celia took hold of Liddy's hand. Liddy was more of a guardian to Celia than Celia's own aunt was. Every night before a performance the three of us gathered in the green room to put on costumes and makeup and discuss the crowd we might have that night. She and Celia let me into their company as though they'd been waiting for me, and I couldn't help but compare this to Comfort's manner, her jealousies and petty remarks, her way of keeping me out, which I thought I hadn't minded—at the time I didn't think I wanted to be included. But I enjoyed those minutes with Liddy and Celia before every show. I had never heard Liddy be petty, not once, and I understood why Pinky watched her, waiting for his chance. It was not just because she was pretty. She had a big heart, and I admired that. I wasn't surprised that Liddy would take the boy's side.

But she was young, too. By the time we got to the shop, she had already forgotten about the man with the waxed moustache. She laughed at something—maybe the wind or maybe the thought of her new dress—and she swung her hand forward with Celia's and then back again.

"Let's see if they have some pink fabric," she said. "A pretty pink ingénue."

Thaddeus's sense of importance hadn't diminished, and he came to me that evening with ideas about his costume, which involved "as much shine as you can manage"; he suggested a gold cape. When he had played opposite Comfort in Pittsburgh, Thaddeus wore a very large top hat with a red feather, and he wondered if I might make one just like it for *The Midnight Hour*.

"I thought the action took place in Spain," I asked.

"Spain or France, but that doesn't matter," he said. I disagreed. It did matter. If the play took place in Spain, he should wear Spanish clothes.

"The main idea is to make me stand out," he said, "like you did for your cousin. Comfort always looked better than—than the rest of us." I had the feeling he was about to say *better than me*. He looked at me curiously. "What word do you have of her?"

"None," I told him. "Remember, she thinks I'm back home."

"Does she? Oh, yes, that's right," he said, and I was amazed he could have forgotten our little scheme so quickly. Like Comfort or Aesop's grasshopper, Thaddeus lived only for the day at hand. But, also like Comfort, his days playing the charming young lead were numbered, what with his thinning hair and swelling paunch. I resolved to make as shiny a cape for him as I could.

However, a week or so later I did come across a notice about Comfort, one that confused and worried me. I could not say that I'd been looking for news all this time, but I did make it a point to read about any forthcoming lectures advertised on post office walls, a habit I started while waiting for Postmaster Mundy back in Jacksonville. Hugo's new play was now in closed rehearsal, and I was under strict orders to stay away from the auditorium—which was fine with me, since I was spending more and more time each day searching out fabric and props.

The notice had been put up in Birchfield, Indiana, where we had landed one hot, humid morning. The river was swollen high from a week of rain, and the pecan trees lining the bank looked like a wall of fresh, green leaves. As I walked into town with Hugo I could hear heat thunder in the distance. He took my arm, which he usually did now. We often climbed up muddy banks or slippery paths to get to the dirt roads that led to town, and I appreciated his steadying hand, though it meant we walked rather close to one another. That day Hugo smelled like freshly cut wood, and I asked him if he'd been repairing the boat.

"Just a bit of prop making," he said, and then he abruptly changed the subject as though it were a secret; I found out in due time that it was. "Now, May, how did you come to be so good at sewing? You should have seen my sister sweating over a needle."

I told him about my mother and how she never needed a rule to keep her hems straight, and about my father, who was so particular about his wheels of cheese. I came from a family of perfectionists.

"Have to be a perfectionist," Hugo said, "and patient, too, to make cheese."

We were beginning to know each other's pasts, and to my surprise I liked that he asked me questions about myself. Hitherto I had thought of myself as a private person, like my mother. It occurs to me now that perhaps I just hadn't had much chance before this to become acquainted with another person, a new neighbor, a new customer; I had lived quietly alone with my mother, and when she died, I lived alone with Comfort. And Comfort, I was beginning to see, took great pains to keep me away from anyone else. As on the *Moselle*, she laughed at me and changed the subject if I drew too much attention.

Hugo and I stopped off first to pay our landing fees at Birchfield's business office, which was in its own small building between the post office and the saddlery. It had a tin roof, and inside it was even hotter than outside. While Hugo paid our fees, I went over to look at the notices pinned up on the far wall, mostly to be closer to the open window.

"Showboat, that right?" The clerk smiled, holding out a pen for Hugo to sign his name. "Wife and I go to your show every year. Still have the dog?"

Outside, the thunder rumbled again and I saw that many of the notices had been folded over by the wind. I straightened a few out— one advertising sperm oil and another offering brown French linens at a discount. As I turned over a third one, I saw printed in heavy block letters:

COMFORT VERTUE,
The Abolitionist.

Even though I'd been prepared to see, had even sought out, such a notice, I still felt a ripple of warm shock go through me as though

I'd come upon something wholly unexpected. Her name spelled out in letters as large as a half-smoked cigar made her seem like a villain, and my shock increased as I read further. It wasn't an advertisement for her lecture, as I first thought, but rather a call to arms.

COMFORT VERTUE,
The Abolitionist.

That unvirtuous *New York* actress COMFORT VERTUE, will hold forth *tomorrow evening*, at the Quaker Meeting House in Viola, Indiana. The present is a fair opportunity for the friends of the Union to *snake Vertue out!* A purse of $50 has been raised by a number of patriotic citizens to reward that individual who shall first hit the fair lady square above the neck with fruit or vegetable of their choice so that she may learn what happens to those who invade our soil and try to rally our men in an unjust cause! Friends, we must be vigilant!

As I read over the notice again I felt a sharp twinge in my bad ear. "Unvirtuous"—was that even a proper word? And Comfort was no more a New York actress than she was an actress from anyplace else, although I had a feeling she would like that moniker. But the real problem was the fruit or vegetable of choice. If nothing else, I should warn Comfort about what was brewing if I could. How many inns were there in Viola, Indiana? There might be rooming houses, too. Would a letter reach her in time?

"All right, then," I heard Hugo say, and the sound of coins clinking on the desktop behind me. I quickly pulled the notice off its pin, folded it up, and put it in my pocket.

"We'll get to Green River in a couple of days," Hugo said as we went out the door. "That's a pretty spot, and we always get a good crowd. What's tomorrow, June second? Why, isn't that your birthday, May?"

"My birthday is June third," I told him.

"Oh, that's right, that's right," Hugo said. He had a card file in his office with all of our names, winter addresses, birthdays, and next of kin written down in case of emergency. "The day after that, then. Sunday. Now, that's convenient, what? Very convenient."

I was hardly listening to him, I was still thinking about Comfort. "Where do we go tomorrow?" I asked. "To Viola?"

"Either Viola or across the river to Beswick," he said. "I haven't made up my mind."

His words beat a rhythm with that particular English staccato, as if every fourth syllable was a bullet or a bee. I could see the flag of the *Floating Theatre* in the distance flutter like a handkerchief. The wind was getting stronger now, and a sheath of dark clouds had begun to crawl over the river.

Alpha, beta, gamma, delta.

"I've always wanted to see Viola," I said.

"Have you, then? Why is that?"

I knew as little about Viola as I did any other town on the river. I cast around in my mind for something that might give it distinction.

"My friend was born in Viola," I said.

"In Viola? But wasn't it platted out only ten years ago or thereabouts?"

I didn't say anything. The first lie wasn't the trickiest, I was learning; it was the one that came after that.

Hugo pulled out his handkerchief and swiped it across his forehead. Then he took off his straw hat, wiped his hairline and nape, and then folded the handkerchief back into a damp square and pushed it into his pocket.

"Well, it's all the same to me," he said, replacing his hat. He smiled at me. "Viola it is."

10

The next morning I woke early, before the sun rose, even before Leo and Hugo got up to move the boat to Viola. I dressed and made my way down in the darkness to the green room, where two box irons were kept like metal turtles in their shells. Liddy and Celia always ironed their costumes at the very last moment before we started in on makeup, because Liddy wanted her dresses to look their best and Celia liked the smell of hot starch.

I was pleased because last night's audience had been our best one yet: seventy-two tickets sold, mostly adults. In the front row a line of look-alike brothers, five of them, laughed heartily at every joke, emitting a fresh waft of onions each time. They all had round red faces with wide noses, and the middle brother slapped his knee at the end of every act. He was a jovial fellow with a deep laugh who looked as though he enjoyed every single thing that came his way. Afterwards, when the players had taken their bows and everyone was filing up the aisles to leave, he stepped up to the piano to talk to me.

"Finest playing I've heard outside of Akron," he said. "You take lessons?"

"I did, yes."

He held his hat in front of his chest. His hair was thinning but neatly combed, and there were straight lines where the comb teeth crossed his scalp.

"Well, I can tell. Mighty fine," he said again. "My name's Joe Alton. My brothers and I own one-third of the boats down here. Alton Brothers—name's getting to be known! We export mussel shells to New Orleans, where they make 'em into buttons. Here!" He pulled a pale paper wrapper as small as a child's hand from his vest pocket and gave it to me. "Some samples. Buttons, not mussel shells!" He laughed easily, his cheeks and scalp turning the same shade of red. "You here tomorrow? You fancy a walk together 'long the river?"

I said we were not there tomorrow and he smiled just the same. "Next year, then. Don't forget: Joe Alton! Alton Brothers Boats and Buttons," he said.

Down in the green room I built up the fire and put the iron slugs on top of the stove to heat them. Then, turning up the gas lamp, I looked at the packet of buttons Joe Alton had given me, which were pearly white and perfectly even and smooth. I planned to sew them onto my good dress, a dark blue silk with small white polka dots— one of the dresses Mrs. Nedel had given me. The buttons were the same shade of white as the polka dots, and I thought they looked very fashionable, almost like tiny pearls but flatter.

From the window I could see the dark sky with ribbons of stars hanging like intricate embroidery stitched in by someone with no sense of design. Along the river, two or three musselers' boats were docked alongside ours. They were no bigger than rowboats and had ropes strung across them end to end like clotheslines attached to poles. Snakes of rope hung down from the clotheslines where the men tied the mussels they brought up from the river so they could dry. They made a pleasant jingle when the wind blew against them, which I could hear as I sewed on the buttons. When I finished, I tested the iron slugs, which were now good and hot. I took one slug off the stove and fitted it inside the waxed iron, and then I sprinkled starch on my dress and began to iron.

By the light of the moon I could see a couple of musselers coming out to dive, so I figured it must be high tide. My iron grew cool and I replaced the slug with the hot slug still on the stove and put the cooled slug in its place. A few minutes later I heard Hugo calling in a low voice to Leo, who was sleeping as usual on his mattress on the stage.

"It's time, my friend," Hugo said.

When my dress was ironed, I hung it carefully over the back of the chair while I unbuttoned the dress I was wearing. I could hear Hugo out on the guard giving instructions, and then the boat began to move backwards away from the bank. I stepped out of my old dress and pulled the freshly ironed one over my head and began buttoning the white mussel buttons up from where they started at my middle. The new buttons were silky-smooth and smaller than any buttons I'd ever had, a novelty, a delight to the touch. I went over to the washboard and felt the collar that was hanging over it—my best lace collar, which I'd washed out last night before going to bed. It was dry, so I buttoned it onto my dress while looking in the long mirror fixed to the back of the door.

My face in the mirror looked very pale and somewhat ill at ease. I smiled, as if trying to console my reflection.

"Crooked river ahead!" I heard Hugo shout. That meant there were a lot of sandbars coming, which they would have to zigzag around. I pulled a chair in front of the window and sat down to wait, arranging my shawl over my lap and a blanket over my shoulders. The boat shifted and swayed as it avoided the sandbars, and through the window I caught glimpses of the southern bank, then the northern bank, and then back to the south, where the trees grew right down into the water.

I must have slept. When I woke it was fully light and I could feel the boat jerk a few times against the current as Leo tied it up. We had landed in Viola. Liddy, in her dressing gown, was standing by the chair, looking down at me. Her long hair was in a single messy braid.

"May! Did you sleep here all night?" she asked.

"Oh!" I said, confused. Then: "No."

"What are you doing?"

I looked for my shawl, which had slipped off my lap. Liddy picked it up from the floor and handed it to me. "I'm meeting someone," I said. "In Viola. I wanted to go into town as soon as we landed. I guess I fell asleep."

"A man?" she asked. "No, that's all right," she went on when I hesitated. "You don't have to tell me."

I don't know what kept me from saying it was my cousin. I wanted Comfort to know I had a new life, but if she came on board the *Floating Theatre*, or if someone like Liddy came with me to see her, I was half-afraid I would shrink back into my old self, the one who couldn't talk to grocers and give out tickets. The one who lived in Comfort's shadow, as Mrs. Howard said. I stood up and shook out the blanket I'd had around me, and then I draped it back over the couch, saying I would be back soon.

"Come here a moment first, will you?" Liddy said.

She moved me in front of the mirror and stood next to me. Her soft face looked like something still asleep, and it made me think of my mother's soft face and her soft arms, getting softer as she got older. Taking the jar of lip salve from the shelf, Liddy found a little brush and painted some color on my mouth very lightly—not as much as she did on her own lips for a performance, but a little.

"Smack," she said.

I rubbed my lips together and pulled them apart with a cork-freeing pop.

"Yes, that's better. You look nice," she told me. "How about some powder? Just a dab?" I nodded. She pulled out the powder puff and gave a few sweeps to my nose and cheeks and neck. "There." She stood back so that now my face dominated the mirror. "You're very pretty, May," she said. No one had told me that before, and I wasn't sure if Liddy was just being nice. She went to the couch and picked up her yellow purse, which I hadn't noticed and which was probably the reason she had come down here in the first place. She was fine with secrets; she had secrets of her own. She held the purse against her stomach.

"When you enter a room," Liddy told me, "push out your chest and pull in your chin. That will give you confidence."

The town of Viola was very close to the river, without a thought to spring flooding, or so it seemed. At the public stable I scraped my muddy boot heel against a cobblestone and asked where the inn was; there were two, I was told. One was across the street—a sign I should have noticed—and the other a little farther up, close to where the merchants kept their houses.

There was no Mrs. Howard registered at the closest inn. The second inn, called the White Crow, was in a line of buildings designed to look like small manors but really housed mostly specialty shops. I could see how such a stopping place would appeal to Mrs. Howard, for it satisfied the outward appearance of money without being too costly—or so I guessed, since the inn, which was small, had no stable attached. From around back I could hear the clucking of poultry.

Inside, a man sat dozing in an armchair pulled over by the staircase. My only fear was that I would run into Mrs. Howard, whom I did not want to see. But I would have to leave that to chance. When I closed the door behind me, the man in the armchair startled awake and looked straight at me as if he'd been waiting for me all this while. He was dressed in a blue velvet coat with brass buttons, blue pantaloons, and dress shoes with ribbons—a sort of "footman-out-of-place" look, as I'd once heard one actor describe another.

"Yes, yes," the man said to me, standing up. "What may I offer?"

"I'm looking for the innkeeper?" I asked, although I was pretty sure I had found him.

The man bowed his head in subservience—something else I

guessed Mrs. Howard would like. "William Whitlock," he introduced himself. He smiled and blinked—he was a man given to blinking—and then walked over to a spindly desk, took up a pen, and turned a page of the inn roster. "At my first inn, burned down now, I used to sleep by the stairs, you see, in case someone got it into their head to sneak out. That was in a rougher town than this, clientele not as fine—it was almost a blessing it burned—and then my wife's brother gave me a good rent on this place. But I got in the habit, you see, and now if I don't sit upright in an armchair, I don't sleep at all. Your name?"

"I'm not looking for a room. I'm looking for Mrs. Howard of Cincinnati," I explained. "And her companion, Comfort Vertue. I'm Miss Vertue's cousin."

He lifted his chin to look at me, taking in the quality of my purse and my shawl, and then confirmed that, yes, they were staying here; might he knock on their door for me?

Alpha, beta, gamma. "Thank you, but I need to run a few errands first. I'll call on my way back. Please don't disturb them. I'd like my visit to be a surprise."

He licked his already wet lips, not quite ready to let me go. "You're her cousin? Must be proud! She's a mighty speaker, Miss Vertue is. Gave a sample last night to me and my missus in the dining room. She comes from New York; I guess you know that, ha! Trained there, she tells me." He lowered his voice. "Course, as a man of business, I can't be seen to take sides. Plenty of Kentucky men ferry over and stop here after concluding their business." He blinked and blinked. "But between you and me and the floorboards, I'm with you."

To me he seemed like a man who would take any side offered at that moment. His eyes were very small and close to his ears, and he was altogether too conscious of the art of ingratiating himself. As I was turning to leave, he said, "Oh, ahem, you didn't say where you come from? New York, is it? Like Miss Vertue? Your cousin, you said?"

I didn't bother with my Greek. "Actually, we're both from Oxbow, Ohio," I told him.

I found a place across the road where I could watch the door to the inn, a small side yard attached to the farrier's that was not, at the moment, in use. I spread my shawl on a very unevenly hewn tree stump and waited in the shadow of the building. Women went in and out of the herring shop just next door to the inn, and I hoped that Mrs. Howard found rooms on the opposite side of the building. Comfort was very sensitive to smell. Her lecture was set for eight o'clock that night and I wondered if we would lose some customers to her. I found myself thinking how she would ask, when she saw me, how it was that I was here instead of Oxbow. I was looking forward to telling her that I'd found a job and was making my own way. Doing what? she'd ask. I debated whether to gloat that I was still in the theater or if I should be sensitive about it, since she was no longer a working actress, although I didn't know if she missed it. But in either case I could perfectly picture her initial surprise, culminating in an increase of her favor. *Well, I'm impressed,* she might even say. I had never before impressed her outside of something I did exclusively for her: made her a new dress, or found us a better seat on a coach. *I am impressed.*

None of that happened, however. I'd been waiting about three-quarters of an hour before I saw Mrs. Howard leave the inn wearing a large yolk-colored dress with a matching silk purse looped over her wrist. She paused a moment, looking up the street. And then, to my surprise, I saw her mute manservant Donaldson cross the street to meet her. Where had he come from? Like me, he'd been waiting for her. I wondered if he'd seen me and if he would communicate my presence in some way to Mrs. Howard. I'd never seen a slate on his person, though I suppose he could easily carry an inkpot and quill around in his pocket. But he was so distant, I could almost believe that he used a more ancient method of communicating, a spiritual-ist's way of giving and receiving messages through the air.

Donaldson took Mrs. Howard's purse for her and followed her down the road, a tight black umbrella over the crook of his arm like a gentleman's cane.

"Oh, but you just missed Mizz Howard!" William Whitlock said, blinking at me when I came into the inn again. This time he was sit-ting at the desk. He pushed his pink tongue a little ways out to lick his wet lips like a frog or a young boy. I said that was all right.

"And earlier—you'll excuse me—but I forgot to ask your name, if you please?"

I was beginning to think there was very little chance that my visit would go unremarked by him when Mrs. Howard returned, but that was the risk I had taken. Anyway, did it matter? Whitlock ushered me up the creaking stairs, past pictures of half-rearing horses and men in red coats—hung there, perhaps, for the Kentucky men he'd men-tioned—and down the second-floor passage, lit only by a squat lamp on a squat table between two squat doors. Whitlock stopped at one of them and, bending so that his wet lips nearly touched the keyhole, shouted through it: "Visitor for you, Miss Vertue! A Mizz Jasper Sin-clair." For that was the name I had given him—Comfort's old married name. That ought to get her attention, I thought.

There was a rustling, and then Comfort's trained voice sang out, "A Mrs. Who?"

"Mizz—Jasper—Sin—*clair!*" shouted Whitlock through the key-hole. After a moment Comfort opened the door wearing a tangerine silk dressing gown and an incredulous expression. When she saw it was me, she raised her eyebrows dramatically.

"May!" she said.

For a moment she couldn't do anything but stare. Her hair was down and her face looked very pink; probably she had just been doing her knee bends, which she liked to do every morning to stay limber.

An ancient feeling of happiness swelled up in me, a feeling from childhood almost as old as I was. "Shall we visit Cousin Comfort today?" my mother would ask me, and then we'd walk the mile and a half into town. I remember the feeling of excited anticipation as keenly as I remembered the little blue dress I liked to wear with its pocket shaped like an acorn.

"Morning, Miss Vertue!" Whitlock said, stepping back, clearly a little in awe of her, and I saw that she had him in her sway like so many others. Remembering Liddy's instructions, I pushed my chest out and tucked in my chin as I walked into the room. It was nicer than I'd expected, with a decent red and green carpet on the floor, a plush armchair near one window, and a small round black table set for breakfast with a loaf of bread and a bowl of cherries the color of fresh dark bruises.

Comfort's face still held the same look of deep surprise, and one end of her dressing-gown belt swung loose like a snake on her hip. She was not wearing slippers. She said good morning very cordially to Whitlock and then shut the door very nearly on his nose.

"May!" she said again, turning to me. "May!"

My chest deflated as she pulled me into a hug. Her hair, freshly washed, smelled like lemons and hay. The door to the bedroom was open and I could see two unmade beds pushed together, with Mrs. Howard's necklaces hanging over one of the bedposts. When Comfort and I had roomed together, I always slept on the sofa or a settee in the sitting room, while she had the bedroom to herself.

She stepped back to look at me. "Don't tell me you're in trouble."

"No, no, nothing like that," I assured her.

"How did you get here? Steamer?"

"Yes—in a way. Well, not a steamer. A flatbed." Her bare throat and bare feet disturbed me. "You'll catch cold," I told her, but she ignored that.

"A flatbed? Why?"

"A barge. A riverboat. I—" Now I was in a bit of a tangle and I tried to work my way back. "I got a job," I said, "on a boat."

To my surprise, Comfort burst out laughing. "What, are you a rouster now?"

"Of course not: as a seamstress. A costume designer. Well, that and other things." I felt the old, familiar compulsion to tell the exact truth. "Selling tickets and putting up show posters . . ."

"What?"

"It's a riverboat theater," I said.

At this she cocked her head. "A *riverboat* theater?"

"We're docked in town. I saw a notice that you were speaking."

"You docked in *this* little town? At the same time I was here?" She looked me over again and an unbelieving smile crept over her features. "What a coincidence!"

"Oh, as to that, well . . ." I was thinking about how I had coerced Hugo to land here, but she must have thought I was trying to come up with a plausible explanation, because she tilted her head and gave me an indulgent, knowing smile. I saw that she didn't believe me.

"Oh, May. May. You've come *all this way* to hear me talk. Imagine!"

"I didn't come from Oxbow," I insisted. "I told you. I have a job on a riverboat theater. I make the costumes. We're going to do a three-act play . . ."

"Well, now I *know* you're teasing me! These little riverboat jaunts do only short acts, you know, singing and dancing, not three-act plays!" Now she was schooling me. She knew all about riverboat theaters, her tone implied, and I did not. Was it really more plausible that I'd come all the way down from Oxbow just to hear her speak, rather than that someone would hire me to sew for them?

"It's true," I said stubbornly.

"Oh, May, I don't care, it's just good to see you! And fancy you coming now, when I could use your help so particularly! Mrs. Howard really cannot sew," she said in a lower voice, conspiratorially. "We stop at seamstress shops constantly. And just last night my lovely gray silk ripped when I was taking it off. Under the arm it doesn't show, but if you could . . ."

My moment of happy reunion was gone. I looked around the room trying to regain my bearings, but it was all too unfamiliar.

"I didn't come to sew. I came because of this," I told her, holding out the notice that I'd found in Birchfield.

"What is it?" She looked down at the circular. As she read it a smile came over her lips. "Oh, dear," she said. She shook her head almost laughingly, looked up at me, and then looked down to read it again. After that, she did laugh.

I was baffled by her reaction. "Comfort, this isn't a joke! Those men mean to harm you!"

"Yes, yes. I know. It's a dangerous game I play. Oh, dear. May, you should see it: it's really quite a spectacle sometimes, these speeches. The way some men shout! And the more composed I am, the more they hate it. Flora says she's never seen anyone as composed as I am. We have a laugh about it later."

"You like it when they shout at you and throw things?"

"They never actually hurt me; they aim for my clothes. But, May, these men! If you could only see them—but you know the type. They absolutely riddle you with snide remarks, and then they are shocked and insulted if you return the volley. As though they have every right to do the shooting but the only right you have is to duck or to bleed. They say that I am assaulting their principles. It doesn't once occur to them that I might have principles, too. To them I'm only a New York actress."

"*Do* you have principles?" I asked.

"Of course! Flora has educated me ever so much. I had no idea how bad it really is down here. They say slaves are happy, but they're not happy! They say at least they have work, they have regular meals, they have homes. But do you know that a slave man can do nothing about the breakup of his family? He can't even stay with his wife if he chooses to, and his babies might be sold away from him at any moment."

"That is terrible," I said, and I meant it. But I could tell Comfort was still thinking about the white men at her lectures.

"Of course, they only come to spar. They all stand together in the back with their hands behind them. As if I don't know they're carrying smashed fruit! And, oh, my dresses." She laughed again. "May, you're lucky you can't see how bad they get. It would make you very unhappy."

Sparring with men—I suppose that was a little like flirting. Comfort always liked to flirt. And I had certainly seen her bristle enough times when she thought anyone felt superior to her. But I didn't like this reaction of hers. I thought she would take heed of the notice and thank me for bringing it to her attention. Instead she folded it up with a smile and tucked it into her dressing gown pocket.

"I'll paste this into the scrapbook later," she said.

She looked at me as if waiting for the next thing I had to say, only there was no next thing to say: the notice had been all I had.

"Well, now," she said with another smile. "Isn't this heat something else?"

My spirits sank even further. She was talking to me as though I were just a common acquaintance, a chance meeting on the street—maybe an actress she'd worked with once and was reasonably glad now to catch up with, starting with her own news. She told me that they'd left Cincinnati almost three weeks ago; Flora wrote Comfort's speeches and booked the lecture halls, and Donaldson drove them from town to town—"on the circuit," Comfort called it. While she spoke she went to the window and pulled up the cheap shade: the morning fog was dispersing and the street below was busy with carts. She was doing important work, educating people about the real conditions of slave life, she told me, looking outside. Then she said something that I thought about later.

"You can't imagine the lives these men in bondage lead."

Again that light tone, as though she was thinking about something else while she said it, and I wondered if it was simply a line that she had memorized. She sat down at the small round table and began cutting a slice of bread. Her face, I noticed, looked older. She was no longer pulling her features in order to look young or pushing her teeth against her mouth to make her lips appear fuller. Now her face was softer, the peachy flesh of her cheeks a little closer to her jawline. Compared to her relaxed figure—she still hadn't closed her dressing gown properly—I felt like a twitchy bird that flew into the room through an open window by mistake and now couldn't get out. There was something more I wanted from Comfort but I didn't know what. Perhaps I just wanted her acknowledgment that I was all right without her. I was independent, I had a job, I was traveling just as she was. But she didn't believe any of that. It didn't fit her idea of who I was, and that idea came first. A warm anger began seeping into my chest.

Comfort spread some marmalade on the bread with the back end of a spoon, sprinkled sugar on top, and handed the slice to me. Flora had gone to check on the seats in the lecture hall, she was saying. She sliced another piece of bread and again covered it with marmalade and sugar. "I'm glad you're coming to hear me tonight," she said, taking a large hungry bite. "Come early so you can sit up front."

I wasn't going to hear her lecture—I couldn't; I'd be playing the piano for our show—but it was no use trying to explain that. A burst of sunlight came in through the window, showing up stains on the carpet, and I regretted taking the slice of bread, because now I would have to eat it before I could go. Liddy had told me how to enter a room, but had she ever told me how to leave one? I took a small bite, but the marmalade felt unpleasantly rough in my mouth. Sugar on marmalade was how Comfort liked to eat her bread, whereas I took mine with plain butter. Once, not too long ago—less than a month, I calculated—Comfort knew that.

11

After her second husband died, Comfort's mother, my aunt Ann, tried her hand at acting, but she was not very good. She made enough money to support herself and Comfort if they lived frugally but was never able to save anything. However, the reason she finally retired wasn't her own mediocrity—that could still be put to use, Comfort explained to me, as long as her looks held out—but rather a scandal in a play she was in that involved an actress, not even the lead role, who lifted the skirt of her costume up over her knees when walking upstage to take her bow.

At the time they were in Bristol, England, and this wanton show of leg caused the play to be shut down by the Bristol police and the theater manager to be fined. In France, ankles might be displayed in certain circumstances, Comfort explained, and even perhaps a knee, but only to a crowd of men. Not so in England. In America the fine would have been even worse and the actress put in jail.

She told me this story for the first time when I was a girl and we were playing together in the Tiffin River. The second time she told it to me was on the night of her acting debut when she was shaking with nerves, suddenly afraid that she could not, after all, perform on the stage. Only this time when she told me the story, she said, "It wasn't someone else. It was my mother. My mother was the one who lifted her skirt. She was a little out of her mind, I guess. Oh, it was a bad play to begin with, but that night she forgot some lines, and a man in the first row threw a piece of bread at her like she was a street monkey. That's what she told me later: that she felt like a vendor's street monkey."

Throughout all the months of Comfort's training—the arm exercises, the voice coaching, learning to draw her breath in through her nose before a stage laugh, and so forth—we both assumed that she would be more successful than her mother. "I have more courage" is how Comfort put it, whereas I thought she was more outspoken and liked no one else to command center stage, both good attributes for an actress. But now I saw she had another worry besides mediocrity: a tendency toward spitefulness, perhaps, like her mother. Comfort said her mother always knew that she was not very good.

Still, it was too late now, the night of her debut. We were standing in her dressing room, which was as small as a closet, with only a few strips of baize passing as carpet. Just as she finished telling me about Aunt Ann, clutching my hands (hers were icy cold), there was a knock on the dressing room door and a little ruffian call boy poked his head in. "Pauline," he said, which was the name of Comfort's role, "you are called."

"Called for what?" asked Comfort, who had never heard this term before.

"Why, for the stage, to be sure!"

He waited for her outside the door. Comfort still held my hands. "What if I do something awful?" she whispered. "I can't go back to Oxbow and live with Mama."

Aunt Ann was still living in Oxbow and had grown odder by the years with her diet of eggs and her intense suspicion, almost hatred, of the village postmistress. My mother and I had lived in the house next to hers for the last few years of my mother's life, sharing a hedge, which also became a source of irritation with Aunt Ann (too little clipped, or too much).

"You will not do something awful," I told Comfort. "You have never done anything at all remotely like that."

But now I was the one, walking back through the village of Viola, past the public stable and the straw yard and onto a dusty road that led out of town (I was too agitated to go back to the boat right away), who felt angry enough to lift my skirt at an audience. For the first time since I heard the story, either the false story told to me as a girl or the true story I heard later, I understood how Aunt Ann had felt: she had done this commendable thing—mastered lines and moved across stage and showed herself vulnerable in public—but, instead of being praised, she'd had food thrown at her. Comfort had not thrown food at me, it's true. But I felt very keenly the sting of her disinterest in my accomplishments—her disbelief, even, that I had any. How many times had she teased me for not being able to lie? And yet she could not believe that I had gotten a job without her, that I could be as independent as she was. More so, for I had no Mrs. Howard to help me.

The road snaked down to a slight hollow and narrowed, becoming dustier and full of rocks. Just as I was thinking of turning around, I heard something that sounded like singing, and when the road turned I saw four or five figures in a line: black men wearing straw hats with the widest brims I'd ever seen, working their hoes over a scrabbly acre of something or other. Free blacks. They were singing a spiritual about Noah, although the man with the deepest voice made it sound like "Norah."

Norah he built hisself an ark
Made it out of hickory bark
Animals came in two by two
The elephant and the kangaroo

They sang the last verse and then started all over again with the first. And why shouldn't they? It occurred to me that I had done just the same thing myself back at the inn with Comfort, gone back to the same old song. As I stood there listening, one tall man with a hole on the side of his straw hat walked over to take a drink from a girl who'd appeared with a water bucket. That was when I noticed a tiny little shack at the far end of the field, and I wondered if they all lived there together and, if so, how they all fit. "You can't imagine the lives these men lead," Comfort had told me. But could she? On impulse, I walked over to where the man and the girl were standing.

"Were you ever slaves?" I asked the man. In my haste to know, I forgot to say hello first.

To my surprise, the man gave me a quick scared look. He wiped his dirty hands carefully with a handkerchief before drawing out a piece of folded paper from his pocket. The paper had yellowed and looked as soft as cloth from being carried about every day. "No, ma'am. Our father bought his freedom before we was born. You can see here."

He held out the paper but I shook my head. "I was just wondering. What it was like. But I guess you don't know." We looked at each other hard for a moment before he looked away, and for the second time that morning I had the sensation there was more that I wanted. The young girl was still standing next to the man, a tin dipper in one hand and the bucket in the other. After a moment she made a motion with the dipper and said to me, "Thirsty, ma'am?"

I nodded and she seemed surprised. But she quickly filled the dipper and handed it to me. "Thank you," I said before taking a sip. The water was lukewarm and tasted like moss. I gave her back the dipper.

"You with the showboat?" she asked.

She was looking at me with the same expression now as the man, wariness and curiosity mixed with fatigue from standing in the hot sun. I supposed that they didn't see many strangers and simply put two and two together.

"Yes. Our show's tonight just after sunset." A thought occurred to me. "I can give you a couple of complimentary tickets if you tell your friends. We're tied up the pier. But I guess you saw us there already."

The girl looked at the man. He looked at me and then said, "We allowed in?"

"There are risers in the back." I gave him two tickets. As I handed them to the man, who looked at them in my fingers for a long moment before taking them, I wondered why we never gave complimentary tickets to free blacks? They could draw in business, too. "Only ten cents for the riser seats. We also take yams, peaches, whatever you have. We're a family business. The owner started it with his sister. Tell your friends to come, why don't you?"

The girl took one of the tickets and looked at it. Her dress was a blue-and-white flowered print so faded, I could not make out what kind of tiny flowers they were supposed to be. It was too short for her, but it was clean and ironed. Were they brother and sister? Husband and wife? She was barefoot, and her feet were shaped like narrow, strong boats. Her fingers, too, were long and tapered, and she held out the dipper again for me but I shook my head no.

That night the risers in the back were full for the first time, and I wondered if Hugo would remark on that. I picked out the girl, but either the man didn't come with her or I didn't recognize him in his good set of clothes. When eight o'clock came, the time Comfort's lecture started, I couldn't help but think of her on stage and the men throwing their fruit or vegetable of choice. But it was time for me to start playing the introductory music, so I tried to forget about her and the state of her dress. I played a quickened version of "The Wolf Is Out" while offstage Hugo nodded his head to the rhythm. He liked songs to be fast.

"The house was rather good tonight, wasn't it," he said to me after the show, giving me my share. He didn't specifically mention the crammed risers, but I was pleased nonetheless.

The next day was Sunday. On Sundays we didn't move the boat and everybody slept late and then more or less did whatever they wanted. I liked to sit on the riverbank next to Leo, sewing, but sometimes I sewed in the dining room if it was rainy or too buggy outside. Mrs. Niffen, wearing her good black dress and a straw hat covered with silk flowers, always went into town in search of a church service with Celia and Liddy. Mr. Niffen practiced on his violin, which was his excuse for not going to church with them, until his wife's shock of white hair was out of sight. Then he stretched out on a shady spot on the bank and pulled his hat up over his face to nap. Hugo either sat with Leo and me with his own fishing pole, or he looked over his books in the office, where it was cooler.

Today, however, the actors didn't seem as relaxed as they usually were on Sundays, and although Mrs. Niffen put on her good black dress, she did not take Celia and Liddy to church. Perhaps it was the heat, which felt like a weight of invisible bricks on my back and shoulders. The air was still and cloudless, and the sun was a sharp bright coin overhead. It was my birthday today, and I wondered if Comfort would remember that.

Some of my anger from the day before had dissipated, although I still felt a lingering irritation that spiked if I thought about Comfort too much. I told myself that I would not go back into town—Comfort had probably already left anyway—but I found myself getting out my purse and counting the coins inside. I needed more dark blue thread, and my white thread was running low, too. But then I remembered that, it being Sunday, all the shops would be closed. I put my purse away. A little while later I thought, *Perhaps Oliver would like a short walk?* He was sleeping under the ticket window awning, curled up in a bitten-off rectangle of shade.

"Oliver," I called. Oliver didn't move. "Oliver, let's take a walk!"

Hugo came around from the other side of the boat looking very red-faced from the heat, his shirtsleeves rolled up. "Where are you going?" he asked, seeing me with my shawl draped over one arm. But before I could answer, he said, "I have some letters to write; could you tally last night's numbers for me? While you're at it, you might just recheck my calculations from the week. But do you mind taking the ledger up to your stateroom? I need the office."

It was something Helena used to do, work on the ledger, but this was the first time he'd asked me to do it. Maybe he was beginning to trust me. Mrs. Niffen was leaning against the guardrail as if waiting for a river breeze before she went off to church, and I waited for her to say how good she was with numbers and how happy she would be to help out. But she just patted her silver-white hair and pursed her mouth shut. When I turned back to Hugo, I fancied he'd just winked. Quickly he began rubbing his eye with his handkerchief.

"These insects, uncommonly bothersome," he said. "Fly right into your face, eh?"

His manner was strange, but I had no notion anything was really amiss until a few hours later, when I took a break from the books to get a cup of tea. No one was in the dining room, and the room itself did not have its usual lingering scent of coffee and warm bread. I went back into the galley; Cook was not in his hammock and the stove was dead cold. I had a slight moment of uneasiness then, and for the first time since I'd been on board I thought of the *Moselle*. But when I went to the window I saw that everything was fine: our boat was still tied to the pier and we were even with the line of flatboats and keelboats tied up beyond us. I scolded myself as I stood looking out. Obviously if we were listing I would feel it. I wiped my wet palms on my dress.

Just then Hugo popped his head into the dining room. "May! There you are! What do you say we go for a walk?"

"A walk? Isn't it nearly one o'clock?" That was when we ate our supper on Sundays. I looked at my father's watch. It was almost one thirty.

"There's a couple of plum trees up the bank; I want to get some fruit for Cook. He's making a . . ." he trailed off, and let me walk first along the narrow guard.

"Plum pie?" I guessed.

"Yes!" Hugo said.

At the bottom of the stairs he took my arm and steered me toward the gangplank with rather more force than seemed called for. I had the sensation of being a horse driven to market, and I did not like it. I tried to pull my arm away.

"Where is everyone? Where's Cook? The stove's gone cold."

"Oh, sleeping, sleeping, they're all sleeping!" Hugo said.

"But what's going on in there?" Shuffling noises were coming from the auditorium. It sounded like my piano was being moved. One of the piano wheels was loose and I didn't want anyone to move it except Leo or me.

"Oh, nothing—wait," Hugo said as I opened the auditorium door.

But he was too late—I was already inside—and when my eyes adjusted I was surprised to see Liddy on the stage wearing the ingénue costume for the three-act play, which I had just finished sewing last night. She was helping Cook push my piano. I'd never seen Cook on the stage before. "What are you doing?" I asked them.

Liddy turned around just as Thaddeus, also wearing part of the costume I'd just made, came onto the stage. I looked at Hugo for an explanation. He squinted his eyes at me and then decided to smile. He spread his arms.

"Happy birthday!" he said.

"What?"

"Happy birthday! Isn't today your birthday?"

Liddy came down off the stage. "May!" she said. "What a surprise we have for you! Sit down, sit down! No, up here in the front row. Right in the middle. You've caught us getting ready, but that's all right. You're a little early is all."

"A little early for what?"

"Your birthday play!"

It took a minute of explaining: they were going to perform their new play for me—at least, the first two acts of it. A birthday play, for me.

"Helena and I always had birthday plays growing up," Hugo told me. "The great fun was trying to keep the other one out of rehearsals.

Or trying to find out where the rehearsals were, if you were the one with the birthday coming." He was smiling hard, very pleased with himself. "We practiced in the mornings when you were in town. If I didn't need Liddy or Celia, they went along with you to keep you there nice and long."

I was still confused. A birthday play? Everyone was smiling at me. I never took much notice of my birthday, and I was embarrassed by this attention, but also a little pleased. After my mother died, most of my birthday presents had been from Comfort, small things she no longer needed: perfume or a shawl—once a shawl I'd made for her myself— and usually a day or two late. I felt a warm, almost liquid sensation go through me, as though I had just drunk a too-large sip of wine.

After Liddy settled me on my seat, Hugo got up to make a quick introduction to the play—Thaddeus in the role of a young Spanish Marquis in love with a general's daughter—and then he jumped off the stage with no more fanfare than a cat.

"Jemmy's going to play the General for me so I can get a look at the whole and also give you some company," he said, sitting down beside me. I could feel the warmth of his shoulder and something of the rest of him—not a smell, not a touch, but, like all performers, he emitted a presence that extended beyond his physical self. He looked at me and smiled again. Because of the pleasure of the coming per- formance? Or the surprise itself? I didn't know, but I found myself smiling back—a real smile, not just showing my teeth.

Thaddeus came on the stage wearing the green doublet I'd fin- ished only that morning, and I was pleased to see that the brown vel- vet ribbons showed up as stripes on the fabric, just as I had intended. He paraded up and down the stage for a moment looking around him, with his servant, Mr. Niffen, at his side. Then he began:

"This is my native place—the town that gave me birth—and in spite of my attachment to the capital, dear Madrid, I must prefer this town to every other spot in the world."

Sebastian (Mr. Niffen): "Ay, my Lord, you came hither to take possession of the estate of a rich uncle just deceased. But if I was not in love, and if the object of my passion was not living in this very town, I could not be happy in it."

"Give me your hand Sebastian—for once my equal."

"How so, pray, my lord?"

"For being in love, as am I."

Mr. Niffen, or rather Sebastian, took his hand away and said proudly, "Ay, sir, but we are not all equals in love for all that. You will always be above my match; for I never could love more than one woman. However, your Lordship I have known to love sixteen—and all at the same time."

Here I laughed.

Sebastian went on: "And all so well, it was impossible to tell which you loved the best."

I laughed again.

The two actors moved upstage and began to argue, for all that one was master and one servant. A few of the windows on the port side of the theater were open, and a hot breeze brought in the familiar smell of seaweed, mud, fish, and the wet, slow-rotting bark of all the tree trunks partially submerged in the water. I was sitting on the very first bench with my shawl in my lap and my hands on my shawl, watching the play unfold. At first my fingers danced a little, wanting something to do, and naturally I looked critically at each costume as it appeared for the first time, but after a while I forgot about them. I noticed that Mrs. Niffen's wig was askew, but she must have fixed it offstage, because I forgot about that, too.

Perhaps it *was* a strange thing that I'd never before seen a play from the audience side. When you are standing in the wings as I always do, you can see the actors drop out of character as soon as they exit, and how the mantle goes on again when they walk back on the stage. You see the ties in the backs of their costumes, and places where a wig has lost some hair. You are so close that you can see spit fly from their lips as they speak their lines. And you never lose the sense that what they are saying is false. At least, I never did. Whenever I waited offstage for Comfort, holding a glass of water and a handkerchief for her, because she gets very hot behind the footlights, I could feel all the actors' urgency without ever having that feeling myself. Perhaps it was just that small distance, sharing the same space with them in the wings while never stepping foot with them on stage, that held my disbelief in place. Or perhaps I was so busy anticipating what Comfort would need next that I didn't pay sufficient attention to the play as a whole.

I don't know. I only know that, sitting on the front bench in the auditorium, watching Thaddeus transform himself into a man in love and Mr. Niffen speaking his lines as though all he wanted in the world was to speak and be heard—a fact I knew to be wholly untrue—something shifted in my mind and I gave myself over to them. It was just as Hugo said. I wanted to know what would happen next, and I stopped for a brief time thinking about anything else.

Jemmy stood in for Hugo as the General, and Pinky came out in the costume of an old woman, a servant named Cecily, wearing a long, unbecoming nightgown of a dress (not my creation) and an old-fashioned mobcap.

Marquis: "That severe air you put on agrees but little with your gentle and beguiling looks."

Cecily (Pinky in a high but growly voice): "What do you mean? I am old and ugly and, what is more, I have, thank heaven, as bad a temper as any woman in the world."

Hugo and I both laughed, and when I looked over at him, Hugo winked. Why was it so funny to see a handsome man dressed as an ugly woman? But it was. Even Leo participated, for at the end of the second act he came out onto the stage and, looking down at his boots, recited in his wonderfully deep voice:

And thus we deliver our gift this day,
In honor of our most excellent friend, Miss May.
We wish we could for longer stay
But we have not yet memorized the last act of the play.

I clapped until the palms of my hands itched. At the same time a proud warmth seemed to pass between Hugo and me. I had no idea Liddy and Thaddeus and Mr. Niffen—the principals of the play—were so good. Hugo was pleased with them, too. We clapped very hard, and this time I did not turn my good ear away from the noise. But the actors were not looking at us as they bowed, I noticed; they were looking beyond us at the risers, smiling their professional smiles. I had the thought that this must be something they were trained to do: bow to the very back row. But Hugo turned around to look, and in a moment he stopped clapping and was up on his feet. And although I stopped clapping when he did, the sound of applause continued, followed in the next moment by the rippling voice of an older, confident woman, a woman who was just as proud of her voice as any trained actress:

"Bravo," Mrs. Howard sang out.

Comfort was sitting next to her, also clapping and smiling. Both of them were bareheaded and Comfort had her shawl folded up into a rectangle beside her. They looked quite comfortable there, straight-backed and lordly in the middle of the very top riser. When had they come in? Mrs. Howard was wearing a dark purple dress and I would not have been surprised to find a cape made of ermine at her side or a golden chain-link belt across her vast hips; but when she stood, the dress showed itself to be nothing more than a fitted day dress. Comfort stood up next to her. Why had they come? Hugo started up the aisle toward them and I followed. I could tell from his stiff back he was angry.

"Who are you?" he began in a loud, rough voice, the voice of a coarse Englishman. "What are you doing on my boat? There's no show today! This is a closed rehearsal! Who gave you leave?" and more in that vein. Mrs. Howard came down to meet him in the aisle with Comfort right behind her, and the four us stood facing each other. There was something of the smell of church coming from Mrs. Howard: dusty hymnals, overly oiled wood, and sweat. She waited Hugo out patiently, a slight but provoking smile on her lips that seemed designed to convey her sense of superiority even when being scolded. No matter what he said, she knew better, the smile implied. From time to time Comfort glanced at Mrs. Howard in the way that a very young wife might look at a husband she is still learning the ways of, gauging her reaction to this tirade.

But when Hugo broke off at last by saying, "Well? And what have you got to say, then? Why are you here?" Comfort was the one who spoke first.

"Why, I've come to see May, of course. My cousin. What a delight-ful play! You must be the director. Mr. Cushing? That was very well done, very well done indeed. As May might have told you, I was an actress myself once." She spoke as though that time was many years ago instead of only a few weeks. She held her hand out to Hugo. "I know quality work when I see it."

"Captain Cushing," Hugo corrected, not taking her hand. He did not look at me but I was aware of his attention shifting sideways.

"I did not invite them," I told him. "I don't even want them here."

"May! May!" Comfort laughed at me. She turned to Hugo with a flirtatious look I knew well. "You'll have to forgive my cousin; she's very direct."

"You don't need to tell me about May," Hugo said sharply, and he leaned closer to me as if he was the one who knew me thoroughly and my cousin was the intruder.

"She came to our rooms yesterday . . ."

"But not to invite you here," I said. "I hardly even told you. You didn't want to know."

"Not want to know! Of course I want to know. I'm delighted that you're working in a theater." She flashed me another look I recognized: *Don't say anything more.*

"All right, you've seen her now," Hugo said. "I'll thank you to leave."

Comfort flushed. I wasn't sure if she was surprised by the reprimand or that her brand of charm wasn't working on Hugo.

Mrs. Howard decided to take over. "Comfort is perfectly right: the performance was very amusing. For a play, you know, that sort of thing. A light diversion." Her brand of charm, as usual, held the sting of an insult. She took a deep breath as though settling in for a long speech, but Hugo got there first.

"This is a Sunday," he said. "I could get fined for performing a show on a Sunday. How dare you just walk in and sit down."

Mrs. Howard talked over him: "My dear man, we left some money at the ticket office window, right there on the ledge, more than enough for two tickets. And if—"

Hugo interrupted her: "You left *money*! A paid performance? I could get shut down for that, don't you know that? They wouldn't just fine me, they would shut me down! It's Sunday! Don't you know it's Sunday?"

"Of course I know. We were at church only this morning, and I told the reverend how we planned to make a visit . . . and, you know, the interest of someone like me will certainly lend a much greater respectability to your . . ." She looked around the auditorium and I saw through her eyes how narrow it was, and how the benches weren't nailed perfectly straight. ". . . your charming little outfit."

"You told the *reverend*—" Hugo took a step back and for a moment I almost thought he would strike her. My heart was beating fast. I had never seen him so red in the face. He cut through the benches and went to a window, pushed aside the curtain, and looked out.

"If he tells the constable . . . You *are* a foolish woman!"

I don't think anyone had ever called Mrs. Howard foolish in all of her life. It took a moment to sink in, and I watched with great interest how the purple of her bodice seemed to bleed its color up from the neckline and into her cheeks. At the same time a vein in her temple rose angrily and her mouth opened slowly like a baby getting ready to cry.

"Impudent man!" she barked.

But Hugo had a voice trained at the Covent Garden Theatre and he could easily outshout her. "Get out!"

I looked at Comfort with mixed emotions as I tried not to laugh. Not that I thought it was funny exactly—or maybe just a little. Comfort looked back at me angrily as if all this was my fault. But it wasn't my fault.

"Well, May!" she said. "You might intercede on our behalf."

"On your behalf? Why, the whole company could be in trouble for this, you know that. You of all people should know that." I was thinking of her mother, and she understood me. Her face grew red.

"No one would mistake us for an audience!" she replied angrily. "There are only two of us! Or is that the number you regularly serve?"

She said this last over her shoulder as she turned to go, whisking her hat up so that its crimson ribbons flew up and then down. I wanted to remind her that she was the one who chose Mrs. Howard. The hat she was waving around was new, her dress was new, and she was plumped out from all the good meals served to her on Mrs. Howard's second-best china. As for me, I would soon go upstairs to eat soup made from fish stock: whatever Leo happened to catch yesterday—something spiny and black, I remembered, which I had gutted for him. But I was fine with soup. I liked it, in fact. I liked being on the winning side. Hugo, I decided, was the winning side.

Mrs. Howard closed her mouth and put her hat on her head but her face was still mottled and her expression was as close to being chastened as it was ever likely to get. She thrust a long hatpin violently into her hat like a jouster blindly attacking the air, and then she

settled her fierce eyes on me. "May, might I have a word with you?"
Each syllable a jab.

"Oh. . ." I said, getting ready to refuse.

"Just a quick moment," she said. "I have a piece of news about
your family."

Hugo glared at Mrs. Howard as she passed him, and she lifted her
chin right back at him. I had no family except Aunt Ann and a couple of
cousins in Germany whom I'd never met, but my curiosity got the better of me, and after a moment I followed after her, not looking at Hugo.

Outside, clouds were rolling over the river in the fast way they
sometimes do. A couple of geese pecked around at the bottom of the
stage plank while Comfort stood watching them from the rail, her hat
still in her hand. She didn't turn to look at me. The tide was going out.

"Now, my dear," Mrs. Howard said to her, "you go on up to Donaldson. He'll be waiting on the road."

I looked at Comfort's back. Her collar was crooked and not altogether clean. I could see how easily I might fall back into my old pattern, looking after her clothes and feeling as though in this way I was
part of a certain life. Her life. Yesterday I had fallen back into the old
pattern, but today, here, on Hugo's boat, I felt stronger. What I had
now was better. Comfort was never going to give me all this. Before
this summer, I didn't even know that I'd wanted it.

"Good-bye, May," Comfort said in a strained voice, turning to look
at me at last. "I hope you can come to one of my lectures. I'll write
you out a list of the towns we're visiting."

Her face was like stone, still angry, but I saw that she was making
an effort and I relented a little myself. "How was the lecture yesterday?" I asked.

"A mashed peach hit me on the shoulder."

"Is your dress ruined?"

"Oh, I hope I'm not so shallow as to care overmuch about the state
of my clothes." A parting insult to me.

I watched her walk carefully down the plank and up the muddy path that led away from the river, picking her way around splats of dark green geese droppings. She had said nothing about my birthday. When I turned back, Florid was pulling on a stiff pair of buttermilk-colored gloves, and without buttoning them she turned to scoop up the coins she had left on the ticket window ledge. Not so much as she led us to believe, I noticed: only four dimes.

"Your captain thinks he's teaching me a lesson." She opened her purse and dropped the dimes inside. "Well. Lesson learned."

She turned to face me. "That man is trouble, May." I watched her pull again at her glove; the leather fingertips, I noticed, were very soiled. "Tell me this: Where exactly did you go when you left my house? Did you come straight here to this boat?"

"I needed a job and I found one."

"That money I gave you—that was only a loan, you know. I expect to be paid back."

That was not what she'd said when she had given me the money. I considered telling her that the color she chose for her gloves was the very worst color for showing stains next to white, but at that moment Leo came out from the office. He didn't look at Mrs. Howard.

"You all right, Miss May?" he asked.

I told him I was fine.

"There's a celebration upstairs. Don't be too long, now." He smiled at me, still ignoring Mrs. Howard. She noticed this.

"We're perfectly well here, young man. *Miss Bedloe* will be with you in a moment."

I suppose she thought "Miss May" was too familiar for a boatman, but Leo ignored the implied reprimand. He just touched his hat and went back into the office.

"What was the piece of news you had?" I asked Mrs. Howard impatiently.

"Just what I said. I expect you to repay my loan."

So. No news about my family—that was only a trick to get me out here. "You told me that money was a gift."

"It was meant to get you home. You used it for another purpose entirely. I don't know what you used it for, but that means less to me than how you plan to pay me back."

From the galley above us I could smell a warm floury smell: cake. Birthday cake. Underneath the rattle of cutlery in the dining room I could hear voices, and I knew they were all waiting for me. All at once I was tired of Mrs. Howard. I started to go around her to the stairs.

She put a hand on my arm. "Wait a moment. Where are you going?"

"To get you the money. I have almost ten dollars. I can send you the rest a quarter a week."

"Forty weeks," she calculated. "That's a long time for me to wait." I noticed a shrewd expression on her face, or maybe that expression was always there. I took a step back so that her arm fell away from me. At the same time a wind came up as it will suddenly on a river, and she put her hand on her hat, still watching me. In the play I'd just seen, *The Midnight Hour*, bets are wagered. "Half my estate to half yours," says the Marquis to the General, "if I can carry Julia off tonight to marry her with her consent." Mrs. Howard had the same look about her, braced as she was against the wind. The look of someone about to place a wager. I put my arms around myself as if to hold my whole body down.

"I've come up with a better idea," she said.

12

There is an embroidery stitch I used once on a costume of Comfort's called the spider web, which is really only a complicated backstitch but still very striking. You begin by making two or three long stitches that will be hidden, eventually, by the finished embroidery, and then you lay your yarn across them in an imaginary circle, like a line of spokes. When the spokes are all laid out, as many of them as you want, you tie them together at the center. The tricky part comes next: weaving another strand of yarn under and around the spokes in order to make spirals. The spirals should be worked close together, and the ridges should be even and stand out. The first time I made one I thought, once the design was finished, that it looked less like a web and more like a golden sun with bent rays. But I certainly felt like a spider when I was making it, weaving the yarn in and out.

On the day of my birthday play, watching Liddy on stage in the costume I'd recently finished, I could see that her dress needed something more. And as Mrs. Howard outlined her plan for how I might repay her loan, the solution came to me: the spider web.

"It really will be quite easy for you, traveling down the river as you do," Mrs. Howard was saying. "No one will suspect a thing."

I didn't answer. Her proposal unsettled me, and when I'm un-settled I like to think of something complicated to distract myself. I envisioned a line of these little embroidered suns the size of silver dollars on the wide Italian collar of Liddy's costume. But the spider web requires a tapestry needle with a long, flat head, which I did not have.

"I'll send you a note with our itinerary," Mrs. Howard told me. "We can talk about the details later, in a more *private* setting." She put her finger to her nose, signaling secrecy.

"What happens if I say no?" I asked as she started down the stage plank.

"You won't say no," she said without turning her head. "You're a compassionate girl."

I wasn't sure that I was. Like Comfort, mostly I thought of myself. After Mrs. Howard left, I went up to the dining room, and Cook brought out a frosted cake and two strawberry whipped-cream pies to celebrate my birthday. Hugo produced a bottle of mulberry wine and another bottle of apricot wine, and we ate slice after slice of cake and sipped the sweet wine and talked about the play. The tables were all pushed together and no one was in a hurry to leave. It should have been a happy, relaxed evening, but it wasn't for me. I was sitting at the far end of our long makeshift table, and my temples felt as though I'd pulled my hair back too tight. I wondered if a headache was coming on.

"May, give us a smile! Weren't you surprised?" Thaddeus asked. He looked at me sideways as if assessing me. "A good birthday treat, eh?"

"I saw you laughing," Liddy told me. She squeezed my arm.

"You were very good," I said, trying to push my worries away. I wanted to tell Liddy how much I enjoyed it; her face was shining like a young girl's. "I completely believed you."

She laughed. "Well, now, that's a great compliment!"

"But weren't you surprised, May?" Thaddeus asked again. "At least tell us you were surprised. Tell us you had no idea what we were up to."

His cheeks were pink from wine and he leaned forward across the table at me. "It was all Captain Cushing's idea."

"Needed to rehearse the act straight through anyway," Hugo said roughly, but his eyes were smiling.

"Thank you," I said. I told them all it was a very nice surprise.

"That's all you have to say about it?" Jemmy asked. "'Very nice'?"

"It was lovely. I enjoyed it." I did enjoy it, but they wanted more. "I forgot that I was watching a play." I looked at Hugo, who smiled a small, private smile at me, a smile for me alone, although everyone was watching.

Leo brought me a present: a pincushion in the shape of a steamboat. "From us all," he said. "I found it a few towns back." It was lovely, about the size of my hand, though the white fabric would get dirty in no time. I stopped myself from saying this, however, and just thanked him with all the emotion I could muster, which was quite a lot. For a moment I forgot about Mrs. Howard as I turned the pincushion over in my hand.

"What did you think of my costume, huh, May?" Pinky asked. "Stole it from our Mrs. Niffen here." He put his hand next to his mouth and said in a stage whisper, "Her nightgown!"

"And who let you into my trunks, I'd like to know?" Mrs. Niffen replied, staring at her husband. Mr. Niffen, naturally, continued eating his cake without looking up.

"But you know," I said to Pinky, "you didn't really look like a woman."

"Hah-hah—har-har-har," Pinky laughed, as though I had just made a joke.

He kept stealing glances at Liddy, who seemed not to notice, but I saw that tonight she did not take any letters out of her purse to read under the table. Her face was rosy—glowing, I would almost say—happy with her performance and with the play as a whole. An outward face, although I could hardly explain what I meant by that— perhaps that she seemed like a person who had no secrets, although of course she did. In some ways she reminded me of Comfort, but when Liddy looked at me, it felt like she saw me as someone she was getting to know, not someone she already knew through and through, which was how my cousin always looked at me. But Comfort did not know me through and through, and I fell back to thinking about Mrs. Howard. Was breaking the law the same thing as lying? I wondered. For that was what Mrs. Howard was asking me to do.

Mr. Niffen took out his violin and played for us between sips of wine, and when the wine ran out he pulled out a flask, and when the flask was empty he put down his violin and sat with his long legs stretched out before him and his hat over his eyes. But even with the hat partially covering his face, I could still see his faint smile as if pleased with himself—perhaps for remembering so many lines, I thought, for he was back to his usual reticence and hadn't said five words all together since the play ended. Leo gave Oliver his own little piece of cake on the floor and then sat with the dog on his lap, both of them listening to Mr. Niffen on his violin until Oliver let out a wheezy snore. Then Leo said good night and took Oliver downstairs. A short time later Hugo put his arm around Liddy and said, "When are we going to meet this beau of yours, eh?" Later still, Celia—unused to any wine, let alone two half glasses—fell out of her chair and had to be carried by Pinky to her cot. Liddy soon followed, and I said good night when she did, although I did not go to my room straightaway.

"Swim tomorrow?" Liddy asked me.

"Of course," I told her. "If it's fine." Then I said what for years I'd heard actors say easily, blithely to each other, without ever once saying it myself—"Good show tonight"—and I meant it. It seemed to me then, and now, as though that little phrase coming from my mouth, almost unbidden, cemented my feeling more than anything else that I was one of them. I had endeavored to fit in and live with them—*with* them, not *among* them—on that little boat, and I had succeeded. I thought of the moment when Hugo and I had clapped together at the end of the play, before Mrs. Howard interrupted. Those few moments of happiness. But then Mrs. Howard roared in.

Liddy smiled broadly and yawned, and I watched her go into her stateroom. When the door closed behind her I went quietly down the stairs and stood on the port side of the boat, where in the purple light I could just make out the other side of the river. The boat rocked gently with the tide, and below me the ever-present geese slept in a feathery group with their sides pressed together. From where I stood, Kentucky did not seem so far away. If Hugo took a sudden fancy to move the boat, Leo could pole us over in half an hour in calm water. I heard soft splashes as some night critter swam about looking for food, interspersed with the creaking of the cottonwoods.

"Rain coming," I heard behind me. Hugo came up to the railing next to me and stood so close that I could smell wine and cake and the damp linen scent of his shirt.

"I love that smell," he said. For a moment I was confused—how could he know that I was thinking about his shirt?—before I realized he meant the coming rain. I looked out at the river.

"So you had a good birthday, eh? You enjoyed my play?"

My play. I liked that he felt so personal about it.

"You've convinced me." I meant about plays in general, and he understood.

"I knew I would," he said with a smile in his voice.

Our hands were on the rail, nearly touching, my right next to his left. Sudden strong laughter came from the dining room as someone began playing Mr. Niffen's violin, not very well. When Hugo turned at the noise, his finger briefly brushed against mine, and I thought again of the sensation I felt when he put the key in my pocket. As if he could read my thoughts, Hugo said:

"How's that key working out? Any more break-ins?"

I smiled. "It's doing its job brilliantly."

He laughed, and this time he did touch my hand on purpose with his own. But he covered my fingers so briefly that I didn't have time to feel uncomfortable.

"Well, I'll say good night, May. I'm glad you had a good birthday. Don't let yourself get rained on," he said.

I watched him go up the stairs, my heart pumping strangely fast. Then I looked out toward Kentucky again. I could no longer see it. After a moment I walked over to the auditorium and opened the door.

Although it was too dark to see, I knew that Leo must be stretched out on his bedroll up on the stage with Oliver beside him. He had doused all the lanterns, but the smell of hot glass and lamp oil still hung in the air.

"Who is that?" Leo asked in a thick voice from the stage floor.

I closed the door behind me. "I'm sorry. I woke you up. It's May."

"What do you need, Miss May?"

"Nothing. I just had a question for you." I hesitated for a moment. "I was wondering: How hard is it to get across the river? I mean, if you rowed."

"What d'you mean? In a rowboat?"

"That's right."

"Not hard. Depends on the tide," he told me. "Why you ask?"

Alpha, beta, gamma, delta. "No reason."

"Don't row across this river 'less you know how to swim. You know how to swim?"

I told him I did.

"Good. That's good. Now, I have to get up very early tomorrow. You need anything else?"

"No," I said. "Nothing else. Thank you again for my birthday play and for the lovely pincushion."

Outside, the rain had started: hard, heavy drops that I could hear on the surface of the river. I felt my way up the stairs with my left hand on the guardrail, raindrops bouncing onto my head. The spider web stitch, I remembered, had a variation in which you wove the thick yarn loosely without any fill. You still needed a tapestry needle to slide the yarn crosswise under the spokes, but if you took care to space the strands out evenly, it would look less like a sun and more like a trap.

There were no tapestry needles in the next town, Delmore, which was on the Kentucky side of the river. Nor did they have any regular sewing needles with large enough eyes. The following day we crossed back to Indiana, where I had more luck. The morning was moist and hot, and chalky-blue clouds patterned the sky. The general store was lodged in the first set of buildings after the wharf, and the proprietor found a box of tapestry needles in the back room. She also brought out an array of silk thread: one a beautiful gold that I couldn't resist. Yellow was unlucky on stage but gold was not considered yellow.

There were a few notices pinned to the wall next to the door, but nothing about fugitive slaves. As I was paying I said, "Do you get many runaways here?"

The shopkeeper gave me a sharp glance but said nothing. She was very fair, with thin hair, and with the light behind her—she stood in front of the window with her cash box on a desk—she looked like a young girl. Maybe she did not understand me.

"I mean runaway slaves," I told her.

At that, she pursed her narrow lips and suddenly looked older. She shut the lid to the box with a sharp crack. "I know what you mean. You an abolitionist?"

"I just wondered."

"Because we don't take kindly to abolitionists around here. We need our Kentucky business."

Like the innkeeper, William Whitlock, she put the slavery question in the context of business. I was not sure how they fit together, and I asked her.

"Oh, really. You people. It's simple!" She was holding the change from my purchase in her hand without giving it to me, and she looked me over as if I were a simpleton. "If those farmers are paying out wages to every man working their fields, they won't have money to come to my store and buy what I'm selling. Not only that, if they let go their slave men, who'll work their fields?"

"Who works the fields up here in the North?" I asked.

"May."

I looked over and saw Hugo standing in the doorway. He did not look angry, but he wasn't smiling, either.

"Have you made your purchase?" he asked me. "I'll walk you back."

He took the tissue-paper package containing my tapestry needles and thread, and opened the door for me. I was beginning to understand his moods a little more, and I'd figured out that when he was excited—angry, passionate, afraid for the safety of the boat—his English accent became more pronounced.

It was very pronounced now. "May," he said as we started back along the narrow dirt road, "I want to tell you a story. No, no," he went on as I started to protest, "it's a short enough story, and it's just this. When my father was a boy in England, he once saw slave ships along the coast of Dover. He was quite young, my father, and on holiday, and as he ran along up the coastline with his sister collecting shells or some such nonsense, his sister spotted the ships, three great big beasts beating along against the waves out in the sea, but not so far out as you'd think they would be. And my grandmother said, 'Those there are slave ships. They've got black men in their hold instead of honest English linen.' 'What's honest English linen?' my father asked her. 'Something meant to be sold,' she told him. Not men."

Hugo began beating his walking stick against the heads of long barley grass beside us. The river rippled below us, the color of thick green milk.

"My father never forgot that. He told my sister and me about those ships many times. It made a great impression."

I said, "I was curious, that was all. That's why I asked her."

"It was a deplorable sight, those ships. I understand that. Uncommonly bad. More than bad—unjust and ungodly. Sinful. Yes, I do, I think it's sinful. But the English slave trade did end, you know. It ended by law. Nothing to do with my father or my grandmother. What could my father do, anyway, a boy of six?"

"I'm twenty-three."

"We will not be the ones to change the laws," he told me. "We're here to give a little entertainment to the people, these hardworking people, you understand? Give them a bit of a holiday. They don't want to look out at the slave ships, no more than my father did."

"Some of them do."

"They come to us for a rest from all that. We're not to get involved."

I glanced at him. His jaw seemed very set. We were coming to the first boats tied up to the shore, most of them already unloaded and ready for new cargo. For once, the *Floating Theatre* seemed stately and calm, heavy in the water.

"Why this curiosity now? Is it because of that woman?" Hugo asked as walked down to the boat.

I understood which woman he meant. I thought about lying and even started my Greek to myself, but instead I just said, "Yes."

"Don't get mixed up with her, May," Hugo said in his strongest accent. He stepped aside to let me go up the stage plank first, and his eyes narrowed as he looked at me. "She's trouble."

I thought to myself: *That's the very thing Florid said about you.*

A few days later I received a letter from Comfort addressed to general delivery, Anderson, Indiana. She listed the towns where Mrs. Howard had booked lectures, mostly places on the Ohio River until they reached Missouri.

I'm sorry we ended on a sour note, but Flora says that you are not to be blamed. It was simply a misunderstanding, and really if you think about it Captain Cushing was the real villain. He was so very rough! And he did not at all allow Flora time to explain, as a gentleman would have. Take care of yourself, Frog, and take the first steamer out of there if he troubles you.

I noticed that she did not write, *Come to me if he troubles you.* Florid added a postscript in brown ink:

May, we will be staying at the Gladwell Arms in New Paul, Indiana. After that at the Creekside Inn at Roseville. I am always in my room at teatime.

This, I understood, was a summons. But I didn't know what I was going to say to her. I had never broken the law and I wasn't sure I could do it even if I wanted to. I could perfectly picture myself blurting out something unwise, Greek alphabet or no. What I kept thinking was that it was foolish of Mrs. Howard to ask me, but I'd already seen what happened when she was called foolish.

As I was rereading the letter, Thaddeus came up to where I was sitting in the dining room. "Is that from your cousin?" he asked. "She was looking very well the other day, I must say." He had a pair of trousers in his hand and asked if I could alter them for him.

"They've gotten a bit tight—too many pieces of Cook's pecan pie, I suppose."

Like Comfort, Thaddeus came to me for all his little needs; he couldn't so much as sew on a button, unlike Hugo or Pinky. Pinky even mended his own ripped shirts. We went down to the green room, where my sewing things were, and as we walked along the guard I couldn't help but look out at the river as though I might see Mrs. Howard come sailing up to us at any moment, although as far as I knew she was traveling only by coach. Meanwhile, Thaddeus was prattling on:

"I wonder, did Comfort say anything about me? About my performance? How we used to laugh together at the other actors in Pittsburgh! Do you remember old Mrs. Goulder? Always trying to get her voice up, poor thing. And her brother—blind as a bat! He oughtn't to be allowed near a stage. Oh, well, these old actors, you know, they're like old horses, and you can get them to go neither with begging nor beating, ha-ha! Or so the saying goes. I'll be there soon, I suppose." He didn't look as though he believed that for a minute. "But the worst," he said, holding the door to the green room open for me, "are the ones who think they're above you. Second-rate. That's what one chap called me, just because he understudied for Kemble." He eyed the letter still in my hand. "Did Comfort say anything about the play at all?"

I had the feeling that Thaddeus wanted to read the letter for himself, and although I couldn't say that at that moment I felt my first twinge of danger, I did realize that I now had real secrets. I couldn't let anyone see the letter, carefully worded as it was, and so I opened the cigar box I still used for my sewing supplies, and while I was taking out pins I tucked the sheet of paper inside.

"I don't think you're second-rate," I said, though I didn't know very much about it. Comfort was always worried about that, too, even though for the most part she received lovely notices. Looking back on it, I'm sure this added to her haste to take up Mrs. Howard's offer and abandon me to look after myself. Thaddeus was just as pragmatic. I looked at the center back seam of the trousers he had given me and began to unpick the thread.

"Yes, well, at least it's not farm work," Thaddeus went on. "That I couldn't abide. I suppose one of these days I'll have to find a rich young widow to marry. Someone whose late husband kept a good cellar. But what I'd really like is to live in the country with some money to my name and a good pair of hunting dogs. I had a bitch in my youth who never left my side until the day my father kicked her in the stomach when he was three sheets to the wind. Annie, her name was. I still dream about her."

What would Thaddeus do, I wondered, when the summer run was over? What would I do, for that matter? I took a pin from my new steamboat pincushion and angled it into the trousers' waistband. Well, I couldn't worry about that now; Mrs. Howard and her proposal was all I could think about. And since she was such a large woman— or "somewhat troubled with flesh," as Pinky always delicately put it—that seemed fitting.

But there was no chance of meeting Mrs. Howard anytime soon, for we stopped in three Kentucky towns in a row, and she and Comfort kept to the North. They never lectured in the South, as Thaddeus had predicted back in Jacksonville, and now I had Comfort's list to prove it. So I was safe from making any decision for a while.

When we finally landed in New Paul, Indiana, we were too late to meet up with Mrs. Howard, who had already moved on. Instead I spent the afternoon cutting shad for Leo, who liked to use it as bait. I wondered if I could just avoid Mrs. Howard altogether. But, I reasoned, she would then probably come looking for me, and the *Floating Theatre* was easy to find—indeed, we advertised our presence.

A few days after that we landed in Carney, Kentucky, a town that was either dying or already dead, depending on your level of optimism, and not a place you would think could fix my purpose, though that is just what happened.

No little boys met us at the landing, and, walking up to the town, we saw only a couple of women out shopping with their baskets.

Storefront after storefront was boarded up and abandoned. Even the horse manure in the middle of the road was old and dry, caked in the sun. The postmaster told Hugo that coal was being dug up ten miles to the south, and what with the run on the banks last fall and the bad tobacco crop three years in a row, half the able men had gone off to dig in the pits. But even without his explanation I would have known that we'd draw a small crowd. The town felt like a dead eye with no mind behind it.

"Damn coal," Hugo said as we left the post office. "They told me about it last year but I didn't think anything of it. If I had my steamboat, we could steam up there and back in a day. What town did he say? Those miners deserve a show. What's our earnings at, May?"

"A hundred and two dollars and fifty cents, less whatever you spend today."

"By the end of August, God willing, I'll have enough for that steamer. But not if our audiences all go inland before then."

We made our way toward a cluster of farm buildings where Hugo, as if intent on reaching every single body that still remained, wanted to put up notices. After we plastered up a few, Hugo noticed an old tobacco barn on a little rise in the distance, clearly not used for years.

"We should get a can of paint. Paint our name up on top there so everybody can see it. That'll get the word out. Maybe even the miners'll see it."

"Won't the farmer mind?"

"We'll give him a couple of free tickets. He might have the paint, too, or some whitewash."

Clouds coiled above us like dark puffy snakes. I could feel the rising wind push the skirt of my dress against my legs as though trying to keep me back, but even so, Hugo just kept walking across the spongy pasture, which had once been planted with tobacco. Some of the old plants were still struggling to live, not taking to their abandonment. Their thin leaves were yellow at the edges and spread closer to the ground than to the sun, and the dewy stalks found ways up under my skirt, wetting my stockings. The long gray tobacco barn, listing to one side, looked more dilapidated the closer we got, and I wondered why Hugo didn't give up on his plan. But, like me, once he set a course for himself, he had to see it through to the end.

"I don't see a farmhouse anywhere," I remarked.

While Hugo inspected the back, I went around front to look inside. The barn was built with no windows and only one door, which was off its hinges and propped up against the outside wall. What prompted me to step in I don't know, for the roof beams were half-rotted and the unevenly planked walls with their dark-eyed knots felt like ghosts watching me with disapproval. An old smell of tobacco and wet wood mixed with the earthy scent of whatever wild creatures lived there now.

If the town behind us felt like gloom, this place felt like despair. I heard Hugo come in behind me. I was about to step back when I noticed something at the far end, a little structure built out of rough-hewn logs and fitted with barred windows, a kind of animal cell, but it was too narrow for a horse and too tall for a pig. As I got closer to look at it, I could see iron rings fastened to one of the thick wooden joists.

Hugo followed me. I heard him take a sharp intake of breath. "Look at the irons. Jesus Mary. That's a slave hold."

"A what?"

"They must have chained them up here while they waited to sell them at market."

For a moment I didn't understand him. Then I did. Something cold settled on my shoulders, and I heard a noise like a broom sweeping back and forth between my ears. I look back at that now as my first real moment of understanding. The ghosts in the knotted wood and the dark, rotting, windowless walls shifted from details to setting, and I felt that just by looking at the iron fetters I was somehow a culpable witness to all the dark deeds that had happened here. The cell was too small for a person to lie down; in fact, the fetters might even have been too high to allow for sitting. I noticed there was a pair of smaller iron rings farther down on the thick wooden beam that divided the cell in two.

"To shackle the children," Hugo said.

The silence in the barn was suddenly overwhelming. The small irons rings had been made to fit the tiniest wrists, and the splinters of rust speckling them were the color of dark, dried blood. I spied a second pair of small rings attached to the other side of the beam. Manacled, the children would have been facing away from each other. There was a small mound of very old, very dry human feces on the compacted dirt, and I thought of the little Negro boy with his frog named Happy. I tried very hard not to picture him there.

Hugo's face was half in shadow. I wanted to say, *Do you still think we should wait for the law?* Only I was afraid of his answer. He was English, after all. I didn't know if that gave him license to withdraw himself from the issue or not.

"Doesn't look like they use it anymore. There's that, at least." He reached out as if to take my arm but I turned away; I couldn't speak. As we walked back across the tobacco field, Hugo thrashed at the dying plants with his stick. We didn't paint anything on that barn, or look for whoever owned it. All I wanted was to leave it behind me, and I walked in front of Hugo listening to the rhythm of his thrashing.

That night, as he predicted, only a handful of people came to the show: eight men, six women, and two children. The women's pale faces were gaunt but freshly scrubbed, and the men sat with their hats in their laps. After the show they brushed off the brims with the open palms of their hands and then offered their arms to their wives. Each one of them was a storekeeper or a farmer. Maybe one of them owned that barn. Still, I couldn't help thinking that, in spite of their small number, they looked like every other audience we played to, both north of the river and south.

13

Mrs. Howard began unpacking the most extraordinary little bronze-colored box—Japanese, she told me—that had within it a miniature tea service: a silver hot-water pot the size of a shaving mug, an equally small silver tea scoop and tea canister, two silver cups without handles, a silver creamer, a silver teapot, and a wool caddy in the shape of an Elizabethan country cottage. I watched in amazement as each tiny item came out, feeling like a doll at a tea party.

"The teapot was an English invention," she was saying, "though it was based on a little pot that the Chinese use for drinking hot wine. I always take this set with me when I travel."

We were in her rooms in Kenilworth, Indiana. Comfort was standing near the window wearing a pretty forest-green dress, and when I first walked in she'd said, "Oh, Frog, I'm so glad you've come!" Hearing that, a sour feeling spread beneath my ribs. I had wanted her to say this in Viola but she didn't, and now it was too late. She came to embrace me but I kept my arms at my sides. Mrs. Howard noticed.

"Girls," she said in her thunderous voice, "let's begin all over on a friendly note. What's done is done. Today is another day, a beautiful day!" she said, although it was humid and overcast. "Now, let's see, where are my tea things?"

Once the tea things were laid out on the little table before us, they seemed too numerous and large to fit in the Japanese box; but I had seen them come out, so I knew it was possible despite appearances. Likewise, Mrs. Howard seemed generous and friendly today, an appearance that did not reflect what I knew to be true.

When Comfort went downstairs to fetch hot water, I asked, "So this is all a ruse? Comfort's lectures? What you really do is help runaways?"

"Not a ruse, precisely, no, not a ruse. Two with one stone, you know. But it's a good cover in its way, a very good cover."

"Does she know?"

"Of course! However, I may have exaggerated her importance somewhat."

Mrs. Howard was a shrewd woman, but I knew that already. She leaned forward, her silver chains rocking over her bosom, her piercing blue eyes narrowing. "Now, then, May, let's talk about what you will do for us."

I will not bore you with the long preamble Mrs. Howard indulged herself in before getting to the point a good twenty minutes later—the stories she told about runaways and their midnight departures and how in two cases Donaldson himself had outwitted their would-be captors (in one instance he ran off their horses and cut up their boots while they slept). Early on in this narrative Comfort came in with hot water and promptly left again, this time with her basket, to go to a shop. I drank tea from Mrs. Howard's miniature teacup, which held about three sips of liquid, and was offered but declined some shortbread, red grapes, the end piece of a cherry cake, and a plate of sliced smoked trout.

Mrs. Howard ate a little of everything but food did not slow down her speech. However, when she opened her mouth for a larger-than-usual forkful of cake, I took the slight pause as opportunity.

"How much am I to do for twenty-five dollars?" By now I was tired and I wanted to get the instructions I needed and leave.

Mrs. Howard shifted the cake in her mouth and said without swallowing. "Oh, my dear, don't be so mercenary! You can't sell off good deeds."

"But that is just what you asked me to do," I reminded her, "back on the boat. However, if you've changed your mind . . ." I stood, knowing she would not let me go so easily.

She lowered her voice. "If you would just deliver some packages," she said. "That's all."

"By 'packages,' do you mean people?" I asked in my regular voice.

She hushed me and then stood up and went to the door. After listening for a moment, she opened it suddenly. No one was there.

"We have to be careful," she said, coming back to her armchair. "I told you those stories as warnings. We have to watch what we say."

"I think you know by now that that's hard for me to do."

"I trust you, my dear."

"It's not a matter of trust."

"Just deliver a few packages as you go down the river," she told me. "They may be small packages. You understand."

"Children?" I thought of the tiny manacles in the slave hold. "What do I do with them?"

"You pick them up in the South, of course, and take them across the river. Donaldson will be waiting with the carriage on the road; you find him and give him the package. That's all. He'll take it from there."

I had more questions but the first bell was ringing, signaling that supper would be served downstairs in a quarter of an hour.

"How will I know when there is someone waiting for me to cross them?" I asked.

"I'll see that you know."

She stood and began brushing the crumbs off the bosom of her dress with wide sweeps.

"But where do I row *to*?" I asked. "And how will I know where to find Donaldson?"

"You'll be told when the time comes," Mrs. Howard said, rearranging the chains on her neck. "The less you know the better."

"Better for whom?"

"Why, for everyone, my dear. None of us knows very much. It's a piecemeal affair. You're one of the pieces." The second bell began ringing. "Now, where is your cousin? I wonder. You won't stay for dinner, of course; I don't think the inn allows guests. Besides, we should really not be seen together now."

You would think that thought would comfort me, but it didn't.

The designs I was embroidering on Liddy's costume were complicated enough to hold my attention for ten minutes at a time. But when those ten minutes were finished, or when my length of yarn ended and I had to unwind a new length, or turn the cloth over to knot the end, or hold the costume up to make sure the line of embroidery was straight, then my mind went right back to Mrs. Howard and her small "packages."

On the one hand I did not want to know too much, because if anyone asked me anything, I was in danger, even with my Greek, of blurting out whatever I knew. On the other hand I did not like to undertake any activity without specific directions. Push the needle up, wind the yarn around the stitch, push the needle down. Step A, step B, step C. This was how I liked my instructions. Mark the cloth at one-sixteenth of an inch. Start the stitch and measure it again; if it's in line, then pull the yarn taut and begin the next stitch.

Several days passed and then it was Sunday. In the afternoon I sat outside as I usually did on one of Hugo's canvas chairs next to Leo, who was fishing off the pier, while Hugo sat on another chair next to me. The *Floating Theatre* was tied up behind us with the little rowboat attached to its stern, drifting slightly against the mossy edge of the river. I noted to myself that the line was knotted around a hook on the stem post. Could I figure out how to untie the knot and then, more importantly, re-knot it? Would there be enough moonlight to see? Or should I bring a lantern? I hadn't heard anything from Mrs. Howard since I left her in Kenilworth. Waiting was safer than the not-waiting would be, but I did not like the uncertainty.

"That for Miss Liddy?" Leo asked me, unhooking a small brown fish that was trying to wiggle its way back into life. He put it in a separate bucket for me to gut and clean when I was ready to take a break from my work. I told him that it was.

"Pretty. She'll like that."

Hugo was wearing a broad-brimmed hat and he angled it to lengthen its shadow over his face. He held a copy of *The Midnight Hour* in one hand and his fishing line in the other. Leo took an angle-worm from a second bucket and dressed his hook while Oliver eyed him with interest.

"If all goes well, we'll debut the play in Paducah or Florence," Hugo said. "How are you coming along?" he asked me. He meant the costumes. He had begun to take an interest in them—even went so far as to make some suggestions. "I was thinking maybe the General should have epaulettes. That would mark him as a military gent."

"I was thinking the same thing. And a broad sash; that's easy to make."

"A striking color. Red or gold."

"Gold would match this." I held up Liddy's costume with the gold embroidery.

"Gold it is," Hugo said. He leaned over to look at the embroidery more carefully.

"Lovely. Maybe add a blue tuck in the center," he suggested. "To draw in the eye."

I smiled to myself. If Comfort had taken this kind of interest in my sewing I would have never sewn scratchy feathers into her costumes, no matter how much she laughed at me. I was pleased that he noticed my work, although I had no temptation to follow his suggestion, since the blue dot would ruin the design. Hugo went back to his play, and when he bent his head I could see the tanned line of his neck just under his thick, dark hair. In the morning, after he and Leo had landed the boat and he'd gone upstairs to wash his face and hands and write in his logbook, he had a certain talcum-y smell. Also his shaving cream gave off a richly sweet scent, though he did not shave every morning. Sometimes he waited until just before the evening show, after he had napped and eaten supper, and on those days it seemed to me that his stubble had its own rough but not unpleasant odor, like pine needles. He was proud of being a riverboat man and proud of his captain's papers, and he was also very proud of his theater. If Leo had not whitewashed the floor to his satisfaction, he got on his hands and knees to spot paint himself. Then he smelled like the lime in the whitewash.

I unthreaded the yarn from my needle and pulled out a stitch that was not quite loose enough. "Have you noticed how full the risers have been this week?" I asked Hugo. "I've been giving out complimentary tickets."

"To free blacks?"

"I ask them to tell their friends and family. I calculated that our net is up twenty-eight percent from last week." I wanted to remind him I was good at math in case he was thinking of letting Mrs. Niffen take over the books.

"I hope you haven't done that in slave states," Hugo told me. "None of the whites will come if there are Negroes in the audience."

"Whyever not?"

Hugo put down his fishing line and wiped the palms of his hands on his trousers. The script fell onto the pier by his foot. "I agree, it's not right. But there it is." He picked up the script, held the fishing pole under his armpit, and turned down the page he was on. Then he sat on the script to hold it in place and began fussing with his line. Oliver was sniffing the bait bucket and Leo snapped his fingers at him.

"What's it like to be a slave?" I asked Leo.

Beside me, Hugo shifted uneasily in his canvas chair.

"You know I don't know that," Leo told me.

"Your mother didn't tell you any stories?"

Hugo shifted again. "Now, May . . ." he said warningly. But Leo just shrugged.

"She found herself a better life. Don't look backwards behind you, she always said."

Hugo cleared his throat, a growly whisper of a noise. He took off his hat and I could see his eyes, which seemed wet and unfocused in the sun. "Listen, May, Leo was never . . . Leo is a free man, you know." He looked at me with an expression I couldn't read. "You shouldn't be asking him such questions. You shouldn't ask anyone that."

"Why not?"

On the river, a large steamship blew two sharp whistles. As it passed I watched its slow side wheel send up sparkling white water and then dash it back down. Leo didn't want to talk about his past, I understood that. But on that day I felt compelled to keep talking. No one seemed able to tell me what I wanted to know. Maybe I wasn't asking the right questions.

"Why don't you ever go into town in the South?" I asked when the steamer had passed.

Leo tested his line. "There are slavers there. Man could catch me up and make me a slave."

Now Hugo became even more agitated. "They can't do that: there are laws!" he said. "You're a free man, Leo, you know that. Born that way." He stopped and then said, "Not that I want you to go to towns in the South. If you're not comfortable, why, then, of course . . . but you should know you're perfectly safe."

Leo shrugged again but he was right. Ten years later I read in a newspaper that men were trying to write new laws that would allow a white man to do just what Leo feared: catch a black man and take him back to the South as a slave, no matter if he'd been a slave before or not.

Leo reeled in another brown fish, identical to the last one, and cursed. He was searching for a large catfish he'd seen early that morning.

"I'll gut all those," I said, gesturing to the fish bucket, "as soon as I finish this bit."

Leo baited his line again. "I just know that cat's down there."

But Hugo hadn't finished with me yet. "I don't understand, May," he said. "We've been out here for over a month and now, suddenly, you can't get enough of the slave question? Why is it you didn't wonder about it before?"

"I don't know. That's how I am."

"I hope you're not corresponding with that woman, the abolitionist." His eyes searched mine. "She's a bully, May. Don't let her dictate your thoughts. You're independent enough not to mind her."

"She's not dictating my thoughts. She started me wondering. And now I keep wondering."

Hugo began to say something and then stopped himself. He reeled in his empty fishing line and stared at the bucket on the pier. After a while he said, as though talking to the bucket, "You pick up the thread of something and then you can't put it down."

I wasn't sure if that was a question or not. "Is that bad?" I asked.

Hugo and Leo looked at each other. Then Leo deliberately worked his line, not answering.

"No," Hugo said. After a moment he added, "Well, I don't know. It can be."

I waited for him to say more. He took a long breath and then he put down his fishing line. "I suppose I feel some responsibility." He glanced at Leo. "For both of you. For everyone. I don't want you, May, or anyone else, to get hurt. As the captain, you know. I feel I should . . ." he trailed off. He looked out at the water where a couple of boys were drifting by on a makeshift raft, one wearing a bent hat made from newspaper.

"Bother," he said. "It's too hot out. I'm going back to the boat."

I'd pulled my stitch too tight again and I bent over my work to hide my face as I loosened it because I could feel an expression on it, something I didn't want him to see. He felt protective, he said. Hearing that gave me a sort of ballooning feeling, a great expanding pleasure, just under my skin. At the same time, however, I was aware that I wanted something more, something more singular and for me alone. I listened to his footsteps go down the pier and onto the boat deck. When I heard the office door slam, I looked up. Oliver was already curled up in the canvas chair where Hugo had been sitting a moment ago. Leo was standing in the same place, looking out at the water with two hands on his pole. The tree snags caught in the muddy shallows bobbed a little as though in expectation of gaining their freedom, but they were stuck fast until a government overseer could come along and put them on his list for removal.

Leo began reeling in his line. He said, "My mam told me that at Christmastime she always got new clothes from the Great House. Caps and such, or boots and shoes. They also gave 'em molasses and sugar and flour. Every family with a bucket."

A hot breeze blew in from the river, pushing his long hair to the side. With it loose, he looked more like an Indian and less like a black man.

I smoothed the fabric on my lap with my fingers. "That doesn't sound bad," I said.

"When she were punished, the master put her in a potato sack and hung her up in an oak tree and beat her with a stick. She once told me that she would wade in blood and water up to her neck before she went back to that place."

I looked at him then but he was staring down at the glassy water as if hoping to spy the whiskers of the fish he was chasing. I couldn't think what to say. Like the child-sized manacles in the empty slave hold, it's worse when you let yourself imagine it. The bottom of the Ohio was muddy and dark, the way catfish liked it. It must be cool down there. The fish stayed well hidden.

I went over to the bucket and picked up a fish to gut and clean for him. I could do this, at least. As I knelt on the pier Leo said, "It ain't hard to row across this river. My rowboat, now, it pull a little to the right. But it does just fine."

At that, I lifted my head and stared at him. Did he know what I was planning? Had he overheard the conversation I'd had with Mrs. Howard? For the first time it occurred to me that he could have stayed in the office after telling me about my birthday celebration instead of going back to tidy up the stage, which is what he usually did after a show, and what I had assumed. But if he had stayed in the office, he might have heard Mrs. Howard's proposal to me. Had he? The side of his face gave nothing away.

14

I don't remember if it was that night or the next that I began to have nightmares about Giulia, the little Italian girl from the *Moselle*, I only know that it was a few days before I made my first crossing in the rowboat. In my dream, Giulia was holding on to me while I swam across the river. Suddenly something caught my leg and began pulling me down. As I was trying to kick it off, my attention shifted from Giulia, and when I finally got loose I found that I was alone. While I was fighting, Giulia had slipped from my hold and drowned.

I jolted awake, but the horror and dismay and absolute failure stayed with me like a line of bitter smoke around my heart. Why did I trust that she could keep her little arms around me? Why didn't I keep a stronger hold myself? It was only a dream, but I still felt the weight of my guilt even after I washed my face, dressed, and walked down the guard to the dining room for breakfast.

As the days went by, people began to notice something was different, although I tried hard to act just the same. The problem was I didn't know what "just the same" meant. Unlike the actors around me, I never took much to studying my own habits or characteristics. When Pinky said, "May, you haven't watched us land the boat lately. You all right?" I realized I'd been sleeping later than usual due to the nightmares, which woke me every night, and I resolved to get up earlier the next day. When Liddy said, "No breakfast for you this morning? That's three days in a row!" I put a slice of ham on my plate. Each day I waited for someone to come up to me with a piece of paper, my instructions. At first I imagined it might be Donaldson, since he was the one who would meet me afterwards and take the children. Then again, as a black man he would be more conspicuous. Maybe it would be a stranger, then, someone I had never seen but who was involved in this business. An abolitionist. It turned out I was right about that. He might come to one of our shows, I thought, and I was right about that, too.

Hugo said, "May, is this your watch? I found it in the dining room." He held my father's watch in his palm, the chain looped around his fingers. I could feel his eyes on my face as I took it from him. I did not remember taking it off.

"You're not suffering from any more seasickness, are you? You've looked a bit pinched lately."

"No, it was just that once." I was surprised he knew the watch was mine, and I told him so.

"Used to have one like it, but someone nicked it in Surrey. A fine piece."

"It was my father's."

He smiled. "Ah, the glass factory gentleman."

I was surprised he remembered that, too. His dark hair was growing long, and he looked weathered and healthy from all these weeks and weeks of standing on an open boat, calling out the names of sandbars and directing the men to heave this way or that. What would he think of the danger I was putting him in—putting all of his company in? Not to mention this boat. Well, I knew what would happen: the smile would be gone and his accent would become very pronounced as he ordered me off.

We wouldn't get to Paducah for another few weeks, and the players were still performing their sketches and songs while I accompanied them on the piano. I couldn't help but scan the benches as I played, wondering if someone sitting there would be the one to tell me that I had to go out that night in the dark and fetch a couple of children and bring them back safely to shore. There was a man who wore a slouch hat throughout the performance as if he might have to leave at any moment; could he be the one?

During the intermission, Mrs. Niffen said, "You're coming in late on your cues tonight. That's not like you." She gave me a long look, as though she'd had her suspicions about me and they were being confirmed. "Are you ill? Shall I take over? I only have a walk-on next half. Celia could do that for me."

I'd begun feeling easier around her, but now I reminded myself that I must watch my back. She would take over playing the piano and anything else that she could.

"I'm fine," I said. I repeated my Greek to myself but I could not think of a lie to tell her to explain why I would be late on my cues. "Just fine," I said.

There was a man with darting eyes and a clipped Vandyke beard, and another man who kept looking behind him . . . It could be either of these men, or anyone. I tried to keep my attention on my playing, but my fingers felt like stiff bones and the melodies all sounded ridiculously light and happy, even the sad ones.

"I'd like to run through the new play tomorrow," Hugo told me after the show as he helped me move my piano back off the stage. "Costumes all set? Of course, I've noticed you like to make changes as we go along . . . refining your art, what?"

I did not consider sewing an art and I told him so. But I was pleased that he noticed. His cuffs were rolled up, exposing the fine dark hairs of his wrist, and as we pushed the piano he adjusted his movement for the one uneven roller, his arm briefly resting against mine.

After he jumped off the stage, I put my music sheets in order. The auditorium was empty, but as usual after a show the feel of all the warm bodies lingered. Someone had dropped a lacy pink handkerchief on the floor and I picked it up. Then I went into the office to see to that night's take, putting all the change in the long silk bag to give to Hugo.

When I went outside to find him, I was hit by the warmth of moist, summer air. The crowd was walking home, most of them not bothering to light their lanterns, since the moon was full and bright, but a few still lingered along the pier. I could see Hugo speaking to a couple near the water's edge, and when the woman saw me, she stepped forward, smiling.

"My handkerchief!" she said, seeing me with it, and she walked up toward me away from the men. "I'm so grateful to you." She had a long neck and a long nose and wore tight sausage curls on either side of her bonnet. Artificial, I guessed, and so shiny I wanted to touch one to see if it was wet.

I held out the handkerchief. As she took it from my hand our fingers touched, and she said in a low voice, "You're the friend of Mrs. Howard's, aren't you?" My heart jumped and then started racing. I glanced at Hugo, who was standing out of earshot. The woman's back was to him, blocking him out. Deliberately, I realized.

"Yes. I'm May Bedloe," I said quickly. Then I thought: *Should I have told her my name?* I didn't know how this worked, but it didn't matter, I believe I could have said anything as long as I started with *Yes.* She came to deliver information, not receive it.

"Your package will be waiting across the river tonight," she told me.

After my father died and my mother sold our dairy farm, there were not many occasions for me to go outside at night. Certainly not in New York with Comfort, or in Boston or Baltimore, either. Sometimes, though, as a girl, if my father had to see to one of the cows or check on a batch of cheese, I would go with him to the barn in the moonlight. Nighttime, or I suppose I should say the dark outside, never frightened me. As a child I had the strange fancy that darkness was more honest than daylight, that the shrubs and trees and the creatures that lived among them were more themselves at night, and that the ashy shade of the grass was in fact its true color rather than the bright hue it took on during the day. Even the darkened river bellowing along below our house assumed its rightful character as it hurried past our farm. Perhaps at night I felt more like a spectator, and I suppose that was for me a comfortable role. I remember the smell of Nicodemus flowers, which bloom after sunset, following my father and me as we walked to the barn.

Stepping into Leo's rowboat that night and waiting while it stopped swaying from my movement, I was keenly aware of the deep color that descends after the sun goes down, and of all the night noises: the cicadas, the soft gulps of wind, the creaking of the trees. I was glad for the noise, since it masked the sound of my oars pushing the boat away from the dock and the soft plash of the water as I rowed. Leo was right: the boat pulled a little to the right. The water around me shimmered like sealskin, a dark smooth expanse that once in a while caught the moonlight and then quickly absorbed it. At midnight I was supposed to be halfway across the river, where I would make my signal and then get a signal in return. That was all the instruction I got from the woman with the pink handkerchief—no letter with points A, B, and C.

I had to row backwards, of course. For a long time I could still see the squat chimneys of the *Floating Theatre* that ran up every two staterooms—my room shared its chimney with Hugo's—each like a little neck topped by a Chinaman's hat but no face. They seemed to be waiting for something. I pulled the oars back and then back again, making a neat swoosh in the water like scissors cutting through fabric, and when I guessed that I was just about in the middle of the river, I turned the boat around so that I was facing Kentucky and took out my father's watch.

The warm air settled palpably on my shoulders like a short felt cape while I waited for the last few minutes to pass. When it was exactly midnight, I got the lantern I'd brought along out from under the thwart and lit it. Then I counted to sixty and doused it.

My dress was damp and sticking to my skin from nervous sweat. Under the round melon of a moon—still bright—I could just make out the Kentucky bank, although the land above it was a long black shadow. I counted to sixty, lit the lantern again, and then doused it. Still no answering light from the shore. The water lapped around me and I heard a fish flop over its surface. The rowboat was drifting downstream and I pulled on the oars to correct it. I wasn't sure if I should go back or go on, when at last I saw a flicker of light that blinked once or twice before it caught. Sixty seconds later it went out.

Turning the boat around again, I picked out a treetop on the northern bank that was, I thought, more or less opposite from where the light had come from, and I rowed away from it in a straight line. If I'd had someone with me they could have directed me, but I was alone, and my neck began to hurt from looking back so often. When I felt the first scrape of the rocky river bottom, I was convinced that I was way off course. There was no town and no pier on this part of the river, nothing at all to tie the boat to, since the trees here did not come all the way down to the water, so I had no choice but to get out and pull the boat up the bank. The tall trees in front of me hid the moon, and the scraping of the hull against the pebbly dirt sounded overly loud, both out of keeping with the other noises and amplified.

I thought about calling out but I'd heard there were lookouts along the river. As I was trying to make out the face of my watch again, a figure stepped out from behind the trees, and although I was waiting for just exactly this, at the sight of him my body lurched back a little in surprise. He was a white man carrying a large basket and he was alone. He probably wanted to make sure of me before he brought out the children. He was shorter than I imagined he would be, and dressed like a farmhand. When he came closer I could smell barn animals and hay.

"Friend of Mizz Howard's?" he asked. I affirmed this. "This your boat?" I nodded again and then said yes. My voice came out in a whisper, which I hadn't intended.

"Here," he said. He handed me the basket, which had a rumple of clothes inside. When he drew back I saw a long gun tucked into his trousers.

"There'll be a light on the other side," he said, "once you land your boat. Walk along the road until you see it."

"Where?"

"Somewhere on the road."

"Which road?"

He shook his head at me. "I don't know—main road!" Even in a whisper he sounded exasperated. "Just keep your eyes about you."

"How many children?" I asked.

"What do you mean?"

"You can see how small the rowboat is."

"Just the one baby boy," the man said.

For a moment I was confused. Then I looked down at the basket of clothes. I pulled back the edge of a pair of trousers and saw an infant's tightly sleeping face.

"I thought . . . I was led to expect children."

The man shrugged. "We hear about a baby coming, we approach the mother. She sends for us when her time comes. Easy enough to say the baby was born dead. Most of the land agents turn a blind eye; they mostly want their women back at work. Or maybe they believe it. I don't know. Course, some of them never even know a baby's coming. The women conceal it."

The baby's head was hardly bigger than my fist. His hair was still wet. When I asked how old he was, the man looked at his watch. Eight hours, he told me.

"Oh, aye. I almost forgot. Look here now." The man pushed aside the clothes at the bottom of the basket and produced a feeding bottle made of clay, shaped like a little upright boat with a goatskin nipple at the top. I'd seen these devices before, once in Oxbow and once in a theater in New York: a young actress gave one to her husband to feed her baby when she needed to be on the stage. I remembered how the husband cradled the infant's head on his elbow, the rough woolen material of his coat itchy, I thought, against such sensitive skin, but the baby sucked down the milk without pause. Afterwards the baby burped a lot and the man laughed as though this was the greatest of jokes. He wasn't an actor, the father, but shifted sets and acted as general carpenter.

"They call it a pap feeder," the father had explained. "Bad thing is, air comes in through this thing and that makes him burp. But better than nothing, am I right?"

After he tucked the feeder back in among the clothes, the farm-hand showed me the jar of milk that was also nestled there. Then he pulled the boat back down into the river for me and held the basket while I got in. "If anyone asks, this is your laundry."

"In the middle of the night?"

He looked back at the line of trees. Anybody could be hiding there, watching us. I wedged the basket under the forward thwart next to the lantern, and when I looked up again he was wading back to the bank. Leo's rowboat, freed from his grip, began rocking a little downstream. I fitted the oars to the oarlocks as the farmhand lifted his arm in farewell without looking back.

I rowed as hard as I could and kept my good ear trained on Kentucky. Thick clouds were beginning to roll in, masking the moon-light, but the river itself was calm. We were about halfway across the river, when strange noises began coming from the basket, like a small coughing pig. I lifted the oars for a minute but the noises didn't stop. Although they didn't seem loud enough to draw attention, that might change if we got closer to shore, so I felt around in the bottom of the basket until I found the little pap feeder and the jar of milk.

The jar was warm at the bottom from the clothes and cool at the top from the night air. I held the feeder upright and poured some milk into it, and then I tried to feed the baby as he lay there in his nest of shirts and trousers. That proved impossible. Milk spilled down his cheek, and he cried his coughing cry even louder, turning his face this way and that so I couldn't keep the nipple in his mouth. I needed to hold his head straight, so I pulled the oars up into the boat and lifted the baby from the basket. His lips were dark raspberry and reminded me of candy I had eaten as a girl, and his wet little eyes were scrunched tight. He had waterlogged cheeks and a smooth, curved forehead that led gracefully up to his damp dark hair and dark rounded skull. I gently held his little head and tipped the milk into his mouth, and soon he began sucking and swallowing in even beats.

Meanwhile we were drifting farther and farther west with the current. When I looked up, the clouds had completely covered the moon and I could no longer see anything at all to the north. For a moment my chest tightened in panic as I saw how easily I could lose my bearings and row back to Kentucky. I put the baby back down in the basket a little more roughly than I meant to and covered him up and secured the pap feeder. The jar of milk was empty. Now the river was beginning to roll a little higher and the wind grew heavier.

I remembered that, before I stopped to tend to the baby, the wind had been blowing on the right side of my face, so I turned the boat with one oar until I felt the same sensation. The clouds thinned briefly, enough to see the outline of the moon, and looking over my shoulder I saw what I took to be the stern light on the *Floating Theatre*.

It wasn't, but I made my way to it anyway until the light flickered off and then I made my way to the spot where I thought it had been. By this time I was looking over my shoulder so often that the muscle in the back of my neck began sending out fiery flames, and with every pull of the oars I could feel my left arm bone moving back and forth within its socket like a mortar and pestle. But finally we reached the bank, and, with the last of my strength—or so it seemed at the time—I pulled the boat out of the water with the baby inside it.

I'd landed us in some very wet, overgrown countryside: we might have been in an African jungle for all the humid green growth and the variety of insects, all of them hungry. A swarm of gnats hit my face like a welcoming party as soon as I picked up the basket and stepped toward the trees, but with my hands full I couldn't wave them away. When I looked down I saw that the baby was sleeping with one arm out of the clothes and his hand at his face, for all the world like a little old man annoyed at the noise of the world and trying to shut it out while he dozed.

My good ear was still trained on the river, and happily I heard no voices, no sound of oars. But the *Floating Theatre* was nowhere in sight, nor was any other boat. I began looking for a road. After only a few steps, however, I didn't think I could carry the basket any longer—my arms were that tired from rowing—so I put it down and made a sling out of one of the shirts. When I was a girl I had once seen a short Indian woman carry her baby this way, though at the time what struck me was the beadwork at the hem of her dress and her wide bare feet in October. Whoever this shirt once belonged to had long arms, for which I was grateful; I was able to tie the sleeves into a knot behind my neck. Then I wrapped the baby in the shirt sling and pressed the side of his warm, new body against me, holding on to his back. I tucked the empty jar of milk and the pap feeder into the sling and then with my free hand I picked up the basket, light enough now, and looped its long handle over my arm.

I felt I could just about manage.

It was so dark that my eyes couldn't make out anything but shapes. The weeds and brush that began at the edge of the bank seemed to spread out indefinitely in the darkness. I stumbled and put my arms under the sling to hold it steady. I could feel the baby's round bottom sagging down like a little ball, and I moved my hand under the small curve of his back and up to his tiny, hard skull. Then I checked the other end for the feeder: still there. But where was the road?

"Heyya, who's that?" a deep twangy voice rang out.

I was so surprised that I made a short, sharp noise before I could stop myself. A shadow ahead of me moved and formed itself into a tall man wearing a fur hat made from the whole of some animal: the furry head was over one of the man's ears and the tail over the other. In the darkness I could not tell whether it was raccoon or possum. The man wearing it carried a broken hunting rifle over one arm, and a potato sack heavy with some kill was slung across his back. As he came up to me he brought with him the smell of gunpowder and wet leaves.

"Well, it's a lady now. Hello, ma'am. What have you got there?" he asked me in a voice that seemed at once both friendly and mean. He had a strong southern accent, but a lot of people on both sides of the Ohio spoke like him; he might be a northerner for all that. Still, I couldn't take the chance that he would help me.

"A baby," I told him. "He's sick."

"He breathing?"

He took a step closer, as if he wanted to check for himself. He was as thin as a string bean and a little bent at the neck as some string beans are. I didn't know how much he could see in the moonlight, but the baby was certainly a little Negro baby, which he might notice if he looked closely.

I stepped back. "I'm looking for a doctor," I said. "I'm trying to find the road."

"You one of them river people? Got yourself a shanty boat or some such?"

I said that I was.

"Where's your boat docked? Not on my land, I hope."

"I don't know. It's back there a ways."

He laughed. "Don't worry, this ain't my land." *So,* I thought, *a poacher.* "You a panicky woman," he told me. "Shouldn'ta come out here without knowing which way to go."

He took off his hat by the snout of the animal and rubbed his forehead with the crook of his arm. Then he replaced the hat at an angle. "Jes' keep goin' the way you're goin'. Up at the road go left. You see a stile on the right, and after that's the doctor's donkey path. You can take that on up to his house."

I needed to turn right to get back to the *Floating Theatre* and, hopefully, to whoever was waiting for the baby on the road nearby, but I thanked him and started walking, hoping that this was the end of it. It wasn't. He followed me through the brush, and when the trees cleared and the road presented itself he said, "There it is, ma'am. Go that way 'bout a quarter mile." I turned to see him pointing west. Then he took off his hat again.

I could feel him standing there, watching me walk, and when the road turned I stepped to the side, out of sight, to listen with my good ear. Sure enough, I heard the faint clop of boots following along down the road in my direction. I hitched up the baby in his sling and kept walking. The one good thing about this poacher, whoever he was, was that he kept me in such a state of nervous fear that I could not fall from exhaustion even though I knew that every step I took I would have to retrace and then walk even more to get back to the *Floating Theatre.*

Leo would get up around three to unmoor the boat. I had to get back by then. I didn't know how far downstream I'd drifted in the rowboat. As I walked along the road—avoiding as best I could in the darkness the deep grooves made by wagon wheels and the rocks that seemed to jut up between them out of spite—I was aware of my own swaying walk, which put me in mind of my cot as it rocked gently on the tide. The baby could wake at any time and want more milk, but there wasn't any. My stomach grumbled, wondering at the many hours on my feet and not understanding that by rights it should be shut down for the night.

At last—it may have only been a few minutes but it felt like an hour—a low gray stone wall cropped up on the right side of the road with trees behind it pushing branches out over the top. I came to a stile, just as the poacher said, and then a donkey path. I turned my head again so I could listen with my good ear. The poacher was still walking behind me. A thin frosting of clouds drifted over the moon, but up the path I could make out a long pointed roof behind a line of spindly fruit trees. My thought was that I would go near enough to the house so that the poacher couldn't see me anymore, and then I would wait him out.

But as I got to the top of the donkey path, I saw that lights were blazing inside the house. Through the half-curtained windows I could see two people moving back and forth in the rooms—a man and a woman. As luck would have it, the woman glanced out the front window as she passed, and although I'm sure she could not have seen me in the darkness, she stopped, moved closer to the window, then pushed the curtain back farther to look.

I stepped backwards on the path and a twig snapped under my foot. A dog that I'd not seen on the porch stood up and started barking, and I felt the baby stir against me.

The woman went to the front door and opened it.

"Someone there?"

I held my breath and rocked the baby, one hand on his head and one on his small ball of a bottom, while the dog kept on barking. I couldn't see a rope but I saw that the dog was straining against something; I guessed he was tied to the porch.

A minute later a man came outside and hushed the dog. He must have been the doctor; he carried a doctor's heavy bag. Now the baby began making soft mews and I stepped back behind an apple tree. The woman went inside and came back with a hat, which the doctor put on his head. His horse was tied up to a post in the yard, already saddled.

He was about to ride down this path, I realized, so I went farther into the apple trees to conceal myself. The trunks were no higher than my waist and split into long fingers of skinny branches, none of which were thick enough to properly hide me. But it was still dark, and I tried to stand very still. The air felt moist and sticky under the trees, as if the sugary liquid of the budding apples rose and congealed there. I listened to my pulse pound in my ears.

The woman had come down off the porch and I heard her talking to the doctor as he mounted his horse. She did not have the poacher's southern accent; it was more like New England, I thought. I rocked the baby and put my little finger into his mouth to suck. The doctor nudged the horse into a slow walk and the woman watched him leave with her arms folded over her stomach. As he went by, I saw his straight back and the good seat he kept on his mount. The dog started barking again.

When I heard the horse break into a trot on the road I exhaled, not realizing I'd been holding my breath. But the woman was looking at the apple trees now, a little to the left of where I was standing.

"Is someone there?" she called out again. Her voice was throaty and confident, unafraid. Educated, I guessed, and definitely from New England, maybe Boston. I could imagine her reciting poetry in front of a roomful of schoolchildren; no one would dare fidget under that voice. As luck would have it, while she was still scanning the apple trees, the baby pulled his mouth away from my finger and started to cry, the same weak spurts as before, like a small wild creature coughing out something in the back of its throat.

She walked up to the porch and untied the dog. Then she stood there holding his lead. "Come on, now, out of my trees," she ordered. "What are you, hungry?"

I put my hand to a gnarly tree branch, which felt like something had been taking tiny bites out of it. The problem was I didn't know friend from foe.

"I hear your baby," the woman said.

She had a New England accent, it was true. And her husband was a doctor. I was suddenly very tired and I felt it in my temples, a heavy throb that spurred me into concession.

As I walked out of the trees I must have looked to her the way she looked to me: a dark shape with details slowly emerging as I got closer to the light of the house. The woman was not tall but she held herself very straight. When she turned to pick up the lamp inside the door, I saw that her hair was in a long braid down her back, messy from sleeping on it. Turning back, she held the lamp up to look at my face and then she looked at the makeshift sling with the baby.

"Are you here for the doctor?" she asked.

"No, ma'am," I said. "The baby is just crying because he's hungry."

"Well, then why don't you feed him?"

"He won't take the breast. Do you have any milk I could give him? I have a pap feeder."

A moment's silence. Then she said, "Just a minute."

She didn't ask me inside and she didn't tie up the dog. The dog and I watched each other warily. He was bigger than Oliver, with short brown fur and a deep, throaty bark—rather like his mistress—and looked as if he'd been bred for rat catching: jumpy and wiry and probably fast. I gave the baby my finger to suck but he had cottoned on to that trick. I got out his feeding bottle and warmed it in my hands.

After a minute the woman came back with a small glass jar of milk. But when she pulled away the side of the sling to look at the baby, she stared at his face. His eyes were open and wet and his little raspberry lips were stretched wide. For a moment she did nothing. Then with her index finger she gently pulled his blanket away from his chin to see more. After a moment she stepped back, still holding the milk.

I don't know why I let her look at the baby; I'd been careful with the poacher. But I was tired and I didn't think fast enough. And she had a northern accent. And her husband was a doctor. The woman looked at me and then she looked at her dog and then she looked at the baby again. She picked up the dog's lead and held it. Her face was shaped like a beautiful pale pear, and her cheekbones were as fine as ice.

"Get off my land," she said evenly. She did not look angry. She was too poised for that.

"I didn't want to come here," I told her.

"You get off."

"I haven't done anything wrong," I said, going down the porch steps sideways so as not to turn my back on the dog. Well, of course I had done something wrong, but I wasn't thinking about how I came to be carrying this baby, I was thinking how there was nothing wrong in asking a doctor's wife for milk. There was nothing wrong with that.

She watched me cross the yard while the baby cried and cried, her hand holding the dog's lead very loosely as if she was determining the best moment to let go. I kept looking back, half expecting each time to see the dog running after me, even after I passed the line of apple trees and could no longer make out the woman's shape or the dog's.

The baby cried his weak, young cries all along the road. Having nothing else, I gave him my pinkie finger again and again until at last, exhausted from crying, he fell asleep with it in his mouth.

The poacher, thank goodness, was nowhere in sight. Stands of scrub trees to my right hid my view of the river, but nevertheless I could hear it moan and stir like a conversation held behind a closed door. The moon gave up and let itself be completely hidden by the clouds, and the darkness seemed to get both darker and warmer as I walked along the high berm of the road. I was beyond tired; I was like something moved on a pulley, mindless, worked by levers. My head felt like a wooden puppet head. When at last I got to the *Floating*

Theatre, I saw that a lamp was lit in the auditorium, which meant Leo was awake, but he wasn't yet out on the deck, nor was Hugo. A dark carriage stood in the road just above the pier.

As I approached it, the driver climbed down. It was Donaldson. He said nothing, of course, as I handed the baby over to him along with the basket. The baby woke and began crying again, and I told Donaldson he was hungry but I had no more milk. Donaldson pulled a bottle from under the seat and filled the pap feeder. But before he fed the baby, he took from his pocket a cylindrical tube no wider than my thumb and shook out a drop of liquid onto his index finger, and then he put his finger in the baby's mouth. The glass tube had a brown paper wrapper that I recognized from apothecary shops: opium. I have learned since that this is a common practice for keeping slave babies quiet, but at the time, even in my exhaustion, I was astonished.

Donaldson looked at me pointedly: my part of this business was done. I knew I would not see the baby again—his little raspberry lips and his coughing cry. I hoped he would be safe, and I hoped that Donaldson had plenty of milk. As I walked toward the *Floating Theatre*, I could hear the faint squeak of the carriage wheels starting up and rolling away behind me down the road. I went straight to my room, thankful not to run into Hugo or Leo. It was not until I had pulled off my boots and was lying down on my cot, still wearing my dress, that it occurred to me that I had lied many times that night without once using my Greek. I had lied to the poacher and I had lied to the doctor's wife and I didn't even think about it. That, I guessed, was fear.

15

To hear Leo say it, boys in short pants caused all the evil taking place on this earth. They climbed up trees along the riverbank when they saw our boat coming and yelled and hollered and threw down apples in their excitement. They tried on "the Cap'n Hat," as they called it, and let it fall into the muddy dirt. They let their ponies loosen their bladders just off the stage plank, making pungent puddles where the ladies would walk. As day turned to night they became worse, trying to sneak into the show without paying or waylaying our customers afterwards with quack concoctions to remove freckles or moles or promised relief from rheumy eyes, which they hawked for a dime a dose. They wore their caps backwards and their faces were as muddy as their hands. They were lazy, mischievous, disrespectful, ignorant . . . Leo had countless insults that he hurled at them one by one. Sometimes they were cowed by his large, hulky frame and ran off, but not always. Once last year, I was told, in the middle of a performance, some rascally boys cut the boat's mooring lines and the boat drifted a half mile downstream. The audience was good-natured enough to walk the extra distance back home after the show, but Leo was furious.

Naturally he blamed boys now for the missing rowboat.

"Untied it, took it for a pleasure ride, left it to rot somewhere. My only wonder is why Oliver didn't bark."

He was talking to Hugo at the guardrail. I could hear them from my stateroom even with my door closed. We were still at the same landing as yesterday; Hugo didn't want to leave without the rowboat. Maybe Leo could hire a mule and go look for it? Hugo suggested. "Could be just a little ways downstream. Up on the bank or in the mud."

"Now I got to go do that, too, today," Leo complained.

"I know. But it's a good boat. Set me back some to get another."

"Those boys are bad boys. You shoulda never gave them no tickets."

"Oh, now, Leo," Hugo laughed. "We don't know which ones did it. You want me to never let any young boys into the show from now on?"

Leo grumbled something I didn't hear.

"I have a feeling we'll find it," Hugo went on pleasantly. "We'll get a mule to tow it back. I can beat my way down the river myself if you can't get to it."

No, Leo said, he would do it. Hot as it was today, he would do it.

In the dining room the actors seemed only mildly interested in the missing boat.

"Coulda come untied in the middle of the night," Pinky said. "Didja hear that wind?" He turned his attention to the pancakes and eggs that Cook was dishing out.

"A wind untying a boat?" Jemmy laughed, pouring molasses with a slow spiral motion over everything on his plate, even the eggs. "How about a ghost, eh? Or one of the willow trees on the bank? With its long, fingery branches?"

Pinky paid him no attention but began cutting up his pancakes with the side of his fork. "Now, May, listen. I was thinking, for Cecily's costume, I use that old nightgown. What if I rip the hem a little? Think that would be more dramatic?" Pinky and the others had begun consulting with me over every aspect of their costumes, and naturally I was happy to talk about that for as long as they wished. But today I was feeling tired and remorseful.

"You'll trip on it up on stage," I told him. "But a tear is not a bad idea. Maybe your sleeve."

"The sleeve—that's good, that's good. Thanks, May! Say," he said as I pushed my plate away and stood, "aren't you going to eat that?"

I felt terrible that Leo had to go out of his way to find the rowboat I'd lost, and I decided I should go with him to get it back. Besides, I was the only one who knew where to look for it. The problem was I didn't know how I was going to tell him where it was without giving myself away. In town, Leo and I were directed to the coffin maker, who sometimes hired his mule out if there was nobody at the moment who needed burying. We were in luck: the coffin maker was idle and he let us use his mule—a squat gray beast with long eye-lashes—for a dime.

The mule was used to pulling a wagon with a nailed coffin to the graveyard while the coffin maker led him by a short rope and the family walked behind. With Leo and me, the mule kept stopping and putting his head down, confused about the turn of events. This wasn't the way to the graveyard and he knew it.

We were walking down a little hog path that ran alongside the river, which the coffin maker showed us. If I had known about this path last night, I thought, what a lot of trouble I might have avoided. I looked at my father's watch. I knew I'd walked for about thirty min-utes last night, which was all I had to go by. It was still morning but the air was heating up and moistening into a hot, sticky day.

"We got ourselves an unhandsome fix here," Leo grumbled. He kept taking off his hat to wipe his head with his handkerchief.

An acrid scent like dying flowers in a vase wafted in from the water, and I turned my nose from it. My shoulders and neck still hurt from last night, and even in the bright sun I found myself yawning. The mule stopped every few yards to try to eat the white buttonweed flowers along the path until Leo smacked him on the rear with the palm of his hand. The path dipped closer to the river, and we came to a shanty boat tied to a cottonwood tree with clothes and sheets hanging off the rail to dry. A group of skinny children were wading in the water around the boat, and Leo scowled at the boys. A couple of them were wearing shirts with nothing but holes cut out of the material for their arms.

"Boys are trouble," I said carefully to Leo as we passed. "But girls aren't so bad."

"Hunh." The mule stopped and Leo slapped him going again.

"And babies . . ." What were babies? I wondered. "Cute, aren't they?"

"Some people like 'em, I guess."

"Of course, slave babies . . . well, that's just wrong, don't you think?" I had two doughnuts wrapped in a handkerchief in my pocket that I'd taken from the dining room before I left, and now I took them out and gave Leo one. He took a large bite and chewed it.

"Little slave babies?" I prompted, hoping to get a response.

He pushed the rest of the doughnut into his mouth, chewed it a couple of times before he swallowed, and then wiped his hands down his trousers.

"Ain't gonna cross this river with you," he said. "Not at night nor in the morning, neither."

I stopped and looked at him but he tugged on the mule's halter and kept walking. I said, "How did you know?"

"Oh, Lord, Miss May, I'm not both sides of a fool. Now, come on and tell me where my boat got left."

"Does Hugo know?"

"Not from me."

"But does he?"

Leo shrugged. "I guess not."

"I need help, Leo. They're giving me babies. I can't row a boat with a baby in my lap."

"I don't set foot on that side of the river, you know that."

I'd been thinking about this. "What if you stayed in the water? I'll just wade in by myself, fetch the baby in my arms, and wade back to the boat to meet you."

But even as I was still speaking he was shaking his head: *No, no, no.* My heart sank. I needed help, last night taught me that if nothing else, and I knew I could trust Leo. But he wouldn't do it.

"Best I'll do is turn a blind eye when I see someone fussing with my fishing boat in the middle of the night," he told me. "And I'll go to fetch it back on a hot morning, taking along with me an ornery mule. That's as far as I aim to go."

He slapped the mule's backside again.

"This heat gonna kill me," he said to the mule, "and I guess you'd think that was fine, wouldn't you, so you could pull my poor old body along behind you just as you like. Now, where is my boat?" This last was to me.

I pulled out my father's watch. "We're just about there," I told him.

My next idea was Thaddeus. I hadn't heard Mr. Niffen speak enough to know his opinion on slavery or anything else, and although I'd had more conversations with Pinky and Jemmy, they mostly spoke about acting and what they thought of Cook's food and the fluctuating price of cigars.

After Leo and I returned with the rowboat, Hugo moved the *Floating Theatre* across the river to a little village on the Kentucky side, and that night we played to a scant audience there. Normally we would never stop at such a small landing, but it was the best we could do. After counting up the ticket sales, I calculated that we had lost a good three dollars by my folly.

The next morning we continued our way downriver as usual and landed in Fairview, Indiana, a sizable town with a gristmill, a tanyard, and two warehouses facing the river. Here we could expect a larger crowd, Hugo told us at breakfast, "so no fussing about"—a reference, I supposed, to Jemmy and Sam's lackluster performance the night before.

"Hard to make a crowd of twelve laugh," Jemmy said under his breath.

"Playing to an empty room," Pinky said.

Sam, as usual, contributed his one syllable: "Yup."

Thaddeus didn't come in for breakfast that morning. I found him in his stateroom holding a dose of castor oil and turpentine that he told me he'd gotten from Cook. His hands looked yellow and his face looked yellower.

"Bad clam last night," he said. "Have to fix up the insides well enough to stand up tonight."

He was sitting on the edge of his cot with a bucket between his feet. His shoes were off, and his straw hat was on the antler of a stuffed elk head he'd found in a little curiosity shop somewhere in Ohio and paid good money for. The head was so old that the eyes had been replaced with yellow marbles, which gave the poor creature the look of a child's toy, and the fur on one side of the neck had been so rubbed down that it looked like brown cloth. The elk faced the river, as though contemplating how to cross it without body or legs, and if you stood in the right place it seemed to be staring right at you.

I always turned my back to it, and I did so now.

"Can I get you anything?" I asked. "A piece of bread or some crackers?"

Thaddeus groaned. Even sick and in stocking feet he dressed in his usual foppish style, with a bright blue cravat tied around his neck.

"I'll fetch you some lemon water and soda," I said. "That will help your stomach better than castor oil."

He groaned again and put his hands up over his ears to hold his head. He was in no condition to agree to anything; I could see that. I helped him stretch out on his cot, his face toward the bucket on the floor, and I remembered how lazy he was. After we left Cincinnati I never again saw him help move the boat in the morning, probably because he slept later than anyone else, and while he slept he wore cold cream on his face like a woman; I'd discovered this once when I called on him before he'd risen, wanting him to try on the vest I'd finished sewing. Now, seeing him stretched out in bed, I realized how unlikely it was that I could convince him to get up in the middle of the night to do any physical labor, like rowing a boat.

"This river life is too rough-and-tumble," Thaddeus said, looking up at me with watery eyes. "Oh, May. What I really need is to find a wealthy benefactress like your cousin did. Or a young widow in the country. Remember that idea? And my pair of hounds. Yes, I'd like that."

That's when I got the idea of money. Thaddeus always spent more than he had, and he often complained about it. He dressed too well for his income and he bought ridiculous items like the elk head on whim.

After I brought him the soda and lemon water I went back to my stateroom and wrote the following letter:

Dear Mrs. Howard,
I hope you are well. I need more money. Will you send some, please?
Ten dollars will be fine.

Yours very truly,
May Bedloe

I didn't want to say too much. She would know what it was for, I reasoned. After reading it over and feeling satisfied, I sealed it and put it in my pocket to post.

A short while later Hugo walked with me into town. Although it was not yet midday, the sky looked baked and still, and it was already too hot for my shawl, which I folded into a rectangle and carried under my arm like a book. Hugo was in a good mood, whistling as we walked. He spoke continuously about *The Midnight Hour*, which was very nearly ready.

"We want a packed house for the premiere. After that, we'll have word of mouth to keep us going. No one does a full play on the river. No one. We'll be the first."

It was a refrain he kept coming back to—how we'd be the first boat to do a three-act play—and I could tell this pleased him almost more than anything else about the endeavor. He smelled, this morning, like cake batter; he'd been helping Cook in the kitchen while I spoke to Thaddeus. It was a comforting smell. We passed two men engaged in nailing clapboards over the log frame of a house, and just beyond them stood a grand oak tree that shot straight up without a single branch for fifty or sixty feet.

The oak was so large, we could post three notices around its trunk. While we were engaged in this, two passing gentlemen stopped to tell us about a family of raccoons that lived in its hollow. They were known affectionately as the Shakentales, and were pets or mascots of the town.

"Mrs. Shakentale were out late last night lookin' for berries," the taller man informed us, pronouncing "late" like "light." Although we were in Indiana, he and his friend both spoke with marked Kentucky accents. He wore a low straw hat, and the shape of its crown mirrored the long shape of his nose.

"Our own Dr. Early leaves a bowl of corn mush every night by his back door, but I guess that hadn't been enough for her lately. We're thinkin' maybe a new litter is on its way."

He laughed and his face re-drew itself into wrinkles while his companion nodded with all solemnity.

"Don't forget the show tonight," Hugo called out as the two men walked away. That was when I saw Liddy walking down the sidewalk with a small lilac parasol I'd not seen before and holding the arm of a very upright man who bent his head to hear what she was saying.

Hugo saw them, too. "That'll be Liddy's correspondent, I'll wager," he said, and he was right. When Liddy noticed us, she came over and introduced the man as Dr. Martin Early—the same man who fed the raccoons mush every night.

"Honored," Dr. Early said, shaking hands with Hugo. He spoke without a trace of the local accent and was a handsome man, with a fine full head of chestnut hair and long sideburns. I noticed his ears were very large but he kept his hair long, partially covering them.

"Caught your show when you were docked in Cincinnati last month," he told Hugo. "Fine show, decidedly fine; I was sorry indeed when it ended. Afterwards I told Miss Liddy here that I could have sat there entertained for three more hours at least."

He wore a striped tie and a crisp white vest with a watch chain showing. His boots were made of the best leather, and his hat was so white that it seemed to emit its own light.

"Cast has changed since then, I'm told," Dr. Early went on. "I was sorry to hear about your sister."

Hugo bowed his head, acknowledging the loss. I looked at the black handkerchief he still wore in his jacket pocket. He had but one that I knew of, and he washed it out every night and folded it into a triangle for his pocket again every morning.

There was a short silence. Then I asked the doctor how he kept his hat so white.

Liddy laughed and reached over to squeeze my forearm affectionately.

"This is my friend May Bedloe. I've told you about her: our very own costume designer. She is very curious about anything to do with clothing."

"Ah, tricks of the trade. Well, I'll tell you: repeated sulfuring. That's what does it."

His dark eyes crinkled when he spoke, and whenever he looked at Liddy, her cheeks flushed pink with pleasure. He began to make himself agreeable to me, asking about the costumes and expressing his interest in seeing them that night.

"I'm bringing the mayor and his wife," he told us. "The mayor's wife in particular is very fond of the theater, and she drags the poor man to Cincinnati as often as the new moon. I say 'poor man' only because he gets very sick on the water, you know, although they've recently purchased a new carriage and the roads this time of year are not as muddy as their reputation. Of course, the mayor is happiest when the theater comes to him, like today. Will you stop at my house for tea? It's only a step."

Liddy looked very happy when Hugo said he'd be delighted. I thought about my letter to Mrs. Howard in my dress pocket, but it could wait. I was curious to see the sort of house this man kept. He seemed unusually cosmopolitan and spoke like a politician I'd once heard in Philadelphia, with a well-pitched voice that seemed to listen to itself and give out information at the same time. He dressed as though he lived in Philadelphia, too, with his white vest and his white hat. He had a city man's flare for finery without ostentation. And yet the town he lived in was barely settled. I wondered why he chose to live here.

We put the town square behind us and crossed over a stream with a narrow bridge, barely wide enough for a cart. The doctor's house was made of logs, very neat and well made, with blue curtains in the windows, and it stood by itself on a little rise above a cleared field. Inside, Dr. Early took Liddy's parasol and my shawl and put them on a high-backed chair against the wall. The main room was large but somewhat dim, having only two windows in front and one in back. It served as his office, his kitchen, and his study, Dr. Early explained. He had built the cabin himself, though he admitted having help with the roof, and he'd had the floorboards shipped in from Cincinnati. The room was crowded with tables full of specimens—preserved reptiles and insects under glass—as well as an array of lancets and a nested stack of bleeding bowls. Some tools hung by nails on the wall, both for healing and for cooking. A closed door led to his bedroom, I guessed, and that was the extent of his home.

We sat on cane chairs and watched as he built up the fire and boiled water for tea. While we were waiting, he set out a large white bowl of dewberries sprinkled with sugar and urged us to eat, all the while talking about his doctoring practice, new cures he was try-ing with French brandy and angelica root. He made me think of a friendly dog that fancies himself a scholar.

Hugo seemed to think it an interesting place, for he got up from his chair while the doctor bustled about and began going from table to table, looking a long time at every specimen with his hands clasped behind his back.

"It's a great treat to meet with another learned man," he said. "It's rare that I have the pleasure." I found myself feeling a little jealous at that. "Another learned man"! I had gone to high school for a year, and I knew for a fact that Hugo had only gone up to the eighth grade before he left to work at his father's theater.

When the tea was brewed, Dr. Early cleared off a jumble of jars and capped bottles from a lacquered tray table, then he set down the tea things and the last of a pound cake, which he had made himself the night before.

"Ate most of it for breakfast, I'm afraid," he told us.

"Delicious," Hugo said, taking a bite. He winked at Liddy when the doctor's back was turned. "A man of varied talents."

"I don't need much sleep," Dr. Early said, wiping four teacups with a cloth and then filling them up. The cups were very pretty, red and green with a clover and honeysuckle pattern. "Five hours at most. And I need something to occupy myself with out here all alone."

He looked at Liddy and for some reason she blushed. "Besides your pets," she reminded him. "The Shakentales."

I looked around as if I might see them. Instead my eye caught the red marble eye of a small stuffed muskrat standing upright by the back door. Was the doctor a taxidermist as well? I found I didn't like him as much as the others seemed to, though I didn't know why, exactly. Something about his easy manner, deliberately not boasting, only underscored how accomplished he was. This was on purpose, I felt.

"So you're traveling on the alligator's eye, are you?" he said. "How are you finding it?"

"What's the alligator's eye?" Liddy asked.

"Why that's what they call the Ohio around here. The state of Kentucky is shaped like an alligator's head, don't you know, and they say that boats along this part of the Ohio River are going down the alligator's eye."

"We're in Indiana," I pointed out. "Not Kentucky."

Dr. Early laughed. "Only marginally," he said.

Hugo smiled at me. "May likes to be precise."

"A very good trait. I only meant that there's not so much difference as you might think. I come from Louisville originally and studied medicine at Jefferson College in Philadelphia. Those two cities, though hundreds of miles apart, were not so unalike, I found. New York, however, is a different beast altogether. Well, all great cities. New York, Vienna, London."

"I spent a great deal of my life in London myself," Hugo told him.

"Only three years," I said.

Hugo frowned slightly. "You mean when I managed the Covent Garden Theatre. That is true. But"—turning back to Dr. Early—"I went back and forth between London and the provinces with my parents before that. My parents were from London."

"I see what you mean about being precise. It's good to keep us on our toes," Dr. Early said to me with a wink.

I resolved to say nothing more. I was beginning to feel grumpy and wished I hadn't come. I had a letter to post and I still wanted to give out a pair of free tickets to the grocer. The tea was rich and fresh-tasting, and the dewberries were just exactly, perfectly ripe. I don't know why I was feeling peevish. Perhaps it was the closed heat of the room. As if he could read my thoughts, Dr. Early stood up and opened the back door, then crossed the room to open the front door.

"Main thing I thought about when designing this cabin was that there'd be two ways of getting out in case of fire."

"Very smart, very smart," Hugo said.

"But I wish I'd laid in more windows." Dr. Early smiled at me showing sharp, white, even teeth. "It gets a mite warm, don't you think, Miss May?"

An accommodating man, but I did not like him.

It was Liddy who spied the piano against the far wall wedged between two low tables, one serving as a bookcase and the other with stacks of plates and teacups and saucers, all of them with the same clover and honeysuckle pattern.

"Why don't you sing us something?" Dr. Early asked when Liddy exclaimed over the beauty of the instrument.

Liddy blushed again. "Well, if May would accompany me . . ."

The piano was indeed a beautiful upright, constructed of caramel-colored wood with round globes and leafy vines carved into the legs. However, I guessed that way out here with no musician to care for it, it must be hopelessly out of tune. Again, as though reading my mind, Dr. Early said, "I tune the contraption myself. Hope it's not terribly off."

For some reason I did hope it was terribly off, but when I tried a few notes with my index finger they sounded just fine. Was there nothing this man could not do? I thumbed through a stack of music on the piano lid. And here I can say that, although I was not aware that I was looking for anything in particular, at this moment I found it. Intermixed with the musical scores were printed broadsides, and as I read the first one a warm flood of uneasy recognition came over me, followed by disgust.

FIFTY DOLLARS REWARD! Ranaway on the 27th of May, my Black Woman named Emily. Seventeen years of age, well grown, black color, has a whining voice. She took with her one dark calico and one blue and white dress; a red corded gingham bonnet; a white striped shawl and slippers. I will pay the above reward if taken near the Ohio River on the Kentucky side, or SEVENTY-FIVE DOLLARS if taken in the North and delivered to me.

Certain words had been circled: "seventeen years," "gingham bonnet," "seventy-five dollars."

Dr. Early was a slave hunter. This must be where he got his money for his specimens and china teacups, certainly not from his angelica root remedies or by bleeding a shopkeeper or two. I took a long breath and an acrid odor filled my nose, something false and unnatural, perhaps from all of his jars and bottles. It could be that the odor had been in the room the whole time but I was only just noticing it. I looked out the small back window to the scrubby woods beyond Dr. Early's cleared field. He probably would have his own path down to the Ohio River. He would go down there late at night to watch, and he would stay until morning. He already admitted that he didn't need much sleep. Maybe he had a special hidden place, like a deer stand, where he watched for anyone crossing over from Kentucky.

"Look at this," I said, handing the broadside to Liddy.

Liddy's fingers around the sheet of paper seemed as small as a child's, and she took a long time reading it. She did not look up but a faint blush of color rose in her neck. Dr. Early came over to see what she had. She took the next broadside from my hands and gave the first one to Hugo. She did not meet my eye, nor anyone else's.

100 DOLLARS REWARD

For my negro fellow STEPHEN who RANAWAY on the 17th September last. He is between twenty-five and thirty years of age, is about six feet high, copper-colored, with a high forehead. He can read but I do not think he can write. Has some use of tools, and was purchased as a rough carpenter. The above reward will be paid for said boy if apprehended out of the State, and eighty dollars if caught within the State and confined to jail so I that I can get him. I will also pay for the capture of any white thief who offered assistance to him, and will mete out my own justice to that unhappy rogue.

I passed along a few other broadsides, and after reading three or four Liddy looked up at the doctor as though she were trying to see him more clearly, or perhaps she just wanted to see him the way she had seen him ten minutes before.

"Well," Hugo said in a broad English accent. "I mean to say. Of course, I can't opine . . ."

"Yes, yes, quite right, it's a local issue," the doctor said. He was still smiling, but there was a sharp look in his eyes. "Something your lot worked out a long time ago"—I guessed by "your lot" he meant the English—"and I wish we had, too. It's tiresome really. But it's the law, and what can you do? Can't break the law, you know." He turned to Liddy. "Now, my dear, I feel for these poor souls just as much as you do, which is why I originally offered my services."

He began to speak at length about the difference between conditions in the North and in the South and how slavery was deplorable but that the law was the law. Moreover, in his case he was raising money for the sole purpose of helping anyone who was ill, rich or poor. And he was very good to Negroes, he went on: some white men captured them in a most humiliating and painful way, but he himself never carried a whip, and it was better by far that he found them and not someone else . . .

He kept talking and talking and I wanted to stop my ears up. I was watching Hugo as intently as Dr. Early was watching Liddy, trying to gauge his reaction, but, like Liddy, Hugo was wearing almost no expression. I thought, not for the first time, how handy it was to be an actor and have all your physical expressions under control. I badly wanted to sit down, and when I did I felt the letter to Mrs. Howard bend awkwardly in my dress pocket. I'd forgotten about that. I took it out and held it, address side down, on my knee.

"I must mail this," I said when at last Dr. Early paused. "I have to be going."

I put the broadsides back on the piano lid, all except the one about the man Stephen, which I'd folded up and put in my pocket when no one was looking. I wanted to read the bit about the white thief again. Arrest and conviction—would Dr. Early do that to me if he caught me in the rowboat? Anxiety pricked my chest. Of course he would. There was a hundred dollars in it.

Outside, Liddy walked a little ahead of Hugo and me. We didn't say a word as we made our way across Dr. Early's field, nor as we walked over the wooden bridge and into town. As we approached the Shakentales' tree, I saw that it was deserted. No one stood in the square, and all the window shutters in all the shops had been closed up against the sun.

"Why did you show me those notices?" Liddy asked me suddenly, angrily, stepping around the tree.

I was surprised. Was she angry at me? "I don't know. I thought you would want to see them."

"I *don't*! I *didn't*! It's nothing to do with you or with me."

I wasn't sure if she really thought this was true or if she was trying to work her way toward believing it. Hugo glanced at her and then at me.

"Well, now, it's a difficult issue," he began carefully.

"Martin is not breaking the law," Liddy interrupted. Her face was tight with anger.

"You think what he's doing is honorable?" I asked.

"You heard what he said. If he doesn't do it, someone else will—and someone with less compassion."

We parted at the post office, and I watched Hugo and Liddy walk back to the boat without me. All at once I felt worn down by Mrs. Howard and everything associated with her. Liddy was my friend. I didn't know what I was doing. I didn't know why I was doing it. First I learned how to lie, and now here I was, breaking the law. I didn't know what to think about any of it, but I posted the letter to Mrs. Howard just the same and hoped that she would forward me some money before she had me go out in the rowboat again.

That night I dreamed I was on the *Floating Theatre* with Giulia. It was sinking, but we stood in the auditorium as though rooted to the floor. I knew I had to get her off the boat but I could not seem to leave the room. As I watched the wall descend and felt the floorboards slant beneath my feet, I reasoned to myself that the water would soon come in through the window and we could swim out that way.

For the next few days Liddy avoided me. Twice she got up and left the dining room just as I came in, one time with the chop on her plate only half eaten, and I realized that she was coming in early for her meals. There was no swimming in the mornings, and poor Celia sat with Leo and me on the riverbank looking dolefully out at the water. Leo offered to teach her how to reel in a fish but she wrinkled her nose, and so I gave her a piece of rough linen, a large needle, and some embroidery thread to amuse herself with.

Mrs. Niffen noticed our rift and made the best of the situation, as usual. Whenever I saw her she made sure to mention Liddy's name and if possible to ask if I had seen her. To this I could only say no. After the third or fourth time she said slyly, "Well, you haven't seen Liddy at all lately, have you! I'm beginning to wonder if you two have had a quarrel." Of course I could tell by her manner that she knew all about it.

Alpha, beta, gamma. "No," I told her.

She stretched her lips into the kind of smile that a child would draw, two broad lines connected at the edges, like a boat. For a moment she seemed all pointed nose and teeth, and except for her creamy-white hair she looked like a fox. "Thank heaven. You two are so close."

My heart seemed to plunge a little lower in my chest when I heard that, since her manner clearly conveyed that she meant just the opposite. I hadn't had many friends in my life, but I thought of Liddy as one of them. And, not having many friends, I also did not know the rules for arguing and making peace, if such rules existed. I wished they did.

The next day, instead of sitting outside next to Leo, I took my sewing up to the dining room, where it was cooler, and sat near a window that overlooked the bank and the little town of—what was its name? Although I had been there only that morning with my posters and my tickets, I couldn't remember it. We had been to so many towns in such a short span of time that they were beginning to all seem alike with their flat-fronted warehouses and boatyards, their horse carts waiting on the dusty road near the pier. Even the difference between north and south felt negligible. The fact that some people had been thrown down on one side of the river or on the other seemed arbitrary, and they could cross to the other side with no change of purpose. They might condone slavery or they might not, but for the most part, I was finding, they would live with the matter. Only horrid people like Mrs. Howard were bullies enough to try to effect any change. And she was a bully, no mistaking that. Was every good change made in the world the result of successful bullying? I wondered. It certainly seemed that everything bad happened that way.

I finished the last spider web design on Liddy's costume and spread the bodice out with my fingers on the clean tabletop to look at it, thinking that in a moment I would go down to iron it, although I didn't particularly want to, since it was so hot. Just then Hugo poked his head into the dining room door, saw me, and walked in. He looked into the galley asking, "What's soup today?" and I heard Cook tell him corn fritters and hash.

"Lovely," Hugo said. Then he came over to me. "Well, well," he said, looking down at the decorated costume splayed on the tabletop. "All finished, is it?"

He leaned over to look more closely at the small embroidered designs. "I like how these turned out. You were right to leave the blue dot out of them." I was surprised he remembered that suggestion. He stepped back and rubbed his hands together, and I noticed they were gray and dusty: he'd probably just come from filling the firewood bins in each of the staterooms. That meant he'd been to my room, and I suddenly wondered where I'd left Mrs. Howard's letter, which a little boy had delivered this morning with ten dollars enclosed. Money to pay Thaddeus to help me cross the river. I reminded myself I had to be careful now about what I left about.

"Have you seen Liddy?" Hugo asked me.

"Why does everyone keep asking me that?" I said irritably.

"Oh, now, May, don't take offense. It's hard when we think well of a person, a man like that, educated, a doctor, only to find . . . and especially someone, in Liddy's case, well, her beau. We have to make some concessions. You two are friends."

"*She's* the one not speaking to *me*," I pointed out.

"That won't last," Hugo told me, but how could he know? I thought how easy it would be to iron into Liddy's costume a small prick of a feather shaft, as I used to with Comfort's costumes when she vexed me. But I didn't want to do that. I touched her costume, flattening the collar with my fingertips. My mother used to say, "My brain is in my fingers," because she touched what she was sewing so often.

But she had a sharp mind at all times, and a clear sense of right and wrong. I remember how horrified she was when a man came to town, claiming to be a land agent, to sell lots in Missouri that weren't his to sell. No one bought any, thank goodness, but a sheriff rode in looking for him the day after he left, and that's how we found out.

"Why would someone set himself against another person like that?" my mother asked my father. "A stranger, someone's who's done him no harm?"

"It's the money," my father replied. "Quick money."

"Well, he'll soon be in jail for it," my mother said, though we never found out if her prediction came true.

Quick money—that's what Dr. Early wanted, too. Did the fact that he could do so and stay within the law make it right? The question made my head hurt.

"Don't you think it's wrong, too," I asked Hugo, "what Dr. Early is doing?"

"Deplorable." He unclasped his hands. "It's deplorable. But what can I do? And besides that, I have a business to run."

My irritation mushroomed again, and I turned my good ear away from him. "That's exactly what everyone says." I gathered up the costume, determined now to go downstairs to iron it no matter how hot the day was.

16

I think there were a few things that excited Thaddeus about the whole enterprise right from the start. One was the furtiveness associated with it, and the thrill of having a secret. Also the idea of acting out a role in real life seemed to appeal to him, like Hugo with his blanket coat and boatman language. Both Hugo and Thaddeus—maybe all actors—warmed to an activity that might combine theater and real life, if that was possible. They could not resist playing a role. I don't think Thaddeus ever much considered the plight of the babies.

"When do you go out again?" he asked in a low voice, leaning forward on the rail. We were on the top deck, so that I could see anyone underneath us. There was still mist on the river but the early-morning chill was wearing off. Leo had finished tying us up at the new landing only about an hour ago, and most of the company was still at breakfast. I caught Thaddeus as he was coming out of his stateroom.

We stood together at the rail looking out toward the steady stream of flatboats and steamboats passing by. Thaddeus held one of Mrs. Howard's coins in his hand, rubbing it every so often with his thumb.

"I don't know," I said. "I don't find out until the last moment."

"How *do* you find out?"

"The last time a woman stayed back after our show. She told me."

"Someone in the audience?"

"I suppose they could find some other way next time."

"You'd think they'd give you more warning than a couple of hours," Thaddeus said, looking out at a snag boat engaged in clearing dead-wood from the river. A white captain with a blue government cap directed a team of Negroes, some of whom were using long hooks to direct the sodden river logs, while others pulled the logs up onto the boat. The captain had his hands clasped behind his back, while the darker men did the heavy work. I wondered if I was beginning to see everything in black and white.

"They're just-born babies," I told Thaddeus. "There's little warning for something like that."

Thaddeus took his foot off the bottom rail. His blond curls looked almost white in the sun, and there were fine wrinkles around his eyes. I had a sudden vision of him as an old man.

"What happens if we're caught?"

I thought of the broadside concerning the abolitionist thief. "Jail, or worse. A fine, certainly."

"I've never been in jail," Thaddeus told me. But he said this as if it was an exciting thought rather than a fearful one. The snag boat was now chugging around the bend up ahead. The river looked marginally cleaner, but not much.

"There's a compass in the green room," Thaddeus mused. "A prop, but it could be useful. If it still works."

Just then Liddy came out of the dining room, saw me, hesitated, and then walked up the guard toward us. I saw her push her chest out as she approached, as if she were entering a room. Thaddeus carefully pushed the coin he was holding into his trouser pocket.

"I want you to know, May," Liddy began in a tight voice, "that I've broken off my friendship with Dr. Early. So you don't have to worry about that anymore."

"You broke it off?" She was wearing her oldest dress, and her hair was unbrushed. I was relieved she was talking to me again, but she did not look well. "Because of the slave hunting?"

"Yes, because of that. I can't be with someone who chases down men and women."

"And children," I said without thinking.

"Don't you lecture me!" she snapped, turning her head.

"I didn't mean . . . no, I know . . . Liddy—" I broke off. It was important that I say the right thing, but I didn't know what the right thing was. I tried to think of what I'd heard other people say at an argument's close, if that was what this was; I hoped it was. "I was a fool," I've heard Comfort say, but that didn't seem relevant, and in any case I don't think she ever meant it. *I was wrong. I misunderstood. I hope you'll forgive me.*

I just wanted Liddy's friendship again. "I'm sorry," I said, but that wasn't right, either.

"Why are *you* sorry?"

"I wish I had never found those broadsides." I meant this with all my heart.

Her face relaxed a degree. "I know. Oh, May! Well, it all comes to the same thing. I would have found out, I suppose. I mean, of course I would have."

I thought about what Hugo said. "A man like that, and your beau . . . It was just surprising."

Liddy agreed. Her pretty, downward mouth drooped even more. She was wholesome and honest and open—that was her character, why it was easy for her to play the ingénue. I felt she was not a girl who should wrestle with anything difficult. No one likes the story of the ingénue breaking.

"Are we friends again?" I watched her face anxiously.

She started to give me her hand and then stopped. "I know you don't like shaking hands. But let's pretend we just did."

Thaddeus was watching us with his thumbs hooked into his trouser pockets and an amused expression on his face, as though we were on a stage, part of a play put on for his entertainment.

"I can imagine that Pinky writes a beautiful letter," I suggested to Liddy, and she blushed.

"Ha-ha-ha!" Thaddeus laughed callously. "And now onto the next."

"So speaks the roué," Liddy shot back, and I thought that was a good sign. She wasn't broken; she was merely growing up. Who here on earth is able to avoid trouble? I reminded myself. Comfort clung to her ingénue roles long past the time they suited her, and it did not do her any good—rather, the opposite. There was a lesson in there somewhere for me, I sensed, but at the time I could not quite grasp it.

Two nights later I received my next message. This time I was taking money at the ticket window, and wrapped inside a one-dollar bill was a note:

Tonight. Signal at quarter past midnight.

I stared at it for a moment, not understanding the wording. Was I supposed to send a signal, or receive one? I looked up, but whoever had given it to me—a man; I couldn't remember more than that— had already left without receiving his change. When Celia came to relieve me at the ticket window, I was so flustered that I began to walk off with the stack of tickets still in my hand. But once I sat down at the piano, my hands did the work they were used to, and the show went off remarkably well. In fact, the audience clapped and stomped so much at the end that Liddy and Thaddeus came out to sing an impromptu song:

When love gets you fast in her clutches,
And you sigh for your sweetheart away,

Old Time cannot move without crutches,
Alack! how he hobbles, well-a-day!

It was an old ballad, and one that I never liked. How could time be on crutches? Time was time. But the audience loved it. While he sang, Thaddeus looked down at Liddy as though she embodied all the joy he knew of in the world, and she looked up at him in the same spirit. I marveled at how they could pretend so convincingly. The song was very slow, and I tried to pick up the pace to move them along to the end. Hugo was standing in the wings on the other side, and he frowned and thrust out his chin at me at me as if to say, *What are you doing there? Don't run up the beat!* But I wanted the show to be over.

I let Thaddeus know about the note when he came to give me his costume, which I pressed for him every night. He brightened up so much that I worried someone would ask him what good news he'd had that day. Pinky in fact did say something to that effect when he came in a minute later with his own costume in hand.

"What is it, old chum? You see one of your sweethearts in the audience?"

"There's always a sweetheart in the audience," Thaddeus replied. "Come and have a drink with me: I bought a pint of Jamaican rum off an Irishman today. Said he always travels with a couple of cases to pay for his meals."

"Smart man," Pinky said. "Rum's better than currency to a dime."

I hoped Thaddeus would not drink too much or stay with Pinky too long. But when I went to his stateroom a little before eleven, he was sitting on his cot looking perfectly sober and waiting for me. He wore a cape and a dark hat somewhat flattened on the crown, and he held his boots in one hand. In his other hand he was holding the compass from the green room. His face was shining with a child's excitement.

"I've been wondering," he said in a low voice as we went down the stage plank. "Is this the real reason you wanted a job on this boat? May Bedloe, Secret Abolitionist?"

"Hush," I said.

Since we were not docked at a pier this time but just tied up to a bunch of trees, the rowboat was pushed up on the bank. It was not tethered as securely as it had been before, and I found the knot easy to loosen. But the real surprise came when we were in the water and I found a paper bag underneath the forward thwart with an apple and a ham sandwich inside. I smiled, pleased with the gesture. *Leo,* I thought, but how did he know I was going out tonight?

Thaddeus threw his elbows out from underneath his dark cape and began rowing backwards. The sound of cicadas faded as we left the shore, and water hit the rowboat softly in regular intervals. I had a small brown vial of morphine in my pocket that I'd purchased several days before, in case I needed it for the baby. When we were far enough from the bank I lit the lantern I was holding in my lap. My stomach was a tight ball, the same as my heart, but the river seemed empty except for us. Still, I couldn't help but think of Dr. Early, and others like him, watching for an opportunity to make quick money. No one returned my signal.

After a minute Thaddeus said, "I'll row us to the bank. We can wait there."

"We're supposed to wait here until we get a signal."

"I don't want to keep rowing just to hold our position."

He consulted the compass, tapping the glass case to get the needle moving, and then began rowing south again. As we approached the Kentucky bank he began testing the depth of the water with one oar, and when he hit bottom he said, "Got it."

He pulled in the oars and then prepared the two jugs that Leo used as anchors: filling them with river water, stoppering them up, and then dropping them by their lines over the side. As we rocked a little on these moorings, Thaddeus took from his inside pocket a jar of beer, untwisted the lid, and offered it to me. I took a long sip and handed it back, then I tore the sandwich in two to share with him.

Taking a bite, he said, "Now tell me truly, May. Is this the reason you were so eager to get a job with Captain Hugo? So you could float up and down the river ferrying slaves?"

"Certainly not," I said. "I was blackmailed."

"Blackmailed!" Thaddeus laughed and then whistled. "Why, May, you and I are more alike than I thought."

"Why? Are you being blackmailed?"

"No, no. I just did not take you for a woman of principle, and indeed you are not."

"I have principles," I told him.

"To be sure, to be sure." He took another sip of beer.

"I don't lie," I reminded him.

"That's not a principle, that's a condition. Would you have thought of doing it yourself? That's my question."

I didn't have an answer. The weak moonlight glittered unevenly over the water like a shroud. Still there was no signal, and no sound except night sounds. The last time everything had happened very fast. After a while Thaddeus took up a line and began practicing knots.

"It's been a long time since I've rowed a boat at night," he said.

That reminded me of something. "Thaddeus, tell me, was your father really a boatbuilder?" I asked him.

He laughed. "No. Why?"

I reminded him about how he had helped Hugo with the boat when we first came on board. "You said your father was a boatbuilder. I've also heard you say your father was a playwright."

"My father has been many things in my telling, but in fact he was only a farmer," Thaddeus said. "Oats mostly. He fished a little, too, and sometimes I went out with him on the Chesapeake. Lord, did I hate it. By the time I was ten I'd set my sights on the finer arts."

I could perfectly picture him sitting behind a barn with paper and a stub of a pencil. "Writing poems, no doubt," I said.

Thaddeus shrugged. "Turns out I'm better at speaking another man's lines than producing my own. My father was quick enough to tell me I would never succeed as a poet. Course, he didn't like the theater profession any better. You know, I think I enjoyed telling him I wanted to be an actor. He couldn't be more disappointed in me, he said. To which I said, 'Let me see if I can't help you with that.'"

"You wouldn't speak to your father like that."

"Oh, yes! If you saw us, you wouldn't believe we were related. He had the longest nose you ever saw. When my mother died, my sisters raised me—four of them, and they doted on me, but he didn't. A constant disappointment, he said about me."

But he spoke lightly, as if he couldn't be bothered with anything at all troublesome. Then he drank the last of the beer and wiped his lips with his cape. The cicadas were loud again now that we'd reached a shoreline, and our little rowboat rose and fell on the water. The tide was a bit rougher than when we had first set out. I looked up. Clouds were moving in from the east.

"There's the light," Thaddeus said. I turned my head to see a small flicker of lantern light shining briefly before it went out.

We decided that Thaddeus would stay with the boat while I went to fetch the baby. Just like before, a white man dressed in farmhand's clothing—but not the same man; this one was thicker and taller—stepped out from among the trees carrying a basket. And, like before, the infant was sleeping. But when I held my lantern up to look, the baby's face did not seem so waterlogged as the last one.

"This one came yesterday," the man said. "Had a time of it hiding her all day. Lucky she slept so much or we'd have been found out for sure. My man thinks I'm off drinking, so now I'll have to get the smell of alcohol up on me." I supposed he meant the farmer he worked for. I checked for the pap feeder and milk, and then I took up the basket in one hand and my skirt in the other and waded carefully back to the rowboat. My boots were soaked through and would smell like river mud in the morning.

Thaddeus held the basket while I climbed in. "Tiny mite," he remarked, looking at the baby's face, and I told him the last one had been even tinier. "I like babies, you know," he said, and the way he was looking down at the basket made me believe him. "They don't hide anything. They can't." When I was settled, he handed me back the basket and checked the oarlocks before steering the boat around.

"Some weather coming," he told me, pulling back on the oars.

I looked out over the river. In the few minutes I'd been gone to get the baby, the current had gotten choppier. The water was pushing us farther west than we wanted to go, and Thaddeus had a time of it. After a few minutes, growing hot with the effort, he stopped rowing to take off his cape and at once the wind thrust us heavily downstream as if it were a hand just waiting for this opportunity. Now I could see tiny forks of lightning to the east. The wind blew off my bonnet and my hair whipped around my eyes. The sky was getting worse by the second.

I checked the baby, who was still sleeping. Despite Thaddeus's efforts, we were moving west as much as we were moving north. I wedged the baby basket under the thwart and turned around to sit next to him, taking up one of the oars with both my hands, and after a few pulls Thaddeus began counting aloud so we could find a rhythm together.

"One. And two. One. And two. That's it, May."

Together we rowed hard, trying to get to the shore. The sky was very dark now and the lightning moved nearer, but the rain had not yet reached us. Every so often the wind dropped for a moment as though catching its breath, and when it came up again, sprays of water hit our faces and chests. At one point the wind tipped the rowboat dangerously, and a rush of water came over the side.

"May, get the bucket!" Thaddeus shouted.

I found the bucket, knocked Leo's bait over the side of the boat, and began scooping water up and throwing it out while Thaddeus took over both oars. The boat seemed smaller to me now and made of the thinnest pieces of scrap wood imaginable. At any moment it would tip over and sink, or the boards would split and the whole thing would fall apart. The baby was still wedged in her basket under the thwart. While I was checking on her, more water came in, and I knelt on the bottom using the bucket like a shovel. I couldn't see the *Floating Theatre* or anything else along the bank. But when I looked a second time I saw a light flicker and catch, maybe on one of the mussel boats: someone looking for something in the storm.

"I can't read my compass," Thaddeus shouted above the wind.

"I see a light. Veer a little more to the right."

By this time the water on the bottom of the boat was only about a couple of inches deep. I got up again to help row. My shoulders were numb and the back of my dress was soaking wet. I was shaking with cold and fear and I hoped the baby was all right. I could see the outline of her basket still upright under the thwart, but sitting in an inch of water. Would she get wet? Every so often I turned my head to check our progress.

"Too far to the left!" I shouted.

"One. And two. One. And two."

His voice was getting hoarse from shouting. More twigs of lightning flickered above us.

"It's the *Floating Theatre*!" I shouted.

"What?"

A lantern was lit in the office window. Leo. He must have looked out and noticed the weather; I wondered if he always lit a lantern in the rain to mark the boat's presence, or if the light was for us. When we hit the river bottom, Thaddeus and I jumped out into the water, me with the basket, Thaddeus with the boat line. The baby was awake now and crying. I pulled the little bottle of opium from my pocket while Thaddeus began dragging the heavy, waterlogged boat up the bank. As I let the baby suck on the drop on my pinky finger, I saw Donaldson scrambling down the bank, half falling. I'd never seen Donaldson do anything undignified before, and that surprised me as much as anything else. But he righted himself soon enough and helped Thaddeus get the boat up. Donaldson's clothes were so heavy, the wind hardly wrinkled them, and he wore no hat. He was too far away for me to see his expression but I could imagine it: stern and respectable even after nearly falling down a muddy bank. A servant doing the next thing that had to be done without complaint.

Meanwhile my dress was wet through and my hands and arms shook with fatigue. I could not even hold the basket properly. I thought about climbing up to the road so I could sit on the carriage step with it, but I knew at once I would not be able to manage that, so I stayed where I was, rocked by the wind. When at last the boat was secured, Donaldson came for the basket and then he picked his way back up the bank toward the road, holding the basket's handle with one hand and grasping a low tree branch with the other to help pull himself up. Just as the rain started, Thaddeus and I got to the stage plank and ran up in our squelching boots. To my surprise, I saw from the light of the office lantern that Thaddeus's face was bright with exhilaration.

"What a team we are!" he said when we got under the roofed deck. He shook out his wet cape behind him.

I didn't understand his reaction but I wasn't going to stand there and talk. It was raining in earnest now and the sound was like horses cantering over our heads, with a separate patter of articulate drops on the wooden deck. It quieted a moment as if listening for a signal, and then it gathered its strength and let down in an absolute fury. I lifted my wet skirt and took the stairs up to my stateroom two at a time. All I wanted was to take off my dripping clothes and get under a blanket. The rain knocked against the boat, making a noise loud enough to drive off thought or fear, and I wrapped myself up in my blanket as if it were my shroud and fell on my cot the wrong way around, with my head at the foot and my feet on the pillow. But I was too tired to shift myself. My arms and shoulders ached, and my backbone hurt from all the twisting I'd done. I pushed my feet under the pillow to warm them, and in all of two minutes, even as the boat rocked and creaked in the storm, I was asleep.

It's one thing to float on water that is as smooth as a bedsheet, once in a while riding a small wave as though a great hand has taken up the fabric to give it a gentle shake before smoothing it out again. It's quite another thing to have a man shouting over a screaming wind to bail out the water that is rushing into the bottom of the boat as it reels from side to side. One thing I knew for sure: I'd been right to engage Thaddeus. I could not have handled the rowboat alone in the storm, and we would have capsized and drowned, both the baby and myself. It would be too much to expect that I could swim the river twice with a child. My nightmare that night was so intense that I made helpless groaning noises in my throat that woke me, and yet when I opened my eyes I could not remember what, exactly, I'd dreamed.

It was still early but I did not want to go back to sleep. I could feel the boat moving in the water, so I dressed and wrapped two shawls around me and went out to the guard. The sun was not yet up and the sky was still bruised from the storm, although it had stopped raining and the air was still. Below me, Hugo stood on the deck with his little enamel coffee cup, and as I watched he lifted the lid, blew on the coffee, and took a sip. He shouted some instruction to Jemmy or Leo and picked up the gouger. Thanks to the storm, the river was clogged with more snags and driftwood than ever. Nevertheless a steamboat was already chugging past us, lights shining out from the bow and the stern, and another one was not too far behind.

The chill morning air felt its way through my two shawls and into my shoulder blades. Compared to the rowboat, the *Floating Theatre* was heavy and solid and perfectly safe, but some of my fear from the previous night lingered like a clammy layer of gauze over my skin. I wanted the assurance of a strong hand, some confidence that for the moment I lacked. When Hugo put down the gouger—satisfied that the boat was where he wanted it in the current—I fetched a few doughnuts from the dining room and went down the stairs to see him.

I wished him good morning and handed him one of the doughnuts. When I looked back, I could make out Leo's rowboat tied to the stern and floating behind us in our wake, as usual.

"Surprised to see you this morning," Hugo said.

I looked at him quickly, worried about what he meant by that. It was true that I'd gotten very little sleep, but I hoped he didn't know the reason.

"Why is that?"

"You haven't been out here much lately. Thought maybe the magic was gone."

"What magic?"

He grinned. "I mean the thrill of watching the boat leave the bank. Maybe 'thrill' isn't the right word, either. Have to be careful with you, don't I? I like how you keep me exact."

"I still enjoy watching you all move the boat," I told him, but I didn't offer any explanation for why I hadn't been up to see it lately nor why I was up to see it now. To say that I was plagued with nightmares would surely only invite more questions.

Hugo leaned against the rail with me as he ate a second doughnut from my offerings. A dusting of deep-purple light spread out over the water, proof that the sun was on its way up, and there was a dewy, mineral tang in the air. I'd forgotten how good the soft wind of movement felt on my face. The river traffic was picking up. Heavy steamers pushing out smoke passed flatboats and long barges laden with barrels. I felt a sort of intimacy with them as we all started the day's journey together, everyone heading west, everyone hoping for good weather and prosperity.

I thought about my first day on the *Floating Theatre*, which seemed like a hundred years ago.

"Why did you face west in Cincinnati?" I asked Hugo.

"What do you mean?"

"When the bells rang out for the victims of the *Moselle*. Everyone else turned east toward the sunrise, but you turned west."

I watched the side of his face, which tightened a little. He was still looking at the water. Finally he replied, "For my sister. For Helena."

The morning fog was lifting and I could make out a narrow island near the opposite bank, or maybe it was a sandbar. I waited for him to go on.

"Helena loved going west," he explained. "She loved going west, and she hated coming back." Never mind the barely populated towns, he told me, or the lack of culture. No theaters, no lending libraries, and not one proper cup of tea to be had between Pittsburgh and St. Louis.

"But Helena loved it. She loved life on the river. She liked to watch the birds and she liked fishing from the guard. Every summer she competed with Leo over who could catch the biggest catfish. They had a standing one-dollar bet."

She was learning how to shoot a gun, and last August she'd shot three ducks on the wing; she considered it poor sportsmanship to shoot something in the water. Her dream was to buy a little cottage in the country where she and Hugo could spend their winters, he said, instead of the hotel in Pittsburgh. They were saving up money for that.

"I thought you were saving up for a small steamboat?"

"That's right: first the steamer. With a steamer we could make twice as much money, because we could do twice as many shows. Six weeks down the Ohio and six weeks back up. We'd change our bill of fare after Cairo, when we turned around. Maybe we'd go up the Illinois River. We definitely wanted to make jumps up the Wabash, and the White River, and the Green."

His face was shadowed with a fine stubble of beard, thicker on his chin. "Was that your dream, too?" I asked. "A cottage in the country?"

Leo shouted to Jemmy to bear hard against the bank, and Hugo looked over but he didn't add any instructions. The boat clipped along now, gaining speed.

"Well, I guess not," he finally said. "But it seemed fine. It seemed a good plan. There was a man we knew in Golconda. Raised horses just outside of town, came to our shows every year. I thought maybe between him and Helena there was an understanding . . . I wrote to him about what happened, of course. Edward Case. No reply. Maybe it was my imagination. But she might have settled down with him or someone else, and as for me, well, what I really wanted to do was set up a little theater somewhere with a permanent company. Do real plays, three-acts. But on a theater fronting the river, you know, so that passengers from the steamers could come in for the show."

"And Helena could fish."

"And Helena could fish," he agreed. A gust of wind came off the water and blew against his blanket coat so that it looked like he was shrugging his shoulders. "Well," he said. That was that.

I could easily imagine Helena, because she sounded like Hugo, all movement and energy: shooting ducks, fishing, laughing with Leo. I remembered her energetic conversation with the violinist after she finished singing on the *Moselle*. And then there was me, sitting still enough to fit in a box while I sewed. I've never thought much about being anyone other than who I am, and to be honest I didn't much think about it then. But I did see how Helena's energy would be exciting to a man—to Edward Case. Just as Hugo's movement and energy were exciting to me.

The thought took me by surprise. But as soon as I had it, I knew it was true. I did like that about him. I liked his intensity and the great care he took of his boat. I liked the way a shock of brown hair curled down over his forehead, and his woody smell, and the slant of his eyes, and how his accent became more pronounced when he was upset. A rush of details came at me, and for a moment I felt a couple of hard heartbeats crash against my ribs. When I looked down I saw that I was pinching the inside of my wrist, something I hadn't done for a long time.

Hugo was looking downstream, which is to say west, and for a moment I stared at the back of his head. I had the strangest compulsion to touch him. I wanted to say: *I'm breaking the law. I'm afraid. I need your help.* The fact that I didn't blurt all this out immediately upon thinking it is a measure of everything I'd learned in those few short weeks.

"Well, now, what's she doing up so early?" Hugo asked. I followed his line of sight and saw that Liddy, still with her hair in a messy braid down her back, was standing at the rail on the upper deck looking out at the river. She raised her arm in greeting to someone, and Hugo and I looked out to where she was waving. A small black-and-red passenger steamship was just then passing us, and I could see a man standing on its upper deck facing Liddy, his right arm raised in greeting. The steamship blew its high-pitched whistle three times. On the third whistle, the man took off his hat and waved it. The hat was brilliantly white.

"It's Dr. Early," I said.

17

All the rest happened in less than a week. Looking at a calendar later, I had to check and recheck the dates, because at first I couldn't believe it. Sometimes your life moves slowly and sometimes it whirls like a spinning wheel under the guidance of a very skilled hand, the hand of a woman who is not necessarily kind. I remember having a sort of frozen feeling in my chest that week, and although I planned and plotted and tried with my very best reasoning to find a way out for everyone involved—well, almost everyone involved—at the same time I suspected that reason would be of no earthly use against that fast-spinning wheel. Whatever happened in the end would come about through good luck or its reverse, and not as the result of my efforts.

But still, I did try.

Dr. Early's passenger steamer stopped at a larger landing a few miles downstream from where we tied up for the day, so that Dr. Early needed to hire a horse to carry him back to us—or, more precisely, back to Liddy. Meanwhile, Liddy had time to pin up her hair and eat breakfast and tell us all what had happened.

He had given up hunting for runaway slaves, and she had reconciled with him. He'd sent her a note two days earlier that she did not answer, although it was a very pretty note ("I couldn't help but read it once I broke the seal," Liddy said). Then, to her surprise, he showed up the previous evening for our performance ("Did you not see him in the back row?" she asked), and he was very unhappy to see her sing that last love duet with Thaddeus, for all that he knew there was nothing between them. Afterwards he waited for her outside and she consented to walk out with him, and as they went along the river Dr. Early assured Liddy again and again that he would never have anything to do with slaves if it upset her, and that he meant to have her always with him. In short, he proposed.

"I didn't see him sitting in the audience," I said, although I recollected that at the time I was nervous about going out that night, so I did not much look up from my piano.

"You didn't? I saw him straightaway!"

Her eyes were shining. We were gathered in the dining room, and as she told her story Liddy shyly drew her hand out from under the table to show us her ring.

"That's a pearl! A big one!" Celia cried out. She was bouncing with excitement. Two small diamonds flanked the pearl, and when Liddy waved her hand, the diamonds sparkled.

Cook poured us all a finger of whiskey to celebrate, even one for Celia. As he poured mine I glanced at Hugo, who was across from me and down at the other end. He was smiling with the others, all except Pinky, whose face seemed like a crumpled piece of discarded paper.

"To Liddy!" Hugo said, raising the thick white coffee cup in which the whiskey was served. "To good fortune and happy days ahead."

Dr. Early arrived not too much later on a large roan horse wearing his impeccably clean white hat and a straw-colored suit. Jemmy and Sam went up the bank to see the horse, whereas Mrs. Niffen and Celia and I accompanied Liddy to see the doctor. For my part, I was curious about how Dr. Early would account for his actions, if at all. He came with a present for Liddy: a sweet leather pouch that he had bought, he told us as he tethered the horse to one of the trees, from a native man who set up shop between two enormous oaks.

"He stores his goods right there in the hollows of the trees," Dr.

Early told us. "It was all very compact and snug. Wouldn't be surprised if he slept there, too."

Jemmy and Sam, once they had examined the horse, wandered away while Dr. Early untied Liddy's gift from the back of the saddle. The pouch, made from pounded deer hide and sewn with dyed-blue deer sinews, was very pretty. But more surprising was what was inside: a tiny baby raccoon the size of Dr. Early's hand.

"One of Mrs. Shakentale's," he explained to Liddy, holding the raccoon out to her with his fingers under its belly. "I'll tame it for you. It'll be your pet."

"How sweet!" Liddy looked up at him as she took the animal, blushing. She had changed her dress after breakfast, I noticed, and added an apple-green ribbon to her hair.

"To celebrate," Dr. Early said.

Liddy blushed even deeper and handed the raccoon to Celia, who was begging to hold it. Dr. Early seemed taller and broader as he listened to Celia praise the creature's little paws and tail.

"And so you no longer are in pursuit of runaways?" I asked him when Celia paused.

His eyes turned to Liddy. "Oh, yes, I've given all that up for good."

"What made you change your mind?"

Now he smiled and looked over at me. Liddy looked up, too, and he moved closer to her. "When it appeared that I had lost this dear girl," he said, drawing her arm underneath his, "I realized very clearly what I wanted: to hang up my bachelor hat. Nothing else mattered."

I looked at his white hat and he caught me looking. "Ha-ha-ha," he laughed. "I like you, May. You're very straightforward. And I am hoping I can convince you to like me now, too."

"Isn't it enough that Liddy likes you?" I asked.

His smile faded a notch but he quickly brought it back up. "Ha-ha-ha," he laughed, as though I were joking.

Mrs. Niffen said quickly, "Oh, Dr. Early, we all like you very much indeed. Very much indeed. And we are all very happy for Liddy. But no one can be happier than I am. I am the happiest of all. I always say to Mr. Niffen that no one likes to see a couple come to an understanding more than I do. No one gets more joy out of that than I."

"Well, I might argue for that right in this case," Dr. Early said, but Mrs. Niffen was not listening.

"No, no, no, I am beyond doubt the happiest of all." She touched the small puffy pouch underneath her eye with one finger as if checking for a tear or hoping to inspire one. "Liddy is like a daughter—no, not a daughter; I am not yet that old!—say, rather, a young cousin to me. A favorite young cousin."

"And what will you do to supplement your income?" I asked. "For your patients? Your experimental medicines? Now that you are no longer off catching up people for profit."

"Oh, I will always find a way to make money, no need to worry about that."

"Perhaps you could make cakes and sell them," I said.

A moment's silence. Mrs. Niffen and Liddy looked at me with horrified faces. Only Celia was not paying attention, as she was still engaged with the baby raccoon.

"I remember your pound cake was very good," I said.

Then Liddy laughed. "Oh, there, May is just joking!"

Mrs. Niffen took up the thread. "Yes, how droll, a man baking."

"There are plenty of men who are bakers," I told them.

Dr. Early resettled Liddy's arm on his and glanced up at the clear sky, unconcerned. Even the clouds seemed to part for him. "Perhaps we should go for a stroll before the day gets too hot?"

"Oh, yes," Mrs. Niffen said. "I'll just get my shawl."

As she hurried back to the boat, Dr. Early and Liddy looked at each other and smiled. Even I understood they wanted to be alone. Celia, meanwhile, was still holding the baby raccoon, only a day or two old. Surely it was too young, I asked, to be taken from its mother?

"Well, May," Dr. Early replied in a professional voice, "in my experience it's better to take them right away and feed them yourself. Bonding, you know. Without a mother she'll be as tame as can be. She won't know how to be wild." I thought of the slave babies I had ferried across the river. I could not think of any creature on earth that would be better off without a mother, and I said so. But Dr. Early just smiled at my comment as though it merely reflected my ignorance.

"What shall we name her?" Liddy asked, stroking the raccoon baby's nose. The animal was remarkably docile—stunned, perhaps, from being snatched from its family and the subsequent long journey in a pouch. I would not like a forest creature with such claws for a pet, but Liddy seemed delighted.

"Whisker?" Celia suggested. "Stripe?"

I found myself watching Dr. Early closely, and he met my eye in an easy, casual way. The sharp look he had back at his cottage was gone. He was making every effort to be agreeable, and in this way he reminded me a little of Thaddeus. Thaddeus was still up in his stateroom, sleeping. He'd missed all the excitement of the morning.

"What about 'Rascal'?" I asked.

Dr. Early looked at me and smiled, showing his beautiful teeth. Everything about him was so clean, it was hard to remember that he was a doctor who regularly attended fevers and putrid sores, who placed leeches on bare arms and wrapped festering wounds. He looked, then as always, as though he'd just finished scrubbing himself from head to toe. Mrs. Niffen came down off the stage plank with her shawl, ready for their walk.

"Rascal," Dr. Early said. He held out his other arm for Mrs. Niffen to take. "I like that."

Hugo did not take kindly to a pet raccoon on his boat, and he made Dr. Early tie up Rascal outside during the performance that night.

The poor little shackled creature clawed at the ground with some unease, but Dr. Early just laughed.

"I'll come out when the captain's not looking and put you in my pocket," he told Rascal, but then he forgot all about her just like everyone else did.

The next day he came with us to our new landing, announcing that he meant to follow the show for a while. That's when I felt the first seeds of anxiety: Did he somehow know what I was doing at night? Would he follow me? I told myself that my worries were silly and unwarranted. Illogical. Just my uneasy conscience making trouble. Breaking the law—breaking *any* rule—was not in my nature. It was like making a seam crooked on purpose. But once I started to suspect Dr. Early, I found I couldn't stop myself.

Pinky alone shared my dislike of Dr. Early, but in Pinky's case it was from jealousy. That night Dr. Early sat in the front row with his white hat in his lap. At each song he tapped his hat against his knee, and after the show he lingered to be with Liddy, who came down from the stage in her costume to talk to him. Although it was a clear summer evening, I was very glad that no one came up to me to say I must go out in the rowboat that night. I did not trust Dr. Early.

When at last the theater emptied, I pushed my piano to the side of the stage and went outside. For a while I stood on the bank breathing in the warm night air, which smelled of the muddy river and the heavy green trees along the water's edge. The townspeople lingered with their lanterns, exchanging gossip and laughing. In the near darkness a circle of women resembled a stand of short trees, and when they laughed they shook a little.

No one paid any attention to me, and I felt, for the first time in weeks, sadly alone. I wished there were someone I could confide in, like Hugo or Liddy. I did not want to talk to Thaddeus because I did not want to worry him; I could not risk him changing his mind about helping me. And Leo had already made it clear that he did not want to know. A poem that my mother taught me came into my mind: *Allen gehört, was du denkst; dein eigen ist nur, was du fühlest.* What you think belongs to all, what you feel is yours alone.

Leo was standing a little ways away from me with his arms folded across his broad chest, watching some boys in short pants playing along the bank or climbing the oak trees that shaded the boat. Two of the bolder ones approached our stage plank and pulled at the knot once or twice as if testing it before Leo shooed them away. His shout excited them to no end, and they giggled their way up the trees, shaking the branches with their scrambling.

I heard Hugo's voice rise above the laughter: "Paducah's the place where we'll open it. You think you'll follow us there?"

"I aim to follow you all the way to the Mississippi before I turn around."

My stomach tightened. That was Dr. Early speaking. I traced the sound of their voices to two figures standing at the edge of the wharf a little ways in front of me. Hugo was taller and his voice more commanding. They were looking out at the water. I saw a line of smoke rising before them in the air and realized they each held a cigar.

"That'll be the next stop but two," Hugo told him. The scent of tobacco drifted back to me. "After that, we'll perform it all along the Mississippi."

"What's the name again?"

"*The Midnight Hour.* A favorite not too long ago in London."

"I look forward to seeing it. Ah, here she is."

A figure in a long skirt—Liddy—approached them.

"I've untied Rascal," she said. "Have you brought something to feed her with?"

From behind me I heard Leo's quiet voice. "Not right to capture a wild critter like that for without you're going to eat it," he said.

He came up to stand beside me, and we looked out at the water and at Hugo, Dr. Early, and Liddy, who stood closer to the river's edge. I agreed, and I told him so.

"I had to tie Oliver up inside," Leo said, "he's that excited about it. Listen."

From inside the boat I could hear, faintly, a yowl. "Poor thing."

"You tell the captain that the doctor has to take the critter with him when he go."

I said I would.

"One more thing. Man I didn't know come up to me while you was still inside. Tomorrow night they're expecting another one at midnight."

"'Another one'?"

"Man said you'd understand."

I turned my head to look at him, and as I did so my boot slid on the gravelly dirt. Leo took me by the arm to steady me.

"How did he know you were safe to talk to?" I asked quietly.

Leo bounced his forefinger off his cheek. "How you think?"

"But does he even know where we're landing tomorrow?"

"He asked me that first."

"Leo . . ."

"And that's all I'm involved. Now, good night, Miss May. I need to see to Oliver now. Make sure you tell the captain."

For a moment I thought he meant about tomorrow night, but then I realized he'd gone back to the subject of the raccoon. I watched his large frame walk away in the darkness. When he got to the oak trees, he looked up and shouted "Boo!" in his loudest voice. High laughter came down from the branches.

"You git yourselves home now, it's late," Leo called to the boys in the tree. "Go on, now. I'm watching you."

That night two owls calling out to each other kept me awake, and when I did finally fall asleep my dreams were worse than ever. Over and over again, in a variety of ways, I could not save Giulia. Every time I fell asleep I tried again and failed. At last I gave up sleeping and read a book by candlelight.

When I felt the boat start to move, I dressed and went out to the guard. The air was strangely warm for daybreak, and I watched the mist coming off the water and creeping up the side of the boat. There was no sign of Liddy, and Dr. Early was staying at an inn in town. He planned to follow us to our next landing on horseback.

The run this morning was fast and difficult. Almost immediately upon leaving the bank we came to a bad stretch of the river with lots of sandbars and sudden, low water. Jemmy and Sam had their work cut out for them, pushing the sweeps hard as they tried to keep in the current. I stayed on the top deck out of everyone's way.

"Battery Rock! Battery Rock!" Hugo shouted, running over to the gouger. Leo must have known what that meant, for he steered us into another channel of the river, and as the mist thinned I saw a perpendicular front of rocks jutting out from a tongue of land on our right. Everyone except Hugo turned to look. The rocks shaped themselves into an enormous, earth-wrought castle, and I half expected goblins to jump out from the rock face.

"What's this? We're not on a pleasure outing! Man your posts!" Hugo shouted at Jemmy and Sam.

The land flattened out as it sunk into the river and managed to go along in this way, seemingly half submerged, for almost a mile. Then a new natural fortress came into view: a straight wall of smooth limestone against the northern bank, with horizontal strata like stripes on an animal. It must have been one hundred feet or more in height. A cluster of small red cedar trees stood at its flat summit, and I could see some of their roots dangling through the fissures as though searching deep within the rock for their sustenance. Several birds of prey circled the trees. The morning air was still warm, but the scene before my eyes looked as if it should be cold, with the mist curling over the rock and the birds' heavy dark feathers suggesting life in a cooler climate. A little farther downstream the limestone opened into a dark cave shaped like a keyhole. An old man and two dogs were standing at the edge of its huge entrance, the dogs jumping up to try to eat something that the man dangled just out of their reach. I was close enough to see the old man's ragged coat and the dirty yellow fur of the hounds that he mercilessly teased. The boat picked up speed and then slowed again, and the dogs' barking seemed to rise and fall in pitch with our movement. I turned my good ear away and saw that the heavy dark birds were following us.

A strange feeling came over me then, as though we'd entered a dark, secret world. We crept along the north side of the river and the banks seemed to squeeze in on us while the river itself churned up mud. We passed a stand of bleached white oak trees, dead but still standing guard, and Hugo landed the boat just beyond them. While Leo tied us up, the mist floated upward into a dirty strip of gauze across the sky.

But by the time everyone else woke up an hour later, the birds of prey were nowhere in sight and the mist had dissipated in the heat of the sun. Still, I could not shake the uncomfortable feeling that the rock face and the cave and the dirty man teasing his dogs had brought on, coupled with my uneasy night.

No one else seemed to notice. At breakfast, the sun was streaming into the dining room and the day had found a pleasant mask: windless, warm but not too warm, and a blue sky with only one or two cottonball clouds. No one commented on the strong smell of stagnant water and mud coming in from the open window.

When Cook brought out more coffee, Hugo stood to make an announcement.

"Excuse me, you all, settle down a moment, please. Just for one moment, ladies and gents, if you please. Is everyone here? Thaddeus? Thaddeus, there you are, good man. All right, now. I have a couple of things I want to say. We're going to land in Paducah in a couple of days and that's where I want to premier *The Midnight Hour*. You're all ready; just a couple of tweaks and turns and we'll be all set. I'd like to find a time for a rehearsal today and then a dress rehearsal tomorrow. Maybe two if we can."

"Why Paducah, Captain?" Pinky asked. "We never landed there before. They won't know us."

"It's a big town, bigger than where we normally go, but that's why I chose it. I want a full house for our opening night."

Paducah was across the river, in Kentucky. It had two newspapers and a distillery and its own savings and loan. Also, it had a long row of stores right there on the waterfront, and that meant not everyone was a farmer. Merchants have more in the way of ready cash. Hugo wanted standing room only, he told us; he wanted a great performance from each and every player, and he wanted to put on the best show Paducah has ever seen. "That'll get the word down the river!"

I looked around. Everyone was listening to Hugo with the same shining expression on their faces, and at the same time their bodies seemed to swell or grow taller. I had seen this phenomenon with Comfort. Even her curls seemed to get firmer when she pictured herself on stage. Opening night was always a sea of excited actors and actresses who carried themselves as though a whole world lay inside them, which it did in a way: the world of their play.

"Our friend Dr. Early knows some people there—he'll be our advance man," Hugo continued. At the sound of Dr. Early's name, Pinky shot a dismayed and covetous glance at Liddy. But Liddy was staring fixedly at Hugo, a blush creeping up her neck.

"May, I'll need you here on the boat, seeing to the costumes and props and keeping everyone in line." We shared a smile and a strong feeling came over me, a feeling that we were together in this, Hugo and myself, almost like proud parents overseeing these happy actors and their dog.

"Meanwhile," Hugo went on, looking at the actors, "your job is to get up the best show these river people have ever seen!"

A burst of hurrahs and shouts filled the room. Hugo looked pleased at the noise, which continued until Cook broke up the excitement by reminding us that breakfast was over and would everyone for God's sake get out of his way. Chairs were scraped back and cutlery clattered on the plates like bones while the actors spoke excitedly in their loud, trained voices, hardly listening to each other but getting louder when no one listened to them.

"Remember, two o'clock, everybody, down in the theater!" Hugo shouted as they filed out.

Only I remained apprehensive, knowing I had to go out that night in the rowboat. Later, as I put up our show posters in town, I passed the public whipping post, a common feature of these small river settlements. I'd once seen a man standing at such a post after he'd been beaten, his shirt slashed at the shoulders from the edge of the horsewhip. What was the punishment in this town for helping fugitive slaves? I wondered. Still, I knew I would go out that night unless, I reasoned, it was storming and absolutely unsafe to do so. But the day continued to be clear and calm, with a few clouds and just the lightest of breezes. There was no one tied to the whipping post when I went by.

But on my way back to the *Floating Theatre*, I saw Leo kneeling down at the edge of the dock fishing something out of the water with a net. At first I thought it might be the catfish he'd been chasing all summer, but it was too large for that. As I got closer I could see dirty wet fur. The body was still partially submerged, but when its head bobbed forward I saw that it was one of the yellow hound dogs that had been teased in front of the cave we passed early that morning.

Its eyes were open and streams of muddy weeds were entangled in its fur and lashed its mouth. As Leo pulled it closer the body tilted to reveal a great welt on its belly. It was too recently dead to smell of anything other than mud, but that stench was terrible enough. Leo told me to go on back, he would handle this, but I found I had tears in my eyes and could not leave. Something made me look down the dock; sure enough, there was the old man in his ragged coat, standing there watching us. The other dog sat erectly by his side.

I was suddenly angry. "This is your dog," I called out to him. Leo struggled to bring the net with the dog in it up out of the water.

"No it ain't," the old man called back. His voice sounded like he had a handful of river gravel in his mouth, and I could see the neck of a bottle sticking out of his coat pocket.

"We need to bury it 'fore the crows get at it," Leo said to me, getting the body settled and then working to free the net from underneath it. His trousers were soaking wet, and he bent to untangle one of the dog's ears from the net's web.

"You need to bury your dog!" I shouted to the old man.

"Even if it was my dog, which as I tell you it ain't, I'd say the bitch just got too close to the river edge."

"That was your fault!" I shouted. "You teased her into it!"

In lieu of answering, the old man spat in my direction. I started to walk over to him but Leo put a hand on my arm.

"But you saw him, didn't you?" I asked. "At the cave?"

"No good will come from messing with a mean old nut, Miss May. I can bury the poor creature."

The mean old nut, as Leo called him, was now rubbing his hands as though they were cold, displaying no remorse at all. The hem of his coat had fallen on one side and I noticed that he wore two different boots. He was old and poor and a drunk, but that didn't excuse him. He turned on his heel and whistled to the one hound he had left.

I was still hot with anger. "You killed your own dog!" I shouted after him. "Your own dog!" But the man made no gesture that he heard me. He hobbled down the wharf in his mismatched boots while the second hound, all ribs and matted fur, trotted briskly behind him. I found myself wondering how a creature could stick to a master so clearly bent on its very destruction.

"That's all right, Miss May," Leo said. "Poor thing's out of misery now."

I was not superstitious, not like actors, but I could not help but feel as though omen after omen was piling up. That evening a sweet, rich scent of jasmine floated over on the wind and the sun set in a spectacular show that seemed to glow green and blue and gold and red all at once. Everyone remarked on it: "The end of a glorious summer evening" or "The most beautiful sunset I've seen in all my life." Even Thaddeus, when we were alone late that night in the rowboat, kept remarking on what a perfect day it had been, both for its beauty and its temperature, and for the excellence of the picnic supper that Cook had laid out for us on the bank with chicken and hard-boiled eggs and pie and a bucket of cold lemonade. I was the only one who noticed that we ate our food among sneezeweed and scrub, and who felt the day's beauty to be false.

If I were anyone else, I would have accused me of too much imagination. But the dead dog in particular kept floating up in my mind. Added to that, Dr. Early did not come to the performance that night as expected. Nor did he come afterwards when the players were sitting around the dining room, eating leftover chicken and talking, and he did not send along a note to explain his whereabouts.

It was nothing to worry about, Liddy told us. He may have been called on to attend a person taken ill. "As soon as a place learns you're a doctor . . ." she said, and shrugged, twisting her engagement ring around on her finger.

But I could not help thinking that it was too much of a coincidence that he had been called away on the same night I was summoned to help carry a slave baby across the river.

That night Thaddeus rowed the boat slowly, taking his time, while I listened hard for any noises above the soft plash of our oars in the water. Every now and again I looked up at the dense array of stars overhead. Thaddeus wanted to talk, but in my anxiety I kept hushing him until finally he gave up.

"No one can hear us out here," he grumbled.

"Someone could be in a cove or along the shore. Sound carries over water, you know that."

He blew air from his lips as if blowing my hogwash away, but settled into rowing the rest of the way without comment.

At last we made our signal with the lantern, and almost immediately a signal was given in return. There was really no reason for my stomach to tighten. Dr. Early had seen the show now at least three times already; why should he attend every performance? And there was certainly no evidence that he was out hunting runaway slaves and anyone who helped them. Besides, if he had somehow caught the man carrying away the baby, why would he lie in wait to catch us? I told myself he was probably in the next town already, preparing the residents there to part with their dimes and nickels in exchange for two hours of an entertaining play.

By now I understood how much these river people craved variety and entertainment, and how happy they were to do their part as an audience. Even tonight's performance could be considered a success, although there were fifteen men to every woman and a more uncouth audience could not be imagined. They spat and smelled up the room and kept their hats on their heads for the full two hours. They hadn't bothered to wash their faces and they shouted out jests to the actors on the stage. But, for all that, they laughed at the right places, and clapped their hands and stamped their feet at the end of each act. They particularly liked Oliver in his little ruffle, and shouted for him to dance again and again until Hugo came out with his arms spread, pleading with them that the dog needed more sleep than the actors, being the star of the show. This made everyone laugh harder, but they got to their feet and found their lanterns and made their jostling way off the boat. When they left, the smell of whiskey stayed in the theater, and I realized that many of the men had been drinking from flasks the whole time. My one consolation was that the old man with his hound dog did not attend. He probably didn't have twenty cents to spare.

Guided by the moonlight, Thaddeus got to a few yards of the shoreline and dropped anchor. The water lapped languidly against the boat, a peaceful noise, as though demonstrating that all my misgivings could only be flights of fancy: nothing bad could happen on so calm and gentle an evening. The moon was up, pale yellow and slightly misshapen, like one of my father's wheels of cheese after a buyer cut a sliver to taste it, and the water was as smooth as I had ever seen it.

Thaddeus stretched out his legs and waited for me to do the work of getting wet and retrieving the baby. I still could see no one onshore—whoever we were meeting had doused the lantern again quickly—but I heard a cry quickly stifled, which sounded like an infant. My stomach was still pitted up as I held my skirt and waded up the bank. As I climbed onto dry land, though, I slipped and scraped the palm of my hand against a rock. It burned without actually bleeding, and I couldn't make a fist for the rest of the night.

A cough. I turned in that direction. Now I could see a figure a few yards away under some trees. But when I saw another figure standing alongside him, my heart went into my throat and I stopped cold. Two men were standing there instead of just one.

"Heyya," one of them said, and began walking toward me.

Now I fully expected to see the white hat of Dr. Early and his smilingly invective face as he held out manacles to chain me up. But the man's hat was brown. It wasn't Dr. Early. The other man, who also wasn't Dr. Early, stayed behind the first man, carrying the basket with the infant. The infant gave another short chuff like a cough and the man carrying the basket shushed it. A long filmy cloud drifted over the moon, hiding their particulars, but their gait—especially the first man's—revealed a fair amount of agitation.

I wish I could tell you what I felt as I stood there watching them advance, one behind the other. But I don't remember. Caught, I guess. Even though it wasn't Dr. Early catching me, I knew I was caught; I had walked right into the trap I suspected all day was coming for me. I waited for one of the men to pull out a pistol, although in truth no pistol was needed: I was prepared to go willingly. I had broken the law, and punishment was the answer to that. The one thing I wasn't sure about was whether I should shout out a warning to Thaddeus or if they thought I was the only one and a warning shout would do nothing but alert the slave catchers to the truth.

What would they do to me? They were brutal to the runaways: once the slaves were returned and the reward collected, the hapless men and women would be flogged, or possibly lynched as a warning to others. To me, the law might be merciful: a hefty fine and six months in jail. But that was only if I was lucky and they arrested me. If they didn't arrest me, I could be hanged by a crowd, my clothes stripped off me, my skin burned with torches first for good measure. If they didn't arrest me, it was because they wanted Old Judge Lynch to sit upon the bench. I understood that now.

"Am I under arrest?" I asked the first man as he came up to me.

Clouds moved over the moon. I could hear the river lap at the gravelly shore behind me like the repeated flap of a handkerchief.

"Not yet," he said. "But like as not they'll be looking for us by now, and here's me in the woods without reason. If they find me they'll suspect me for sure . . . ah—" Here he swore.

"Who will?" I asked. "I don't understand you."

"Wouldn't leave it, wouldn't let me leave. I hardly thought I'd get here in time for all the fussing . . ."

"What do you mean?"

"The girl. She wouldn't leave it."

"What girl?"

That was when I realized that the short man standing behind him was not a man at all but a girl. A Negro girl. Holding the basket, hushing the baby.

When she stepped out from behind the farmhand, I stared at her, trying to make out some features. She was short for a man but tall for a girl. And in the dim moonlight I could see now that she was wearing a dress. In fact, she seemed to be wearing several dresses. She was staring at me, too, and then she put down the basket. When she straightened up, I saw that the front of her dress was wet under her breasts.

"You're the mother," I said. She looked all of fourteen.

"Wouldn't leave the baby," the farmhand repeated. "Wouldn't let me go. Her fault if I get caught. If we all do." He swore again, not exactly at the girl but close enough.

The girl said nothing.

"What's your name?" I asked her.

"Lula," the farmhand told me.

"Can't she talk?"

"She can talk a hog into going into the smokehouse on its own cloven feet. Wouldn't leave the baby, she told me, and wouldn't stay behind. On and on like that. Talked a mile a minute till I was just wore out with the noise of it all. But I guess that's your problem now." He looked back into the trees. "Good luck to you."

"Wait—you want me to take her with me?"

"I told her, I said to her, we have to make our plans first. You need to wait for someone to make *you* a plan, I said. But did she listen?"

Lula spoke for the first time. "I'm not gonna wait," she said. "I'm all done with waiting."

"But what will *I* do with her?" I asked the farmhand.

"Same as you did with the others. Same as I just did. Give her to the next one down the line."

That was Donaldson. "What if he won't take her?"

"He'll take her. What else can he do?" He cursed some more. "Now let me be off."

"You tried not to take her," I pointed out.

A quick spasm ran down his shoulders and arms, either from impatience or fear. "All I know is it's the end for me, so if you don't take her, she's on her own. I'll be looked for shortly; I have to get back." And with that, he left without so much as lifting his hat or nodding good-bye. He ran a little bowleggedly back into the trees and away for good. It was hard to imagine how he'd been recruited to do this work. Principles or pay?

Lula put the basket down and turned to face me squarely, as though her resolve that I would do the right thing would induce me to do the right thing. And why not? It had worked with the farmhand. But she wasn't without nervousness, either, for when an owl or some other critter shifted its position on a creaky tree branch nearby, she visibly started.

"How we gettin' across the river?" she whispered.

"I have a rowboat. There's a man waiting. But I'm not sure I should take you."

"You gotta take me! They find me, they'll kill me."

"Across the river's not much better. They might send you back."

"It's the North, ain't it?"

"Yes, but the people aren't always . . ." I thought of the doctor's wife who had shooed me off her land. "Some of them might as well live in the South."

"What you gonna do, take my baby and leave me to be hung up and whupped and killed?"

The clouds had moved off and the dimpled moon lighted the river. I could see the top of Thaddeus's hat just a little ways down the bank.

He'd moved the rowboat into a shallow nook near some river boulders. I didn't know what to do.

"What's your baby's name?" I asked, stalling.

"William."

"What happened to the father?"

"He around."

"Did he run away, too?"

"It were one of the sons. The middle one." She uncovered the baby's face. His large dark eyes stared up at me without blinking and he had curly, thick eyelashes. His skin was very light.

One of the sons. One of her owner's sons, she meant.

"How old are you?" I asked her.

"I don't know."

She covered the baby back up and looked at me. She was waiting for me to say yes or no, but I didn't know what to say. Like a child, I began to have the dread feeling that, since I had broken one rule, I was now condemned to break rules forever—that I had succumbed to my lower nature, which disregarded any law that interfered with my own desire. And my desire, at that moment, was to save her. But that was breaking the law. Of course, I had broken the law before ferrying those babies. And yet, this seemed worse.

I looked at her and at the basket at her feet. She was right: I found that I couldn't just leave her.

"All right," I said at last. "But it's an unlucky day. You should know that."

"All of them are," she told me.

As we began to walk toward the rowboat, Lula, now holding the basket up against her chest, stumbled and lurched forward.

"Are you sick?" I asked.

"My feet are bleeding."

Her boots were caked with mud. Even the laces looked as stiff as brown icing.

"I didn't have no shoes, so the man gave me these. They too small for me."

"Do you want to take them off?"

She looked down at them. "Might not be able to get them back on. My left foot's not so bad. Must be smaller or something."

"Here." I took her arm. "That's all right, just put your weight on me."

Thaddeus had positioned the rowboat so we could step into it from the boulders without wading into the water. When we got up next to the boat, I took the baby basket from Lula and gave it to Thaddeus, who was staring at the two of us. He quickly collected himself and helped Lula and then me into the boat, which rocked heavily as I sat down next to the girl. I realized my heart was still thumping hard and my balance was off.

"This is Lula," I said in a low voice. "She's coming with us."

Lula, who had gotten the bottom of her dress wet getting into the boat, shifted her damp hem away from her legs and looked at Thaddeus cautiously. He touched his hat and then, perhaps for once in his life shocked into reticence, pushed us off without another word.

Although every splash of water made my heart jump, our crossing was as calm as the one coming over. Even so, by the end my eyes hurt from straining to see into the dark night. About midway on the river Lula stooped to bring her baby up to her breast to feed him, unbuttoning the front of her dress and then unbuttoning the dress underneath that one. She had but two dresses in the world, I guessed, and she didn't want to leave one behind. I understood that. While she nursed her baby, Thaddeus kept rowing, but he turned his head away as if it was suddenly important to watch for something coming in from the east. I wondered what he thought about this new situation, but I was too afraid to speak in case the nervous farmhand was right: already Lula had been discovered missing, and people were up and down the river and maybe even on it looking for her. I did not dare to light the lantern to check our direction, and I worried over every sound not made by our own oars.

But we got to the other shore and tied up without incident. Although it was not much past midnight, it felt as if the deepest part of night was upon us already, the time when every creature on earth had settled into silence. Thaddeus arranged the rowboat so that it was exactly the same as Leo had left it: oars crossed at the bottom, bottle anchors under the aft. When I looked back, the river was just a long chasm of darkness.

"We in the North now," Lula whispered. I wasn't sure if she was asking me.

"Have you ever been to the North before?"

She nodded. "Once with my mistress."

Thaddeus had finished tying up the rowboat. "What now?" he asked, indicating Lula.

I didn't think a crowd on the road was a good idea so I told him I would take care of things from here, and that he should go on up to his stateroom. My words conveyed that I knew what I was doing and I didn't need his help, but in truth I didn't know what to expect. "Give her to the next one down the line," was all the farmhand had said.

Lula wouldn't let me take her basket from her even walking up the rough path to the road, where she stumbled on the pebbly dirt, and as before I had to content myself with holding her arm. Once we got to the road, I saw the carriage at the far side of a bend half hidden by the shadow of an oak tree. Without cloud cover, the moon was very bright, and if anyone were to come along the road, flat as it was, they would see us from a long way away. I held my breath so I could hear better, turning my good ear toward the road, but all I could hear was my heartbeat thrumming in my temples. As we approached the carriage, Donaldson climbed down from the driver's seat and clasped his hands in front of him. But when he saw the girl, he unclasped them, and for a moment he did nothing but look at her.

"This is Donaldson," I said. "He's here to take you on." I gestured toward Lula. "This is the baby's mother. Lula."

I was close enough to see him draw a breath before he held out his hands for the basket. She gave it up to him easily, which surprised me. Maybe because, unlike me, he was a Negro. Donaldson tucked the basket up next to the driver's seat, but when Lula moved to get up there with it, he turned and blocked her way.

"She's the baby's mother," I told him again. Then, more boldly: "She's to go with him."

He shook his head.

I felt my heart sink. "She could ride inside. I can get a rug or a blanket or something to cover her up." But he shook his head again.

By this time he had one foot on the bottom step and he turned slightly toward us but not enough to give Lula room to get past him. He shook his head a third time even before I could think of what to say next.

My heart sank further, as if making room for the onrush of anxious fear, which arrived a second later. The moonlight was behind him, so I could not make out Donaldson's expression, but I daresay he probably had none. He took the next step up and climbed into the driver's seat.

"Wait!" I said, louder than I meant to. Lula looked back along the road nervously. "Are you coming back for her?" I asked. "What should I do with her?"

Donaldson held the reins in his hands. The horse stomped his back hoof, wanting to be off, no doubt, and back in his stable for the night. I was hoping for a gesture at least from Donaldson. Some indication of what would happen now.

"What do I do?" I asked him again.

Donaldson looked at me. He moved his head but I didn't know what that meant. He flicked the reins.

"What's the matter with him?" Lula asked. The horse started down the dirt road.

"He's mute."

"Where's he going?" She began to go after them, but with her bad feet she couldn't run very well. She managed to slap the side of the carriage but it didn't slow down. I thought she was going to try to pull herself onto it, but instead she called up to Donaldson, "His name is William!" She wasn't shouting—we were both too nervous for that—but her voice was urgent and strong. By now the carriage was beginning to outpace her. "Tell them he's called William!"

The wheels creaked quickly down the road, and after a minute Lula stopped running and stood there looking after them. When I got up to her I saw that her face wore a shocked and exhausted expression, too worn-out even to cry, and I heard the leaves in some nearby trees lift and shudder in the wind.

"They'll make a plan," I told her, remembering what the farmhand had said. "They will. They'll make a plan for you and come back."

"But what about my baby? I need to feed him. Why wouldn't he take me?"

"Maybe the next place, maybe the hiding place, is too small for anyone but a baby?" I was making things up, speculating, and it felt strange. I gave it up. "I don't know." I gently touched Lula's shoulder and turned her around. There was nowhere to go now but back to the boat. The first thing was to get her away from this open road and off her bleeding feet.

"Please don't . . ." A sob came up from her throat marbling the rest of her sentence, but I understood what she wanted to say: *Please don't leave me.*

"Don't worry." I tried to comfort her. "I'll take care of you. And they'll make a plan and come back. We just have to hide you tonight. And maybe also tomorrow. Part of tomorrow."

She took hold of my arm, whispering something that might have been "Thank you" or might have been "Can you?" Without her basket her other hand hung empty and her shoulders seemed very thin. As she limped along next to me, I was afraid her feet would finally give way altogether and that I'd have to carry her, but it didn't come to that. We made it down the road and then back down the path to the boat.

But I had forgotten about Thaddeus. He was standing at the boat railing, smoking the end of a thickly rolled cigarette, and I had the feeling he had not gone right up to his stateroom on purpose. He looked around at the sound of our footsteps on the plank and then, after a moment, flicked the end of his cigarette over the guard. An owl started up and then stopped mid-call. The silence felt like something hiding. Thaddeus cocked his head at me, a question, as he drew a breath.

"Don't you say a word," I told him.

18

I tried to think of a place to hide her.

My room contained only the barest necessities: a cot, a wash-stand, and a line of brass hooks along one wall to hang my clothes. My blankets were too short to screen her if she hid underneath the cot, which was the only obvious place.

The green room was a possibility, although actors and actresses went in and out of there all day, checking costumes or making them-selves a private cup of tea. But there were crates in the green room, one of which might be large enough to hide Lula inside, although damp and moldy. I could line it with a sheet or a blanket. I would have to make holes for air. A day or two in a crate—after all she'd been through, I thought that she could manage that. But what about during our performances? I'd seen Pinky or Sam shift the crates to make seats for themselves while they waited for their cues or even look inside for a prop they'd misplaced. Any number of things might happen. And there was no lock on the door, as there was on my own door. Could she stay in the green room during the day and then come up here while everyone else was in the dining room eating supper? But that plan seemed too risky. On a boat as small as ours, there was no guarantee of privacy, even during mealtimes. People forgot a hand-kerchief, or wanted a shawl, or suddenly remembered a letter they the same route on purpose. When Mrs. Howard realized I was living on a boat moving down the Ohio River, the natural division between the North and the South, she might have seen it as an opportunity not to be missed. Perhaps she began to plan her schedule around ours. I could picture Donaldson settling Mrs. Howard and Comfort at an inn and then later driving to the dark road above the river to wait for me to bring him the rescued babies. The "packages," Mrs. Howard had called them. A dark snake seemed to wrap itself around me: a feeling of resentment, of being used. She had wanted me out of the way, and then she wanted me to help her. Would she help me now in return? I didn't know anything about getting a runaway slave to safety. I wouldn't know whom I could trust.

As I lay there fretting, Lula began to moan in her sleep, and then suddenly she cried out:

"Don't touch me! Don't you touch me!"

I sat up quickly and took her hand, which was very small. Her fingers were cold. I hushed her and bent to whisper in her ear that she was all right now. She was lying faceup with her two short dark braids splayed out against the pillow, and she looked even younger than fourteen. Perhaps she was. But she'd had a baby only two days before, a child giving birth to a child. A taste like old meat rose in my mouth. I wondered if she'd had a nightmare about the father—one of the sons, she'd said. When I stroked her forehead Lula didn't open her eyes but she did stop moaning. A few seconds later I heard the floorboards creak outside my room and my heart jumped. There was a knock at my door.

"May," Hugo said quietly. "You all right?"

I cleared my throat, hoping to keep my voice even. "I'm fine. I had a bad dream but I'm fine now."

I was watching Lula's face while I spoke. I was afraid she would cry out again or wake up and say something.

"You need anything?" Hugo asked.

"No, thank you," I said.

I hadn't locked my door—a mistake. There was a long, still moment, and then I heard Hugo go back to his room. I listened for the sound of his cot groaning as he lay down on it. When the quiet extended itself long enough, I let go of Lula's hand and, as quietly as I could, got up and locked my door, turning the iron key slowly to keep it from making noise. After that, I stretched back out on the floor, prepared to get up again at a moment's notice. But when I next opened my eyes, the sun was coming up and Lula was awake and turned on her side, looking down at me. I could feel our boat moving down the river.

I'd been dreaming of Giulia. "Someone's coming," Giulia had said.

I went over the possibilities again in my mind. The green room, the dining room, the office—they each had their drawbacks. The main one was that none of their doors had locks.

"Are they gonna find me," Lula whispered, "now that it's day?" It was still very early, the only light the soft gray of sunrise, but I understood her fear. She was curled up in a U on the cot and I sat down next to her, feeling the small nub of her knee against my hip.

"They're not going to find you." I tried to smile—I wanted to reassure her—but the movement felt awkward and pinched.

"They gonna look," she said grimly.

That was true. But who were "they"? We both no doubt painted our own pictures in our minds: mine was a man with manacles hanging from each pocket, a hound at his side, a whip in his hand, and the righteousness of the law spurring him on.

"I've locked the door," I told her. "No one can come in. But we have to think of a good place to hide you."

She slid off the cot and bent to look underneath it, and after a moment I looked, too, wondering if I could make the small space hidden from view. Below us I could hear Jemmy practicing lines as he worked the sweep on the starboard side, "Yes, sir, she put me in a box—she allowed the Marquis to escape and made me take his place. I cried, but she laughed."

A box would be perfect. I thought again of the crates in the green room. And then I thought: Helena's trunks.

They were still at the foot of my bed, since I had never found another place for them. The larger trunk, a dove-colored dress trunk, was big enough to hold a crouching girl. It opened like a book and had a patch of soft wood on one side, having once been left—this was my guess—in standing water. It was not the trunk of a woman who cared about appearances. Comfort's trunks, in contrast, had shiny latches (shined by me), and if just one strap began to show wear, she bought a whole new trunk, bargaining in her dimpled way with the trunk maker, trading the old one in for the latest model and getting a better discount than anyone but me thought she could. Helena's second trunk was smaller than the gray one, a long, black, workmanlike box with fraying straps.

However, the problem with Helena's trunks wasn't their shoddy condition. The problem was that they were both filled to the brim.

I'd taken all the costumes out of the larger trunk, but even so, it still had many of Helena's personal effects: two fishing rods of different length, waxed twine, a gutting knife, a hunting rifle, a few hats crushed in different ways, and one hefty teal book: *Birds of America, Volume I.* I read the words on the flyleaf: *Happy birthday to my sister, who is most happy outdoors. Love, Hugo.*

Lula and I discussed it in whispers. "Maybe we can wedge the smaller things into the other trunk?" "What doesn't fit we can just put under the bed." I heard shouts below us as the men landed the boat, but it was still too early for most of the actors to be up. The gulls and the shorebirds were loudest at this time of day, and I could also hear men calling out along the pier below us. I was thankful for the noise, and for having an end room. I knew Hugo wouldn't come back up to his stateroom until after breakfast. Still, I kept my good ear trained for footsteps on the stairs or along the upstairs guard: someone walking about before breakfast was unlikely but not impossible.

We packed everything we could into the smaller trunk, although I was loath to smash the hats more than they were already smashed. But the hunting rifle? I picked it up. It was on the short side, as befitted a woman, but not short enough to fit in the smaller, black trunk. With no better options, I put it under my bed and covered it with Helena's old shirtwaists and a shawl.

Lula had to sit on the trunk lid so I could latch it. She was in my hands completely: my responsibility. She could make no movement by herself toward freedom. What was worse, I realized that Hugo had landed the boat on the other side of the river. We were back in the South. I didn't tell Lula this. I just said, "Stay away from the window." The curtains were closed, but to be absolutely sure I pinned them together with three of Helena's hatpins.

"What's that noise?" Lula whispered.

I listened. "Those are seagulls. Haven't you ever heard seagulls?"

She shook her head and touched the end of her braid.

"But isn't your home . . . didn't you live near the river?"

It wasn't near the river, she told me. She and the farmhand had to travel all evening and into the night in a hay cart. She and William were squashed up in a barrel together.

"He slept mostly. That was one good thing." Below us we could hear the men's voices as they finished tying up the boat. "How many people live here?" she asked.

"On the *Floating Theatre*? Twelve."

We spoke so quietly, we could hardly hear each other, and Lula kept looking at my door. I got up and tested that it was locked, and then I brought over the basin to clean her feet again. I wanted to take another look at her sores.

"Have you ever been on a boat before?" I asked, wiping her heels carefully.

"Once," she said, "when I went to Evansville with the missus. Maybe I heard seagulls then but I forgot. That town was big! I couldn't believe how many stores they got. One store had a whole wall stacked with rolls of colored fabric. I don't know how you could choose just one. If you had the money."

"Do you like to sew?" I looked at her fingers, which were long and strong.

"Yes'm. I sewed both these dresses I have on."

She was still wearing her two dresses. I looked at the top one, and she lifted the hem up to show it to me. It was very straight, with small, even stitches. I could not have done better myself.

"Did you use a rule to keep the line straight?"

"Jes' my eyes," she told me.

The bell rang for breakfast.

"Hungry?" I asked.

She looked at me uncertainly, as though the last question might be a trick. Already her belly was flattening, and her arms were as thin as two twigs. Her curly eyelashes seemed out of place with her suffering.

"I'm always hungry," she said.

If anyone in the dining room had paid any attention, they might have seen how clumsy I was: I dropped my fork on my plate three times before I stopped counting, and I knocked over the pitcher of maple syrup, which was luckily empty. Fortunately, everyone was caught up in the thrill of dress rehearsal later that day and opening night tomorrow. No one paid any attention to me, although Hugo did look up briefly when, as I was rising, I pushed my chair back so abruptly, it fell.

I brought Lula folded pancakes that were moist from being in my pocket, and hot coffee in a large mug that I went back to refill twice. There was always a pot of coffee on the side table in the dining room, along with crackers and biscuits and sometimes cake. When I went back for Lula's second refill, I saw that Cook had just put out a fresh batch of biscuits, so I carried three of them back to my room. Lula drank the coffee quickly, hot as it was, and ate three biscuits one after another without stopping, then licked the tips of her fingers and felt the sides of her mouth for crumbs.

"That's a good biscuit," she said.

I locked my door again. By this time everyone had gone down to the theater for rehearsal, but I couldn't take any chances. After breakfast I'd asked Leo, whom I found in the office, if I could borrow a screwdriver. At the same time I gave him Helena's fishing rods, which did not fit in the small trunk. Killing two birds with one stone.

"What's this?" he asked, taking both the rods in one hand.

Alpha, beta, gamma. "Hugo wanted you to have them. They were Helena's," I said.

Leo ran his hand up one of the rods, the longer one, and felt the line between his two fingers. Then he spun the reel, which was sticky.

"Got to use a fishing rod," he told me. "Else it's unhappy."

"Just don't say anything to Hugo—thank you or anything. He might feel bad. You know, remembering."

Leo stooped to hunt around in the oversized tin bucket where he kept his tools. He handed me a long screwdriver without asking why I needed it. I was hoping I wouldn't have to tell him about Lula, not wanting to get him in trouble. "I know he would," he said about Hugo. "But those who've passed don't care if we remember or not. That's only for us. I'll be thinking about Miss Helena when I use it."

Back in my room I twisted the end of the screwdriver into the soft, rotting wood of the largest trunk, the one that had been left in standing water and was a little bit warped, while Lula worked at brushing her teeth. She had never brushed her teeth before, she told me, so I showed her how. Her eyeteeth were very white and slightly pointed, like a fox's, and her gums bled a little. While I worked on the trunk, she held my little square mirror in one of her hands and spit every so often into the basin.

After I decided that I'd punctured enough holes in the wood, I moved the trunk behind the door and turned it so that the hole-ridden side stood an inch from the wall, hidden from view. Since this particular trunk was for dresses—or fishing rods, in Helena's case—it stood upright, taller than it was wide, and inside there was a hook hanging down from the top for hangers. I worried that the hook would be in the way, but after Lula got herself curled up in there, sitting cross-legged with her knees raised, she said, "No, but look here." She took off her shawl and hung it on the hook, making a curtain in front of her. It wouldn't hide her from anyone really looking, but if the trunk was open a crack, all you would see was fabric.

I closed the trunk up.

"Can you breathe?" I asked.

"Yes'm," came the muffled reply.

I opened the trunk again.

"You don't have to stay here," I said. "I'll lock my door. You can just go in if you hear someone trying it."

"I don't mind," Lula said.

"I don't want you shut up inside all day."

Her large eyes looked watery, she blinked so little. "I'll just sit here with it open. If I hear someone come, I'll shut it up on me," she told me.

I watched her practice pulling in her legs and closing the trunk from the inside. When I was satisfied she could do it quickly and quietly enough, I said, "All right."

Then I handed her the *Birds of America* book that Hugo had given his sister.

"I don't know my letters," she told me.

"You don't have to read, you can just look at the pictures. See these words here?" I turned the cover toward her. "They say *Birds of America*. It's a book of birds."

"What's America?"

What's America? I glanced quickly at her to see if she was joking. "It's the country we live in. This big stretch of land, all the cities and farms together, they make America. Don't you have a mother or father to tell you these things?"

She shook her head no. "I have my auntie, but she never said nothin' like that." She opened the book to a color illustration covered by a thin piece of rice paper, which she lifted carefully by one corner. She breathed through her mouth like a child, but I noticed she was cupping her left breast with her free hand.

"Does your chest hurt?" Her milk wouldn't stop for a while, even without a baby to feed.

"Not so much to signify."

"I'll get you some ointment. You shouldn't be in pain."

She blew air out from her nose. "This ain't pain." She turned the page with one hand while keeping her other hand cupped under her breast. She wasn't looking at me anymore. As I'd hoped, the pictures caught her whole attention.

"Will you be all right while I'm gone? I'll lock the door. Don't make any noise, now."

"Mm. Mm-hmm."

I hoped she was right to trust me.

Earlier that morning, even before I went in to breakfast, I'd found a boy on the pier to carry my letter to Mrs. Howard to the ferry, where he was entrusted to commission another boy to take it across the river to the inn where she and Comfort were staying. This was faster than the post office, and even with paying two boys it did not cost any more. I'd asked for a return reply, and, after locking Lula into my stateroom and putting the key in my pocket, I leaned over the guard-rail to see if the ferry was on its way back. Below me in the theater I could hear Jemmy speaking some lines: "Flora, Flora, you are in the plot!"

And then Hugo in his director's voice: "Show us your eyes, man! Show us your eyes! No, no, don't stop, keep going."

There were a good many boatmen along the pier, but I could not see the ferry on the water. As I was coming down the stairs Pinky came out of the theater. He was dressed in his old-woman's wig and cap and had a gray flannel wrapped around his neck. He said hello to me and then coughed after his words. A strong waft of garlic came from his mouth.

"Are you ill?" I asked him. Actors superstitiously believe that garlic helps anything from a sore throat to a bunion.

"Just a bit of a throat, nothing more," he said. "I'm popping up to see if Cook won't give me some more garlic to crunch."

"That won't do anything. I'm going to town; I'll stop at the apothecary there." Which I was already planning to do, for Lula, but I didn't tell him that.

Pinky thanked me several times. "Oh, that's very generous done, very generous done to be sure. It's only a scratch I'm thinking, but I can't lose my voice—" Here he stopped and swallowed laboriously. "Tomorrow's the big night!"

"Rehearsal going all right?" I asked.

"Booming! Only that Jemmy, he needs to learn his lines better. We still haven't run all the way through without stopping. But our Liddy is wonderful, don't you think? Pity she should forsake all that talent of hers for a man . . . a man like that," he said.

"A man like what?" I asked with interest. Had he noticed Dr. Early's sly behavior? But he was only jealous, being in love with Liddy himself.

"Oh, any man, really," he said pulling his face back as if speaking into his flannel scarf. "Any man except me."

I thought he was the better of the two, and I told him so.

"Pity only you and I know it," he said with a self-effacing grin.

When I got down to the pier, I looked up at my stateroom window and was relieved to find that I couldn't see anything through the pinned-shut curtains. Maybe it was a mistake to leave Lula alone, but at the same time I couldn't arouse suspicion. I had to do what I always did when we landed in a new place: put up posters and give out some free tickets, no matter that ever since breakfast I felt as if I had swallowed a walnut whole and it was now lodged in the side of my stomach.

The day was cloudless, like the day before, but hotter. Although the town, Smithland, had a reputation for lawlessness—there were a good many taverns up and down both sides of the street—as I stepped inside the apothecary shop I could see that people there took their health seriously. The shelves along both walls were lined with covered glass bottles and jars, and in front of the shelves stood low glass cases displaying metal canisters and round disks of ointment as well as the inevitable cigar boxes. At the far end of the shop I spotted a low doorway closed off by a green velvet drape. Above it hung two signs: "Open All Night" and "Inquire Apothecary Within."

I could hear voices coming from beyond the velvet drape, but no one else was in the shop. Unaided, I looked along the shelves for what I wanted: spirits of ammonia and niter for Pinky's throat, and dragon's blood to stop Lula's milk. As I went along, I breathed in a mixture of wood polish and fish oil and a dry, powdery odor that I could not identify.

I found the jar of dragon's blood and pulled it off the shelf. Then I found the ammonia. The voices in the back room, although not loud, became more discernible as I got closer, and as I crossed in front of the doorway I thought there was something familiar about the voice of the man speaking.

". . . you may have heard it called Irish moss. Good for rickets, too. A bit of lemon juice will help it down the pipe."

Another voice responded in a low tone, and I couldn't catch his words. But when the third man spoke, I turned abruptly. It was Thaddeus.

"Thanks, Doc," Thaddeus was saying. "Lucky for me I ran into you."

"I see it all the time," the first man said.

Now I recognized the voice: Dr. Early. I immediately turned to leave, but in my haste I forgot to put down the bottles I was holding. A man came into the shop just as I was exiting, and he held up his arms when I nearly plunged into him.

"Whoa there," he said with a grin. But he didn't step aside.

The apothecary lifted the green drape and came scurrying out of the back room, saying, "Well, now, I didn't know anyone else was in here."

"The lady was just leaving, I think," the man at the front door said. He took off his hat.

I saw the apothecary look at the bottles in my hands. He was a little man wearing spectacles and a green vest that matched the green drape over the door.

"No," I said. "That is, I wanted to pay for these first, of course. I thought . . ." I paused. *Alpha, beta, gamma.* "I thought I might have dropped my purse outside. But here it is right here in my pocket."

Thaddeus had come out of the room after the apothecary, and I was aware of him watching me and grinning. He could probably tell I was lying, but he just said, "Well, Miss May. This is a surprise. On a particular errand? Dr. Early is here, too. Our Liddy's future happiness. I've finally met the man."

He spoke with his usual light tone, and I could not tell if he was sincere or not. I could never tell with Thaddeus.

"I'm here to get Pinky some things for his throat."

"Pinky has a bad throat?"

"Also some lozenges, if you have them," I said to the apothecary, who had begun wrapping up the small bottle of ammonia in brown tissue paper.

Dr. Early came out from the back room carrying a dropper bottle, which he gave to Thaddeus. When he saw me he came up and took my hand as though we were the best of friends, apologizing for missing the show the night before. "Completely unavoidable. I was called on to help deliver a baby. Up all night. The life of a doctor." He looked impeccably clean and not the least bit tired. In his left hand he carried a pair of spotless gray gloves.

"Dragon's blood?" the apothecary asked me, picking up the next bottle. "That won't help a bad throat."

Dr. Early looked at the bottle the apothecary was holding. Then he looked at me. Something in his eyes changed very slightly and my brain wouldn't work for a second, even to summon my Greek.

Thaddeus said, "Oh, that's for makeup."

Dr. Early turned. "Makeup?"

"For the stage," Thaddeus explained. "We mix a drop or two with talcum powder to make our cheeks red."

The apothecary took out a large white handkerchief and sneezed into it. Then he said, "Even the men?"

"Makeup," Dr. Early said. I wasn't sure if he believed Thaddeus or not. "Well, Miss May, you do a bit of everything, don't you? And here I thought you simply sat in a corner and sewed."

There was something not very nice in his voice, and I saw the apothecary glance at him. But I understood. He wanted to let me know that he had still not forgiven me for showing Liddy the runaway slave advertisements. He would never forgive me for that.

"Oh, I do much more," I said with some feeling. "You would be surprised at how much I can do."

Dr. Early eyed me again with that shrewd look of his. A bully, I was thinking. That was what he was. The apothecary looked from me to the doctor and then back again.

"That will be thirty-eight cents," he said firmly, as though that number would settle all differences between us.

Dr. Early touched his hat. "I will see you this evening," he said as he left us, but I did not know if his remark was directed to Thaddeus or to me or to both.

Back on the boat, I mixed the throat gargle and gave it to Pinky, I gave Lula a draft of dragon's blood to stop her milk, and I stole a half loaf of bread and two broiled chicken legs for her dinner while Cook was napping in his galley hammock. In the afternoon I watched the end of the second dress rehearsal and made minor adjustments to Mrs. Niffen's dress. I fitted the actors up and helped them change and listened for any sounds coming from my stateroom. Not hearing any, I nevertheless made excuses to go upstairs so I could check.

Lula sat half inside the trunk the whole day looking at the bird book and jiggling her knees to get out her energy. Whenever I came into the room, she asked if I'd gotten any news. But although I'd been sitting in the auditorium watching by the window, no boys came running up to the boat with a note for me. Finally, toward evening, I told her that it might take another day.

I could see she was scared, and to distract her I asked if she liked the book all right.

She showed me her favorite page. It was a bluebird with a caterpillar in its mouth, feeding a baby. "Look at all the legs on that thing," she said. She meant the caterpillar. "Someone spent a whole day I bet just drawing those little bitty legs."

"You like it because of that?"

"Well, that's one thing. Also the blue color of her wings."

I fingered the holes I'd made in the back of the trunk, wondering if they were large enough, and I re-pinned my curtains to keep them closed. Meanwhile, Dr. Early spent the afternoon on the pier with Rascal. Sometimes I saw him speaking to the riverboat men, and once in a while he wrote something down in a small notebook. Just before supper I noticed he was talking to Thaddeus near the stage plank, and my throat seemed to close a little when I saw them. Rehearsal had finished and everyone else was resting for the show that night—our last performance of songs and jokes and jigs. Thaddeus should have been resting, too.

When he came up on the boat I asked him what he and Dr. Early had been talking about. It was the first time we'd been alone together since the previous night. But instead of answering me he said in a low voice,

"Are you still hiding her?"

I hesitated and then nodded.

"The doctor is a slave catcher, you know," Thaddeus told me. "He's on the lookout for a runaway right now."

My breath caught in my throat. "For Lula?"

"For a man named Jackson."

I was relieved, but only for a moment.

"I knew he was still doing that," I said about Dr. Early. "I knew it."

"Twenty-year-old man who ran away yesterday. One-hundred-and-fifty-dollar reward." Thaddeus looked at me sideways. "That's a lot of money."

"They wouldn't pay so much for a girl," I said quickly.

"Of course not," Thaddeus said smoothly. "Not for a girl."

It was impossible for me to guess what he was thinking. I was never good at that sort of thing. Was it my imagination, or were his blond curls darker this morning? I wouldn't put it past him to put a rinse on his hair like an old actress Comfort used to laugh about in Boston.

"Well, keep it to yourself," Thaddeus said, turning to go up the stairs. The supper bell was ringing. "He told me he's only doing it once or twice more. He wants money to buy Liddy a nice wedding present is all."

I believed that Dr. Early would want money to buy this or that for this person or that person from now until every runaway slave was caught in every corner of this country, but I kept that opinion to myself. He would never change his ways. He knew it and I knew it. Maybe we were the only two.

"I wonder how much they would pay, though," Thaddeus added as he went up. "For a girl."

Everything above my waist seemed to stiffen at once, the back of my neck in particular.

"Thaddeus," I said. "Wait." I followed him up to the guard. I didn't want to raise my voice in case anyone overheard. "Thaddeus. You can't be thinking about that."

"Oh, I know," he said. "Only it's hard to be on the wrong side of the law. Makes a fellow uncomfortable."

"My . . . my connection"—all at once I was afraid to say too much—"is coming to get her tonight. He's coming here to get her." *Alpha, beta, gamma, delta.* "I've had a message."

"You're lying," Thaddeus said evenly, without turning around. By now we were walking in single file toward the dining room, Thaddeus leading. On our left, the river glistened silvery-gray, pushing a small keelboat west.

"You can't even see me!" I said.

"I don't need to. Remember, I was the one who taught you how. But don't worry, May. Ten or twenty dollars doesn't much signify. Or whatever the reward for a girl might be."

I thought of those broadsides I'd found on Dr. Early's piano. Some of them named rewards of up to one hundred dollars, even for women. "I can get you more money," I told him. "After supper, if you want, I can give you some more."

Thaddeus stepped aside to let me go into the dining room first. A gentleman. I could see his face now, which was pale and expressionless. "That would be helpful," he said.

It may sound strange, but after this encounter with Thaddeus my anxiety, although not exactly lessening, shifted a little. Even as I went into the dining room, taking care to sit at a different table from the one he chose, I felt something alter inside of me. It was as though my fears had been suddenly repacked in my body, like the contents of Helena's trunks, moved and fitted into a corner somewhere to make room for other, more necessary considerations. I could not afford to be anxious; maybe that was it. Just like that day on the deck of the *Moselle* when I found the scissors in my hand and proceeded to cut away Giulia's dress and my own so our clothes wouldn't drown us, all my attention went into the task of survival.

Certain facts ordered themselves in my mind: we were in the South. There were no bridges across this river, although there was constant talk of building one. Safety for Lula meant finding a passage north, and since there were no bridges, that meant going either by boat or by ferry.

The next day the *Floating Theatre* was landing in Paducah, another town in the South. But after that we might go back to Indiana. I resolved to ask Hugo. If the next landing was in the North, that would mean only one more day of hiding her. The question of where she would go in the North was still open. I would take her myself, if necessary. I would go all the way to Canada with her if I had to. Part of this resolve was fear and part of it was anger. At Mrs. Howard, at Thaddeus, at Dr. Early, even at Hugo. At everyone who wasn't helping me. It was not logical to be angry with Hugo, but I was. I was angry at the world, for making such laws.

On the other hand, why wait for Hugo to move the boat? I could

row her to the North myself that night in the little rowboat. At dinner
I pushed the limp stewed greens around on my plate and cut up my
chicken without taking a bite, trying to work out what to do. Pinky sat
next to me. He was feeling worse, I could tell. He spoke very little,
saving his voice, which was fine with me. Cook was railing against
someone who had stolen a couple of chicken legs (me) and I dared
not look at him, fearing it would show in my face. Meanwhile, Mrs.
Niffen was telling everyone what she thought they should do tomorrow in preparation for opening night—rest, a lemon gargle, followed
by a short walk in fresh air—and everyone but Mr. Niffen made a
show of listening to her. Thaddeus sat at a table across the dining
room near the windows, eating heartily.

After dinner, as I was unlocking the door to my room, Hugo came
walking up the guard.

"May, a word?" he asked.

I assumed he wanted to give me some instructions for tomorrow,
and I followed him into his stateroom. He pulled his desk chair over
to the window and took a white towel from a hook.

"I wonder if you would do me a favor. Helena used to cut my
hair for me, but now, well, you can see I haven't managed it myself, and tomorrow being opening night . . . do you think you could
give me a trim? The back is getting long. I meant today to go to a
barber."

He handed me a pair of scissors. I lay the open blades against my
thumb; there were small specks of rust along the bottoms, and in one
spot the metal was so worn down, it looked as if it had been nibbled
on by an impossibly small rabbit. They probably hadn't been sharp-
ened all summer. "Let me get mine," I said.

Back in my stateroom I looked at Lula and put my finger to my
lips. I pointed to the wall, and she nodded. We had already gotten
used to not speaking to each other when we heard Hugo in his room,
since the wall between us was about the width of a pancake.

"These will do the job," I said to Hugo, returning with my own scissors.

He sat on the high-backed wooden chair with his back to the window, giving me the light. The summer sun made the evening feel like afternoon, although our show would begin in an hour or two. Outside I could see other boats tied up for the night, and no one was left on the pier rolling barrels or bargaining sales—only Dr. Early. He was sitting on one of Hugo's canvas chairs, looking out at the water. I wondered why he had not eaten dinner with us. Keeping vigilant watch for the slave Jackson, no doubt.

Hugo's hair was very soft and dark. I combed it out and began taking small snips at the ends, using my fingers to measure straight lines.

"Pinky tells me you went to the apothecary for him today. Is that right?" Hugo asked.

"Don't move your head," I told him.

"That was very well done, May. Thank you for thinking of it. But that's not what I wanted to speak to you about."

"I thought you wanted me to cut your hair?"

"Yes, yes, quite right," Hugo said. He blew out some air, maybe a laugh.

"Don't move your head," I said again.

"Sorry." He stiffened his shoulders as though to make a sturdier base. "Right, then. Besides cutting my hair, I did want to speak to you, to take this opportunity to tell you something I've been thinking about. Now. May. It occurs to me that you are beginning to feel at home on this boat of mine. Am I right? You know our ways now, more or less, and you can anticipate our needs, Pinky's gargle, for instance, and you take it upon yourself to help out even if it's not sewing. That's new for you. I had the impression when you first started that you only cared about sewing. The costumes and so forth. You felt that was your job. Whereas I felt your job included a number of things, really anything that might need to be done. And I can tell you now that I was a little worried for a while that you might not be quite capable. Well, we both were, weren't we? But you *are* capable, and more, and I want to thank you for that. I know Pinky is grateful for the gargle."

"I was going to the apothecary's anyway," I said, and then I stopped because I hadn't meant to tell him that. But Hugo did not ask me why else I would go. Instead he said:

"Well, I hope with the medicine and a good night's sleep Pinky will be just fine. However. There's something else I noticed, and that is . . . well, I'm sorry if I'm trespassing into your personal life here, but I've noticed, being in the next room over, I've noticed that you sometimes call out in your sleep. Last night, for instance. I heard you."

I stopped and brought the scissors toward me, away from his head. I looked at the blades and then at my hand. Hugo seemed to be waiting for me to say something.

"I have nightmares sometimes," I told him.

"Yes, nightmares. That's what I thought. Any idea why?"

"I . . . well, you know . . . the *Moselle*."

"Mm. Yes, of course, indeed. But I mean to say, May, that your fears may be more than just about the *Moselle*. It's occurred to me that your fears may also have to do with your situation at present. Your life now. You know what I'm getting at?"

I pulled away again. Now I really was shaking. I started to say, *How did you find out?*

But Hugo kept talking. "You probably think that, after the summer is over, your employment will end. You're not an actor; you can't move onto a stage theater in some town or another. You're part seamstress, part stage manager, and part advance man, but most of the actors in towns see to their own costumes, and most stage managers are men. And of course an established theater doesn't need an advance man to advertise its shows. So I want to tell you that I've made a decision. If you'd like, you can come with me to Pittsburgh after the summer and wanted to read aloud, and they popped back to their stateroom to get it. They might see us coming up the stairs: me and a runaway slave girl. That would be the end.

I took Lula up to my stateroom, not knowing what else to do, and she looked all around at the small space, the cot and washstand and the brass wall hooks illuminated only by the moonlight coming in through the window. I pulled the curtains closed and then pulled down the blind that covered the window on the top half of the balcony door. After that, I carefully wiped her blistered and bloodied heels with the rag I used to polish my boots so that her feet began to smell like blackening. She had delicate, curved arches and long toes. I gave her a clean pair of stockings in lieu of bandages, and then I dipped a clean cloth into the water basin, wrung it out, and washed her face.

"Thank you, miss," Lula said when I was done.

"Call me May," I told her, but she had already begun crying in quiet gulps and might not have heard me.

I made her lie down on the cot, pulling the blanket up to her chin and touching her forehead as my mother used to do for me. Then I stretched out on the floor beside her, using one shawl as a blanket and another as a pillow, and I listened to her quick, low, muffled sobs, wishing I could say something helpful or in some way ease her mind. After a while her sobs fell away and she went to sleep.

Exhausted as I was, I stayed awake for a long time studying the ceiling, trying to think what to do. I had certainly made a mess of things. On the other hand, I couldn't help but feel that it was hardly my fault. Anyone would have done the same. I would write to Mrs. Howard in the morning, I decided. I still had Comfort's itinerary, which I'd tucked into a book of verses that Liddy had loaned me. By now Donaldson had probably informed Mrs. Howard about Lula anyway. It was lucky for me that they were following the Ohio River, as we were. Or was it luck? For the first time I wondered if we were on work in the theater there. I can get you a job with me. Mostly sewing, probably, but maybe other tasks as well; I'm not sure. My point is, you don't have to worry about how you'll get your bread and butter after the *Floating Theatre* closes. I don't want you to worry about that. I don't want you to have nightmares over it. Life can be hard for a single woman, I know that."

"Oh," I said. The back of his head was very still, and the late-afternoon light, past its gloaming, cast a weak shine on his hair, making it look like something metallic, a helmet. I tried and failed to think about my future. Pittsburgh, he had said. At the moment my imagination could go only as far as the northern bank of the Ohio River. He wanted to help me, but he was thinking too far in advance.

"You've done very well here," he told me. There was a pause. I wasn't sure what to say. I looked at the scissors, which were open above his head, and I carefully pulled the blades together. Through the window I could see that Dr. Early was still sitting in the canvas chair, smoking a cigar. I suddenly realized that he could be there all night. That meant no chance to sneak out with Lula in the rowboat.

"Are you finished?" Hugo asked. It took me a moment to realize that he meant his hair. I pulled my fingers through it. It was as fine as a child's. I could smell the soap he used on his face and hands before dinner. I was glad I could not see his eyes and that he could not see mine. I didn't know what I might look like to him.

I glanced out the window again. Dr. Early, of course, hadn't moved. I said to Hugo's back, "Where are we going after Paducah?"

"Joppa, Illinois," he told me. "Is that all right, then? What I offered? Do you think you can rest easier now?"

"I'm not sure," I said honestly. "I'll try."

He stood up and looked in the mirror. "It seems the right side is a tad longer than the left," he said gently, and I realized that I had neglected to cut the right side at all. He smiled at me, amused, and in spite of my worries I smiled back.

But before he could sit down again, someone spoke from the other side of the wall. "*What* is *this?*"

It was Mrs. Niffen, and her voice was coming from inside my room. I ran to the guard, feeling in my pocket for my key as I did so. It wasn't there.

When I threw open my door, I found Mrs. Niffen standing in the middle of my room holding a dinner plate.

"What are you doing in here?" I demanded. My voice was shaking from fear but it might have sounded like anger. From the corner of my eye I could see, partially hidden by the open door, Lula's trunk. It was closed, and Lula was nowhere in sight. Her discarded stockings, though, had not made it inside the trunk with her. I stepped back and pushed at them with my foot, at the same time thinking I could claim them as my own.

Hugo was behind me. "Margaret, who gave you leave to go into May's room?" he asked Mrs. Niffen.

"I thought I heard something, a scurrying sound like vermin. And look at this." She showed him the plate with two gnawed-at chicken bones. "Cook's chicken legs. It was you who took them."

"Now, Margaret," Hugo said.

"This whole room reeks of chicken."

"Margaret, it's all right."

"All right? Now, Captain, you know it isn't all right. I don't want to scatter rat poison all over the boat. It's bad for Celia to breathe that in—she's a growing girl—and what if Oliver got hold of something? He'd be dead in a thrice and it would be your fault." She turned to me. Her eyes were red and her white hair seemed very shiny, as though righteousness gave her an angelic glow.

"We are not permitted to eat in our rooms," she told me, holding the plate out as proof.

I spotted my room key on the bed next to my sewing box. Where I'd left it after I fetched my scissors. Again I looked around for signs of Lula, but her extra dress and her boots were still where I'd stashed them, under my bed.

"All right," I said. "I'm guilty. I brought food into my room."

Mrs. Niffen kept staring at me with her little red eyes. "That's it? No apology?"

I wasn't going to apologize to her, but I did turn to Hugo and said I was sorry.

"Margaret should not have come in here, but she's right about the rats," Hugo told me. "River rats are the worst. They're the size of baby cows and will eat through a brick wall to get to a chicken bone."

Baby cows? "You mean calves," I said before I could stop myself. I was not being sarcastic. My father was a dairy farmer, after all.

Mrs. Niffen said, "Cheek!"

But Hugo's eyes crinkled into a smile, though his mouth didn't follow suit. I had the thought that, just as I had learned the ways of the boat, maybe he had learned the ways of me.

"Calves. Of course." He waited for me to say something more, but I did not. "Will you promise not to bring food in here again?" he asked me after a moment. Mrs. Niffen harrumphed, as if this was too little a penalty for my serious crime.

I didn't need my Greek. I was getting quite skilled at this. "I promise," I lied.

19

As I suspected, Dr. Early stayed out on the pier all night.

At breakfast the next morning, when this was discovered and discussed, Liddy told us, "He writes poetry. He looks for inspiration in nature."

"What?" Hugo asked with some amusement. "A doctor and a poet, too?"

"What a fine man, my dear," Mrs. Niffen said to her.

From across the table Thaddeus mouthed to me, "Jackson." The runaway slave. But of course I had already guessed what Dr. Early had been doing all night.

"He's sleeping in the office now," Hugo said. "He came on board when I woke up to move the boat. Pretty good hand at the sweep."

"Let's bring him a plate of pancakes," Mrs. Niffen suggested. "He shouldn't have to stay at an inn tonight, all that expense. Don't you think, Captain? Since he's doing so much for the show. I'm sure he'll fetch such a crowd today as never before." This with a significant look toward me.

But before she could fetch him a plate, Dr. Early came into the dining room looking as fresh as ever. With all the attention on him, no one noticed the slices of ham I slipped into my pocket. All my clothes had begun to smell like past meals.

Back in my stateroom, I gave Lula her breakfast. Today she was keeping herself closed into the trunk except for a crack, understandably nervous after yesterday's scare. I had given her the steamboat pincushion to look at as a curiosity, and it was still in her lap.

"I think I could make something like this," she said, turning it over in her hands. "If I had the right material and real good scissors."

I locked my door from the inside and came over to look. Crouching down, I saw where she had pulled back the steamboat's little cloth side wheel to see how it had been sewn in. "See?" she said. "You just need to cut out lots of parts and stuff them, then sew them together."

"You'd need very good eyes."

She nodded. "And a long nail or something to push in the wool. But not sharp."

"Maybe a tapestry needle," I said. "That has a flat head."

I gave her a basin of water and a clean cloth. Then I turned around so she could wash herself with some privacy.

"I received a note this morning," I told her. "They're coming for you tonight."

The note had been brought by a young boy who had eyes more for the boat than for me; I spotted him walking around the lower deck, looking into all the windows and running his hand idly along the painted wood beneath them. The message was written in Mrs. Howard's large scrawl: *I've made everything ready. Our friend will wait for you on the road above the pier; meet him with the package just after the show begins, and he will take care of things from there.* By "things" I assumed she meant Lula.

"Will they take me to my baby?" Lula whispered. "To William?"

"I don't know what they'll do," I said truthfully. "But it seems as though they've made a plan at last."

"Like the man said, they do like their plans." I was sitting on the bed with my back toward her, but I could hear the bitterness in her voice.

"Would you rather cut and run?" I asked. "Take your chances?"

"That's what I did do," Lula reminded me.

There was a small nightstand between the bed and the window, and on a sudden hunch I picked up the book of verses there. It was the book Liddy had lent me, into which I'd tucked Comfort's itinerary. The book was small and beautifully bound in dark brown leather, the title etched in gold: *Crossing the River at Night and Other Poems* by Dr. Martin Early.

I pushed the pinned curtains aside to look out. There he was, walking toward a group of rousters. A moment later I saw that Thaddeus was following him. Thaddeus must have called out, because Dr. Early stopped, turned around, and then waited. My hands felt suddenly sweaty, and I nearly dropped the curtain.

"What is it?" Lula asked me. She seemed to be able to know what I was feeling by reading my back.

"Nothing, really," I said. I was watching Thaddeus and Dr. Early talk to each other. Thaddeus was standing very still, his legs apart, like someone keeping a fine balance. "It's nothing. I just wish it was tonight already."

I heard someone walking along the guard. When the footsteps stopped at my door, Lula's face went stiff and scared, and we looked at each other for half a second before she folded herself into the trunk and quietly closed it. I glanced around the room for signs of her and picked up the basin of water from the floor. As I carried it back to the washstand I saw by the jittery water that my hands were shaking.

"Who is it?" I called out.

"Hugo and Pinky. Can we come in?"

I took the key from my pocket. Hugo was frowning when I opened the door.

"What's this, you're locking your door from the inside now? Is this because of the chicken?"

"I've had things disappear from my room," I said.

Mrs. Niffen must have been out on the guard, or maybe the door to her own room was open, because she called out, "Only things that belonged to me!"

Hugo's face contorted a moment, trying not to laugh. He said, "You should be able to guard your things while you're here, though, don't you think? Or are they all taken by force?"

"I've never taken anything!" Mrs. Niffen called out again, belying her previous statement.

Hugo looked around and spotted Lula's trunk behind the door.

"There it is, Pinky."

Pinky walked over to the trunk and laid his hands on it. "Ugh," he said in a very rough voice as he tried to tilt it back. "What's in here?"

For a moment I couldn't move. Pinky's grip slipped and the trunk knocked back down to the floor—only a couple of inches, but I could imagine the terrified Lula inside. Out on the pier a dog started up a string of short, loud barks.

"What are you doing?" I said. "Don't!"

"We need it for the show tonight," Hugo told me.

"Lend us a hand, will you?" Pinky growled. His voice had gotten worse, not better.

I stepped between Hugo and the trunk. "Wait—no—I have things in there . . . Helena's things, and some of my own . . . since, you know, this room is very small. I needed the storage. For some of my things. Some of my private things."

I was babbling, and I stopped to take a breath. "Just let me empty it first."

Pinky stepped away and he and Hugo both looked at me, waiting for me to empty the trunk so they could take it downstairs.

"I'll call for you when it's ready," I said.

"How long can it take?" Hugo asked.

"I'll call for you," I said again.

"Well, all right." But instead of leaving he walked to the window, pushed aside the curtain, and looked out. "That Thaddeus has become very interested in Liddy's doctor," he said.

I wanted to look down at the pier, too, but at the same time I was afraid to move too far from Lula's trunk.

"Thick as thieves," Pinky said hoarsely.

Hugo looked back. "That's the other thing, May. Pinky's voice is going. We may need you to stand in for him tonight."

"What?"

"You've been to enough rehearsals. You must know the lines by now, and if necessary I can prompt you from the wings. There aren't many."

"But I'm a woman!"

Hugo grinned. "It's a woman's role, as you might recall."

"What about Leo? You don't want to miss the joke of a man dressed up as a woman. That's a good joke."

"Not playing in the South. Not with his color," Hugo said. "More's the shame and pity. But I know you can do it, May. Remember our talk last night? You've proved yourself very able, very able indeed."

Too able, I thought. There was no chance that I was going to step foot on the stage. All those people looking at me. The lights of the lanterns glaring up into my eyes. As if reading my thoughts, Hugo reminded me that I was on the stage every night playing the piano.

"That's different," I said.

"Not by much," Hugo argued good-naturedly. Pinky was looking at me. When my eyes met his, he grimaced in sympathy.

"I'm going to fix you another gargle," I told him.

"I just had one before breakfast."

"Well, I'm going to fix you another. We've got to get you in shape for the show."

To say that as the day wore on the excitement on the boat became ever more palpable would be like saying as the sun went down, the daylight faded. Although what I really wanted to do was wrap a flannel around my neck and claim a bad throat like Pinky, keeping to my room all day and watching over Lula, I was far too busy to do that. The last-minute costume alterations, the inspection of each small lantern that lined the edge of the stage, running lines with Liddy, helping Cook make sandwiches, since everyone was too busy to sit down to a meal—all this and more fell to me. Meanwhile, I brought Pinky so many gargles and cups of hot tea with lemon that I thought he would need three extra chamber pots in his room.

Luckily, as planned, Dr. Early went to town instead of me to promote the show. I supplied him with complimentary tickets and posters, and he slid the pieces of paper from my outstretched fingers with a slight smile and a thank-you that could have meant anything.

What had Thaddeus told him out on the pier? The night before, I'd given Thaddeus ten dollars more and he took the money graciously, as graciously as Dr. Early received the complimentary tickets today. But I could trust neither one of them. Scenario after scenario rose up in my mind: Lula caught, Lula shot, Lula with manacles locked to her wrists. If this is imagination, I thought, then it is a painful part of the human condition.

As I was watching Dr. Early's figure disappear on the road to town, Thaddeus came up next to me and leaned against the rail and watched him, too. We were standing on the lower deck near the office, and I could feel a slight breeze coming in off the water. I looked quickly around; there was no one on the deck now but us.

"Did you tell Dr. Early about Lula?" I asked him in a low voice.

"Of course not," Thaddeus replied. "But, May, listen. We should think about this. I believe we could get eighty dollars if we released her. That's forty dollars each."

"Released her," I thought. As though we were talking about freeing a bird. He looked at me earnestly, and I noticed again how he was

aging. He ate too much; in a few years he'd be good only for portly characters—mayors and city bankers.

"When we started, you were sympathetic," I reminded him.

"May, May. Listen to me. It's not that I'm unsympathetic, but we're on the wrong side of the law here. Surely you can appreciate that."

I did. And I didn't like being on the wrong side of the law. I thought of the whipping posts I'd seen in every river town, and the corner jails without windows. Also the threats on the broadsides—Old Judge Lynch. For a moment I felt something cold coil up my spine. It was difficult for me to break a rule so deliberately. I wish I could explain how it felt, like a twist in my body that cried out for straightening.

But "I'm abiding by my choices," I told Thaddeus.

"You don't have to. That's my point. You can come around to the right side of the law. You're a practical person, May. We both are. We're alike in that way. We'll just tell the authorities we were tricked by the abolitionists. The rabble-rousers. But now we see the error of our ways, and we want to rectify that."

I looked at his puffy, bland face. Back in Pittsburgh Comfort sometimes called him Fatuous Mason. *Alpha, beta, gamma, delta.* "I understand," I said.

"You're reciting Greek to yourself," Thaddeus said sharply. "I can tell."

"All right, all right. But what would you have me do?"

"Don't do anything. I'll handle it. Whatever happens, we'll split it fifty-fifty."

"If I get caught and hung, you'll split that with me fifty-fifty?"

"We'll be on the right side of the law," Thaddeus repeated. "You don't need to worry about hanging."

Voices floated down from the upper deck, and Hugo and Liddy appeared at the top of the stairs. "What are you two whispering about?" Hugo called down to us.

"The sleeves of my costume," Thaddeus said.

He could lie, I noticed, without any hesitation at all.

"Well, I have some bad news, May," Hugo said coming down. "Pinky's lost his voice entirely."

I felt the hard shell of a walnut again in my side. I took a breath but could not seem to exhale afterward. "Cook?" I suggested weakly.

"Cook's been drinking since lunch; all the excitement has got to him. I'm afraid it'll have to be you. But it's only one scene. And I'll be right next to the stage feeding you lines if you need them."

"Don't worry, May," Liddy told me. And Thaddeus said, with a smile that seemed to convey worlds, "You'll be fine."

The walnut being now permanently lodged on the left side of my stomach, I went up to my room to sit on my bed. I felt nauseous and a little bit cold. It wasn't just the play, of course. I had never before kept a secret, or at least something I was consciously protecting from being exposed, and the long wait for help was wearing on me. Not to mention the threat of Dr. Early, and now Thaddeus. I felt like I was back to being a small child when more was expected of me than I could possibly give. Lula sat halfway inside the trunk, as she had yesterday, watching me. I had my arms wrapped around my middle.

"What's wrong?" she whispered. "You sick?"

"Hugo wants me to act on the stage tonight. Captain Cushing, I mean."

Next to me, on the bed, lay Pinky's "sides"—his part in the play—on a thin roll of foolscap. Lula could see I was upset, I guess, because she got out of the trunk and sat next to me on the bed.

"Have you ever seen a play?" I asked her.

"Not a real one. Just back home, you know, a couple o' the men used to act out the family sometimes. Pretend to be the three sons, the young masters. If no one could see."

"Do you know what you're going to do when you get free?" Talking to her made me feel marginally better.

"I'm going to learn how to read."

"I meant for money."

"Oh. Cooking or cleaning for someone? Same as I did before, I expect, only for wages. Though I'm not much at cooking. Peeling potatoes and cutting 'em up, I can do that."

"How about sewing?"

"What, like making new dresses?"

"And alterations. Maybe a hotel would hire you. Some of the big ones like to have girls on hand to help with such things."

The sun was slanting in under my curtains on its way down. In a couple of hours it would be time for the show and I hadn't even looked at my costume. I had Pinky's wig—the nightcap with gray hair—and the old nightdress of Mrs. Niffen's. But I was beyond caring if either one fit.

I let out the breath I'd been holding. "Lula," I said, "Listen. Something's come up." I decided to tell her about Thaddeus. Maybe she could help me think of a plan. She was smart—that was obvious. She got herself here, didn't she? And she got her baby away to freedom. Lula listened with a worried frown. After I finished, she said, "I *thought* there were something about him."

"I'm supposed to take you outside to meet your connection while everyone is watching the play, but now that's impossible. I'll be on the stage."

"You'll just have to get me to them before it starts."

"I've thought of that. But so many things could get in my way. It won't be completely dark, for one thing. And what if they're not there yet? You can't wait by yourself. Or can you?" As much as we stopped at these little southern towns, I still didn't always understand what slaves could do alone and what would stand out.

"If I seemed to be doing some chore or piece of work . . ." Lula said. We looked at each other. What would that be? A girl couldn't be a rouster or a boat hand.

"If we can't meet them before the show starts," I said, "I'll be on the stage and I won't be able to protect you."

"You think the doctor and Thaddeus will come looking for me while you on the stage?"

"They could come up here even now. Thaddeus knows you're in my room. The only thing saving us is that Dr. Early is caught up in looking for another runaway."

But even that was changing. I didn't know it then, but Dr. Early had finally discovered the runaway Jackson hiding behind a boiler in one of the steamboats tied up at the pier. One of the rousters had turned Jackson in.

Released him.

I looked at Lula, at her dark eyes with their thick curly lashes, her two short braids, her wide cheekbones and pointy chin. I did not want Thaddeus to get her, it was that plain and simple. Lula looked back at me, both of us waiting for the other one to come up with an idea. I tried to think.

An hour later I was up on the stage with Leo, when Hugo, Liddy, and Thaddeus walked in.

"There you are," Hugo said to me. "I was looking for you."

"I asked Leo to bring down my trunk. Here it is."

Leo had placed the trunk in the exact middle of the stage floor. For some reason this symmetry pleased me. Hugo jumped up onto the stage and walked over to it. "This trunk?" he asked. "You brought *this* trunk down? But this isn't the trunk we wanted!"

I'd brought down the smaller, black trunk instead of Lula's big one.

"I just couldn't get everything into one trunk," I said, "unless it was the bigger one."

"Then make a pile under your bed! It's only for a night or two; I'll get another when I can. Thaddeus is too big fit in this trunk! Remember, we have to carry him onto the stage in it!"

"I can't empty the other one," I insisted.

Liddy and Thaddeus were standing together in front of the benches. Thaddeus looked at me steadily but didn't say a word. He'd probably guessed why I didn't want to move my large trunk. I felt my pocket for the key to my room and I saw Thaddeus's eyes follow the movement. However, his face, as usual, revealed nothing.

Liddy said, "Oh, my goodness, we can use my trunk. It's bigger than Helena's anyway."

She went up to her room to make it ready. To her credit, she did not look put out. Hugo said irritably to Leo, "Might as well put that one in the green room. It's no use to me."

Leo said, "All right, then, let me just go help Miss Liddy first."

When Leo was gone, Hugo looked at me for a long moment, and then he seemed to take a breath and tell himself something.

"All right. All right, then. No harm done. Liddy's trunk will serve us fine." He patted his trouser pocket, pulled out his pipe, put it back in. "You have a case of nerves, May, that's understandable." I could see he was trying to make allowances for my stubbornness. "I know we're asking a lot of you tonight. Now, listen, though, I don't want you to worry. You can look at me anytime and I'll feed you the line. The audience, they won't care. By the time you make your entrance, they'll be engrossed in the play. That's Thaddeus and Mr. Niffen's job. They do that job very well, very well indeed. You're jittery, of course you are. That's to be expected. But remember what I always say: Nerves are good. Nerves make us better actors. If we feel bored, the audience will feel bored. Nerves invigorate us."

He was right: I was nervous, very nervous, only not for the reasons he thought.

"I don't want to be a better actor," I said in spite of myself.

Hugo smiled. He pulled out his pipe again and felt for his tobacco. "You always speak your mind," he said. "I like that."

"One of her most charming traits," Thaddeus put in. Was he being sarcastic? His face was smooth and blank. "Oh, and by the way, Captain," he went on, but he was looking at me. "Good news: Dr. Early will be able to make the show tonight. He managed to catch that *poem* that's been dogging him."

"Catch a poem?" Hugo asked. He put his tobacco back into his pocket without filling his pipe, and I realized he was as nervous as I was for opening night.

"Pin it down, so to speak," Thaddeus said, still with his eyes on me. He was staring at me with such significance that I asked, "Do you mean the runaway slave? Is that what you mean by 'poem'?" At that instant I honestly forgot it was a secret. But Liddy wasn't there in any case. Only Hugo looked surprised.

"He's still at that game?" he asked.

Thaddeus looked annoyed and then he shrugged it off. "Early's got the town's justice of the peace coming to the show with him," he told me. "Now's our chance to meet him, May."

"Why on earth would May want to meet the justice of the peace?" Hugo said dismissively. "Now, go on, both of you, into your costumes. The good people of Paducah are on their way. Cook's agreed to work the ticket window. Let's just hope to God he can add and subtract."

The good people of Paducah were a notch above our last few audiences, at least if you took their clothes and manners into account. After I changed into my costume—Pinky's nightdress—I put on a large cape with epaulettes and three brass clasps down the front to cover it while I played the piano. My plan now was to sneak outside as soon as I could, find whoever was waiting for Lula, and let him know when to look for us. I figured I could slip her out right after intermission; there were a few moments when all of the actors except me would be on the stage. As I finished playing the first song and started the next, I looked for Mrs. Howard, although I wasn't sure she was planning to come; her note had been cryptic. But, sure enough, in she walked with her old commanding style, with Comfort beside her. When she saw me, Mrs. Howard lifted her chin and nodded. *The plan is in place,* the nod said. *Everything is fine.* But it was not.

I must have been banging the keys rather hard, for Hugo said, "A little lighter, if you please, May. The ladies and gents want to hear themselves talk while they find their seats." My piano playing was indicative of my state of mind, which was entirely disassociated with my body. I hit the keys with all my might, and then, following Hugo's instruction, a little less than all my might, half hoping I could just play forever. But all too soon Hugo signaled an end to it. Men and women had squeezed into every spot on the benches, and, this being the South, whites sat up in the risers instead of free blacks. Dr. Early was sitting dead center in the front row with the justice of the peace on his right and on his left a rough-looking sort of man who could have passed as a whip master or, just as easily, the offender being whipped.

I had seen the justice of the peace enter. I'd been watching for him just as I'd been watching for Mrs. Howard, wondering if I would be able to pick him out from among the farmers and tradesmen who were ducking through the doorway, removing their hats and looking around with the expression of blank dislocation that I'd seen on almost every man stepping into our theater. But the justice of the peace, it turned out, was easy to spot, since his expression walking in was not one of dislocation but of ownership, never mind that as far as I knew he had never once been on the *Floating Theatre* before. He was not an overly tall man, nor an overly rugged man, nor particularly handsome, but he swept into the room with a dusting of energy around him like a cloak, as though he carried his own world with him wherever he went and imposed it on others as a matter of course. He wore a dark, well-tailored coat and his face was sun-creased and craggy, dominated by a pair of bushy eyebrows. When I saw him, my heart seemed to change its rhythm for a moment, as though my blood decided to turn around and go back where it came from. I retain the impression that he came in alone, and that there was a space before and after him, as though others preferred to give him a wide berth.

Hugo walked onto the stage and said, more to the audience than to me, "Thank you, Miss Bedloe! Thank you very much!" and a few people clapped. I stood up from the piano bench and faced them, as I did every night. The justice of the peace looked at me without clapping, and Dr. Early's eyes were bright and alert. I must have stood there longer than usual, for the scant clapping died away and Hugo had to walk over and escort me across the stage toward the wings. His hand on the small of my back felt warm and heavy.

"All right, May?" he asked quietly.

Behind us, Jemmy and Sam were busy pushing my piano out of the way. I said without thinking, "Hugo, I need your help." I don't think I'd ever called him by his first name aloud before.

"I'll help you, I'll help, don't you worry," he said, and then he went back on the stage with his arms up to start his welcoming monologue. Too late, I realized he thought that I meant my part in the play.

I started to open the back door, which led to the outside guard, so I could look for whoever was waiting for Lula and tell him my plan. But Jemmy and Sam, coming up behind me, said, "This way, May!" and laughed at the thought of me losing my way to the green room, its door only a few steps behind the stage. "We can't mislay you now!" Jemmy teased. "We need you tonight."

In the green room the rest of the company were sitting on the chairs and sofa or pacing the few steps between them—everyone but poor Pinky, who was out in the audience with a chamois cloth wrapped around his throat. As Hugo began his introduction, I heard the audience settle itself into a quieter state, and my anxiety quickened. The little room felt crowded and hot. My small, discarded trunk was where Leo had left it, triangulated against the corner like a corner table. Mrs. Niffen was sitting on the closed lid while Liddy adjusted her wig, a dull brown shade that reminded me of a squirrel in winter. Mrs. Niffen was holding her red wig in her hands and fussing about which would be the better choice.

"The red will clash with your costume," Liddy told her.

"It's too bold," Jemmy agreed.

Mrs. Niffen frowned. "But the red will help me be seen from the last row."

"Brown," Sam said in his usual succinct way. Celia, wearing a boy's shirt and trousers—both of her two small parts being male—took the red wig from Mrs. Niffen and carefully fitted it over the wig stand on top of a crate.

"I put on my own makeup tonight," Celia told me in her quiet voice, turning to me with a tiny, proud smile.

I smiled back and nodded, the best I could do, since I couldn't pretend to be anything other than wracked by my own problems. Was Lula all right? Were there enough holes for her to get air? *We tested it,* I reminded myself. *She said it was fine.* As I stood by the door, trying to think of an excuse to go outside, my anxiety enlarged to include myself. Would I be all right? Would I remember to keep my face turned toward the audience? Would I forget my lines?

Liddy said, "May, let me draw you some wrinkles on your forehead: you need to look like an old woman. My goodness! You're shaking."

"I'm afraid," I said.

"That's all right." Liddy squeezed my shoulder. "Here, sit here." She pulled a stool over, and I bent my knees a little too quickly and sat down hard. "Turn toward me," Liddy said. "Now look up. Tilt your chin a little. There we are." She bent over me with a brown grease pencil and I felt her draw a few quavering lines across my brow. Then she put a little more rouge on my cheeks with the tip of her pinkie. "I know you're afraid. That's normal. But you'll be fine. And as the captain says, it's good to be a little nervous."

"There are so many people!"

"Don't think about the audience, just concentrate on your part."

Her warm hand was on my chin, keeping my head steady. From the corner of my eye I could see Thaddeus watching us. "That's right," he said. "The play's the thing. Eh? Am I right?"

"Yes, absolutely, the play's the thing," Mrs. Niffen agreed. "Don't worry, May. It will all be over soon." She couldn't bring herself to say that I would be fine.

Thaddeus pushed himself off the wall he'd been leaning against and came up to me. His small eyes seemed closer together, and his lips were very red from the stage makeup, giving him up close a debauched appearance. "Just as Mrs. Niffen says. It will all be over soon." He bent his head and whispered, "During intermission."

"What? What do you mean, 'intermission'?" I asked loudly, drawing back from him.

Liddy said, "What are you saying to her? Oh, Thaddeus, don't frighten her."

"I just said that she should keep her voice up." Thaddeus cocked his head. "Sounds like the captain is wrapping up his speech. We're on." He turned to Mr. Niffen. "Ready?"

"Sir," Mr. Niffen said, extending his arm.

They walked out of the green room together, and the rest of us listened to the audience clap and stamp their feet, followed by a sudden falling away as Thaddeus spoke the first lines of the play. The rise and fall of sound put me in mind of my first day on the boat, when I felt so ill. Was Dr. Early going to search for Lula during intermission? Was that what Thaddeus meant? If so, I had to get her away before intermission and not afterward, as I'd planned. As I wiped my sweaty palms on my costume, I realized I was still wearing the Austrian cloak that I played the piano in, but my hands were shaking so much, I had trouble with the clasps.

"Let me," Liddy said gently. I felt a stab of emotion, like remorse. She was kinder to me than Comfort had ever been, and yet I would certainly ruin her happiness with Dr. Early if I could. We heard the General—Hugo—join Thaddeus on the stage, and Mr. Niffen came into the green room, having made the audience laugh with his exit.

"Good house tonight," he remarked.

When the time of my entrance approached, I went to the narrow space we liked to call the wings to wait for it, and Liddy came with me. As I looked out onto the stage I was momentarily mesmerized by the short, fat flames in the small stage lanterns around the proscenium. My eyesight blurred and I took a step back.

"Ah! My Lord! By heaven, here she comes, just returned from church."

That was my cue. I waited for my feet to move. When they did not, Liddy pushed me.

"Donna Cecily, Donna Cecily!" Thaddeus cried out to me.

We two were now alone on the stage. The space felt both wider and more cramped, and very near to the benches of people. I turned to speak my first line: "Signor." But nothing came out.

Thaddeus paid no mind but went on: "I think you are one of the domestics in the General's house?"

"Domestics?" I whispered, trying to find my voice. "Why, I am the *governante general* of the whole house!"

"Can't hear you!" someone shouted from the audience. I turned to see a man in a green quilted jacket push his way into the front row, squeezing the justice of the peace and Dr. Early. "Speak up," he said as he settled in, looking straight at me. Something moved underneath Dr. Early's jacket and I saw the head of a baby raccoon peep out. Rascal. He must have smuggled her on board.

"Cecily," Thaddeus said loudly, to cover the man's voice, "I have something of the highest importance to communicate to you."

I began to speak, but my words seemed to fall into my nightdress.

"Louder!" the man in the green jacket said again.

I turned to him. "I'm trying!" I snapped. From the corner of my eye, I could see Hugo in the wings in his General's costume. He was waving his hand away from the audience, signaling me not to look at them.

Thaddeus said in a low voice, "Look at me." Then louder: "You are severe, Cecily. That air you put on agrees with you but little."

I stared at him, trying to remember the next line. From off to the side of the stage, Hugo prompted: "And do you think . . ."

"And do you think to cajole me?" I said, getting my voice up a bit louder now. "If you come hither after my young lady," I went on quickly, skipping a few of my lines and Thaddeus's, too, "I have the pleasure to inform you, you won't get her."

Somehow my voice stayed up and somehow we made it through the scene with no more missed lines or feedback from the man in the green quilted jacket. As I spoke I tried not to look at him, or at Comfort, who was staring at me from the second row in utter astonishment: I was on the stage. I was acting. I had taken her place, and now she was the one watching me instead of the reverse. Standing there in my servant's costume and cap, I waited for Thaddeus to finish speaking his line, and then I spoke my own. Within a few minutes I was duped by Thaddeus, turned out of Hugo's house, and humiliated. The only thing that was left was my dismissal.

"Hear me, General—" I said to Hugo.

Hugo: "Not a word. Be gone this instant, and tomorrow I'll send the wages after you that you have so little merited."

When Hugo left the stage, I turned to Thaddeus.

"Young gentleman, the General has provoked me so far, that I'll serve you against my inclination. Therefore command me, and I will do all I can to obtain for you his niece, out of spite."

At this, Thaddeus turned to the audience and smiled triumphantly.

Exeunt, as they say, and the end of the act.

That should have been the beginning and end of my stage career, since Cecily made no more appearances in the play. But I had no time to be relieved before the next act began without pause. From there on the play would move quickly toward intermission.

"You were wonderful!" Liddy told me. It wasn't true, but I loved her for saying it.

She walked with me back to the green room, where Celia congratulated me. I spoke a few words to her before muttering that I needed some air, and went out to the guard.

Outside at last. I closed the door behind me, took in a long breath, and looked around. My heart was still pumping fast, but the fresh air was calming and the night was clear, with just the faintest last traces of purple sunset. I could smell lingering smoke from the day's steamboat traffic, and one small steamboat was docked for the night at the far end of the pier. I looked up at the road that led to town but there was no sign of Donaldson or anyone else who might be waiting to carry away a fugitive slave, just a line of empty carriages and a solitary farm dray without a driver, the horse hitched to a post, his head in a feedbag. How was I going to get Lula out before intermission without anyone noticing? I leaned over the rail, trying to see farther up the road.

Celia opened the door. She said, "You wanted me to tell you when Thaddeus was in Liddy's trunk. Well, he's getting in now."

I followed her to the wings, where Sam and Jemmy, wearing porter caps and moustaches, were closing the lid over Thaddeus's head. On a silent signal they lifted the trunk and carried it out to the center of the stage. Liddy also stood in the wings, waiting for her next cue.

"This chest contains a few trifles from India, which I mean to present to my destined bride," proclaimed Mr. Niffen on the stage. In a moment Hugo and Mr. Niffen would exit and Mrs. Niffen would open the trunk to let Thaddeus out. It was time.

"Liddy," I whispered. "You have to help me. There's a young girl, a young slave girl on our boat. A runaway. I need to get her to safety."

Liddy and Celia both turned their heads to look at me. "What!" Liddy whispered. "Here now?"

"She's young, only just Celia's age. She was raped by her master; she had a baby . . ."

Celia put her hand to her mouth. Liddy looked shocked.

"Get everyone out of the green room, will you?" I asked. "I have to get her off the boat before she's caught."

"Where is she?" Liddy whispered.

But Hugo was exiting to the other side of the stage. From the trunk, Thaddeus called out in a loud but muffled voice, "Open the lid! Open the lid!"

Still in my servant's costume, I quickly stepped out onto the stage before Mrs. Niffen could open the lid.

"Excuse me!" I said loudly.

Mrs. Niffen stared at me. "Why . . . Cecily?" she said, and then frowned and made a jerky motion with her head for me to get off the stage. A few lanterns flickered for a moment as though they were surprised, too. Hugo was standing in the wings on the other side but I dared not look at him. I swallowed, trying to moisten the roof of my mouth, which felt like a rough, dry stone, and I made myself look at the justice of the peace, who wore the blank expression of someone witnessing an event without participating in it. Someone only there to witness events—well, if that was anyone, that was me, that was my life with Comfort; but now that life was over and I was making something happen, or trying to, and I didn't like it at all, my heart was knocking around hard enough to break a rib and I had nothing on my side, not the law certainly, and not even the truth. I didn't care about telling the truth, and for once I didn't feel the need to, although I did.

"I have to stop the show," I said loudly, looking straight at the justice of the peace. "There's a slave on this boat. A runaway slave!"

He looked back at me blankly, as if this might still be part of the play.

"A runaway slave right here on this boat!" I repeated.

"A what?" Now his slack expression began to change into something harder, and he stood up. Beside him, Dr. Early tried to tuck Rascal, who was trying to climb out, back into his jacket pocket. He opened his mouth to say something, but I spoke over him.

"What's the reward for bringing in a runaway?" I asked. "Eighty dollars? I'll bring her to you for eighty dollars."

"Now, wait a moment," Hugo boomed out, walking quickly across the stage. Meanwhile, Thaddeus was knocking frantically on the lid of the trunk, and Mrs. Niffen remembered him. She opened the lid and Thaddeus scrambled to get himself out, saying to me in a snarl, "You tricked me! You want the reward money all to yourself!"

"It's a lot of money," I said.

Dr. Early jumped up and said to the justice of the peace, "Fred, I knew about this. I was going to tell you at intermission so we could go up together and get the girl. She's in one of the staterooms. Come on."

I glanced over at Liddy, who was now standing on the corner of the stage, half on and half off, staring at her fiancé. Her face looked all at once soft and crumpled, older somehow, and more like Comfort's face in the last few years when certain roles were denied her. But she was a good soul, a true friend, and after a moment she pressed her lips together and turned around—back to the green room, I hoped, to get everyone out. She held Celia by the arm while Rascal took the opportunity to jump out from underneath Dr. Early's jacket, knocking over a small stage lantern, which Hugo quickly put right.

"Upstairs!" I shouted to the justice of the peace. "I'll show you."

The rest of the audience was now beginning to stand up to leave. They might not have known exactly what was happening, but it was clear that the stage actors were involved in some wrongdoing and would end up in jail or worse, and they wanted no part of it. Rascal, in her delight in being free, kept knocking over the proscenium lanterns, which Hugo picked up. Jemmy and Sam came out onto the stage to chase Rascal, and I didn't know where Pinky was. I ran out of the auditorium and up the stairs with the justice and Dr. Early following me. Thaddeus was right behind us, wanting his cut of the reward. When I unlocked the door to my stateroom the two men rushed in, and Thaddeus pushed me aside.

"She's in that large trunk there," he told them.

I stood outside on the guard and watched them for a second. Then I shut the door and turned the key. I could hear them inside, hammering on the padlocked trunk, trying to get it open. It would take them at least a minute to discover they were locked in the room. And with all the noise of people leaving the boat, it was possible that no one would hear them for a while.

I ran down the steps. I was so intent that I didn't see Hugo at the bottom until he reached out and grabbed my arm, almost making me fall.

"Hugo!"

His looked at me as if he were looking down a well, gauging its depth. His face seemed very close to mine. "Where is she really?" he asked.

"What?" I breathed.

"Whoever it was you brought over in my rowboat. Someone not picked up, I'm guessing. You had to hide her?"

I stared at him, astonished. His accent was very thick, a sure sign of agitation, but he could not have been more perplexed than I was as I tried to fit this new information into the puzzle of the last few weeks. He knew? All this time? I must have asked him, for he said, "Who do you think left you the ham sandwiches? Who lit the lantern in the storm?"

I had assumed all that was Leo. "But why didn't you say? Why didn't you tell me?" I felt tears prick my eyes.

He made a gesture that conveyed a mistake or a regret, his palms facing out as if wanting something from me. "I thought that if I were directly involved, then everyone here, all the actors and Leo, they could be implicated, too. I didn't care a penny's piece about me, but

I worried about them. Bad judgment or . . . I don't know, but let me help you now, May, let me at least do that."

I heard a crash from my room: they had broken into the trunk. My heart was racing. There was no time to weigh right and wrong.

"She's in the green room," I said.

Hugo led the way, his hand still on my arm, weaving us through the crowd leaving the boat. Leo was in the green room when we got there but everyone else had gone—thanks, I suppose, to Liddy. When he saw me, Leo turned to open the small black trunk that he and I had carried down that afternoon, and Lula uncurled herself out of it. The trunk was too small for a man—Hugo was right about that—but not too small for a girl.

"Are you all right?" I asked her.

One of her braids had come undone and was more of a pigtail than a plait. She was wearing both of her dresses and some slippers I'd found for her among the costumes. Leo stood at the door to the green room that led to the stage.

"That raccoon is gonna burn down this boat," he said, looking out the door.

"Go on," Hugo told him. "You go catch it. We can do this."

I could hear pounding above us. Thaddeus and the others had discovered my trick and were trying to get out of the room.

"Where will you take her?" Hugo asked me.

"There's someone waiting for her on the road."

I grabbed a costume dress from the rack and put it on over Pinky's nightdress. Then I covered her up with a dark cloak we used on the stage for messengers.

"What's your name?" I heard Hugo ask.

"Lula," Lula said. She looked at his face quickly, then down at his boots.

"Lula, do you have anything you don't need, a coat or a cape, a bonnet?"

"No, sir. Just my two dresses I have on. Why?"

"They know that you were on this boat. They'll keep looking until they find something."

I pulled on Mrs. Niffen's bright red wig, the one she had decided not to wear, and found a costume bonnet for Lula. I didn't know what Hugo was getting at. "We have to go," I said.

"How about shoes?" he asked.

I remembered the boots that had made her feet bleed. "In the black trunk." I hadn't wanted to leave anything of hers in my room.

Hugo said, "Good. Those will do. Now, May, come back quickly if you can. May—" He took my left hand and then my right. He pulled me toward him. When his lips met mine, I was so surprised I almost started to speak, and indeed for a moment I felt as though my unspoken words had found physical expression in the movement of his bottom lip under mine, my mouth moving in response, a sudden heat in my chest. It was over in the time it would take to say two or three words. When he drew back and looked at my face, I felt my own face grow warm and I stared at him, thinking he would explain something—what he felt, perhaps, or something about me.

Instead he just repeated, "Come back as quickly as you can."

I was filled with something light and wonderful, one more emotion to pack into my crowded heart; but still I tried to isolate it, because I knew I would want to examine it later and feel it again, the surprise of it and the lovely joy. People continued to make their way off the boat, and I realized that not all that much time had passed from when I interrupted the show, even though it felt like hours and hours.

"I will," I said to Hugo. "As soon as I can." Then I looked at Lula. "Ready?"

She nodded, pressing her lips together in a twitch. Somehow my legs carried me forward out the door and onto the guard with Lula beside me. Her large costume bonnet half hid her face, which was good. Ahead of us, men and women spoke to each other in loud voices, most of them sounding scared or shocked, although one man holding a straw hat in his hand was laughing. I looked for Mrs. Howard and Comfort, hoping they could lead us to whoever was waiting on the road, but I could not spot them in the throng. No one noticed us, not even Celia and Liddy, who were exiting the boat up ahead alongside the man in the green quilted jacket. Liddy was carrying Oliver, who looked back at me over her shoulder. He was wearing the ruff I had made for him that first day, when I felt so ill. Then the crowd closed up between us, and I didn't see anyone else from the company for many weeks after that.

Lula took my hand and squeezed it, and I squeezed back. One of us was sweating, or maybe it was both of us. Our palms were slippery but we did not let go.

Down the stage plank, onto the pier, up toward the road, just two more people in the crowd of people leaving the boat. I still could not spot Mrs. Howard. When a gunshot rang out above us, the crowd panicked and pressed forward recklessly. The men had found Helena's hunting rifle, I guessed, and were trying to shoot the door lock open. I tried to turn my good ear away from the clamor, but this proved impossible since the clamor was everywhere. I looked back at the boat at the very moment that Thaddeus or one of the men—all I could make out was a smudgy figure—burst through my stateroom door, breaking the lock. It was then that I felt something in me shift from urgency to alarm.

The crowd surged up onto the road and we followed. Lula let go of my hand.

"You have to treat me like a slave," she said.

"How do I do that?"

"Don't look at me, not direct."

We kept walking, trying to push ourselves ahead. When we got to the road, people peeled off in different directions and horses started pulling carriages away, one before its door was even properly closed. Everyone was in a panic to leave whatever mischief was going on. Lula and I turned our backs on the *Floating Theatre*, following the road that ran alongside the long pier and the river. I could feel pinpoints of sweat on my scalp, bringing out a woody scent in my hair, and my breath felt like a cold, hard coin in my throat. I looked up at each waiting carriage, hoping to see Donaldson or Mrs. Howard or Comfort, or a stranger who was also on the lookout for us. It was fully night now, but the moon was high and full. Lula walked behind me and the dark horses snorted or stamped as we went by as though they, too, were eager to leave this place behind.

We came to the end of the carriages. I could see that there was nothing farther down the road but trees. Although the *Floating Theatre* was at some distance behind us now, I didn't want to turn around and recheck the carriages for fear that by this time Thaddeus and Dr. Early had finished searching the boat and were now looking for us along the road, and I did not dare look back for fear of seeing them. So I kept walking with no plan in mind except to look like a woman going somewhere and not a woman with a runaway slave she had no idea what to do with, and I carried a wild hope that Donaldson was here somewhere and would find us. Other people were carrying on down the road, too, ones like us with no carriages or wagons. The moon was so bright that even without all the men and women carrying lanterns I would have felt exposed. One man looked at me a little too long as he approached us, and then he looked over at Lula.

I said to her, "Hurry up, now," hoping to sound like a slave owner. The man walked up to one of the taverns fronting the river and went inside.

Lula said, "You got some lines across your head. That's what he was lookin' at."

I remembered the wrinkles Liddy drew on me. I licked the cuff of my sleeve and rubbed it over my forehead. "Better?"

"A little. Do it again some."

As I rubbed my forehead again, I saw the steamboat I'd noticed earlier tied up at the very end of the pier. It wasn't a good place to hide—I thought of the runaway Jackson who'd been caught behind a boiler—but it was better than being on the open road. Above us was the town, but I didn't want to go there. They would check all the inns. I looked at the boat again. I could try to bribe the captain, I thought, and then I remembered I had nothing with me: no money, only my father's watch, which I wore tucked under my shift. Maybe he would take that.

"Ever been on a steamer?" I asked Lula.

She looked over at the boat. "Won't they look for us there?"

"They'll look for us everywhere."

The boat was small for a steamship, and coming up to it I saw tight bales of paper loaded up and stacked on its lower deck. So, a packet boat, but it might take on a few passengers, too. I hoped the captain would not ask too many questions. As we walked up the gangplank the steamer's whistle unexpectedly blew, and two men wearing caps and smoke-stained jackets got ready to pull the gangplank up.

"The boat's leaving?" I asked.

"Captain's orders," one of them said.

"At night?" I had never heard of a steamer traveling at night.

"Moon's bright enough. Captain thinks it's safer."

"Safer than what?"

He pointed behind me. "Don't want to catch fire if it moves up the dock."

I turned around. Down at the other end of the pier, a boat was on fire. I saw its flames leap up over the water and lick at the wooden dock. It was the *Floating Theatre*.

"All this paper—we'd be gone in a wink," the man said, nodding toward his cargo.

I looked at the bales of paper. Then I looked back at the fire. It was simple addition but I could not do it.

"Our boat!" Lula breathed. I couldn't answer, couldn't even nod.

"You two can go up top if you want," he told us. "Less noise."

But Lula and I stayed where we were on the lower deck, too shocked to do anything but watch the *Floating Theatre* burn, while behind us the steamship's boilers started up and the paddle began its first slow rotation. Liddy had left the boat, I knew that, with Oliver and Celia. But the others? Hugo? Did Hugo get out? From where I stood, I could see only hot, bright destruction. Shoots of orange flame began wrapping themselves in a tight embrace around the boat's wooden frame, and now I could smell the pungent scent of smoke drifting toward us in the air.

I felt the steamer lurch as it began backing away from the pier. My throat felt thick, as though already filled with ashes from the *Floating Theatre*, but I didn't cry. Lula and I were holding hands again, and even though I normally hated anyone touching my skin, I believe it was I who first reached out to her. The two men went off to help with the boilers, and Lula and I were left to ourselves to watch the *Floating Theatre* burn up. It hurt my throat to swallow. It hurt almost to breathe. The steamer slowly crossed the river, and the men tied up at the first landing we came to on the northern side. But even there, half a mile away, I could still see a spot of bright white flame against the night sky.

20

It was nearly August by the time I found a job at the American Hotel in Cleveland on Superior Street, a street that had sixteen-inch-wide sidewalks and, by law, no pigs. Cleveland, like Cincinnati, hailed itself as an up-and-coming modern city, but the canal boat that I took to get there was as slow as a farm cart, with clumps of sheep congregating beside the locks and weeds clogging the culverts. It took me five days to get to Cleveland, two weeks to find a job, and two weeks and a day to secure lodgings in a run-down brick house that was somehow forgotten when the neighborhood turned from residence to commerce. But I didn't need anything better. The rooms were cheap, they were close to the hotel, and I had a door key the length and width of a rat's tail.

At the American Hotel, I worked in a square, low-ceilinged room behind the kitchens, with one cracked window looking out over the back alley. Housemaids brought me trousers with buttons off of them or dresses with hems coming undone, given over by the hotel guests. I was paid very little but I was given dinner and supper every day that I worked, which was six days a week. Once in a while I was called on to go up to a guest's room and perform some alteration there. I knelt on the carpet with pins in my mouth and my fingers on the hem of a lady's silk skirt while she spoke to someone else in the room. Some days I did not get much work, and other days I had more than I could do myself. On those days a young Negro girl named Bella helped me, and afterward, if we had time to spare, I showed her some embroidery stitches. She wanted to set herself up as a "fancy dress maker," as she called it, on the street where her family lived. Her father owned his own barbershop and had come to Cleveland when he was twenty; Bella told me that he had been born to free parents in Virginia. Bella told me quite a lot while we worked. She had a pleasantly high, light voice and spoke without pause, changing subjects here and there like a bird flitting from branch to branch. I learned about her family, her father's family, the church regulars, and "that bold boy Simon across the way" who had taken a liking to her.

After work, Bella turned right to go home—sometimes bold Simon would be waiting on the corner to walk her there—and I turned left, but I did not go back to my rooming house right away. Cleveland had been bitten by "the theater bug," as one newspaper put it, and there were many options for an evening's entertainment. Newly formed companies performed Shakespeare or French melodramas; or I could see American comedies at Cook's Theatre, built by the brothers Cook, or I could see musical productions at the Italian Hall on Water Street. I went as often as I could and studied each playbill for names I knew: Miss Lydia Fiske, Mr. Sam Trotter, Mr. James Grieve. Captain Hugo Cushing. Usually I didn't even wait until I was sitting down but stood in the aisle near a gas-lit sconce holding the playbill with two hands—two, because I found that just the act of the usher putting the bill in my hand caused me to shake. There was always a moment before I looked at the print when my heart seemed to take a step back in my chest.

Mrs. Margaret Russell, I read. Miss Mary Skapek. Mr. Gregory Roscoe.

And other names like them—names I did not know. But, of course, why would anyone from the *Floating Theatre* be there, playing in

Cleveland? It would be too much of a coincidence. I checked the names again.

"Can I help you, Miss . . . ?" the usher asked as people brushed by me on their way to their seats.

"Sinclair," I told him. "Mrs. Jasper Sinclair."

"Can I help you find your seat, Mrs. Sinclair?"

"No, thank you."

It was unusual, if not disreputable, for a woman to attend the theater alone, but I didn't care about that. I tended to roll the playbill up like a scroll after I sat in my seat and, just as Hugo had once predicted, after a minute or two I forgot everything but what was happening on the stage. It didn't matter that I saw the same roles time and again—the low comedian, the singing servant, the blithe ingénue—I was captured by their plight, and glad to be captured. Watching a play, I forgot what I had done, who I had hurt, and who I had helped. I forgot myself, and I suppose that was the main thing.

Afterwards I went back to my two small rooms, stuffy with the humid summer air, and tried to sleep.

Of course I sent Mrs. Howard my Cleveland address and told her to "please forward it to Captain Cushing," but I had no idea if she knew where he was or if she would write to him if she did know. I did not even know if he was alive. The only news I could find about the fire on the *Floating Theatre* was from a small notice in the *Cincinnati Daily Gazette*, which I read at Mrs. Howard's house a few days after the event.

RIVERBOAT THEATRE

Burned on the Ohio River where it was docked at the Paducah landing last Friday night. Dr. Martin Early, physician and poet, and one member of the company were killed in the blaze. The brave citizens of Paducah extinguished the fire before it could damage the town.

One member of the company. That was all the information I had. There was no mention of Lula—nothing about a runaway slave. I had no idea where anyone from our boat might be, so I had no one to ask. I considered sending a message to the Paducah post office advertising my address, but then thought better of it. I didn't know if the law would be looking for me, and Mrs. Howard didn't, either, but to be safe, she told me, I should use a different name for the time being. And so I became Mrs. Jasper Sinclair.

After our moonlit escape on the packet steamer, Lula and I traveled for three more days before we reached Mrs. Howard's house. The steamer took us nearly all the way to Cincinnati, and might have gotten us the whole way there if I hadn't caught the captain looking at Lula too many times in a thoughtful manner. We skipped off at a smaller landing while the men were loading up barrels of nails to be carried with their cargo of paper, and I found a coach to take us the remaining miles. The driver accepted my father's watch as fare, probably ten times the value.

We had slept very little on the steamer, just an hour or two here and there, but Lula slept heavily on the coach. I kept myself awake in case she had a nightmare and I needed to wake her, and I watched her closed eyelids for signs of distress. There was moisture at the corners of her eyes, but I don't think she was crying. I told the couple traveling in the coach with us that my sister in Cincinnati had just had a baby and that I was lending her my girl here—I nodded toward Lula—for a few weeks to help out. They had their own "girl" with them, a woman wearing a blue headscarf who was a good number of years older than themselves. "My sister's baby is a boy," I told them. "His name is William."

We arrived in Cincinnati at last in the late afternoon under a gray sky threatening rain. Not knowing if anyone might be looking for us—if notices had already been printed up with our descriptions and a reward set for our return—we walked the rest of the way to Mrs. Howard's house, skirting the busiest streets. It was muggy and hot even under the trees. We shared a ham roll that the lady on the coach had given me, and talked about what Lula would do after she found her baby. She liked the idea of dressmaking. Maybe she could make little novelty pincushions, like my steamboat pincushion—lost now, like everything else.

But I couldn't think about what I had lost. We were in the North, to be sure, but still I couldn't shake the fear that at any moment someone might appear before us with a whip or a pistol. I remembered too vividly the look on Dr. Early's face in Paducah as he jumped up to show the justice of the peace where to find Lula: the eager, even joyful look of a hunter. He was going to capture something weaker than himself, a creature who had committed the terrible crime of trying to be stronger than she really was. That was Lula, but it was also me.

When the rain began, Lula and I stopped for a moment and lifted our faces to feel the cool drops. Lula took off her costume slippers, which by now were torn and dirty, and stood in the grass.

"You'll catch cold," I told her. "Why are you smiling?"

"Free soil." She picked up a stray blue jay feather from the ground and twirled it between her fingers. I remembered the bluebird picture she liked so much from Hugo's bird book, with its detailed caterpillar. Raindrops sparkled in her dark hair.

By the time we came to the house, the rain had tapered off and great puddles spotted the drive. We went around to the garden and I opened the back door, which was kept unlocked. Then for a few minutes we stood just inside and waited, wet and dirty and for my part nurturing the new mistrust I felt for every soul—housemaids, who might be anywhere in the house, or errand boys, who would use the back door, too—until Donaldson came through and saw us. He quickly took us down to the cellar, which had a straw pallet and a basin of water among the old furniture and crates. We dried off as he fetched Mrs. Howard, who suggested we both "lie down for a while"—me upstairs and Lula on the pallet. But I was so exhausted that I slept all night, and by the time I woke up it was almost noon the next day. There was a blue jay feather on the pillow beside me— the same feather Lula had picked up the afternoon before. I didn't understand that it was a good-bye note until Mrs. Howard informed me she was gone.

She wouldn't say where she went. "Next stop" is all she told me. "Only Donaldson knows where that is, and I don't ask him. They had to leave while it was still dark."

"Can I send her a letter?" I was thinking someone could read it to her.

"Only if you want her to get caught."

"Is she with her baby, at least?"

"We're not told the details, May. Safer that way. She is free, I can tell you that, thanks to you. And her baby is, too. You were a good soldier back there."

"You should be proud," Comfort added.

They were not good soldiers, Comfort and Mrs. Howard. When she learned about Lula from Donaldson, Mrs. Howard contacted a farmer who owned a dray wagon with a false bottom—the farm dray I had seen from the railing of the *Floating Theatre*—which was often used for ferrying fugitives. But the farmer had been at his brother's house for a few days, hence the delay. He returned in time to hitch the wagon near the Paducah pier during the show, where he waited for someone to bring him Lula. Why he wasn't sitting up in his dray when I looked, I do not know. Maybe he'd gotten impatient, since I was so late, and went out to see what he could see. Mrs. Howard herself panicked and left with Comfort when the justice of the peace got involved. She assured me that she and Comfort had looked for us—they went up to the town, thinking we would remove ourselves more from the crowd—but later Comfort admitted that they did not look for us long. Mrs. Howard was nervous. She was a known abolitionist, and she did not want to get drawn into the chase. She could not afford to be in jail, Comfort explained to me. There were too many people she needed to help.

I still have the blue jay feather. I wish I had been able to say good-bye.

Mrs. Howard gave me Comfort's old room with the furry ceiling full of pig hair, since she and Comfort now shared two rooms down the hall. For two nights I slept so heavily I did not even dream, but still I could not shake my exhaustion, which felt like a thick woolen shawl across my shoulders and over my head. I was happy that Lula had gotten away—exultant, even. We had prevailed against all odds. And yet at the very same time there was a pocket of darkness in me, a great chasm of regret, when I thought of that night. The *Floating Theatre* was gone. I had taken Hugo's livelihood and the livelihood of seven other people. Eight, if you counted young Celia.

"Now, May," Mrs. Howard said at breakfast a few days later, "you have to stop dwelling upon that boat. That's over and done with. It's a pity, to be sure. A great pity. But it wasn't your fault. You did not set the fire. You got Lena out and you got her to safety; you should be proud of this. Dwell on that if you must dwell on anything. Our cause is a just cause, you know."

She said more in this vein—much more—and when she stopped to sip her tea, by now almost certainly cold, I said, "Lula, not Lena."

"Of course," she replied smoothly. "Lula."

I wished I could explain to her how I felt inside, like fabric that's been torn into strips. But, "It's not your fault," Mrs. Howard kept saying, even when we found the small inch of print in the *Gazette* later that day with the report of the fire and the deaths. I left the next morning, and although Mrs. Howard tried to stop me—"You have an obligation to the cause now; you can do important work right here"—

I would not be persuaded. She gave me twenty dollars and a canal boat ticket for Cleveland, and this time I actually bought and used the ticket.

Three days to get to Cincinnati, five days to get to Cleveland, fifteen days to find work; but after that, for me, time seemed to stretch out meaninglessly. I went to plays at night and rose each day to the same humid morning that eventually gave way to rain or a humid afternoon. The wind coming off the lake blew at me like a series of loose slaps, wriggling my hat away from my hatpins, so that I walked to work like every other man or woman on the street with one hand on my head.

One afternoon at the end of August, Bella and I sat sewing in the hotel's little back room with a great swath of light-blue silk between us; we were both hemming the same skirt, which needed to be done in a quarter of an hour so that the lady who owned it could dress for dinner. We had our heads down and were working as fast as we could, but Bella still kept up a conversation the whole while, describing the outing she'd taken that Sunday with her two brothers and four sisters to hear the new Cleveland City Band play at Public Square.

"Eighteen men," she told me. "My brother Petey counted."

I liked to have hard work in front of me that needed to be done quickly, and listening to Bella was also a welcome distraction from my thoughts. She didn't speak about slavery or runaways or the emancipation question—at least, not to me—but of everyday life. And although I felt very far from everyday life—a life that I believed should include family or at least neighbors who know your real name—I enjoyed hearing about her Sunday excursions and her romances, even what she had eaten for dinner the night before and how she and her mother prepared it. Once the idle talk would have irritated me, back when I was a person with no bitter regrets. Now I simply listened and imagined her life as she told it to me, my fingers working furiously over the silk.

"Afterwards we had ice cream, but Petey had two because he dropped his first one, and Momma favors him," Bella said.

Mr. Loran, the sprightly, no-nonsense manager of the hotel, poked his head into the room. "How's it coming along, girls?" he asked. "Alice is ready to take it upstairs when you're done. She's in the kitchen."

I bit off the thread and knotted it. Then Bella gave the silk another turn with the iron while I cut some tissue paper to wrap it in. I found Alice sitting in the kitchen with her legs straight out in front of her, her maid's cap in her lap. "Oogh, it's hot," she said. Then, standing and refitting the cap on her hair: "There's a guest askin' for a bit of help. A lost button, I think. Room four sixteen." Her fingers darted here and there, tucking in strands of her hair without the aid of a mirror.

"Bella, can you get the button jar?" I asked.

Alice shook her skirt out and then took the dress from me. "Wanted you by name. Said, 'Is the lady Mrs. Jasper Sinclair here today?'"

I felt the blood come to my face. No one had ever asked for me by name. No one except Bella and Mr. Loran and a couple of the hotel maids even knew me. Was it the law at last? I wanted to ask but I didn't know how to without sounding guilty. I considered getting Bella to go up instead of me in spite of the guest's request, but after the first rush of fear I felt another emotion take over, as though I had been waiting all these weeks for the consequences of my actions, and now here they were.

Room four sixteen, Alice repeated after me.

As I made my way through the kitchens and the dining room and then across the reception hall and up the wide polished stairs, it seemed like everyone else in the hotel was going in the opposite direction. If it was the law, I reasoned, they would have just come to the back room where I worked and arrested me. But I could not

completely convince myself. By the time I knocked on the door, my
chest felt like it held two hearts, each one pumping out an alternate
rhythm.

"Seamstress," I called out.

After a long moment the door opened.

Donaldson stood on the carpet, the light behind him. He didn't
smile, but he nodded to me and opened the door all the way to let
me inside. To say that I was surprised to see him does not adequately
describe my confusion and the sudden tingling I felt along my arms,
as though my skin had a sudden need to make sure of its place in the
world. I stepped into the room. It had thick cream carpet with a rose
design along its edges, and the heavy furniture seemed to sink into it
as if it were milk foam. I was still turning my head, expecting to find
Mrs. Howard in a corner with her tiny tea set, when the door to an
adjoining room opened and Hugo walked out.

His hair was longer, and he was dressed somberly in a plain brown
suit. It was strange not to see him in his boatman's coat or the old
trousers he worked in, and of course he was not wearing a costume,
either. He looked almost like someone else entirely, but as he walked
across the carpet something escaped me, a sound or a puff of air,
something in between recognition and relief. Hugo took the button
jar from me and put it down on a little side table. I could not seem
to move a muscle.

He took my two hands. He said my name. I saw that his eyes were
kind, and Donaldson was looking at me, too.

A sob came from my mouth as I let Hugo embrace me. But after
a second I stepped back. I knew he was here to give me bad news:
one of the company was dead. Still, I was just so glad it wasn't him. I
wanted to know everything but first I couldn't help asking, "How did
you find me? Was it Mrs. Howard?"

Hugo raised his eyebrows. "Mrs. Howard? No, no, she couldn't
get rid of me fast enough. Gave me my tea in the hallway."

I felt myself smile. "She does that."

"Lucky for me, Mr. Donaldson here stopped me as I was leaving. Man can write bloody fast," he said, and at that Donaldson's face changed. It didn't look like a smile, but it might have been a smile. When I thanked him, he put his hand out and I took it.

"He arranged for some business with a Mr. Loran and drove me up here with him."

"The hotel manager?" I looked at Donaldson with astonishment. "You know him?"

Again Donaldson didn't seem to move a muscle, but something in his face confirmed this.

"Did you get me this job?"

He took out a pad of paper from his pocket and a short pencil, and I saw that Hugo was right: he wrote bloody fast.

We thought you might want to continue to work for our cause.

"'We'?"

I'll arrange a visit when the girl isn't working.

"You mean Bella?"

He took up his hat and made a little bow to me before leaving. When the door closed behind him, Hugo said, "I shouldn't wonder if he isn't the brains behind the whole operation."

We were still standing on the thick carpet in the middle of the room. The light outside, a harsh metallic gray, sliced in through the half-curtained windows. Hugo looked tired and almost ordinary in his brown suit. "Hugo, what happened that night?" I asked.

He pursed his lips and went over to close the window. The sounds from the street, which I'd hardly noticed—the rattle of a horse harness and a couple of men speaking loudly to each other—shut off like a spigot. Hugo turned back to me and lifted his arms in a gesture I couldn't interpret. As he began to talk, I watched his face, looking for—what? Some judgment or anger, I suppose. There was emotion there, but I couldn't tell what it was. He told me that when Lula and I had left, he stayed in the green room, trying to make it look as though Lula had died trying to escape. He put her boots in the trunk and tangled up the bootlaces in the hinges so they wouldn't float away.

"Then I tried to push the trunk out the window," he told me, "but the window wouldn't open far enough, so I carried the trunk out to the dock and pushed it into the river. I watched it for a few minutes to make sure it would float. When I turned around. . ." He looked away from me. "I found out later that one of the theater drapes had caught fire. Everything went up very quickly after that."

Once a fire begins, it can spread as fast as your eyes can travel; I knew that from when my father purposely burned down one of his old, unused barns. I remembered how the flames started along the corners and then quickly found the windows and roof. There was a loud crackling sound as the wood split. Soon the dark gray plumes of smoke were thicker and larger than the building itself, and in a matter of minutes I could see the barn's skeletal frame.

My chest felt tight, as though my lungs were stiff copper pipes. "Liddy?" I asked Hugo. I had seen her leave with Celia, but I had to be sure. "And Celia?"

"They're fine. They're all right," Hugo told me. "Liddy has given up the business and gone back to her family in Akron. Pinky is thinking of following her there. I hope he does."

That meant that Pinky was all right, too. "Then who?" I managed.

"Dr. Early didn't make it out. He went to the green room is my guess, still looking for Lula."

"Who else?" I asked. "The newspaper said Dr. Early and one of the company. Who else?"

Hugo hesitated. Then he said, "Leo."

"Leo?" I stared at him. "It can't be Leo. He's not an actor. He's not one of the company. It said one of the company."

"It was Leo, May."

"No. It can't be." I think I closed my eyes, because all I could see was a sort of dark ashy wall. For a minute I could not even cry. Of all the people I had considered, I had never considered him. I had never worried it was him.

Somehow I found myself sitting in one of the armchairs and Hugo was kneeling beside me. When I began to cry, he took hold of my left hand with both of his. A wave of dark shame and sadness and unbearable regret washed over me. Leo never caught his catfish. He only wanted to do his job and then sit fishing on the pier on the northern side of the river and be safe. But I had ruined all that. Tears streamed down my face. It felt like stone after heavy stone was being piled on my heart.

"I know. I know," Hugo said.

"I'm sorry," I told him.

"I know."

He did not say that it was not my fault, as Mrs. Howard had said. But he was here, he had found me, and he was holding my hand. He told me that two men from town had found the trunk the next day with Lula's boots in it, and, just as he'd hoped, they concluded that Lula had died—drowned was the verdict. The law wasn't after me. Dr. Early, who knew about my role in all this, was dead, and Thaddeus had scampered off to Kentucky.

"Given his own involvement, I doubt he'll say anything," Hugo said. "Probably found a new troupe already. *Floating Theatre*'s dust, of course."

A fresh wave of regret and shame hit me as I thought of the boat, and I put my handkerchief—Hugo's handkerchief, which he'd put into my hand—up to my face. That boat was his child.

"Do you want to stay here, May?" he asked me gently after a while. He was close enough for me to see the dark circles under his eyes, and where his sideburns needed trimming. "Do you want to keep working in this hotel?"

"I want to be with you," I said. That I knew.

"That's all right, then. We can build a new boat. Donaldson said he'd lend me the money. Course, we'll have to wait until next year. Summer's nearly over."

"What do you mean?"

"And we'll make a proper hiding place this time. No more trunks." He stood up and pulled the other armchair up to mine, so close that their edges were touching. When he sat down, our knees rubbed against each other. He took my hand again in his two. "But maybe you don't want that."

Did I want that? I was elated that Lula had gotten away. She had gotten away, and she'd been helped by Liddy, and Hugo, and Leo, and Donaldson. But what if she had been caught? Then I would have counted it as my own failure and no one else's. I hoped she was safe. I hoped she was far away and reunited with her baby, William. I remembered his short, curly eyelashes like her own. But the price had been so very high. Hugo did not speak of Leo again after that afternoon, but I know that he thought of him. My fault. My fault.

Conflicted. That's what the feeling of torn fabric inside of you is called.

"Well, that, my love," Hugo said when I told him, "is the human condition."

From outside the room I heard voices—a man's and a woman's—and the sound of a door closing with a scrape. I didn't really expect to get away with everything, and I hadn't. Hugo gave my hand a squeeze, bringing me back to the room with him.

"What do you say? Are you ready to start all that up again?" he asked.

He looked so ordinary in his brown suit.

Alpha, beta, gamma, delta.

"I'm ready," I said.

AUTHOR'S NOTE

The small towns along the Ohio River changed rapidly in the first half of the nineteenth century, emerging and growing larger or disappearing altogether within decades. For this reason I have fictionalized most of the town names that are mentioned in the story, although I tried to remain true to the spirit of the area. There was a real steamboat called the *Moselle*, which sank near Cincinnati in 1838 after its boilers exploded. Of the 300 people on board, 117 survived.

The events of the novel take place twenty years before the American Civil War began, when the Ohio River was the natural division between the North, or free states, and the South, or slave states. In 1838 the second Fugitive Slave Law had not yet been passed; however, slave catchers did watch the Ohio River for runaways and also ventured north to bring them back.

ACKNOWLEDGMENTS

My deepest thanks go to Sue Armstrong, Lisa Bankoff, Heather Lazare, Kate Parkin, and Trish Todd for all their help and insight; to Alice K. Boatwright, a wonderful writer and friend; and most of all to Richard, John Henry, and Lily for their absolutely unwavering support.

ABOUT THE AUTHOR

Martha Conway grew up in Cleveland, Ohio, the sixth of seven daughters. Her first novel was nominated for an Edgar Award, and she has won several awards for her historical fiction, including an Independent Book Publishers Award and the North American Book Award for Historical Fiction. Her short fiction has been published in the *Iowa Review, Massachusetts Review, Carolina Quarterly, Folio, Epoch, The Quarterly,* and other journals. She has received a California Arts Council fellowship for creative writing and has reviewed books for the *Iowa Review* and the *San Francisco Chronicle*. She now lives in San Francisco and is an instructor of creative writing for Stanford University's Continuing Studies Program and UC Berkeley Extension.